WRITERS REPUBLIC

THE
BROOKLYN QUEEN

S. COLA BISHOP

WRITERS REPUBLIC L.L.C.
515 Summit Ave. Unit R1
Union City, NJ 07087, USA

Website: *www.writersrepublic.com*
Hotline: *1-877-656-6838*
Email: *info@writersrepublic.com*

Ordering Information:
Quantity sales. Special discounts are available on quantity purchases by corporations, associations, and others. For details, contact the publisher at the address above.

Library of Congress Control Number: 2021938444
ISBN-13:   978-1-63728-481-0   [Paperback Edition]
                    978-1-63728-482-7   [Digital Edition]

Rev. date: 05/26/2021

I, dedicate this book to my family and friends
in Aruba, America and Amsterdam.

CHAPTER

1

Come on, three o'clock. Come on. Bell. Ring. Eboni sat in the classroom, counting down the minutes to freedom. She wanted to kick it with her friends; the only time she'd have to spare was on her walk home. When she reached home, her chores were watching over her younger siblings, Elisha and Eric; that was the help that was expected from her by her mother. When the bell rang, she rushed out, but her friends were not around. She lived three blocks from the school and was slowly enjoying the sights of her Brooklyn neighborhood as she walked down tree line blocks with beautiful brownstones. She noticed the group of young guys on the corner; seemed like every day they were out there. She overheard one of them say, "She's going to be a heartbreaker when she grows up." And the rest agreed; she smiled and kept walking along. She waved to a couple—her neighbors. They took pride in their homes—were out cutting their hedges, pruning their trees, sweeping the streets in this 80-degree temperature. A late-model Cadillac rolled by, blaring the latest Michael Jackson sound, and she snapped her fingers to the "Thriller" beat. She was glad to be alone, away from Penny, the chatterbox, and her circle of friends. Tina and Dawn didn't take sides or come to anyone's defense. They would just giggle at the whole situation. Penny's teasing was getting harder to ignore. "Well, Penny is just jealous. Don't you know that?" Her mom had said. "Eboni, all the

1

women in our family have big butts. You're only twelve years old, and the family trait is already showing. So what? Let Penny tease all she wants. Did she mention anything else? Your beautiful pecan skin? Your thick long hair? Light-brown eyes? I bet she didn't." Eboni remembered this and felt better. Ten minutes later, the feeling vanished. She entered the house and froze in fear at the sounds of the screams. "Gail! Open up this damn door and give me back my money!" Henry yelled. His wife had barricaded herself in the bedroom.

"No, Henry. You're drunk."

"Bitch, don't tell me I'm drunk. Give me my money."

"No, it's for the rent. It's the rent money." She cried and crouched lower against the wall. Her dress was torn, and her hair was a mess. She had run upstairs, trying to escape his gin-soaked anger. There she stayed, her arms wrapped around her legs, and rocked back as if to protect herself against a violent storm.

"Gail!" he yelled again above the pounding on the door. "I'm gonna kick this door down and beat the shit out of you if you don't open this fuckin' door right now." She buried her head in her lap. He started kicking harder. Gail stared at the door frame, horrified. The lock was bouncing loose. She crawled to the bed and pulled herself up, ignoring the sharp pain racing down her arms. She braced herself and reached under the mattress for the $1,200 he had given her. Friday night when he had come from work and before his drunken spree started. She walked to the door and caught sight of her face in the mirror. The black eye was turning blue. She jumped as the door gave way, banging against the wall, and Henry was in her face before she could react.

"Where's my money?" He towered over her with his 6'4", 220 lbs. frame. He was mid forties with brown skin and a boxer's build; good-looking and damn good provider. That's what attracted her until the drinking and smoking destroyed his looks and he became resentful. She stood cowering under his stare. She was 5'7" and 125 pounds. Her normally smooth pecan skin was now bruised, and her light eyes swollen, blackened.

"Here's your money." She handed it to him, trembling, and turned her head to avoid the slap, but he caught her across the face. She screamed

2

out in pain, which further enraged him. He knocked her down on the bed with another slap and began choking her.

"Don't you ever, ever take my money!" He pounded her head into the mattress. She felt herself growing weaker, unable to fight him off, and the pressure of his fingers tightened around her neck. She was losing her breath. Her vision blurred, and her eyes filled with tears.

"Mom! Dad! Stop it." Eboni rushed to her mother and tried to pull her father's hands away, but he was too strong.

Gail struggled to focus on her daughter, afraid Henry might turn on her next. "Eboni. Get out! Get out!"

Afraid to leave, Eboni tried to plead. "Daddy, please! Please! You're hurting her." Henry looked down on his daughter's face filled with tears and, as if a trance had been temporarily broken, he released his hold. Gail rolled away from his grasp, crying, "Not in front of my child. Please, Henry, please…" He looked at his wife and his daughter then rose to his feet. In the doorway, he leaned against the damaged frame. "We're not done. I'm not finished with you," he whispered. Eboni covered her ears as the door on the loose hinges slammed against the wall. Henry had left. Gail hugged her daughter. "Eboni, honey. It's going to be all right. He's just upset, but he's calm now. It's going to be alright, baby girl." She smoothed her daughter's hair and stroked her cheek. "He's just upset," she said again. Her voice drifted, moved away to a peaceful time as she embraced and caressed Eboni. The phone rang. Gail and Henry had been married for fifteen years. He worked as a carpenter for a small local firm, but early in the marriage, he had begun to drink up his salary, leaving Gail to provide for the children on her salary as a bank teller. She was now defending him. "Denise, he's a good man. You don't understand." She held the phone under her chin and held a warm cloth against her face as Denise's voice rattled through the receiver. "You need to leave him. He's been doing this for years. It's by the grace of God that you are not permanently scarred, but you are damaged emotionally, and that's just as bad."

"Well, what am I supposed to do? Just pack up and walk out? I have four kids, in case you forgot."

"Hold on, honey. I'm not Henry. I understand you're hurt and upset, but think of the kids. Is it fair for them to see their father treat you like this?"

Gail was silent. She knew her longtime friend was right, but what could she do? Where would I go? she asked herself, with only $2,000 in savings that Henry knew nothing of. If he found out, he would have beaten her so that he could drink on his dry days when he was broke. It's a wonder she managed to save that, what with trying to keep a roof over the kids' head and food on the table and clothes on their backs.

"Gail! Gail? Are you there?"

"Yes, Denise. I'm here. My mind was just spinning."

"I know, girl. I wish I could help you, but you know you and the kids could always stay here."

"But he knows where you live, Denise. He would be at the door, kicking that in too, and I don't want to bring that kind of trouble your way."

"Well, I'm here for you. You do know that."

"Yeah. I gotta go, Denise."

She felt trapped. A minute later, she made her way downstairs to clean up the house, straighten up the mess Henry had made during the fight. All before the rest of the kids came home. She picked up the chair she'd used to block him to put some distance between them. She cleaned up the broken dishes that had gotten in his way when he dragged across the kitchen table. Eboni had gone to pick up Elisha and Eric, and both helped to further tidy up the place.

"Who's going to help me make dinner?"

They both chimed in repeatedly, "I will, I will."

Gail's throat still hurt, but she wanted to appear strong, not weak or beaten down, for Children's sake.

She did not want her daughters to see her as a woman stuck between a fucking rock and a fucked-up, hard place.

Henry returned home late and even more drunk. He stumbled into the bed and lay next to Gail, who was pretending to be asleep.

"Gail, honey..." He blew his sour breath on the back of her neck. "Turn around. I-I- wanna talk to you. Turn, I said! And why do you have all these clothes on for?"

"I'm cold and tired, that's all." She spoke softly, trying to keep him calm.

"Well, take 'em off and come closer to me. For warmth." His words were slurred. "You know I love you. I didn't mean to hurt you. I love you, woman. Don't ever leave me, 'cause I'm afraid of what I might do. I love you. Now come on. Gimme a kiss."

"Henry, I'm cold. Let's just get some sleep," she whispered.

"There you go tellin' me what to do again. First, with my money, now this."

He grabbed her arm and the ache was so painful it had stretched down the length of it.

He squeezed hard. "Take it off, I said."

She wanted to scream but knew that sound would set him off and wake up the kids.

"Okay, Henry. Please. Just lower your voice."

"Lower my voice?"

"They will hear you. See here," she said quickly. "Everything's off."

"Good. About time you listened to me. I'm the man. Just because you bring in a bigger paycheck, may have a better paying job, but I'm the boss of the family."

He stood up to remove his clothing and stumbled. He caught himself, cursed, and removed the rest. He balled them up and aimed for the dresser but missed, and the shirt and pants landed on the floor. "You'll get 'em in the morning," he said and climbed on top of his wife.

Later, Eboni heard her mother crying but was too frightened to enter her parents' bedroom. She didn't hear her father yelling or the furniture being knocked about, so she lay in bed and cried herself to sleep.

Hours later, Gail slipped out of bed. She felt used and trapped, listening to her husband's snoring.

He had finally passed out. She made her way to the bathroom, turned on the shower, and stepped into a soothing flow of warm water. There she stayed, welcoming the feeling washing over her. She closed her eyes and imagined each drop like a tender kiss, loving, smoothing the bruises away. She turned the water on full force. It streamed down her back, washing away the anxiety and fear.

Her mind again flashed back to a more peaceful time. When her husband was so different. He used to surprise her with flowers of the season just because... And he had often taken the kids out, as he put it, to give you a break."

"God, do you hear me? I need help. I can't take it anymore. Please have mercy on me and my family. Paul, my oldest, has run away. He got tired of being Henry's punching bag. Please bring him back safely."

As the water streamed over her, she stared at Henry's straight razor resting on the edge of the sink. It was as if her prayers had been answered. She gripped the handle and brought the blade down on her wrist. She cried out, dropped the razor in the tub, and looked at her wound. She had only managed to nick herself. She ran the cold water over the cut. "God, I can't even do that right. Well, maybe I deserve the mess I'm in." The anger she felt for her husband she now directed at herself. "I'm an idiot. Look at me."

"Gail! You in there?"

"Yes, yes, Henry. Be right out," she hastily replied, frightened, hoping he had not heard her when she cut herself.

"Well, hurry up! I gotta go."

She opened the door and walked past him then got back in the bed.

––––––––––––– ✦✦✦✦✦ –––––––––––––

Eboni was at Penny's house when the phone rang. She arrived at the hospital to find her father crying to the cops. "I didn't mean it, she fell, she made me do it." He buried his head in his hands. She looked at him until he turned away.

"Where's Mommy?"

"In there." He gestured.

Penny trailed behind her, but Eboni told her to wait. She wanted to see her mother alone. In the room, a nurse approached her. "Your name is Eboni?" she asked. She shook her head yes, speechless at the sight of her mother.

"Well, she's been asking for you. Go on over to her dear," she said so kindly.

Eboni approached the bed cautiously. "I'm here, Mommy. I'm here." She touched her mother's swollen face. Gail looked as if she had been in a car accident. "Mom. Daddy did this to you? But why? Why does he keep hurting you?"

"He didn't mean it," Gail said weakly. She was groggy from the pain medication the doctors had given her.

Eboni leaned closer and sobbed on her mother's shoulders. "Mom, don't leave me."

"I'm sorry," Gail whispered. I can't protect us. The nurse came over and touched Eboni's arm. "I'll be right back," she said; she looked in Eboni's eyes and left the room.

"Mommy, Mommy, I'm sorry I wasn't there to stop him."

There was a soft knock at the door, then it opened. "Come here, baby."

Eboni ran crying into Denise's arms. Denise looked over at her friend.

"She has a black eye, a broken nose, six broken ribs, and a broken arm."

"My God." Denise grasped, trying to hold herself together for Eboni's sake.

"Please, Eboni, won't you wait outside for a minute? I want to talk to your mother. I'll come and get you when I'm done, honey."

Along the corridor, Eboni saw the nurse talking to the police as they placed handcuffs on Henry. "Daddy!" she cried out.

———— ·✦✦✦✦· ————

Five years later, when the phone rang in the middle of the night, it startled Gail. She jumped up out of her sleep, grabbed the receiver with fear of the unknown, knowing that all her children were sound asleep in their beds in her house. Her mind raced to Denise. Something had happened to her.

"Hello, is this Mrs. Reid, the wife of Mr. Henry Reid?"

"Yes, it is. Who's calling?"

"This is the correctional division's chief officer, Mrs. Jennifer Watson. I'm sorry to inform you that your husband, Henry Reid, along with several other inmates, died in a prison disturbance this evening."

"Died?" Gail was not sure of what she was hearing.

"I'm sorry to call you with this news."

As the woman spoke on, Gail only half listened. Through the shock and disbelief, a sudden cautious feeling of happiness emerged. Henry had been in prison for five years for repeatedly beating her until the courts finally got tired of him and slammed down a sentence of seven years he had two years left. Even though he had been behind bars, it was Gail who had been the real prisoner. Now a weight was lifted; no more threatening phone calls about killing her for having him locked up.

Why didn't he see she was already dead? He had killed her years ago; he just didn't bury the body.

"Mrs. Watson, you know what I want you to do with Henry's belongings? Burn them in hell. Now if you can't do that, then throw them away or give them away. I don't want anything from that monster. Do you hear me?'"

"I understand. I've read his case file. Well, good luck to you, and once again, I'm sorry to call with this disturbing news."

The line went dead, and Gail listened to the buzz.

"Yes. Thank you. We'll be just fine. I can do it alone just as I've done for the pass five years. My children will be alright. They have me."

She spent the rest of the night in prayers.

CHAPTER

2

The music vibrated through the house. Gail knocked on her teenage daughter's bedroom door as Biggie's "Hypnotize" threatened to tear down the structure of her walls. Gail got no answer and flung the door open. She yelled, trying to talk over music blasting from Eboni's radio. Eboni turned in middance to face her mother and knew she was pissed.

"Turn that noise down or turn it off," Gail said. "Hip-hop! That's all you listen to. You need to hop your ass in your school lesson and pick up a book to hip into how, 'bout that?"

Eboni waited until her mother had closed the door. Then she plopped on her bed and picked up one of her rap magazines, flipping through the pages, when an old school came on. "Rock The Bells" by L.L.Cool J, boomed through the radio, screaming to be turned up on blast. She knew her mother would be marching right back and, this time, might do a little more, like confiscate her sounds. She turned L.L. off in mid scream and went downstairs. Her mother was mopping the kitchen floor. Eboni started to step in, hoping to grab a soda before her mother turned around but decided from the mood her mother was in, even a nice cold soda on a hot day wasn't worth it.

Watching her mother clean, she remembered when her father was alive, how she and Elisha would spend their days helping her mom clean up the mess he'd made coming home drunk, knocking things over, then asking who broke this or that, not remembering that it was him.

Gail was vigorously scrubbing the floor with the mop when she noticed Eboni standing in the doorway. "Oh, girl! You scared the bejesus out of me. I know you didn't come to help, did you?" She paused to wipe the sweat from her face.

"No. Just came to ask if I can go to Penny's house for a while."

Gail nodded yes and went back to her chores. Since Henry's death, she felt as if she was the cause of her kids growing up without their father.

"What's up, girl?" Eboni asked.

"Ain't nothing," Penny said. "Just chilling."

"Yeah, my mom's tripping, so I blew."

"Hmm, I know how that goes," Penny replied. "Yo, bust this. I met this niggah the other day while I was standing at the bus stop waiting for the B12 on my way to the doctor's office for another fake-ass baby test."

"False alarm, huh?" asked Eboni.

Penny turned away. She didn't want her to see the hurt look on her face because she secretly wanted a child, someone to love her back.

Thank God she played it off.

"Anyway, this brother pulls up on me in this broken-down whip, trying to holler at a sistah, asking me if he could play taxi for me and give me a ride."

"Did you go?"

"Hells no, and have someone see me in that buggy bucket stagecoach?" she laughed. "Naw, I just told Mister No Money I don't need no ride. Just give me his digits 'cause my bus was coming. That brother was a buster from his weak ass-whip to his played out gear and fucked-up 'fro."

"I'm surprised you ain't diss him as big as your mouth is."

Penny shrugged. "See, sometimes, you gotta do it with tact when a brother is whack."

"Yeah, so you don't get slapped," Eboni added.

"True dat. Those bumbees niggahs be having mad bags of chips on their shoulders 'cause they broke and tired. What's a sistah to do? Get down with a sinking ship and swim, hoping to stay afloat? I don't think so." Penny was silent for a moment then turned to face her friend. "Eboni, I wanted to ask but don't want you to get upset and shit and start bugging out."

Eboni saw the look on Penny's face. It was a silly grin. "What is it?"

"You, sure?"

"Yeah, go ahead. Ask me."

"Okay then. There was another pause. "Whew. All right, well, I just wanted to ask you… She took an even longer pause, still holding that silly look.

"Girl, stop beating around the bush." She tapped Penny's arm. "Spit it out already."

"Okay. Okay. Are you a virgin still?"

"A virgin?"

"Yes, you know. Someone that's not having sex. Doing the nasty. Getting some. Answer me."

Eboni looked at her oversexed friend.

"Well, answer me."

"Number one, I know what a virgin is. And number two…it's none of your biz."

"Aha. You're still a virgin," she laughed.

"What makes you say that?" Eboni asked, not really wanting to hear the answer. She always told herself that she would not end up like her parents in an abusive marriage.

"I could tell," Penny said.

"Well, so what? Anyhow, I'm saving myself."

Penny was shocked. "For what?"

"For someone special."

"Girl, you need to come off that. You better stop dreaming and leave that TV shit alone 'cause ain't no fucking knight up on no horse out here. Now, what you need is to get you one of those dudes on the corner with a pocket full of easy money and get paid like I do. You do what I said. Look, don't be sounding all naive and wet behind the ears on some newborn shit. You are too big to be a baby. Let me put you on. You see, you're cute and shit, and I know brothers want to holler at you Shit. 'Cause, they done stepped to me asking about you, and that's on the real tip."

"Who?"

"Girl, just listen. Let the brother buy you something. Take you out. Sport him—shit, play his ass like a sport, like basketball, football. Pick, girl."

"Girl, you know I ain't got no time for boys. I got school, where you need to be instead of chasing someone else's pocket. And besides, their asses will be in jail or dead or mad baby mommas and a bunch of kids they can't afford so they walk away leaving broken mothers to raise those kids by themselves. I don't want no man-child. No one makes it off the corner. Look at all those murals tag up on the storefronts. Anyhow, just look at that guy—that old-ass man—what's his name?"

"Oh, I know who you're talking about. Knowledge," said Penny.

"Yeah, that's him. His old ass trying to talk to everyone like he's some young buck. Don't he have a mirror or he so stupid he can't even see how old he looks? Disgusting."

"And besides, you know your mother will kick your ass."

"For real," they chimed and laughed.

"And anyhow, those guys out there are alot older than me."

"Better to teach you," Penny cracked.

"And the only one I would talk to is Jeff 'cause he's fine. What is he, twenty-four or something?"

"So you don't want no young head. They're broke and cheap. And play too many games."

"True dat. I don't see anything special out there anyhow."

Eboni could always tell when Penny had had sex 'cause that's when she starts picking on her. She wore her sexual partners like a string of pearls, one right after the other.

But Eboni has never known Penny to be in a lasting relationship with anybody. Guess that was why she went out like that. Not me. When I do have sex, I'll be married to that man. He'll love me and respect my potential.

"Eboni!"

"Yeah, girl?"

"You hungry? Let's go get some pizza at Lucia's."

"I'm down. And besides, Jeff is out there." Penny smiled. "Well, let's just go. Just walk past him," Eboni said, thinking that Penny had probably slept with most of the guys out there anyway. She was known for her easy access. And Eboni was known for her roadblocks.

They ordered their slices and sodas from the large Italian lady they called grandma Lulu.

"My treat," Eboni said and paid for the food. Then she noticed Tony, one of the guys from the corner, standing with someone new, or so she thought.

"I haven't seen him in a while. Heard he was in jail or down south somewhere," Penny said, nudging her.

Fresh meat for her, Eboni thought.

"Hmmm, he's fine," Penny said, licking her lips. He was heading their way.

"Get his attention," Penny said. This annoyed me being put on the spot, but I told myself to stay cool as he walked up.

"Hello, he said. "Can I talk to you for a second? My name's Shawn. I've been noticing you. Wouldn't mind getting to know you better if that's possible." He smiled.

This fine, dark brother smiled and all Eboni could manage was a hi and blushed and walked shyly away.

Penny stayed to talk to him. Eboni heard her say, "What's up? I'm Penny."

"Yeah, bet you are," he teased as the door closed behind me. She'd tried to flirt, but he cut right to it, shutting her down.

"What's up with your friend?"

"Who? Eboni? She's cool."

"Yeah, Eboni. She's flyy. Tell her I said that."

Then he walked away, leaving Penny standing there. Quick receiver that she was, she'd caught right up to Eboni.

"Aha. Now I got it. You're shy."

"Nonsense, girl. Just eat your pizza..." Before it gets cold with your hot ass, Eboni thought.

"So when are you two going out or hooking up?" Eboni asked, feeling a little jealous.

"We're not. He doesn't want me. He said he thinks you're the bomb!"

"Girl, stop playing." Eboni smiled, hoping she wasn't lying or riding her. But then again, why not? Why wouldn't he want me? Eboni was seventeen but very developed. She was already wearing a 36C on a size 8 frame. At 5'7", 120 lbs, most of that was in her behind, which was plump and round. She jiggled like jelly when she wore loose-fitting clothes.

Her mother teased her, saying she was going to need a girdle to hold down the Reid curse or blessing. "It's a matter of taste," she said.

"Well, girl, what are you going to do?"

Eboni looked at Penny. She was a little heavier than Eboni and attractive. She had a cute face and dimples and rocked the latest hairstyle and gear; she stayed fresh. She didn't have much of a figure. Guess that's why she thought so little of it, Eboni thought. For a black girl, her butt was flat! But she had a very big chest—44 double Ds. She always bragged about them, calling them her solution solvers, saying how they get her out of jams and gets her what she wants.

"Formula 44D please," the guys on the corner yelled between coughs when she passed by. She loved it; she ate it up, all that attention.

"Eboni, girl, he is fine."

"I know, but so what?"

"Look, there he is with Jeff, the biggest drug dealer on that corner," she said, tapping Eboni.

"I know. I can see. Calm down, you get all boy crazy. I see them."

"A'ight. Which one looks better?" she asked.

Eboni had to admit they both were fine. "Shawn," she said.

"Girl, would you look at him? Ouch! He's sooo fine," Penny teased.

"Okay, the next time I see him," Eboni said, stopping to point at Penny's face, "and he speaks first, I'll holler back."

"You go, girl. He's the hottest thing out there, and if I can't have him, then you get him. Lock him down, girl, and no pressure, right?"

"No pressure," Eboni repeated. But her heart was racing yet Shawn was nowhere near them. There was something about him Eboni felt a connection to, even though she had ran out of Lucia's pizzeria like some kid. But he did tell Penny... "Wait, did he really say that to you?" she asked again.

"Yeah, he did."

———————— ·+✦+✦+· ————————

"Yo! Yo! Yo! Who's in the house?" shouted Donny and Johnny, coming down the block.

"I takes the mic, then you pass it back," they clowned with each other.

"What's up, guys?" Penny said. "We'll talk later," she whispered to Eboni. Then turned to the boys. "Hey, fellows, what you up to?"

"You, heard about Dawn's parties coming up?"

"No. Whose party?" Penny said, bouncing her 44s up and down and looking at Donny, the neighborhood DJ.

"Dawn's, that's whose."

"When is it?" Eboni asked.

"Why? You don't party or hang out. School girl goody-goody," Johnny teased.

"Don't even try it," Penny said, sticking up for Eboni. "Shit, my girl is down for whatever."

"Yeah, all right, we'll see. It's at the end of the summer. Two more months, from now."

"You clowns," Penny said, and Eboni laughed.

"For real! Well, heads up anyway, you know Dawn's party does be off the hook said," Donny.

The next day, I thought a lot about what Penny had said to me. I was seventeen years old and bitten by the shy bug. I hurried home with his eyes burning a hole in my back at the pizza shop. I could still hear him chuckle as I left. Embarrassed, I decided to go over to Penny's house; she was in her room, as usual. It seemed the men she dated. Gave her a sense of purpose. I needed to confide in Penny about what had taken place. I needed reassurance on how it wasn't that bad—some girlfriend courage—and to plan our attack for later on when we see him. Girl power. I was somehow convinced that I was going to make him mine, not in the sport him kind of way as Penny put it but, in the way, he was going to be my man. Penny has been my friend for years; she's been with me through thick and thin—from my father's abusive behavior to my mother's hospital trips. She's been there by letting me stay at her house when I was too scared to go home. Even though she was only a year older than me and I found her to be a close friend, she's a little boy-crazy for my liking.

They spent the rest of the evening going over Shawn and the boys. Out there from old man Knowledge to Jeff, Little Tony to Markus and Dave and the rest of the cats on the corner.

As her mother ate her breakfast—eggs, and butter toast—and sat drinking her tea, Eboni's mind was playing over what had taken place with Shawn, and she was left wondering what she'd done wrong and what he probably thought about her and how immature she must be compared to the women he dated and who hang around him. And I'm going to be the one to knock them all out the box.

The next day, Penny stopped by. As they were heading outside to go to the park and play some handball, they had to pass the famous store corner. Eboni never really thought of herself as shy, but then again, she never really had much contact with the opposite sex. She then realized the boys that she was attracted to she was very shy around. And the ones she wasn't attractive toward, they became her best friends hung out with. You know, the type the guys who thought it was safer to chill with the girls than to form their own crew. You know the type 55 boys, not quite 100 percent, always hanging around us girls, cracking jokes, rapping, doing impressions—just straight clowning, keeping me and my friends laughing. They didn't start no trouble didn't want no problems. Wasn't looking for competition or confrontation from the other guys and crews in the neighborhood. That's why they played us so close. We were headed to the park, only stopping to pick up the rest of our click. So cool to hang with but too foolish to keep. Donny and Johnny. They always carried a boom box even though it was played out. They didn't care if people were laughing at them. That's what made them so cool.

Donny was cute; he was a tall light-skinned dress fly. Lives to party and an up-and-coming DJ like the next Kid Capri. Johnny was short, pudgy around the middle but had an effective, contagious laugh that had everyone rolling no matter how corny the joke was. Was dark-skinned with even skin tone for a guy. So with Donny and his sidekick Johnny, who always toted the box, they partied all the way to the park. Penny and Eboni passed the corner store on their way to pick them up.

Shawn and his crew were out there. "Look, girl, there's Shawn." I know, I got eyes. I'm not blind, just nervous, she said to herself. "You're going to talk to him, right?" Penny asked, all persistent and too much in Eboni's business. "Let's just go. All his boys are with him. . I'll catch him later when he's alone."

"Yeah. Okay." She smirked. Soon as they were about to pass him with Eboni's head purposely turned to look away from Shawn, he said "What's up?" to Eboni. And she managed a girlish "Hi" with a little girl's smile on her face. Very immature, she thought; her mind was saying run, but her body was frozen. "Not bad, not bad at all," Penny said as they passed them. Good, she didn't notice. She guessed it was because Penny was by her side and she had something to prove. Or was it my outfit—pink and white shorts set that hugged my body just right—that kept him smiling after we passed him?

<hr>

Shawn thought out in the open with a smile on his face, "Yo, shorty right, Imma holler at that for sure. 'Cause I'm for sure wit it!"

Tony was pressed up on the wall with his arms crossed. He looked at Shawn. "I just don't see it, son."

"Whatever, man. Remember Sandy, Lisa, Tina, Robin, and Chantel, who were they sweating?"

"Son, it ain't even about that. All I'm saying is we got money to get out here. So put shorty on the back burner. Tony knew Shawn was his boss but was also his boy; they had been friends for years and did time together. They even shared women. But he saw something different when he talked about Eboni.

"Yeah, back to this money, how much you got for me?" Tony dug in his pocket and pulled out a wad of money and handed it to Shawn. "The count is on point," he said while looking at Shawn, hoping he did offend him. Shawn counted his cash slap Tony on the back stuff the $3,500. In his pocket.

"Yeah, we're good. Come on, give me a walk to Lucia's."

"All right, I'm down for pizza."

———————— ·+++++·· ————————

At the park, we had to wait for our turn on the court. I still enjoyed the game. The Puerto Ricans had the court on lockdown. They were the better players, like they were born to play handball. So as we waited for our turn, the sun was beating down on us. Donny turned up his radio and started to dance, doing his pop and lock to an oldie but goodie rap classic. "Ah-hah," he said to the beat of that old-school sound.

He always knew how to get things started on an upbeat. "Go, Donny," Penny chimed. That was some game, and I guess the Puerto Ricans had enough and wanted to rest and kick back to the music and watch us play to see if they had any competition. They let us play one another then called next. But after ten minutes of watching us play, they left. They shook their heads and laughed, got up, and headed back down the hill. The Latinos were the kings of the handball court. We played a couple of sets; the guys won. It was getting hotter; the sun was now standing on our backs, so we gave it a rest. Handball is a hood sport. "There's no handball on TV," joked Donny, "so I'll never be the next great Jordan, Kobe, or O'Neil of handball," as he lay down on the grass. "And besides, they take that game way too seriously anyhow."

Two hours later, we were heading back down the hill. We had to pass the corner store once again. Shawn and his crew were still out there. I was too exhausted to be bothered, and that's when he walked right up to me and took my hand and held it. I started to pull away but was held by his sexy slanted eyes that were hypnotizing me, setting me in a trance. I stood there.

"I would like to talk to you."

I looked down at my arm. My hand was engulfed in his beautiful hand. He noticed my glance and, with his sexy bedroom eyes, said, "Oh, this," moving, my arm a little. "It's just to make sure you don't run off, this time." He said with a smile, revealing rows of perfect white teeth that would make a dentist broke. What was I hearing? He wanted to talk to me. I slipped and repeated. "Yes, to you a little later on. I'm going to walk down your block, hmm, around six o'clock. And we could go for a walk so we could get to know each other better," he finished.

"All right, sure" was all I could manage, terrified and excited, then I walked away with my crew.

"Girl, you did it!" exclaimed Penny.

"Turn around and see if he's looking at us."

"Us, no. But you, yeah, he's cold staring at you. You got him hooked. Now pull him in. Nice and slow." As we sat down on my stoop, Donny looked at me then asked, "Yo, you know what he does on the corner all day," in a big brother manner.

"She knows what he does out there!" yelled Penny in a sassy way, defending me. I shook my head yes to his waiting answer, ignoring Penny's look.

"Eboni, all I'm saying is be careful with him. Seems a lot of girls mess themselves up by guys like them getting on drugs or having babies too soon. Look, just be smart about him and not be blinded by the cash he might wave at you. You really don't know him, but he runs with a dangerous crowd, and bullets have no name."

I could see how worried he was for me. "I know, and trust me, I'm no fool. It's nice to know you care," I said with a smile and a wink. He winked back at me. I knew everything between us was all right again. He was just trying to protect me.

"What time is Shawn coming?"

"Around seven," I said; just in case he was late, I didn't want to look like I was waiting for him. Which I was! So Johnny turned on the box, and we listened to the top 10 countdown on Hot 97.1 with FunkMaster Flex. One of Jay-Z's songs blasted, and the DJ has spun that record too many times for my ears. "Damn, Flex could spin," said Donny. "Yo, I'm just like that, cutting and scratching." He mimicked with his hands just like Flex. "Yo, next week, Tina's having a party. You playing?"

"Nah, she already got Dawn's cousin, Troy, then it's Dawn's party after that, and you know, it's going to be fly. Everyone's going to be in the house," said Donny.

"Well, I'm not feeling Tina's party." I couldn't stand Tina. I don't like her ways. Heard she was a thief, and things always seemed to disappear when she was around.

"Even though I haven't seen Dawn in weeks, I know I'm invited," said Penny.

"It's BYOB," said Donny.

"Yeah, bring your own bag," said Johnny in between beats. "A-huh!"

This was the hood; it wouldn't be like crashing hood parties since they didn't have any guest lists. It was word of mouth, not mail.

"Yeah, so at the party, I would be shaking my rump, on the dance floor—or should I say Dawn's mother's living room," said Penny. "And, girl! I know you're coming. Donny said he talked to Dawn about DJ-ing."

I shook my head, yes. About the party.

"So I'm going to hear you play," Penny said.

"For sure. I just gotta cop the hottest summer jams that was about to hit the radio stations," he added. "'Cause I'm gifted like that. So who's riding with me to the city? All I'm saying is that it is one record store."

"I don't care for a bunch of cute guys standing around talking about beats and records and not paying me any mind," she said while stretching her arms in the air. "Eboni, you down for the ride?"

"I don't know yet. I'll let you know."

"All right, cool."

"Huh, unless you could spin like the rest and best of them, that was one trip I didn't want to take," finished Penny.

As we sat there waiting for Shawn to come walking down the block, Donny and Johnny were in their own world, talking about all the girls that would be at this party. Then Johnny asked if he could do a little rap for the party. "You know, rock the mic. One time, like RUN-D.M.C meets Mister Rogers, two very different neighborhoods."

"I don't know cuz it's a paying thing. You know how that goes."

"I'm your boy. Let me run it by Dawn and Troy first. I'll get back to you." Johnny was smiling as if he'd had a definite yes. "Cool, 'cause my rap is tight."

Penny was joking and teasing me about my meeting with Shawn. Donny made a sound that caused me to look at him. He was frowning. I knew what that frown meant, so I didn't ask. Johnny was putting his rap together when my mother called me inside, and it was still early, so I told them to wait. My mother was in the kitchen cooking, which she only did on the weekends. She was making her famous rice and chicken cook-up. "Eboni, I need you to make the salad."

I was getting the vegetables out of the fridge. That's when she said to me, "Your Aunt Nancy and her kids are having problems, and they will be moving in with us. So I need you to make room for your cousin, Justina. She'll be staying in your room."

"When are they coming?"

"Tomorrow," she replied.

"Oh, that's good."

"And Paul is going to help."

"Paul?"

"Yes."

"Why? Cause he's hardly home?"

"Well, he's upstairs, so he'll be moving your aunt's furniture up in the attic. So I need you to mop and dust it out for me. You could do it now or in the morning, but it needs to get done before they come." I heard her yell after me. I haven't seen my cousin Justina in a while. I was happy they were coming to stay with us. I thought, on my way back outside, Shawn is coming, and I am not about to be stuck in the house, cleaning. At least not this night.

She thought Penny was rapping along with Johnny while Donny was making the beat. Like Biz Markie. Eboni's mother was now cleaning up the living room and the dining room even though it wasn't messy; she just couldn't stand dust. It was embarrassing for her. She always told her girls, "Dust is a sign of a disorder." That's how she would put it. Elisha was dusting the furniture; she was spraying lemon Pledge on the dining room table. While her mother was vacuuming.

"Mom, why are we doing this? 'Cause it's just going to get messy when they move in here," asked Elisha.

"Because if you want people to respect your house, you have to set the pace in other words. She'll see how I like my place and help keep it that way," replied her mother.

It was getting closer to five o'clock, and I still hadn't had dinner. Shawn would be here. I told Penny and the crew I was going inside and that I needed to get ready! They got up to leave. "Girl, I'll be back before he comes. I'm going home to eat."

"Yeah, me too," Johnny said.

"Ditto," said Donny with a look of warning to me. With a smile on my face, I went inside to have dinner. Mom was still talking about making room for our aunt and her family. How she wanted to keep the downstairs part of her home clear of clutter. One thing about my mother, I learned she would let fifty people come live in her house, and not mind making room for them just as long you didn't leave your clothes or shoes or books or belongings in any part of her home unattended. If you left something, she would be hitting the roof and packing your bags, sending you on your way. Now I would be doing double chores with them here.

<hr />

Eboni thought while deciding if she needed to change. Nah, what I have on is good enough. It's okay, my pink-and-white shorts set with white Nike tennis shoes. She didn't wear any makeup as she sat downstairs, waiting for him. Shawn knew off back that Eboni was the girl for him. He liked her style, the way she didn't try hard to get noticed. It was all natural as he studied her. She was a beauty and was down to earth. That's how he phrased it to Tony, who kept on insisting it was a fuck thang! "Naw, man, she's different."

"I'll give you that, and by that, I mean, I haven't seen her with no man. She wasn't hanging out in the streets like the rest of these young chicks. Her girl Penny said she was smart too. Already in college. Yo, man, she outta your league. You better off with Sandy."

"Shit. Sandy who? Ain't no girl out of my league. Look at me, man, fly money, fly clothes, and fly honeys. Shorty is mine for the summer. I'll check you later," Shawn said, looking at his watch. "Gotta go scope miss honey," he said walking down the block after slapping five to Tony, who just stared at his man.

Yeah, you might be all that, but she is different, he thought after Shawn left.

While they were still cleaning, I went back outside and joined my friends.

"Tick, tick, tock. The mouse will be coming down your block," Penny joked. And I was a nervous wreck. Keep it together. You got this.

"We're gonna leave, we shouldn't be here when he comes," said Johnny.

"All right, guys, I'll see you later," I said, going back inside to watch a little TV with my family who had just finished cleaning. The phone rang. My mom got up to answer it. Ten minutes later, she was back watching TV with us again, and relaxing, which was rare for her. We were watching reruns of A Different World.

As the doorbell rang, I got up to answer it. My mother was looking to see who it was. As I opened the door, I could not believe it was Shawn at my house, ringing my bell. "Who's at the door?" my mother yelled out 'cause it was late, and she wasn't expecting anyone.

"It's for me, and I'm going outside for a while. I'll be right back!" I yelled out, closing the front door quickly.

"I've been thinking about you all day, so when I walked down your block and you weren't out here sitting on your stoop, I have to admit I was a little nervous about ringing your bell this late at night. I was hoping that you would be the one to open the door and not your mom."

All I could do was smile and think, This fine, really good-looking guy is thinking about me. "Yeah, I'm glad you came to see me," I commented. So as we were heading down the steps after locking the front door behind me, he held the gate open for me, that's when it hit me where were we going, nothing was planned, I thought. As we were walking down the street, my neighbors were staring at us. I guess they had never seen me with a guy before or because he was one of those guys who hung out on the corner and I was with him.

He asked if I wanted to eat something and then go to the movies. I just finished eating not too long ago. "Well, I'm hungry. Let's walk over to McDonald's so I could grab a quick bite then we'll go to the movies from there."

"All right." McD's was only two blocks away anyhow. While Shawn was placing his order, I noticed that there were four girls around his age staring at him. I guess they were flirting with him. But he didn't disrespect me. He paid them no mind as he grabbed my hand as we walked past them.

"Now it's off to the movies," he said. I was thinking about how I have never been to the movies with a guy before. It should be fun and especially a night of first for me: my first kiss and my first time in the city. He must have read my mind. Shawn leaned over and kissed me on my mouth. I was shocked. I hadn't kissed anyone before like this. As Penny would say, "Leave that TV shit alone. This is the real thing."

When we got out of the movies, it was late; and for some reason, I thought Forty-second Street would be closing up; it was just as packed. So I had to pull back air. "You have never been kissed before, huh?"

I looked shyly at him. "No, you were the first."

He smiled and held me close to him while hugging me. He then whispered in my ear, "I'm going to teach you a lot of things that's going to make you a woman that knows her shit. Your ass is too fly not to know what you have and what to do with it. And I'm in no rush, don't want you all scared and nervous. So we're going to start slow, OK, no rush." He kissed me real slow. "How old are you?" he asked again.

"I'm seventeen."

"Wow, you look older. I thought you were around nineteen or twenty, didn't know you were so young. Your body said you were older, and the way you carry yourself, I just figured you were around my age. You are mature for seventeen, though, you had me fooled. And I like you too much already to let you go because of that."

"Age ain't nothing but a number," I said.

"Yeah, you're right. Come on, let me get you home. It's pretty late," he said while he put his hand around my waist. We walked to the train station. "We should go out again. I would like to see you again. I'll be honest with you, I'm not seeing no one, and even though this is the first time we've been out, I would only like to see you. And it would feel right if I had someone who cares about me. And I cared for them."

Wait, is he asking me out?

"I know we just met, but I feel something special with you. I know you are feeling it too. Otherwise, I wouldn't have any feelings for you," he said flat out to me.

"Shawn, I do feel something for you, and I know this is strange, but I do feel like we might have something, so you agree we owe it to ourselves to find out. I never felt this way so fast for nobody before. What about Sandy?" I slipped but glad it was said.

"No, not even her. Word is bond. My word is all I have in this world. Look, I want you to be my girl and mine only. Look, I don't hit women, I don't cheat, and I will never hurt you. You can trust me on that. So can I have your phone number so I could at least call you?" He said while writing his number down for me.

I had been living in a shell, always worried that all men were like my father; but something about him told me differently, and then I jumped out the window. "Yes, Shawn, let's do it. I mean, yes, I want to see you only," I said, giving him my number too.

"It's going to be hard for me to sleep, I'm going to be thinking of you for real all night."

"I would be thinking about you too," I said as he walked me to the door then kissed me good-bye. He pulled me close to him and I felt his hard-on, so I pulled back and looked down at him. This time, he shyly smiled. We said our good-nights, and I went inside. I had no idea what time it was. It was 1:00 am. My mother was up and mad at me. I tried to explain that I lost track of time.

"You're seventeen. Your time is twelve o'clock, not 1:00 a.m." And since you didn't know, that's what it is, you hear me? And you better never lose track or else." I went up to the bed. All I could think about was Shawn and his kiss and how he made me feel. And I know he felt it. Because his pants said so. I couldn't wait to call Penny and tell her about my date—and my new man. "First time out the gate and you land a top dog from out on the corner" is what she would say. She would have to wait 'cause at one thirty in the morning, I was not phoning her to wake up her parents. So as I laid down, my mind went on Shawn. It all came back to me like a movie playing in my head. Except my mother's part. That was edited out.

Everything played back in my mind over and over from Shawn ringing my bell to walking to Mc'Ds to the movies—it was like a dream that I didn't want to wake up from, but he was going to call me tomorrow, I better get to sleep.

As I woke up and got out of bed, Elisha was asking me to fix her hair. She has beautiful thick hair. While I was stretching and yawning, she brought her brush and comb and was directing me on how she wanted it. I combed her long hair. Two ponytails with a part down the middle. "You want a bang?"

"Hmmm, no. I want you to braid the front. Do it like so." She waved her hands to the side. "That's how I want the braids to fall."

I kept thinking about Shawn.

"I'm hungry," she said when I finished. We went downstairs to get something to eat. Mom was in the kitchen already as soon as we walked in.

"You know your curfew."

"Yes."

"Well, hurry up and eat then so we could get ready for your aunt and your cousins who are moving in today. The truck will be here around noon with their things. Your aunt is already on the train so she could beat the moving truck here. Go on and eat."

Just as we finished eating our cereal, the bell rang. They're here, I figured. "I'll get it," I said with Elisha behind me. "What's new, girl, why didn't you call me? I was waiting to hear from you. Should've called me when you got up this morning."

"Are they here?" my mother yelled.

"No, Mom, it's Penny!"

"Girl, what time did you get in? I saw you and Shawn walking down the block when we came back to check on you," said Penny. "Anyway, we just chilled at Donny's house, listening to music. Girl, you gotta tell me everything that happened last night!" exclaimed Penny. Elisha was looking at us all in our conversation.

"Penny, let's talk about this later, but right now, my aunt and my cousins are coming to—you know—to live with us. So I have to help clean up, and you're more than welcome to contribute. I'll tell you while we work. Wait here, Penny, while I get the rags and a bucket," I said then went into the kitchen closet and grabbed some rags and a bucket.

They went upstairs to the attic. "Boy, it sure is dusty in here," said Penny."

"I know. My mother keeps a lot of junk." Elisha was in the kitchen helping Mom with the food. She was making fry bakes and tuna fish for Aunt Nancy and her kids.

I told Penny everything and especially about him kissing me, how he said he's going to teach me everything about being a real woman.

"And then what else happened?"

"Oh, I gave my phone number and took his, we're supposed to be dating!" I yelled out excitedly.

"Dating already? You only had one date with him, what are you talking about? Eboni, you need to slow down. You and him are moving way too fast for real," Penny said with a worried look on her face.

"What?" I responded in shock. "Aren't you the one that was just saying to me get myself a pocket fuller? Now you're telling me to slow down?"

"Yeah, 'cause it seems like he's trying to hook you too. Look, all I want to know is when is the next time you guys are going out."

I could see that Penny's a little jealous. As we moved the furniture around so I could finish mopping, one of the drawers to the old dressing tables fell off. Picking up the broken drawer, Penny said, "I think it's time to toss this." She was using them for storage.

"Just rest the drawer on top of the dresser. I'll fix it later, just hurry up and dust so we could get out of here before I start to sneeze."

Penny dusted up the last old dressing table. An hour later, we were finally done. I heard my aunt and cousins downstairs. Justina and Keith were in the kitchen, eating fry bakes and tuna fish. I and Penny went in to help ourselves.

"Is that Eboni? Child, look how much you've grown from the last time I've seen you, you was five—wait, no, I'm wrong. You were seven. Well, anyway, come here and give your aunt some sugar. Lord Gail, look at this child's backside. Just like how ours used to be. You're gonna have to beat the boys back with a baseball bat. Just keep it by the front door," she laughed, releasing me from her hold. Penny stood there, smiling the whole time. As we were walking out with our bakes, she asked, "Is she from the country?"

"No."

"'Cause that's the same way my people act." We both laughed.

My mother was going over the sleeping arrangements. We were watching TV while my mother and aunt chatted like they were teenagers. Aunt Nancy was younger than my mother. And they both had been working in the city at banks. They were catching up on old times and new ones to come. While I and Penny were sitting there talking about Shawn, I heard my aunt say something about needing some stuff from the store. And before I could get up, Justina was walking past me with the money in her hand and heading toward the front door. I remembered Shawn out there. I then told her to wait for me. She used to live in Flatbush, so she had a provocative way of dressing. She was older than me; she's nineteen, has light skin, and cute and had on the tightest jeans I've ever seen, so I had to let him see her with me. So that I could properly introduce them.

As we were walking down the street, my neighbors were staring. I had to tell Justina about the block, like whom we spoke to and whom we didn't talk to, so that there wouldn't be any surprise with her inviting the wrong people in our home. It was about 80 degrees, and Shawn and his boys were out. As we were walking toward them to the store, I asked her which one she thought was fine, just to see where she stood and see her taste in men.

"That one."

"Which one?" I asked.

"The one right there in the blue."

Penny looked at me and then rolled her eyes before Justina could see. Justina pointed at Shawn, with his baby-blue velour tracksuit on and blue-and-gray suede Puma sneakers and a gray LL Cool J Kangol hat, looking so fine with his perfect teeth, beautiful full lips, slanted bedroom eyes. I guess because when you're alone with him, you cannot say no. He had that appeal.

"The other guys are cute too, but that one in the blue really stands out!" exclaimed Justina.

"Yeah, well, Justina, he's my man," said Eboni.

"Huh? Yeah right!"

And as we walked up to them, Shawn came over and kissed me on my lips, proving to Justina. I turned to look at Penny; she was standing there with her mouth open. I smiled and kissed him back, like we've known each other for years. I guess we shared so much information about one another I felt comfortable around him and in front of others. Then I turned to introduce him to my cousin, Justina. And to Penny.

He looked Justina up and down. "It's nice to meet you." It seemed as if she blushed a little. And at Penny, who he just waved at and said a quick hello to. I was more concerned about the warmest hello that he showed to Justina than the brush-off he gave Penny. And as far as that little blush she tried to hide, I wonder just how long my attractive older cousin would be staying with us.

Shawn called the rest of the guys over to meet us. Copying my move, he then introduced me to Markus, who happened to be just as tall as Shawn, but light skinned, and could dress just as fly too. Markus was good looking, but he didn't have that sexy smile or the slanted eyes like Shawn's. And then there was Dave. Dave was cute too for a group of guys hanging, selling drugs. They were all fine and polite. And little Tony. He was a dark-skinned cutie, just like Shawn—not as tall as the rest of them, just a little taller than me. He could pass for 50 Cent's twin; his body was ripped. I noticed Penny smile when he said hi to her. What's up with that? I would ask her later. Hmm! Does Penny have a thing for little Tony? She forgot to tell her best friend. Or is something already going on? I'll check her on that.

Justina went into the store with Penny. I stayed out there with Shawn. His friends had moved back to their spots so we could be alone.

"I want to see you later. I couldn't stop thinking about you," Shawn said while he was kissing me.

"I don't know if I could see you then. I have a full house. My aunt and cousins are there."

"Try." He smiled.

"I don't know, and besides, I now have a curfew."

"Curfew?" Oh, I got myself a real good girl, he thought.

"Yeah, for coming home so late."

"Oh, I'm sorry."

"It's all right, it's not your fault. But if I could get away, I have to be in before midnight."

"Cool, I'll see you a little later then. I just want to spend some time with you."

"All right later. And we just get something to eat while we talk."

"Right, nine, and we just get something to eat while we talk," I repeated.

Penny and Justina came out with their bags. I kissed and said my good-byes to Shawn.

"Girl, I can't believe how fine the guys are out here in East New York, shit! I'm glad to be out of Flatbush with a bunch of rude boys, and I ain't talking about the Caribbean Islands either."

"How is the Bush?" Penny said.

"Ain't nothing out there. I mean, I was just getting into trouble out there with my friends, y'all know how that goes. But out here, it's a whole different place, like a fresh start."

"Well, I'm glad you're staying with us." I smiled. "Looking forward to having you around.

"Me too," said Justina.

Hmm, just as long as she knew her place, and it is not with Shawn. We dropped the bags off, and Justina too. Penny and I headed over to Donny and Johnny's house. So we could chill at the park and kick back. Donny was his usual funny self, teasing me about Shawn and how he was going to keep an eye on him so I wouldn't get hurt. He was the big brother of the group. He told me this as Penny and Johnny were walking ahead of us, singing to the sounds of the box.

"Yo, Eboni, I want you to take the trip to the record store with me."

"All right," I reluctantly agreed. All four of us would endure the music man conversing with his fellow music men. We played a little handball and watched Donny play some basketball. Then we went back to the block. When we got there, Justina was sitting outside with Elisha. Donny just kept staring at her just like Johnny was. So I introduced my cousin to my best guy friends.

"Yo, Eboni, let me talk to you for a minute," Donny said, pulling me aside. "Yo, your cousin is fly, does she have a man?"

"I don't know."

"But would you find out for me?"

"Sure, can we go back over there now?"

He was whispering, and we were already two houses away from them. We all sat on the stoop, clowning around, except Donny who was not his slapstick self. He was in a "mature" mood, trying to impress her. Justina kept looking and laughing at everything Donny said no matter how corny it was with Elisha, me, and Penny; she was telling us her knock-knock jokes, which was very cute for her to do.

Johnny then tried out his rap on us, and only Elisha was his biggest fan. So Johnny kept on rapping, and Elisha was doing the beat.

Paul, Eric, and Keith had been moving Aunt Nancy's furniture up in the attic.

"Whew, we're finally done!" exclaimed Paul. "I can't move a muscle."

Johnny started his rap freestyle with my cousin Keith, which made him sound better.

"Both of you should consider doing a bit at the party coming up," said Donny trying to impress Justina again.

Mom called everyone in for dinner. Boy it looked like a Thanksgiving meal. Mom and Aunt Nancy went all out. They put their foot in it! Four baked chickens, fried wings, macaroni and cheese, peas and rice, potato salad, fried fish and salad, and two pumpkin pies. Plus ice-cream for later. Mom prayed. We all chowed down. I mean, top buttons on pants were popping open around the crowded dining room table.

After dinner, Mom and Aunt Nancy went upstairs to relax. I and Penny, with Elisha Justina, helped washed, up all the dishes; the guys took out the trash. Paul turned on the TV, but no one was watching it. We were busy listening to Keith and Justina tell us about Flatbush and how dangerous it had become. They talked of the friends they had and how they were becoming pregnant and having kids at such a young age. Keith told stories about shootouts he had seen and friends he'd lost over the years. Every summer, it seemed someone was dying. That made me think about Shawn and his child's mother Sandy, how she was moving so she could finish high school, which meant she had to be seventeen or eighteen years old, which was too young to be a mother. Boy that must be hard for her. I knew I had to take it slow with Shawn, not rush into things with him no matter how fine I thought he was. I don't want no baby at seventeen.

Shawn came by. I answered the door and told him to come in. As I entered the dining room where everyone was still and watching the basketball game, they all stopped talking and stared. He said his polite good-night. "Come on, let us go outside," I told Shawn, looking at my family.

"I see what you mean about a full house, are you having a party or something?"

"Hmm, sort of. It's a blending of the two families."

"Oh, so that's how your house is going to be."

"Yeah, guess so."

"I'm kind of hungry, let's go get some Mickey Ds or something."

"Why don't you just come on back inside and I'll fix you a plate?" We went into the kitchen, and they paid us no mind; the game was in full swing. He was sitting on the chair when I told him what we had left. I began to make his plate. I put chicken wings, fish and macaroni and cheese, potato salad and peas and rice. He ate at the kitchen table, and my sister came into the kitchen to say hi and played with his chain. He took it off and let her wear it.

"You're cute, are you a rapper?" she asked. "Are you Eboni's boyfriend? Did you kiss her?" she then added. I wanted to tell her to watch TV or something. Before I could say it, he replied. "No, I'm not a rapper, yes, I'm her boyfriend." She smiled and went on acting like she was a little Foxy Brown, the rapper, with his chain on. He just laughed and said how cute she was and how lucky I was to have siblings 'cause he was an only child. His house was always quiet unless the TV or radio was on. And how his mother worked to make a home for them. He talked about him getting his apartment soon. My man with his own place—did he just tell Elisha that he was my man? I have got to thank her for being so nosy. I'll get her something like candy and take her to the park with Penny and the guys. Not with Shawn—we had kissing to do.

So after he finished eating, it was almost 10:00 p.m. We had talked so much, and my curfew was at midnight. "Why don't we just stay in?"

"That's cool."

"We could go sit in the living room so we could be alone." Everyone was watching the Lakers game, with O'Neal and Kobe, Fisher the dream team. So as we were walking past them, they were yelling at the TV. Shawn laughed then paused to watch some of the excitement of the game. I pulled his arm and led him into the living room. "You want to watch the game?" I asked.

"Naw I'm tired,'" he said, sitting down on the couch. And closed his eyes. He looked so peaceful. I reached over and kissed him on his forehead. He smiled with his eyes closed. I sat down next to him so I could cuddle on him with my head resting on his chest. I slowly closed my eyes and fell into a light sleep. They were still watching the game and yelling at the players. Heard something about Kobe taking it to the rim. Fisher passed to O'Neal. Shawn managed to sleep through all that noise out there. He must have been too tired for words. When we woke up, it was after twelve. Shawn nudged me. I looked at the time; he got up to leave. I walked him to the door; we said our good-nights. Even at midnight, he managed to look fresh without the little nighttime breath.

I gave a peck on his lips then I closed the door and went upstairs to my bedroom to sleep. I forgot Justina was sleeping on my bed, so as I turned on the lights, she jumped up.

"Had a lovely time with Shawn?" she asked.

I yawned, ignoring her. I went and got out my pj's then went into the bathroom to change then got in the bed and went to sleep. Justina was trying to ask me questions, so I pretended to be asleep. She gave up and joined me and fell back asleep.

The next couple of weeks flew by so quick Shawn was at my house, I wasn't spending much time with my friends. We went out to the city, movies, and dinner. The next time Shawn called, it was early in the morning and told me he wanted to take me shopping and was on his way. "So be ready. And we're going to the city."

So I got dressed in my tight-fitting blue jeans and hot-pink-and-yellow-striped tee shirt. And some Donna Karan pink sandals and matching pink Donna Karan pocketbook. I went downstairs to eat something quick—a toast and orange juice— sat outside to wait. Fifteen minutes later, here comes Shawn wearing dark-blue jeans with a white tee shirt with white Air Jordans.

As we were heading for the train, Shawn told me he wanted us to have matching outfits and that's why he was taking me shopping. And he has a surprise for me later. He said we were going to Macy's and Bloomingdale's and how he made a lot of money and was going to spend it on me to show how much he cared. He then gave me two thousand dollars for my pocket. I never had anybody give me so much money. I was surprised. We hit Macy's. He picked out some sweatsuits for me and some sexy panties and matching bras. He paid for it. We then hopped into a cab to Bloomies. He brought some velour sweat suits that were almost the same color as mine. We did manage to get a White sweatsuit alike. He must have spent $4,000 so far. He grabbed my hand and said, "We need to jump in a cab for kicks." We went to Nike-town. He brought me three pairs of sneakers, and the same for himself too. Then he said, "We should go get something to eat, jump in the next cab, and head for the village. Here, take this twenty and order us some Burger King. I got to make a quick phone call. My cell phone is low, and it went off two times already. I'll be right there, go ahead and order the food." I didn't see him going to the jewelry store.

While Shawn was in the jewelry store, he told the man he wanted to buy two-carat diamond earrings and a love chain with the XOs on a nameplate with diamonds in the Os and diamonds on Eboni's name.

"You could have the earrings now, but the chain would take about a week," said the clerk. He put a down payment and paid for the earrings.

We had about eight bags with us as we sat down to eat. "I got a surprise for you."

"For me?" I smiled, looking at my bags.

"What you think about this: I want to get some platinum fronts," he joked.

"I don't like them. Your teeth are perfect, why would you want to mess them up with some ugly metal in your mouth?"

He laughed, "That's the style, and I'm into fashion. I gotta stay fly. And besides, I wouldn't get them right now since you don't like them."

"Good, 'cause I ain't kissing no metal."

"Yeah, OK, baby girl."

Shawn dropped me off with all my bags. Told me he would be back later to take me out to dinner and the movies. "As long as I'm back before midnight..."

"That's cool."

Elisha and Justina were upstairs, so when I came in with all my bags, Elisha started going through them. "Wow, he sure spent some deep money on you," Justina said, pulling the rest of my clothes out on the bed. I was still holding the bag that had my underwear.

"What's in that bag?" Elisha pointed to me.

"It's nothing."

"It's grown folks' stuff," said Justina.

"Look, don't worry about what I have here. It's just pantyhose."

"Oh," she said then went back rummaging through the rest of my stuff. "What you brought me?"

"Next time I go shopping, I'll pick you up some things, OK?"

"Uh-huh. I like those sweatsuits," she said, picking up one of my outfits. "This blue one is pretty. You gotta let me rock one."

"Yeah, OK, I ain't even wearing it yet."

"I mean after you rock it."

"Naw, Shawn got those things for me, so I ain't letting no one wear them," I said, placing them back in the bags. Elisha got bored and went downstairs. Justina sat looking at me kind of funny, like she was trying to figure me out. Then she just came right out and asked me if I ever had sex before. I told her no.

"You should be careful because when a man buys you things, he's putting a down payment on your pussy. That's just the way it goes. 'Cuz, why else would Shawn spend all this money on you?"

"Why, I know you're going to tell me," I said, insulted.

"Look—and judging by how much they cost—I'll say he's investing in you. But I'll say you're worth it though. And if I was still a virgin, I'll make them buy me things just to even talk to me. But the guys I date—now they buy stuff for me, but not like this. And they do it over a period of time, not like this in one shot."

"Look, cuz, that's you, you live your life—worry about that. And besides, we're only dating. He's my first. The only thing we do is kiss."

"Yeah, for now."

"He's not even trying anything."

"Huh?"

"Look, let's just get off this subject. Why don't you help me pick something out to wear? He's coming later on." I pulled out four outfits and some shoes to match. She ended up picking out my Gucci sweat suit and matching Gucci sneakers. "It'll work," I said, hanging up my outfit. "I'm going to take a shower," I said, grabbing my new panties and bra and DKNY perfume I had gotten last Christmas. The bathroom became like my bedroom since she was sharing the room with me. I no longer had privacy and could not lock my door.

My mother called me in her room to ask where I went so early this morning. And she wanted to meet Shawn, my new friend. "I went to the city, he brought me some sneakers. And we ate a quick bite at Burger King."

"Oh, I see."

"Is it alright if he takes me to the movies later on?"

"It's OK, but I still want to meet him when he comes by to get you, so don't try and sneak off with him. Or the next time he calls, I'll invite him over." I knew my mother meant that hoping she wouldn't think I was too young to date him or that he was too old for me at twenty-two.

I tried to change the subject. I was asking if I could go to Dawn's party this weekend. "I'll take Justina and Keith with me." No mention of Shawn. "Donny would be the D.J.," I threw that in before she could say no. Just then, Elisha came in to bring a sandwich for her.

"Yours is downstairs, do you want me to bring it up for you?"

"No, I'm going down anyway." Keith and Eric were in the kitchen, the rap duo.

"I'm ready for the party this weekend," said Eric. Keith asked me if I wanted to hear them rap. I was never one who liked to stand there and be serenaded to. I felt sequestered, held there out of politeness and respect, not of interest. So I wondered how long I would have to endure this live entertainment. I thought no matter how bad they were, I was not going to criticize them. Just let them have their moment, with Keith rapping and Eric harmonizing. I must say it wasn't that bad or long. I didn't think they were ready for Apollo Theater or that they could stop the sandman from dancing their butts offstage. "Thumbs-up," I said, so

I didn't lie. "Where's the sandwich Elisha made for me?" She was at the learning stage of cooking. So I better eat it, I thought.

"It's right here," said Keith, handing me the food.

"You're going to eat?" asked Eric.

"Yeah, why not?"

"Because she made it, that's why."

"So? I ate her cooking before. And you should eat her food too. She might become a chef and end up on VH1."

"One of those sorry-ass stories,'" joked Keith.

"Whatever. Eric said anything's possible. Look how we're trying to become the next Jay-Z or even Ludacris.

"Yeah, I was going to finish school first, then become a rap star,'" said Keith.

"OK, Mister Rap Stars Wannabes, just make sure you buy Mom a maid," I joked back .

"Yeah, we'll hire Elisha as our private chef."

"Hey, you'll never know!"

I called Penny to tell her about my shopping spree with Shawn and all the things he brought me. "You got me something?" she asked.

"No, why should I? Anyway, he's coming by soon to pick me up, going out again."

"What else is new?"

"Well, at least he's not cheap and selfish. Seems like he knows how to treat a lady. You know we're dating?"

"Yeah, I know you're going out and shit."

"No, I mean, he's my man. Ain't no other woman. He said that he has a surprise for me later on."

"Hmmm, I know what that is. I got news that I've been dying to tell you." She paused to let my curiosity build, just like a news reporter with breaking news when they interrupt your favorite TV show.

"Are you going to tell me, or do I have to tune in at five?"

"Girl, you know I can't keep any secrets from you."

"OK, get on with it, let me hear what's up."

"All right, me..." And then another long pause.

"Penny!"

"OK, OK, Little Tony and I are having sex! And it's freaking good. Been seeing him for two whole weeks now."

"What!" was all I could say. "How? When did you start seeing him. And sex—how long has this been going on. Wait, don't answer that. I know you are using protection."

"Yeah, I'm on the pill. He's the only guy I'm sleeping with now. Oh, now Little Tony and I can double date with you guys," she joked. Went on about how he gave her a promise ring and some money, how it meant forever, how he told her he liked her, that she was beautiful. And how no man has ever said that to her before. Even if he didn't mean it, it was her first time hearing it. Now Penny was not an ugly girl, but her personality could rub people the wrong way at times, but she's a good friend to me. I didn't know if I should be happy or scared for her. I always thought she had a good dose of self-esteem.

The only thing I could muster was congratulations. "We should all go to the party this weekend."

"Yeah, I'll tell Tony. Oh, and by the way, he's not Little Tony anymore because there's nothing little about him."

"Penny!"

"Just teasing you."

I knew Tony was not her first. She was already sexually active; this was just another encounter for her. I told her I was hanging up so I could get ready for Shawn.

"Well, Tony and I are going to a motel. I'm going to get myself ready. So I'll get back to you."

All I could say was, "Have fun!" After all, Penny was older than me, and she was no virgin—that was gone way before Tony. So how could I mourn over something when she was too proud to give it away?

That phone conversation with Penny—I started to think about Shawn and me, what kind of surprise he had for me. And the money he had given me, was it like Justina had said: a down payment on my body, on my virginity? Was his kiss just first base for him and my body home plate? What if I did give myself to him, would we still be together? And his child's mother, was I just replacing her? Was he a baby maker? Did he have any more kids that would pop up later on us? And what if she wanted him back? After all, they were a family.

About Penny—was Little Tony only using her for sex? Did he like her? I would have to find out when we double date, and I would have to see them for myself. Here I was, playing Nancy fucking Drew ghetto detective for what? As if Penny's life had the answer to Shawn and me.

My virginity was my choice. I would have to live with it. It seems like everyone was doing it, it's like sex was just another way to spend time with someone. Like giving a gift that you couldn't return, only exchange when you grew tired of the person. Too bad, there wasn't an "I change my mind" or back see's policy's give me back my virginity. No, sex the first time out the gate was for keeps, a one-time thing. You had to be in love with the person you gave yourself to—that's what I was told. Funny how Penny didn't mention anything about loving Tony. She just said they were having sex and having fun. So I figured it was a fair exchange—there were no robberies, no one got hurt. As I got dressed for my date with Shawn. I didn't feel like going all the way to the city for a movie. We could just go to Downtown Brooklyn instead. I threw on my Gucci sweat suit and matching white sneakers. I wanted to see Donny before I left. I went to his house, and his mother answered the door.

<hr />

"Hello, Mrs. Richardson, is Donny here?"

"Yes, he's in his room, go right up," she said, letting me in.

I could hear the music booming from his bedroom. Jay-Z. It's hov, mix with dust it off your shoulders playing. As I opened his door, Donny looked up from behind his turntables. There were records everywhere; I could hardly see his bed as I made my way over to him by climbing over crates of albums to stand by his side so I could tell him what time I could go with him to the record store in the city. "I want to stop by Delancey first so I could buy Shawn a ring with the money, he had given me."

"That's cool. What's up with your cousin Justina. I saw her talking to Shawn the other day, but it didn't look like anything. You should be worried about."

"Well, you need to step to her quick. Because she doesn't have a man, but after the party, who knows how long she'll be single."

I was leaving Donny's house when I spotted Shawn going up my steps. I called out to him; he turned around and waved to me. He walked up to me.

"You ready?" he asked, kissing me on my lips.

I hesitated. "Yes, but first, you have to meet my mom."

"Sure, no problem. Mothers love me." He smiled. So I gave him the once-over. He had on his white Adidas tee shirt camouflage jeans and matching sneakers. We went to sit in the living room as I went upstairs to get my mother and give her the once-over too. She said she'd be down in a minute, watching the end of her show.

When I went back down, I found Justina and Elisha keeping him company. I told Justina about Donny and gave her his phone number.

"Thanks." She smiled. She got up to leave. Shawn waved good-bye to her.

Elisha climbed up next to him and hugged his neck. He was playing with her when my mother came in. He then stood up and extended his hand. "It's nice to meet you."

"Nice to meet you too, Shawn." She smiled.

"We're going to the movies and dinner," I told her. I could see she was pleased, so I then said we had to leave to be back in time for my curfew.

Once outside, I told Shawn how I didn't feel like going all the way to the city. "Let's just go downtown. They're playing the same thing anyhow." So as I started to walk towards the train station. He grabbed my hand. "Let's drive," he said, pointing to this brand-new white BMW 750LI. I looked at him and back at his new car with the keys in his hand. "Since I met you, my business has been—um—good." Should I be happy for the poison that he was putting out in the streets. That's why I never ask him about work or money. "You are my lucky charm. Don't worry, this is not your surprise." Good, I thought. He opened the car door for me; the leather felt like I was sitting on a slow flame. I felt like that puppy you see with their head hanging out the window, but I knew I had to be cool. So I lay back in the seat, and he turned up the radio. And we were there in no time. He parked on a side street. I kept looking back at his car.

"When did you get it?"

"I picked it up this afternoon. You like it? 'Cause you didn't say much on the ride."

"I like it. I mean, what's not to like, it's a Beamer."

"It's fly. Right?" he said.

"Yeah, it is," I had to admit.

Then he went on about how we were going to do a lot of driving in it 'cause he's not about waiting on trains anymore. "And I'm not standing on the corner either." Those guys out there worked for him. He was just going to lie back and get his money. Little Tony was going to oversee things for him so he would have more time to spend with me, and how he wanted me to come with him when he went to see his child .

"When was the last time you saw your son?"

"It's been about two months. Sandy just called me the other day. I knew the car was coming, so I figured I would wait till it happened, then I and you could shoot out there. I'll give her some cash for my son. That's how Sandy and I worked."

I was dying to see what his ex looked like. "Yeah, OK, I'll go with you.

"Yeah, I knew you would," he laughed.

I smiled too. "Yeah."

After we ate, we went to one of those old Foxy Brown pictures with Pam Grier. When the movie was over, we drove back to East New York. I asked him about Little Tony and Penny and double-dating with them. Since he had a car now, it would be easy for us to get around now. "Just name the time, and we could do it."

"Well, since the party is coming up, we could all go together."

"Hmm, that's cool. And wear your baby-blue white sweatsuit I just brought you so we could match," he said.

"Yeah, we'll be twins up in there."

"And they will know you belong to me," he said as he kissed me. "You're something else."

"What do you mean by that?"

"You, know I told you I have a surprise for you and you didn't even ask for it."

"'Cause you're the one that said you had something for me, so I guess you'll give it when you're ready."

"See, that's why I like you," he said, kissing me again and pulling out a gold jewelry box.

I opened the box. "Shawn, this is just what I needed, and I'm not just saying." I put the earrings on.

"Well, how do they look?"

"They look beautiful on you," he said, touching my face. "I just got one more surprise for you."

"Shawn, you don't have to buy me things. I already like you." I wanted to say love but knew it was way too soon for him to hear it.

"Just one more: you'll get that one a little later or at the party."

We then drove over to the park and sat in his new BMW. He lay on me, and I sat there, stroking his forehead. I kissed him; my shyness finally left. He told me he could fall in love with me and see himself married to me, but he didn't want to rush me and how I should finish school first and ask me what I wanted to do with the rest of my life. I said how I wanted to work for one of those fortune 500 companies or be in business for myself. I'm not sure what kind, but as long as it helps people. He mentioned how he was going back to school and he wanted to have a clothing store. How he would sell the hottest and newest things. He was going to use his money to make it happen. He wanted me by his side to help. He kissed me then his hand went down to my chest. I looked at him, and my heart was beating so fast as if I had just run a marathon. And he seemed to have felt it too and removed his hand from me and just held me close to him, calling me his lucky charm. "No rush."

I asked him what he thought about Tony and Penny dating. He said he didn't care; they were grown. As long as Tony didn't fuck up his money. Who Tony was screwing was his own business, and I should be concerned about us—being happy. Then he turned the radio up, and we listened to Hot 105.1 with Big Tigger. "Come here, let me show you how I like to be kissed."

"Hmm!"

"Huh?"

"You catch on quick. You're easy to practice on."

"You make learning fun."

"Lucky charm." Then he buried his face in mine. I like the feeling I was experiencing while he was kissing me, I ended up placing his hand on my right breast. He looked at me and asked, "Are you sure?" I just smiled at him. He then started massaging my breast. And I felt something warm between my legs. And I let out a sound that surprised me and made me blush a little. Shawn was kissing and licking my ear and neck. The windows in the car were fogging up; I could not see out. Then Shawn put his hands down my pants. I squealed; he kept on playing with me. My panties were so wet. I thought I'd peed myself and didn't know it. He kept on twisting his fingers on my privates, and I was enjoying it.

"Have you ever had a hickey before?" he whispered, knowing he was my first.

"No," I exclaimed. "Well, first, to give a hickey, you have to relax, then I have to gently suck on your neck like so. Umm, mum." He was moaning. He must have sucked on my neck till the color came off.

"I don't like that, it hurts." That's the first time I ever heard that one before he smiled. I looked in the vanity mirror; my neck was pink, turning red. Before I could say anything, he spoke. "Just wear a scarf."

"In the summer?"

"Why not?"

"Because my mother will notice."

"OK, I'm sorry. Don't worry, the next time I do something with you, no one will know."

My neck, my pants—I got to go home, I thought. I snuck upstairs to the bathroom to check my neck. The mark was now red! I knew someone would see it, and then no more Shawn. I went over to check my panties; when I pulled them down, there was white stuff all over them. It looked like I had a cold and forgot to blow! I cleaned myself up and tiptoed to my room trying not to wake up Justina. I didn't feel like answering her questions.

When I turned on the light, she wasn't even there. "Good!" And quickly changed into my pj's and got under my pink sheets that my mother had just put on. I lay down and just a few minutes later, I heard Justina come in. She was tripping over something out in the hallway. When she turned the light on, I got up. I looked at her; she was looking quite red. Her skin was reddish and her eyes too. She said she and Donny were drinking and she had more than she was used to as she stumbled over to the bed. She almost fell on me if I hadn't moved.

Her blouse was half-buttoned, and her neck had red marks all over it as I helped to take off her clothes so she could get in bed. I saw more red marks on her breasts as I gave her one of my shirts. And I put her on the edge of the bed in case she needed to get up. She was snoring, or should I say the liquor was sleeping.

My mother opened my bedroom door to tell me that Paul got approved in the navy and would be leaving tomorrow overseas and she was throwing a dinner party for him. So I better not miss it.

First Daddy, now Paul—why were the Reid men always leaving!

Justina woke up, and she was telling me about her night out with Donny. That she was going to the party with him and how they came close to sleeping together. "Girl, but I passed out!"

Justina, Penny—everyone was having sex. I thought about how I came close to sleeping with Shawn, but we both knew it wasn't the time or the place. I would hate to think of my first sexual experience in someone's car even though it was a Beamer. It sounded so cheap, and I know I'm worth more. I'm glad he didn't pressure me but said he would wait till I'm ready. "No rush." I think I might be ready!

Shawn thought about the party and where it's located. He knew there would be trouble. So he called his boy Markus and told him to get the guys together so they could back him up just in case something went down. Better safe than sorry. Plus, it was not only himself he was worried. He had to protect his lucky charm. Shawn knew Eboni was a little young for him, but he was falling in love with her. She made him think of a future, plus she was different from Sandy. Sandy was dizzy and carefree. Shit, she gave it up so fast and then turned around and said she was pregnant, and his boy Dave had fucked her too.

She would've let us run a train on her if it wasn't for me changing my mind. And I was trying to teach her how to be a strong woman like my moms. Then she hits me with this baby. Damn! I fucked up! But

Eboni is different. She thinks, plus she's smart. And she's a virgin. She special ah'ight. She the only girl I've been seeing and ain't have no sex since! But I can wait 'til Eboni's ready. When I get it, I'll be getting it all the time. No rush!

Markus called him back to say that the crew would be there, packing guns.

Shawn didn't want to worry Eboni with the problems he was having on the streets over his business. There was a war about to start. And that was the reason he brought the car. He couldn't be walking around and get caught out there like that. Now he must move his moms out of this neighborhood. He helped Sandy and his son move out. I have a lot on my mind, and she wants me to go to this party with her. I'm no teenager so I doubt the cats I have beef with would even show up at some house shit. I didn't want to go, but I couldn't let her go without me. So my boys will be there. Eboni would be safe. She said her cousin Justina was coming. I hope she stays out of my way. She's been flirting with me, but I'm not sweating that. She's not even my type. I'm in love with Eboni anyway. But still, I know Justina is easy pussy. The way she's been trying to throw it at me. But I ain't trying to catch it. Imma set her straight and let her know what's up. Naw, fuck it, I'll put Markus on that ass since she is throwing it around! Put your glove on. Hit that shit, back that bitch off of me.

Shawn went to look out of the window to check on his ride. Then he thought about his money and went under his bed where he had cut a hole in the floorboard and took out his stash. He had to pay his mother's rent, so he counted out $1,500. That was for the small two-bedroom apartment he shared with her. He gave Sandy $1,000 for the baby, Eboni $1,500.00 for the chain. He then got dressed and headed for the car. He was on his way to pick it up when his house phone rang when he was heading out the door. He ran back upstairs and caught it on its last ring.

"Hi, you miss me?" said the person. "You have been on my mind all day."

"Lucky, I was just on my way out. What's up?"

"Uh, just thinking about you and wanting to hear your voice. Oh, by the way, Paul is going to the navy," Eboni said, excitedly.

"Yeah?"

"So mom is throwing him a farewell dinner. You are coming, right? I'll see you there at 7:00 p.m. Bye." And then she hung up. She didn't even give him a chance to answer, but he'd see her at seven. "Picking up the chain now. Let me see what my boys are up to," he said while driving back from the city. Checking his money, Shawn parked around the corner from the store where his boys took care of business and walked over to the spot. Little Tony and Dave were out there.

"What's up?"

"Just chilling. Cops are getting thick out here. It's getting hot, man!" said Dave, looking around as an undercover police car rode past them. "See what I'm saying?" Shawn nodded in agreement. "Where's Markus?" he then asked.

"He went to re-up."

Tony then came walking up to them in his usual baggy attire.

"Where you been, man?"

"Went to get some smoke's. Yo, where's your ride?" asked Tony.

"I parked it over there. You know I ain't lazy."

"Yo, Tony, come here a second. Let me holla at you," Shawn said, pulling Tony to the side. "How's my cash flow. It's all right?"

"Yeah, man, everything is on point. You know I ain't going to let no one fuck up your money."

"That's good. What's up with you and Penny? Heard you all been hanging tight."

"She's good company. Give her a little dough, and she gives me a little heady mo. But ain't nothing, just hanging. We ain't like you and Eboni. You know I'm a Mack that goes and goes. Ain't no time for one-on-one hoes C.R.E.A.M. Sun, (Cash Rules Everything Around Me.)" code of the streets. Paying homage too the WU- Tang Clan.

"Yeah, I hear you."

"You know me, and I'm trying to get this money up for a ride this winter. I don't want to be freezing my nuts off waiting for the train."

"Yeah, I hear you. Well, get to work," joked Shawn.

"See you guys later on, gotta go check on things. I'll pass through later on." He slapped five then he walked off. "Guess who's coming to dinner?" was playing in his head. Why does Eboni always wanted me around her family? Not that I mind, but I wanted to spend my free time with her alone, teaching her. He smiled as he rang the bell.

Elisha opened the door and let him in. He kissed her on the forehead then followed her into the dining room where everyone was at. Eboni got up to kiss him but caught herself on her mother's sight. So she hugged him instead after they made their toast and wished Paul well.

It was getting late, so Shawn left. Eboni walked him to his car and told him how tired she was and would see him tomorrow. They kissed some more, and then he drove off. He was so tired he was in the city earlier. And had to do a lot of running around just so he could make it in time for Paul's farewell. I didn't even know him. But ever since he started dating her, he found himself part of an extended family. Eboni thought her night was over; she pulled out her nightgown to sleep when her mother called her into her bedroom. She wanted to talk to her about her relationship with Shawn. She noticed the way daughter's reaction was toward him when he came in then thought it was something she needed to address and discuss with her in private.

Eboni came into her mother's room and plopped down on the bed. "Yes, Mom?"

By the look Gail gave, she got back up and decided to stay standing. "I want to talk to you about Shawn. It looks like he likes you a lot and you share the same feelings—"

"Mom," she interjected.

"I just want to explain what could happen if you're not careful."

"Mom, I'm seventeen."

"And a lot of girls your age find themselves in a situation that could have been prevented, with proper guidance. I love you and don't want to see you stuck in a mess like that. I know it's hard to tell me—your mother—that you have strong feelings for Shawn, but I want you to come to me so I could take you doctor and get you checked out. Now I don't want you to have sex. You are too young. But I was young also. So if you are, or even considering it, I would like to make an appointment with your doctor so we could put you on the pill and get you the proper protection. It's not just a baby, there's STDs out there, which means sexually transmitted disease. There's stuff out there that could have you itching, burning when you pee. Or crying for the rest of your life, or ending your life quickly. So please just come to me. I'm your mother, not your enemy. I'm here to protect you. Now hug me." Gail hugged her little girl like if she was a baby

She knew her baby was growing up and becoming a young lady, and it scared her. Eboni went to the bathroom to change into her nightgown when the discussion she had with her mother came to her mind—STDs, baby, death…STDs baby, death. These kept playing in her head. She had seen girls who look like they were her age pushing a baby carriage or carrying them and a schoolbook bag in the morning when school was in and always thought how hard it must be on them. She didn't want to end up like them. She had her friends and now parties to go to. That was before she met Shawn. Even though he wasn't pressuring her for sex, she didn't want to lose him; she loved him. And she hoped he felt the same way.

Penny called early in the morning. Eboni heard her mother calling her for the phone; she got up then she went to lie back down for ten more minutes before she got ready to go shopping with Penny. They got off the train at Jay Street, Downtown Brooklyn. It was a crowded Saturday morning; the streets were packed with side vendors, taking up city streets as if they couldn't all get together and open up a little flea market to showcase their bootleg items. They knew the stores would be just as packed, and those lines seemed like they were created to make you buy more. You would have time to think while you take your one-inch step toward the cashier to pick up those last items that you know you wouldn't even be thinking about if the lines would just moving and weren't so damn long. Penny picked out an outfit that Eboni thought was a little too dressy for a house party and told her, "Let's find something less formal," not wanting to hurt her feelings. "After all, I don't think anybody would be wearing a cocktail dress," and then went to pick up a mini dress for her to try on that was perfect for Penny's body type, with her large breasts and flat behind—she was robbed in the butt department. This dress she would look like a model. Built just like a white girl. Penny went into the fitting room.

"OK, I'm coming out, tell me what you think."

Eboni told her how sexy she looked in that killer dress. And she did. Penny smiled then said, "Tony is going to love to take this off of me. Shit, he might just fuck me right in it." She then rubbed her legs "Girl, I'm on fire."

"I'm not even trying to hear about you and the new flavor of the month."

"Yeah, I know that's the cobwebs talking, don't know what you're missing," she joked, changing the subject. "Girl, this dress looks good on me." It was a black short halter top that was cut low in the front without exposing everything. Eboni asked if she could bend over without falling out of it. So Penny bent down. Eboni looked to see if everything stayed in its place, and it did. They were standing in line to pay the cashier.

"When we're finished here, I want to walk over to the jewelry store. I want to get Shawn a ring and surprise him with it before the party." Eboni didn't want to tell Penny about the talk she had with her mother. Being that Penny was already having sex. Her opinion would do more harm. And it was her body, which means her choice. They went over to the Jazzy jewelry store where everyone shops for the hottest jewelry. She wanted something for under $1,500 she could buy. So as they were looking, Penny said she wanted to get a chain for herself. But she didn't have any more money after she brought the dress and the latest shoes. She was maxed out and hoping Eboni would spring for lunch.

Eboni picked out two rings then asked the salesclerk to show her. One was a diamond cluster ring she knew Shawn would like it. The other one she liked; it was a diamond-cut ring with an S initial on it and had diamond chips around the S. The cluster ring was more substantial and cost $1,379. And the initial ring was about the same with tax, the clerk told her. She liked the S ring better. The clerk put the ring in a box and a little bag and handed it to her. She thanked him then she and Penny left the store. "It's not a green box, but gold is just as lovely too," she said.

Penny asked her if she was hungry because since they finished shopping, they should grab something to eat and how she didn't have any more money. And promised to treat next time. So they walked over to Ray's famous pizza and ordered two slices and Cokes. They decided to eat and strolled along. They were planning what time to leave so they could make it to the party in time because Shawn was driving them.

"I have to call Tony so he could come by the house in time too." They finished their pizza in no time. As they got back on the train, Penny asked about her hair and how she should wear it. She didn't want to sweat it out and have her hair ruined if she was to put it up in curls or wear it down. Eboni suggested to flat twist the front and pin them back in a roll-on. "Do like me and put your hair up in a ponytail, and nothing fancy. You are starting to have soap opera taste with your cocktail dress. Leave Erica Kane to the TV, not the hood."

Eboni walked Penny home and told her to call later since she only lived four houses down from her. Penny yelled back to her if she could get dressed at her house and call Tony from there. She agreed and then closed and locked her front door and went upstairs to lie down. Shopping and taking the train had drained her energy plus the talk with her mother and what plans with Shawn for after the party had her head spinning.

Elisha came into the room and asked her where she had been 'cause Shawn called and said he would try back later. Eboni asked Elisha to pass her that bag over there, the brown one. There were four other colorful bags on the floor. She didn't throw out the bags from the time she and Shawn went shopping, even though they were empty. She hasn't done much to her room either since Justina moved in. Elisha gave her the bag. Inside of it was a small Gucci shirt Shawn brought that was too tight. She was going to return it. But after seeing Elisha, she realized she hadn't brought her anything in a while. Even though she was too young to know what Gucci was and cost, she gave it to her anyway. Elisha tried the shirt on also. Though it was a little too big for her, she could still wear it. Elisha was happy with the white tee and gold letters. She knew what Gucci was what the rappers were wearing.

Eboni spent the rest of the day in bed, with Elisha watching TV. Rap videos were on, the host: Big Tigger. The pecan cutie. He was playing the top ten countdown.

With Elisha singing along, Eboni told her, "I hope you know your schoolwork this good." Elisha shook her head yes and kept on with the tunes. Justina came in and said she was leaving early for the party to help Donny set up. She wanted to be there with him and didn't see the point in sitting around. "I was never one to sit still." She been there less than a month and already managed to find herself a man.

"Justina," Eboni said. "It looks like you and Donny have something special."

"Yeah, I'm surprised at how well I enjoy being around him, considering we just really met. I guess spending time listening to music and picking out songs have made it seem like we've known each other for some time now. He took me to the record store in the city the other day so he could get some more records. He sure spends a lot of money on his music and been teaching me how to mix and blend. And I'm getting good at it. Might be the next Spinderella."

"If you keep at it and if I see you on TV, or in any rap magazines, just remember who introduced you two," Eboni said, joking.

Justina laughed and added, "Yeah, you could be my manager." Justina kept on telling Eboni about the record store and how they were mixing in there and how she filled out an application for a job there. "And the manager told me he would call me within this week, and if I didn't hear from him for me to call him. And if I get the job, I would get a discount on the merchandise." She was trying to plan her future in music. She was excited about working in a record store. For one minute, Eboni thought she was talking about clothing stores so she could build up her wardrobe. I guess she's not as vain as she looks. Maybe Donny is right for her. I always thought of him as a clown.

Justina went to the closet and brought out the clothes she would be wearing later on tonight, so she tried it on to show Eboni how it looks. When she came back into the room, Eboni had to sit up.

Justina kept turning around, showing off her red catsuit. She looked good in it now, with her in her apple-red catsuit and Penny in her halter mini dress and then me in my white sweatsuit; they're all looking fine; they are going to outshine me. But I'm fine with that 'cause I'm coming with Shawn, the flyest dude out there.

"Damn, girl, you gotta let me borrow that." She smiled then winked. "Trade, yuh!" I laughed. "Penny got a bad outfit too."

"Y'all are going to be the bomb of the party. She said that was the look she was going for."

"OK, I just need you to pick out which shoes went with this suit." She reached under the bed and pulled out three pairs of shoes: one was black high heels, the other was white flats, and the last ones look like Sunday shoes.

"Neither one of them," I told her, went to the other side of the bed, and pulled out my black boots and gave it to her. "Wear these." We did have the same size feet, a perfect seven. "You want me to wear boots?"

"Just try them on and see how they look. You don't have many choices. And besides, don't you see Salt-N-Pepa rocking them in their videos wearing catsuits and boots you're from Flatbush, you should know."

"Eboni, how long ago was that?"

"It still works. It's a black thang that never goes out of style."

"I know you have a fashion sense."

"Would you just try them on?"

"OK, pass me the boots."

As usual, I was right. She pulled them on and checked herself the full-length mirror behind my bedroom door and asked if she could wear them. She laughed and said, "It's like pulling teeth."

"Just don't scuff them up."

"Now, all I need to do is find my little black bag and get my jacket on. 'Cause this outfit is done." She pulled out her suitcase and found her purse and jacket. She emptied her Guess jean bag and put all the contents in her black Coach bag. That was when Elisha and Penny came in. Penny had a little duffle bag with her. She tossed the bag on the chair then sat down on the bed with me and looked at Justina, who was fixing her hair. By brushing it down, it could feather fall on her face and neck. Penny said she was too excited about the party and wanted just to come over and hang out till it was time to leave.

"Justina, why are you getting ready so early? You know black folks' time—this is even too early for white folks."

"I'm helping Donny set up, and I don't think I would have time to come back and change."

"Oh, I see," answered Penny. And I was lying back on my bed with my feet still touching the floor. Elisha came and sat next to Penny, and we all were just watching her fix her hair.

Penny said how she spoke to Tony before she left. He and Shawn were coming to pick us up around nine. And we should start getting ready around eight. "Well, since it's early, why don't we go downstairs and get something to eat?" We all went and sat down in the kitchen at the table, trying to figure out what to eat since nobody felt like cooking anything. We just made sandwiches. I took out the cold cuts, some cheese, some mayo mustard with the deli selections—turkey, ham, and Swiss cheese. Everyone made their sandwiches and washed it down with juice. Justina got up; she had to meet Donny. They would meet up with Keith and Johnny so they could help carry the equipment to Dawn's house. "So, I'll see you guys at the party," she said as she was walking down the hall.

Penny cleaned up the kitchen while Elisha put the rest of the food away. We sat around the dining room table, turned on the TV to kill time. I was looking around, more like thinking about Shawn 'cause when I asked him to go to the party with me, he seemed a little nervous, like if something was troubling him. Maybe I'm making more out of this. Perhaps he was worried about money or an ex-girlfriend being there and causing drama.

The only thing fair is death. I learned it didn't matter how much money you had or how good of a person you are. Air was even; everyone uses it. Some would say that justice was unfair, the prosecution and the process had a price and a finger that pointed on the ones who couldn't afford a proper defense for themselves. But death dealt with an even hand.

Shawn took a shower and checked his nude body out in the mirror. He has always worked out and kept his body in shape. At twenty-two he had a nice muscle build; his biceps—or how he called them his pythons—were his pride, and he showed them off too. He walked over to his dresser to get a pair of boxers. Then he thought about the party and Eboni's safety. He ruffled through the drawer and felt for his gun that he would bring with him. Since he always kept it loaded, he placed it down on his bed. And he remembered Jeff's death. He hasn't touched it since.

Jeff died over money. "Damn, I should have been there. That money was owed to him, and he didn't even have a piece on him to defend himself. It all went down when he was on a drug deal for his uncle. He'd just reach home when Markus called and said, "Jeff got shot." Before he knew what was happening, he was running over to Jeff's home, who only lived a couple of blocks away from him. When he got there, he heard Jeff's mother Mary, yelling and crying.

Jeff's sisters, the twins Belinda and Melinda, were holding her up. He rushed over to them, and Mary embraced him tightly. "They killed my baby, my only son," she cried with hot tears rolling down her face. Shawn held her tight and cried. Jeff was twenty-three years old when he passed away.

They had been friends for twelve years, and now he was gone. He was holding on to Mary when the cops came over to them and told her that she needed to come with them to ID the body properly. She was going to the city morgue.

"I'm coming too." He was going with her; she was like a second mother to him. Now his best friend, his partner, was gone. He noticed Little Tony, Markus, and Dave standing over there across the street. He could see that their eyes were red. He nodded in an attempt to say, "We fucked up." Little Tony and Dave were close friends. It used to be the three of them chasing girls, running from cops after they did a stickup, or got into a fight that Jeff started. He was always the one who would jump up first to fight and plan a robbery he thought as he took the cab back with Jeff's mother and sisters.

Flashed back to when they first met Jeff. He'd just moved into the neighborhood and would be going to the same public school. Jeff was walking down the hall, eyeing everyone like he was the baddest thing out. He was putting his books in his locker, which was next to Jeff's. He didn't see him, so when he opened, it hit Jeff right upside the head. Before he could apologize, Jeff cocked back his fist, and it met Shawn's face, right in the eye. And with one eye closed, he grabbed Jeff up, and they knocked to the floor. And they were picked up by the security guards and dragged off to the dean's office and handed the sentence of one week in detention. It was there they met officially, from fight to friends. Now he was gone. He was still dealing with the loss of his friend was, not feeling in the mood too party. But he promised Eboni.

Shawn went to his closet and took out his white sweatsuit. He knew she would be wearing hers. So then finished getting dressed, he put on his Polo cologne. It was old, but it still did its job, got the ladies open. He threw on his jewelry and put Eboni's own in his pocket. He wanted to call Markus; he picked up his gun, a .9 mm, and tucked it in his waistband. He phoned Markus. Dave was over there, waiting for Tony.

Shawn told them that he would meet him there. He was going to Eboni house and make sure they were ready. Shawn rang Eboni's bell. Eric opened the door to let him in.

"What's up, Eric?" and gave him a pound. Eric yelled out Eboni's name and added that Shawn was here. Eboni, Penny, and Elisha came running down. Shawn kissed her, then he kissed Elisha and said hi to Penny. Then he ask if she spoke to Tony. He said he was on his way over here. Before they could sit down or get the next word out, Tony was ringing the bell. Shawn pulled Eboni aside and gave her a chain and told her that he loved her. She kissed and hugged him and whispered she loved him back and reached into her pocket and pulled out a gold box and handed it to him.

Shawn parked right in front of Dawn's house. There was a crowd of people standing out there grilling them when they stepped out of the BMW. He had put rims on it. Shawn looked around to see if he recognized anyone from the crowd. Deciding he didn't, his gun stayed tucked. Inside, there were more stares, but this time from the girls. Shawn looked at them. "Don't even sweat them," he said and kissed Eboni softly on her lips. "I ain't." She smiled.

"Where's Dawn?" I asked as Penny came in. We found Dawn, said hello and went over by Donny, who was mixing on the turntables while Justina was looking through the record crate. She saw us and came bouncing over, swinging her hips. I looked to see if Shawn had noticed her little act. He was staring at Dave and Markus, who just came in and were walking toward him. Justina told me how many drinks she had and that she was going to make us one. I'm not a drinker, but since it was a party, why not. "Don't make it too strong."

"I won't. Don't want you throwing up all over yourself." She came back with mine and Shawn's drinks and another one for herself. I told her she needed to slow down. As I watched, Justina slipped through the crowd. More people were coming in. The room was packed even though the furniture had been removed. Shawn went over to his boys.

"It sure is getting packed," Justina said, on her way back over to me then asking me if I wanted another drink? I didn't even taste my first yet

I took a sip of it. "Whoa! What kind of drinks is this?"

"It's Alizé Red, and I've been drinking this all night."

"It's strong."

"I know. Don't worry, you can't get fucked up if you don't want to."

"You know I don't drink, so why'd you make it so strong?" I said, taking another sip.

"That's how it is, and it came like that."

"Yeah, well, this is it for me."

"That's all it takes to get you to feel nice anyway."

"Let me go find Shawn."

"Donny is calling me. I'll be back." She and Donny, I laughed to myself. Penny and Little Tony were in the corner, dancing. They were slow-dancing. Feeling a little warm, I went to find Shawn. I needed to feel him next to me.

⸻ ⊹⬥⬥⬥⊹ ⸻

Flip was driving his old, rusted-out green Toyota Corolla. "Yo, man, pass the shit. A niggah ain't put near shit in it." And he went to suck the whole thing down. He said to his man Pump, who's known for carrying a pump shotgun while turning around to look at, him revealing a scar on his right cheek.

"Damn, man, here take the shit," he said as he passed the E&J. "Fuck it. Imma roll this blunt up."

"And pass that shit up here too after you spark it," he said bogarting.

"You niggahs be acting, for real sound, like bitches," said Ricky, who was Flip's cousin, while laughing in the passenger seat.

"Damn, I'm tired. Shit, ain't nothing out here!" said Flip.

"Yo, there's a party on Pitkin Ave., by the projects. We could roll by," said Pump.

"Tru, bet," as he cut car on new lots heading for Pitkin.

"Where's the E&J? Can a niggah live?" said Ricky.

"Yo, you remember that punk that didn't want to fork up the jewels?"

"Yeah, the one you popped. What about him?" said Ricky, looking out the window at a couple walking down the street.

"Naw, saw money. Yester, nigga jetted like if I was po-po."

"Aha, you did shoot him."

"Yeah, punk-ass bitch," said Flip while smoking on the blunt. "He's straight up butt," he joked. "Got me a nice chain though," feeling it while he drove.

"Bump that," said Ricky. "Yo, the party is going to be fly—mad honeys in there. Imma scope me a couple."

"True that, mad bitches up in there," said Flip. "Imma grab me one right by the ass, and if shorty asks funny, Imma tell her to run dat."

"You know how them. Brooklyn skee-yos get down, I ain't talking about no low, low. I'm talking about the flossed-out skeets."

"Word, it's Reynolds." Laughter. "Yeah, I'm with that shit. We should bring some back to the crib and get right," said Pump.

"I'm down with that shit Flip said."

⋅⋅♦♦♦⋅⋅

I walked over to Shawn interrupting his conversation with Dave and Markus. "Excuse him."

"Nah, we understand," they said, and I led him away so we could dance. We looked like twins with our matching sweat suit and sneakers. He pulled me close to him, and I felt him. And this time, I moved in closer and kissed his neck. He was kissing my ear gently. Donny saw us and put on Usher's "Nice & Slow" followed by Ms. Morgan's "Do Me Baby," and I was lost in the song. The living room was filled with couples. I felt something hard on Shawn that was on his waist. I put my hand on it. It was his gun. What was he doing with that? I thought. He looked down at me. "It's for our protection. Don't worry."

"OK." For some reason, I trusted this man. Now I know why he was nervous and I knew the rest of his friends had weapons on them too. But I know Shawn, and I was safe, so I kept on dancing. After all, he didn't work nine-to-five. He was a drug dealer—and was good at it, so he had to have enemies out there.

"Baby, I love this ring you brought me. I know I didn't say much, but you know we were leaving and all."

"I got it when I and Penny went shopping. I was thinking about you and wanted you to know it."

Damn, I got myself something special right here, he thought. Kiss her.

I was no child. I knew as much that with drugs comes guns and death. I was worried more for Shawn. I realized that night how much I love him. And when I thought about him getting shot or killed, I didn't want to lose him. Our life was just beginning. We had plans. I wish he could find another way to make a living. This way was too risky, and I needed him. Shawn was more my world than I could ever tell him.

<hr>

"Yo, the party's right around the corner, on the left," said Ricky.

The Toyota came to a stop. " Yo, ain't that, that nigga's whip?" said, Ricky to Flip.

"Say it ain't so? This is my lucky night!" He had been gunning for Shawn since he was the big moneymaker on the streets. And being a stone-cold stickup kid, how could he pass on that opportunity? "What?" Niggah luck was changing as he spotted Shawn's car. Flip hopped out and tucked his heat under his waistband. Then Ricky stepped out too, quickened his step, and went creeping over to Shawn's car. "He's not in here." Pump, then got out with the shottie.

"Yo, he's inside," Flip said, adjusting his retro nines, walked in, and surveyed the crowd.

<hr>

Shawn was kissing my forehead, and his back was to the door. Then three guys came in. Markus walked over to us and told Shawn that "they" were here while Dave kept an eye on them. The guys at the door saw us and reached under their shirts and pulled their guns out and aimed it at us. Shawn pushed me aside. As if synchronized, he and his boys drew their weapons.

Two of the three gunmen walked up to Shawn. But no one shot. The crowd started running. Someone knocked over Donny's turntables in the mix of chaos. There were thirty people at Dawn's party and only seven people standing. Dawn was hiding behind the table and peeking out. Justina had run over to Donny; they hid by the overturned speakers.

"What's up now, Shawn?"

"What's good, Flip? I see you and your boys coming and threw on some ruckus shit. So what's on your agenda?" he said calmly.

"This is what's up," said Flip, raising his gun to Shawn's head. Eboni jumped in between them. Flip looked at her, distracted by her stance. "What the fuck is this shit? I smoke bitches too."

Shawn interjected, "She ain't got nothing to do with this," as he stepped in front of her, returning the favor with his gun cocked and aimed. "It's all me," he said, looking at Flip and his boys while Tony and Dave held their Gats on point, ready to light the room up. She had blocked Shawn with her body, not thinking.

"Naw, Flip, man, wrong time, too many heads around, man," said Ricky as he looked at Eboni. He had seen her before but was nervous to ever step to her because she was so pretty and, never even noticed him.

"True, true. But, Shawn, Imma see you again real soon, real soon. And, sweetie, Imma see you in black for real!" He stood there for a moment before he lowered his gun, but before he went through the door, he looked back again and shook his head.

The skinny, light-skinned one with the scar on his face, I would never forget. That scar was from his ear to his chin. A jailhouse telephone cut it was called. He told Shawn to watch his back and left with the other two, who were through the door already.

Shawn grabbed me close to him and asked if I was okay. I nodded yes. Then he told his boys to make a move. His boys went out first to see if Flip and his crew were still outside waiting to ambush us. I was too shocked to move. Shawn was talking to me, but I couldn't comprehend what he was saying to me. All I could see was three gunmen coming to gun Shawn down in front of me. Penny and Justina and Donny came over to us. Justina was asking about Keith and Johnny. Donny said he had sent them back to his house to get a fan 'cause turntables were getting hot and could blowout. Shawn then told me and Penny, "Let's bounce." As I was walking towards the door, I almost fell, but Penny caught me. Shawn took my hand and led me out. I was trying to hold back the tears. Stay strong, girl, don't cry, I told myself. Markus and the rest of them were outside with the party crowd The gunmen were nowhere around. I felt a little safe as we got in Shawn's car. I was crying by then. "It's all right, baby. It's going to be ok. I love you and wouldn't let anything bad happen to you, I swear," he said as he kissed me gently on my lips. "I love you too," I told him and buried my face in his chest and cried. We rode off in silence. Markus and Dave rode back with us. Shawn said he was dropping Penny and me off at my house and that he and his boys were going to take care of this. I begged him not to go, but the look in his eyes told me it was useless; his mind was already gone.

Penny and I sat up in my living room. An hour had past, and no Shawn or Tony. I was scared and could see she was too. Penny was trying to remain calm. None of us said a word. We kept switching to get up and look out the window for them. By the time Shawn and Tony pulled up, another hour had passed. We ran out to meet them. Shawn was hugging me so tight; I started crying again. He then wiped my tears and told me not to worry how he drove around all night looking for Flip and his crew so he could get this mess straightened out. I said, cutting him off, how I wanted to be with him, that I wouldn't be able to sleep unless I knew he was safe. "We could go to my house or a hotel."

"Let's go to a hotel."

"I know a nice one in Queens by the airport, the Crowne Plaza."

"That's fine. I just want to be with you. I don't care where we go as long we're together."

Tony then came up to us. "A'ight, Shawn. Penny and I are going to head over to my crib." They left. I got in the car with Shawn and laid my head on his chest. I turn the radio to WBLS, the R & B station. After what happened tonight, I wasn't in the mood for rap. Shawn got to the Belt Parkway; no one spoke. Then he pulled into the hotel parking lot, parked in front, got out, and told me to wait in the car. Five minutes later, he came back with a key card. He parked the car in a garage parking lot. Then we took the elevator to the third floor. He opened the door, and I walked in first like I'd been here before. I was moving in a daze, still in shock about what just happened. I heard Shawn close the door and locked it. I was looking around the room; there were thick green pine carpet and beautiful green-burgundy drapes and matching bedspread. It was a large king-sized bed square in the middle of the room, a large dressing table that had a Bible on it. The TV was inside the armor with the remote. Shawn turned on the TV; while flipping the channels, he stopped at a porno station. He looked at me then changed it to a movie, told me he was tired and going to lie down. I went to the other side and lay next to him. We were watching a movie. Shawn started rubbing my legs. Then he moved up to my arms, and he unhooked my bra. I took off my shirt and pulled my sweatpants down. "You want to take the rest off?" he asked with a smile. I got up and stepped out of my panties. He began rubbing me as I lay naked. He stood up and took his clothes off. I looked over his body, and my heart started pounding, thinking it was going to jump out of my chest. I knew he could hear it. He was nude, and I was naked and scared. He then came over to my side of the bed. "Are you sure?"

"Uh-huh." I nodded, looking into his sexy bedroom eyes.

"Good, let's go take a shower."

"Together?" I sounded so immature.

"Yes, I'll wash you, and then you could wash me," he whispered in my ear. "Or we could wash each other at the same time." He smiled. Then he reached out for my hand and led me to the bathroom. It had a double sink and gold-and-green wallpaper. It had that luxurious look to it—and I was worth it. Shawn turned on the shower jets, and water ran down his back. I was taking a shower with him!

Shawn asked me what I was doing out there; he was already in the shower lathering up. I could smell the soap. I told him I didn't want to get my hair wet while standing at the shower door. "Well then, look on the counter. There should be a shower cap." And more soap in the basket that was there on the sink. I got in the tub with him.

"Shawn, why are you smiling?"

"You look so good naked. Turn around so I could soap you up." He started with my back then worked his hand with the washcloth down to my butt. I closed my eyes when he got to my legs. "Turn around so I could wash all of you." He added more soap to the cloth. He teased me by soaping my neck then arms then wrapped the cloth around his fingers and traced it straight down my body—and it landed right on my cat! Meow! He looked at me, smiled, then ran his fingers back up my arm. All the while, my heart was pounding; it sounded like a reggae beat. Shawn washed the rest of my body. He washed my breast like he would bathe a baby—so delicate. And he washed my cat with a gentleness that calmed my heart down. I rinsed off; then he kissed me on my lips and passed me the cloth so I could finish. He said it was his turn, and that he was dirty and needed a good washing. He stuck his arms straight in the air like a baby wanting to be picked up. I felt a little at ease because of his sense of humor. I chuckled, reached over, and took a new cloth from the rack that was next to the shower door and soaped it up. I started washing his chest and wanted to stay there at that spot. I guess he knew it too and moved my hand to his penis. I closed my eyes and washed him there. "Turn so I could get your backside."

"OK, I think I could do the rest." He then rinsed off and turned the water off. He picked me up and brought me back into the bedroom and placed me on the bed.

"Wait, I'm wet, I need to dry off first."

"You don't need to," he said as he pulled down the sheets and crawled under the covers next to me. "I'm going to teach you!" he said and began kissing me,between my legs. My mind was racing to catch up with my heartbeat. He squeezed my breast, kissed it, and popped the nipple in his mouth; he was sucking on it. I found myself moaning. I thought about getting pregnant, but Penny and I had gotten birth control pills together. I was rubbing the back of his head while I started whispering to him. I don't want to get pregnant. He reached under the pillow and pulled out three packs of Trojan condoms.

"Kiss me on my lips."

"See, I'm careful," he said as he opened it. He told me to put it on him. I tried but kept on pinching him. "Here, let me do that. You're lowering my mood," he chuckled. I looked down at him; his mood had lowered. I laughed too. He kissed me, and it was back on. He began caressing my body, then kissing me all over. I was in a daze not knowing what was happening or what's next. He was kissing me between my legs again, "Oh boy, did I enjoy that. " You're, so ready." He whispered. He rolled on top of me, and I grabbed his back and held tight. He entered me, and I screamed! I was in so much pain and thought I would faint. I felt as if I was choked and pulled apart all at the same time

"Are you, OK?"

"Yeah, I'm all right. Just do it slowly so I could breathe, it hurts so much."

"You want me to stop?" he asked then whispered, "You are so wet, and that's how I love it," in my ear and stuck his tongue in it. His wetness dripped down my neck.

"I do, but then again, I don't. Just go slow," I breathlessly said as my body was heating up. Then he inched inside of me, and my nails dug deep down in his back then he screamed. He went in further; before I could yell, he started rolling around, moving on top, and that was feeling kind of good.

"You're so wet, you feel so good. Damn, Eboni, this feels sooo good," he whispered over and over again.

Before I love you could come out of his mouth, I told him, "I love you."

"I love you too," he said as his body glided on mine. A tear rolled down my cheek; I guess that was my virginity leaving me. I hugged him tight and said good-bye to it. He was so tender with me, and I was enjoying him. A couple more strokes—one, two— on the third then he collapsed on me. I lay back, closed my eyes, and pictured what just happened; I was a woman now! He sat up and kissed me again and started stroking my hair, brushing it away from my face, and looking at me like I was a new person. Then he kissed me, and before "I love you" could come out of my mouth, he said it to me again. "You know, Eboni, I want to be with you for real. I mean, I'm not just saying that so you would keep sleeping with me."

"Shawn, I know. I trust you now with my heart."

"I knew when I first met you, we had something special, and I mean that."

"Wait, baby, I really got to go," I said and kissed him.

As I got up to go to the bathroom, he said, "Eboni, you're bleeding, there's blood on the sheets." He smiled

"What's so damn funny?"

"Oh, nothing." I was her first, he thought. He paused. "Just thinking that I'd wanted more of you."

"Shawn!" I went into the bathroom. After my shower, I went back in with a towel to cover up the spot of blood. He had tossed the sheet in the corner and used the top sheet for the fitted. I climbed back in the bed; he lay on my breast.

"You, OK?"

"I'm all right."

"Good, don't want to scare you off."

I knew that would happen, so I wasn't worried. After talking to the pros, Justina and Penny, I knew it was going to happen. Shawn was telling me about the trouble he was in and how I needed to be careful when I was by myself. I rubbed and kissed his head; he asked again was I all right. "Am I your first virgin?"

He sat up. "Let me see, hmm…yeah, you are."

"Stop playing!" I tapped him upside his head.

"I'm not." He smiled. "You are the first one I took my time with and love, so that's what makes you my first, ok?" Then he tapped me on my nose; he shyly asked, "Could we do it again?" I was too sore to even think about another round, told him not tonight, then closed my eyes and thought how I didn't feel that explosion everyone spoke about, but it was my first time, and all I felt was the explosive pain and how I was trembling and needed to rest. So we lay holding each other. A few minutes later, I heard him snoring while I lay there looking at the ceiling. Finally, sleep.

I forgot where I was when I awoke to see Shawn closing the hotel room door, and wheeling in a cart with four silver trays and a pitcher of fresh orange juice. He pushed the cart over to the bed on the side where I was. He kissed me. "Rise and shine. I know you are hungry after the night we've had. I'm starving." And he kissed me again.

"Good morning. I'm going to the bathroom first. Let me just wash up a little."

"OK, I'm going to fix your plate, so hurry up so your food won't get cold, even though it had just come up," he added.

"OK," I said as I closed the bathroom door. I checked my face out in the mirror. Good, and I didn't look too bad. I was expecting to see my eyes all puffy from crying and drool caked to the side of my face, showing what a deep sleep I had, but I'm proud to say I didn't look bad. And judging by Shawn's reaction to me, I didn't wake up with my boogeyman's face. All I needed was a brush for my hair. I wash my face and brushed my teeth, I stole a quick shower. As I washed my cat, it was still sore—a reminder of last night. Felt like soaking, but Shawn and the food were waiting. As we were eating, he kept asking me how I felt. "Sore, sore, sore," I told him.

"Would you want to do it again?"

"I'm not even hearing you. I just told you how I feel."

"I'm in pain too," he said.

"Oh yeah, how?" I looked confused.

"My back, you had your nails so deep in it."

"Cause of the pain you were cracking, my walls seemed like I was being split in half."

"So it hurt, huh? Sorry, it's just so…"

"So what?" I said.

"Nah, nothing."

"Don't bite your tongue for me."

"I'm not biting anything."

"So say it then."

"It was just so wet, damn, the whole bed was soaking, that's all." He smiled then quickly changed the subject. "You want to get something else to eat?" Damn, that was weak, he thought.

"Naw, I'm good. How much is this going to cost?"

"I don't know, it's billed to the room. I'll pay for it when we leave."

"Oh."

"You sure you don't want something else—you know, something different?"

"I'm fine. I can't eat anything else, besides, I am stuffed." I happened to glance at the clock. It read nine in the morning. "Shawn, I need to call Penny. My mother will be looking for me. She knew I went to the party and told me I could stay late, but here I was, and it's morning. She would tear my butt up if she knew where I was." I phoned Penny's house, and her mother picked up. "Good morning, Mrs. Thomas, may I please speak to Penny?"

"How are you doing?"

"I'm fine, thank you." All of this as I hoped my mother didn't call.

"Hold on. Penny, pick up the phone!" she called out.

Penny came to the phone

"Hello, girl, what's up?"

"What's up, Ebb?"

"Girl, I'm here with Shawn at the hotel. Did my mother call?"

"No."

"Good. Well, I want you to switch over and dial my house and hook us up, but don't say anything, just stay on the line."

"Okay, hold on a sec."

"I'll just tell her that I'm at your house since I always spend nights over there anyway." I knew she would believe that. I hung up from the three-way. Shawn was still in the shower, as he came out of the bathroom, "Is everything straight?" he asked.

"Yeah, it's straight." I was looking at him and patted the bed next to me. He was drying off; he tossed the towel on the floor and dove right on the bed next to me. This time, I took control. "Lie back and close your eyes."

"Huh?" Nothing but a word. I got on top of him and eased him inside me and rolled my hips gently. As I was grinding on him, Shawn reached up and started caressing my breasts. I knew how to move so I wouldn't feel too much pain. What was sore was now wet."

"Yeah, that's it, baby, do it like that."

"You like this. You feel how wet I am?"

"Yeah, so wet."

I was rocking back and forth on him and loving it. "You want more?"

"Girl, you're going to make me cum, slow down a little."

"What slows down ain't no slow motion over here. You'd better hold on."

He grabbed my hips as if he could stop this hum!

"Eboni, baby, do it slowly. Make it last. This is good." I gave him my roll since my rock was too much for him. I exploded. My whole body was tingling, Shawn grabbed my hips and was moving me from side to side then he exploded into a condom. "You're learning well," he said with a smile.

"It's nice to have a patient teacher, and, baby, you haven't seen anything yet." We rested up in each other's arms.

I usually don't even stay this long with a woman four hours in a tellie, then I was out, but I can't get enough of her, thought Shawn.

Because I called Penny and spoke to my mother on the three-way, told her I was okay that we had left the party early because of the trouble that went down (she already knew 'cause Justina had told her—Yeah thanks, cuz) I was safe at Penny's house, and I could relax with Shawn a little longer while her mind was at ease that no trouble or harm came to me. I was free to spend more time with him. Shawn told me how I surprised him when I took control, especially for a newly lost virgin. I told him I was planning this and was not going to let this chance go to waste.

He then asked how I thought he did. I told him he made me feel special. And I was glad I lost my virginity to him. I couldn't compare him to anyone—he was my first. I didn't want to leave this hotel, the paradise that we were creating; 'cause once we left, we would be going our separate ways. Then there was the beef he had with those three guys from the party. I never would forget the one with the scar on his face. The way he stood there at the door as if he was planning on doing a mob hit and gun down everyone in there. Then he realized that he didn't have enough ammo to carry it out. Just ghetto, you know, sugar but no Kool-Aid, peanut butter but no jelly. Thank god they were ghetto, or I might not be here. I wish I could keep Shawn here instead of facing what was out there. Here was safe, just the two of us and room service. No distractions unless we invited it. Hotel heaven was winding down. The phone rang. Shawn answered it, said it was the front desk, and we had noon checkout, unless we wanted to stay longer, he asked me. I told him I could stay till ten because my curfew was at twelve, unless I called Penny and begged her to cover for me, and we booked it for another night.

"You should get dressed."

"Why?"

"So we could shoot to the city."

"For what?"

"Do a little shopping."

"Shopping?"

"Yeah, pick up a few things."

Since the car was in the hotel parking lot, we didn't have to walk far. The traffic was thick; we were stuck in a few traffic jams—where you got an inch every five minutes! That's New York for you, and we had just entered Brooklyn crossing over the conduit. Saw White Castle, it made me hungry, till I thought about the bathroom the next day. "Shawn, when we get to the city, let's stop and get some food for later on."

"For sure, no problem."

We were finally cruising, catching every green light on Atlantic Ave. Until we got to Bedford Ave. and the night of the living dead came out begging for change. There were two other cars ahead of us when a man came up to the car in front of us and started wiping their clean window. "What kind of water is he using?" I asked.

"I don't know, but they better not touch my shit," he said as I sat there praying for the light to change and turn green. The people in the car ahead threw some money down on the street. The man picked them up, counted, dropped them in his cup, and started walking toward us. Come on, light, turn green. He got to Shawn's window with his dirty cloth in his hand, looked at Shawn, then looked at me. He was met with cold stares.

"Come on, man, can I wipe your window?" he asked. Shawn turned his head as if no one was talking to him.

"Give him a dollar," I whispered.

"For what? I don't support no one's drinking or drug habits."

The man was still standing there, looking at us. "You know, I used to have a nice car too when I was about your age."

"Yeah, ole man, what happened?" Shawn, asked sarcastically.

"Lost my job due to the war, and shit went over to fight. And when I came back, nobody gave a damn," he said in his tattered army jacket. "So there you have it."

"Look, you could be telling my ass another eight million New York stories for all I know, but here, take this twenty"—he peeled off his not—"and do what's right for you."

Green.

"You believe ole man?"

"I don't know."

"Good answer, Eboni."

"'Cause you don't know."

We drove on. Next thing, we were hitting the Brooklyn Bridge bound for Manhattan. "Where are we going? I mean, what part."

"We're going to Harlem-125th Street. I know you need a few things, plus I need to pick up something while you wait in the car. I'll just be a minute," he said as he drove onto the FDR, shooting past 34th Street 42-96 Street. I looked at him; he was flying.

"What kind of things do you think I need?"

"Some clean clothes, you know, a few new outfits, underwear—sexy underwear for tonight." He smiled.

"Oh, so you had this all planned out."

"Yeah. As soon as you got on top of me, I wanted to see you in something sexy—not that you need that—you're already sexy. You got it going on. Maybe I should get a whip for you while I'm at it."

I laughed.

"Yeah, and I'll get some handcuffs too cause that's the only way you can stop me from tearing you up is to chain me down," he joked.

He fed the meter, and we went into a clothing store. I picked out a summer dress. It was cut short right before my thighs, almost too revealing for my taste since Shawn had got me accustomed to sweatsuits like a hip muslin covering up. It had yellow and pink flowers on it with thin straps. And I picked out a pair of yellow sandals since I already had pink ones at home and two pairs of jeans and tube tops. Shawn said he had to be at a friend's house within the next hour. "So let's just go to the lingerie section, and after your finish, we could head over there then come back so I could get some things for me."

"All right, let's hurry up then."

We walked over. I picked out a black silk teddy with silk matching panties.

"Hmm, I can't wait to see you in this tonight."

"Yeah, well, I'm going to model this for you."

"Let's go pay for this so we could catch this dude and get back to the hotel."

"Shawn, you are too much, come on where's the cashier?"

He still had ten minutes on the meter. "The way these meter maids came around and gave out tickets, you would think they had a humming device to let them know when your time was up while they sat up in some coffeehouse and ate donuts," said Shawn. "I was in the city the other day and stepped into a store, I mean I just went in must have been no more than five minutes, and when I came out, there was a hundred-dollar ticket."

"So they owe us twenty five minutes, right?"

"Huh, not in this greedy-ass city."

Shawn then pulled in front of a liquor store; he got out and came back with a bag. "This is for later."

"I don't drink."

"Just try some of it. It'll help you loosen up while you model that teddy for me. Besides one, two, even three ain't going to kill you. I'm with you, so be comfortable."

I thought about Justina tripping into the room when she got drunk. I wasn't going to star in that show. Shawn parked in front of this house. "I'll be right back." And he dashed up the stairs so fast. I sat there counting the group of older men hanging out there trying to talk to the young girls that were eyeing me, or should I say whiplash from the Beamer, when I noticed this young black girl with a large behind, cold-staring at me while talking to her friends. So I acted. I pulled down the sun visor to fix my long natural hair—not weave like they all had—and glanced at her. She rolled her eyes at me. Yeah, bitch. Miss me with your drama. I smiled. Check yourself. That shit even ain't yours, and you fronting thinking your shit is tight. Please. They even ain't on my level. And I clicked the visor closed. Fuck 'um. When Shawn came back, he had a bulge on his side. I didn't want to ask because I didn't want to know. We stopped and picked up some food after. Harlem was filled with the best black soul-food restaurants. No Mexican cooking collard greens. You got big momma in the back, putting it down. And everyone knew Sylvia had it going on. Fried chicken and mac and cheese with greens topped off with sweet pecan pie.

"You know what, I don't have to stop to pick up anything for me, especially since I got this weight on me," he thought.

"Why not? Don't you need some fresh clothes too, like underwear?"

"Naw, I'm a guy, I could make do, and besides, I don't plan on being in them for long." He hinted with his sexy eyes.

I patted my cat to see if it was sore or was it purring. It's like Shawn was talking not to me but to my cat.

"Baby, I need to holler at you on the bizniz tip, so I need your head leveled up and focused." He hesitated, which caused me to be a little concerned looking up at him.

"Shawn, just spit whatever you're thinking. I can take it." Before I start bugging out and wonder was it another woman or a baby popping up on us? I thought.

"Baby, take the siren out of your voice 'cause it ain't no reason to be alarmed. Look, I need you on my team in my world, fully understand, and I can't be all worried about you while I'm baking this dough. I move a lot of shit, and nigghas be getting the green-eye. "How, much bags are being moved?" He ignored my silly comment. "I know I could trust you. You ain't no user. Plus, you're my girl, so I trust you even more, and with that being said, I'm going to bring you up to speed on the drug game. I need a person I could trust and depend on."

"What about little Tony, Markus, and Dave?" I asked.

"Yeah, well, they're getting greedy, ever since I bought my wheels. They will still be around, but a little lower on the totem pole, that's all. Well, let me just show you what I just picked up. This is a metric scale, I needed another one. It's used to count ounces. And right here is a half kilo of cocaine. It cost me twelve thousand dollars. And when I'm finished with it, I'll have twenty-five close to thirty thousand dollars. Then I'll go buy two whole kilos.

"Twenty-five thousand? How long does it take to make that much money?"

"It depends on the customers. But first, I'm going to cut this."

"Why?"

"'Cause I'm selling crack and powder. Don't worry, you're going to be inside. In the spot, not on the streets, so no one has to know what you are doing."

"How much money could I make?"

"Slow down, Noriega, let's move this shit first. Don't worry, you're going to get paid," he said with one hand on the steering wheel and the other one on my shoulder. I thought about what he was telling me about getting paid just for bagging up stuff. I wasn't at risk; it's not like I was on the corner dealing and looking out for cops. Or worst, the stickup kids who either roamed in packs or rolled on you dolo. Or gang rivals over tufts and power.

"All right, I'll do it. When do I start, boss?" I joked.

"This week, I'll just re-up Tony and the fellows still moving products out there, and they have about two days' supplies of the shit anyway. That will give me time to cut it and cook it. And show you how to measure it and bag and tag then it's ready to hit the streets.

Me, a drug dealer? I love him so much I would have followed him anywhere, and that scared me. He still had beef over turf, which he said by going to Harlem; he just handled it. That the big boss was going to move some people down there. The big boss owned New York; he supplied the heavyweight buying and dealing. And Shawn was on his way to becoming a heavy. Plus, the big boss was his uncle. Who'd started Shawn as a runner, then moved to the greyhound as a traveler.

Now he was a boss with a staff of five, top leaders, including myself. We then discussed how he was in need of and required more street workers. That was something he couldn't advertise for—huh no job listing in the Daily News or Post.

"Don't worry, and I'll protect you. This way, we'll spend more time with each other."

"Did Sandy go into business with you too?" I asked him.

"No, I told you she was dizzy, plus she used. Nothing substantial like crack—just sniffed little powder and smoked weed. Drank, party—she was a party girl, basically. I told you about her, how dizzy she was."

I just looked at him; we were pulling into the hotel parking lot. He opened our hotel room door and placed all the bags on the dressing table and stashed one under the bed.

"What's that you got there?" I played.

"It's your fashion set, missy," he played back and handed it to me. All I wanted to do was rest until he started talking to my cat again. And there she goes purring as if his words were petting and stroking her. I smiled and headed right into the bathroom.

While I was in the bathroom, taking a shower, I heard him flicking through the channels on the TV. I asked myself a question: could I do this, could I help sell something that was destroying my community that had mothers selling their bodies and self-respect, jewelry, furniture, lugging it around on a shopping cart. Not washing or working or caring for their kids? Kids are just running wild, stealing from their neighborhood stores because they didn't have any food in their house 'cause their mothers sell off her food stamps for a hit. How would it all fall back on us as a people? The chain of destruction. That was a lot to consider as I pictured in my mind those zombie women and men I used to see while I and Penny, Donny, Johnny sat outside chilling on the stoop. And one would walk up to us trying to sell something with their eyes bulging out of their sockets, pleading with us to buy from them. And we all would yell, "Get out of here crackhead" and laugh as they cursed us and walked along to the next group of people, trying to unload their TV set that he probably snatched off the living room table while everyone slept. Well, I don't owe them anything. I didn't force them to use drugs. That's their choice, and my preference is money and Shawn. Besides, I won't be out there handing them the stuff or, looking into they're eyes while killing their souls.

I hurried up and dried off and took the silk teddy out of the bag with its matching panties. I slipped the teddy over my head, pulled up the panties, combed my hair since I didn't wear makeup. I just brushed my teeth. I yelled in a sexy voice, "Here, I come!" Click. Shawn turned off the TV. And with a drink in one hand, he pointed out that my glass was by him.

He licked his lips and told me in a sexy voice, "Come and get it. I sashayed over to him, just swinging my hips, looking him straight in his eyes that were sweeping over my body. "Girl, I can't wait to tear you up," he said. "I'm going to teach you." He smiled. I smiled back, took a sip of my drink, and was propelled back to reality as my facial expression changed from a quiet summer day to a hurricane rainstorm.

"Yuck!" I managed to say between gasping and choking. "What is this? It's awful."

"It's Remy Martin, and maybe you need some soda in it. I drink mine straight and the only mix is the rocks. That's the only thing that chases my Remy," he said and got up to pour some soda in this hurricane of a drink I just tasted. He filled the glass up with soda from the half of the Remy he had given me. I took a sip then swished. Not bad. I didn't want to taste the liquor with no traces of it. I tried to give him a sexy look and began warming up to this drink. I did a little striptease for him, swaying my hips as I've seen on the rap videos. Shawn's sexy bedroom eyes were shining at me. I shook my ass at him; he slapped it and palmed my ass. Then he pulled me next to him. "Girl, I knew you were a winner when I first talked to you." We made love; it was gentle and slow. "You're getting better at this," he whispered in my ear.

"Yeah, I just needed lessons, I'm going to teach you now."

"Ahh, the student surpasses the teacher," he joked.

"You are never too old to learn new tricks," I joked.

We lay in each other's arms, sipping on our drinks and picking at our food while watching TV.

Shawn was telling me how he was going to take this drug-dealing business to a whole new level. That he wanted to be a supplier and move weights like his uncle, how he was going to do it on his own. The only thing he said was that he would have to travel out of town and if I could get away so I could go with him. "You do know that I'm still in school and plan on finishing?"

"I'm talking about weekend trips, and you could get Penny to cover for you. The longer trips, I'll take Tony or one of the guys with me."

"OK, let me think about it. When are you planning on making your first trip?"

"In a couple of weeks, not right now."

"OK, enough shoptalk, I want some more." And with that, he pulled the sheets over our heads. His touches were paralyzing 'cause I just lay there while he explored my body. Sounds came from me that I never knew existed. I enjoyed being with him. When we finished, he asked if I was hungry. He was going to order room service. I knew we were checking out tomorrow and wanted to make every moment last. Then I thought about my bedroom I shared with Justina, how it didn't compare. I'd rather be here lying in Shawn's arms, losing sleep, instead of dealing with a powerful kick Justina delivers.

Shawn ordered us some spaghetti and meatballs with garlic bread and salad and a bottle of red wine, a Merlot. "Let's have a romantic night," he said.

"You're surprising me," I said. You're strong, tough, 'I'll kick your ass,' not afraid to fight anyone, was this soft, romantic, gentle lover who knew. I told him.

"A good woman will calm any man. Look at Tarzan. You're my Jane," he teased. "I'm hunting for food right now. See, I'm dialing room service. I'm Tarzan, citified. I may not have hunted it down to get a meal, but I do have to hunt for the money to get it. Instead of trees to swing from, I swing from buildings. There's no difference. We're in a concrete jungle, baby! Survival of the fittest, that's what's up. Babe, stick with me. I'm going to put you on. And if we were ever to break up, I ain't mad at you 'cause you're good peeps, so I know it would have to be my bad," he joked. "No man could ever step to you with his weak-ass bullshit lines. You'd shut him down with the quickness. He has to come correct on the top steps like me or deeper. You are going to be street-smart, which you are already—just a little more fine-tuning. Guy-smart so you could stop them before they even get out the gate. And school-smart so you'll know your ABCs and 123s and weed from trees so you won't get beat," he joked. "You know, I grew up an only child with no siblings to learn from. So I spent my summer with my mother's brother. My Uncle Pete, the boss. He had three kids. One was around my age. He was dealing back then, always had nice-ass things, nice clothes. My mom's worked hard and provided for me the best she could. But my uncle used to let me go with him and my cousin Raymond—we called him Ray-ray—on his drug buys. I was only eleven then, so I been in this game for a minute. Ray-ray got strung out his eyes, weren't open his ears either. They were closed. I first started with Ray-ray, trying to make some money. Uncle Pete set us up with customers. I ended up getting caught, spent six months at Spofford Juvenile Detention Center. By then, Ray was fourteen and a junkie. He wasn't fucking with crack anymore. He used to smoke rulers."

"What's that?" I asked.

"That's when you take weed and some crack, cocaine, and roll it in a blunt. So from that, he moved on to pure coke. Next thing, he was in the alley shooting up heroin. Said he was on a rich-man's high. Shit, everyone knows rich men prefer coke. Anyway, one month later, he died of drug overdose. And when Uncle Pete buried him, he dropped in the coffin one hundred syringe needles and one pack of heroin.

"Damn, that's deep," I said.

"Yeah, and since then, I never got high. Don't even smoke cigarettes. Just started working out going to school, which I finished with a GED. I did a semester at college, but everyone there was asking for drugs. So I emptied my book bag, hung up my books, and filled my bag with drugs from Uncle Pete, and made a killing. Until some 21 Jump Street–looking cop busted my ass. Luckily, I didn't have any weight on me, just a couple of weed bags left. Coke sold out fast. You know, everybody wanted to stay up. Guess midterms or something. Anyhow, I saw the judge with a couple of bags to my record. Did eighteen months at Rikers."

What could I say? He was opening up to me. There was a knock at the door.

"It's room service," the voice called out. Shawn put the towel around him and got up to answer the door. I made a quick dash for the bathroom. The bellhop rolled the tray in as I came back out of the bathroom. Shawn tipped him fifty bucks, said his customary thanks, then closed the door behind him. He lit the candles, handed me a single rose. Then he pulled out my seat for me as I sat there in my teddy. I removed the robe that was hanging in the bathroom. He sat across from me, poured us some wine, and I poured the water.

"Voila!" he said as he took the tray's cover off, revealing our dinner. "I want to make a toast." He surprised me, with the wine glass in his hand, he began by clearing his throat, and his eyes were a little glossy. "I just want to tell you that I love you and glad that we're together, and here's to making money. Welcome to my world."

And with that, I said cheers, and we clicked our glasses together and began to eat. His world? He was my world, I thought, and wouldn't have it any other way. "Bonnie and Clyde," I said.

"Yeah, that's what we are. And that's your nickname, so if I call you that, that means something is about to jump off and stay on point Bonnie."

"And the same for you Clyde."

"True, we are going to make some team. Now tomorrow, I'll show you how to bag, and we could get to work."

"The quicker, the better," I said. I didn't know if my courage was coming from the wine and liquor, or because he believed in me. I surprised myself.

We ate, made love, and slept, holding each other as if our bodies were making a pact, promising to keep each other safe. I was the Bonnie to his Clyde. I didn't want to end up like them foolish. This was the loss of my innocence.

CHAPTER

3

Shawn drove me home; we kissed, and he told me he was coming back to take me over to the spot. I went into the house and was expecting to hear my mother's voice, but she wasn't even home. Justina said she and Aunt Nancy and Elisha went to Chinatown and were having dinner out there in the city. And that Johnny called for me. I knew it was Penny. So I phoned her, even though she was my best friend, I wasn't going to tell her about my new job with Shawn. I called Penny's house, and she answered.

"What's up, girl? I just got in."

"Had a lovely vacation, didn't you?"

"Yeah, too bad, it ended."

"Well, how was it?"

"How was what?" I knew she was talking about the sex, but I wanted it to drag out.

"You know… Do I have to spell it out to you?"

"All right, since you're prying into my business—"

"Your business! Sounds like you got some. And here I was, thinking he was teaching you spades all night. Your business only means one thing, girl, you got busy to have business."

"Well, if you must know, I'm in the club with you now. Why didn't you tell me how painful it is? I was yelling, biting, pushing, pulling."

"Oh, first time out and you're already into kinky sex? I guess freaks are born, not made," Penny aha, joked.

"Did you hear me? I was in pain."

"That's because you busted your cherry. You did bleed."

"Yeah, all over him and the bed." I wanted to change the subject before she went on about her first sexual experience. "Did my mother call?"

"No, she knows you always stayed over. I had Johnny call to see when your freaky ass was coming home."

"Good. Shawn is coming back for me a little later on."

"Boy you must have a magnet in your pussy," she laughed.

"Yeah, I'm trying to connect with him." I'd rather she thought I was sex-crazed like she was than to know I was a drug dealer in the making.

"Well, girl, don't give him too much, you might wear him out, and he might move on to the next."

"Girl, you are crazy." Before we hung up, she said she and Tony were going out. "Have fun, wear him out, tear him up," I joked.

"Shawn is changing you."

"Have fun, call me later." We said our good-byes. I thanked her for covering for me then hung up.

I went upstairs to lie down and think about the past two nights. Justina was getting ready for her date with Donny and was telling me how she met a new guy named Derrick, who was tall, dark, and fine. She had met him on the train; he lived in Brownsville. They had met at the Junction. I didn't feel like hearing this, and I wish I had my old room back, where I could come in, close the door, and lock it and be by myself. But here I was, listening to her go on about the men in her life.

"What time are you leaving?" I asked her.

"In ten minutes, she replied.

"Oh well, I'm going to take a nap before I go back out. Just close the door when you leave. Thanks!" See? Polite.

———————— ·+++++· ————————

Shawn came over to pick me up. I love the way he looked in his BMW. It suited him. He had on a gray jogging sweat suit and a white

Sean John tee shirt. We drove over to Riverdale on the other side of East New York; it's where one of his spots were. He said he only had three of them and would be making his rounds today to re-up and collect his money. He parked around the corner, and we walked up the block. Spanish and Arab stores lined the neighborhood. We passed a group of guys around Shawn's age. They looked, we looked. Shawn nodded. "What's up." They nodded back, and we went about our way. It's a respect thing that guys do, like saying, "I'm as live as you" and at the same time saying, "Go about your business" among men.

We, as women, we're a little less sophisticated when we pass each other. It was more like, "Bitch! Don't even think you're better. You ain't cute, Miss Thang! I got it going on and could get your man"—all of that in the second it took to pass one another.

We headed up two flights of steps. Shawn did his special knock, and the door went through five locks and a chain then opened. The guy who opened the door was standing there, holding a police bolt pole in his hand.

We walked past him. I followed Shawn into what was a living room. The sofa propped up on cans, in the front of it with bricks in the back. There were two milk crates for a table, a small black-and-white thirteen-inch TV on another container. The guy walked back in and sat down and began rolling up a blunt then lit it.

"What's up?" Dawanye said in between puffs. "Man, Dave just stepped out."

"Yo, where's my money?"

Dwayne got up and went into one of the two bedrooms then came back with a brown paper bag full of cash. Told Shawn it was all there.

"What about the rocks and pow-pow, do you have enough?"

"Yeah, I'm good for a day or so. Shit's been kind of slow."

"So I'm hearing," said Shawn. "Well, all right, I'm outta here."

"Peace," Dawanye replied.

We then drove over to the next spot. Shawn ran in, told me he would be right back, just doing the same thing: picking up money. He was back in no time with another brown bag filled with cash, made another quick stop before we headed over to the main spot. As I later found out, this was a real smoking crib, the main spot—leather sofa sets, beautiful sixty-inch floor model TV, glass and brass-end tables.

"This is where we're going to prepare everything. OK, the first thing I need you to do is count all these money separately and put it next to the bag it came from."

"Why?" I asked.

"So I know who's short with my money," he said. "You count that while I get the stuff together to measure and cook."

"Well, bring it out here so I could see it," I yelled out as he was walking into the kitchen.

He came back holding a plastic Wendy's tray in his hand with the scale and two big mayo jars and a box of baking soda. The cocaine—he walked over to the bedroom and came back with it. "I stash it after I drop you off. Don't want to be riding around with this on me. Shit, that's twenty years right here. Ain't no personal use. This is intent to sell." He then laid everything on the glass table. I was counting the money. I finished the first bag it was five thousand. Shawn poured a large amount of cocaine in one of the mayo jars. Then poured it out on to the metric scale to measure it, wrote down how much it weighed, then poured in the baking soda in a jar with it. "The easy part is over. Now, this is what I want you to do as the business starts picking up speed. Come with me in the kitchen so I could show you how to cook it. He then sat the mayo jar filled with coke and baking soda, added water, and put it on to boil. I stood there looking. "There, this should be done in a few," he said. Then he walked back in the living room and began to double-check the money I just counted. He felt me looking at him, like, "Why did you even ask me in the first place?" "Look, I always do a double-check and sometimes a triple check. You're new to this, and it's a lot of money, so it's easy to miscount."

"Well, five thousand is what I counted." Then five was what he said too.

"All right, you finish the rest of the bags, I'll go get the stuff." And he came back with another plastic tray and some paper towels. He dumped the cocaine out of the jar.

"It looks like a bar of soap," I said.

"Yeah, this is where you come in. I need for you to chop this up real small. Like this." He looked like he was dicing up onions and made the coke look like tiny crumbs, and he filled up one vial and handed it to me.

"How, many of these you want me to fill?"

"All of these plastic vials right here." Then he handed me a bag filled with at least five hundred vials. "When you finish counting."

"I'm on my last count."

He recounted the money, wrote down the totals, and handed me the tray and bags of vials. "Make one so I could make sure you don't put too much coke in it. Don't want to make the crackheads happy, just a little hungry. If you know what I mean," he joked.

I made one and gave it to him. "How's this?"

"You're a natural. That's good. Now make the rest of them like this one." We were in the spot for two hours when I finished bagging up ten thousand vials, with his help.

"Let's order some Chinese food."

"And have them deliver it here?" I asked.

"Yeah, I always let Chino bring it. That way, it doesn't look like a spot from the outside. There are groceries in the kitchen 'cause sometimes, I stay here after a long day's work and don't feel like driving home."

"You stay here alone?"

"Of course, if you don't believe me, go check and look around for yourself. You know women always make themselves known by leaving something behind. Besides, when do I have time for any other girls? You've seen, since you've been with me, anytime my beeper goes off, it's for business, and my cell it's for you and emergency only. I only have time for you, that's why I want you around me at my side. Girl, you put it on me."

"I'm sorry it just looks like a mack pad, you know a love nest," Eboni jokes.

"Look, cut the childish talk. If you don't believe me, then spend some nights here, OK, ?"

"Yeah, maybe I will then."

"Then do that."

The Chinese food arrived; he got up to pay for it then took the food into the bedroom. We ate chicken wings and egg rolls with french fries and made love. It was getting late, and I had to get home, I mentioned.

"OK, I just got to drop the stuff off at Dave's house, then I'll take you back."

I didn't feel safe about riding with the drugs in the car, but since Dave didn't live too far, the chances weren't too dangerous. So here I was, taking a risk for Shawn. What else would I do for him? Does love make you blind? I knew my friends wouldn't understand.

Shawn took me home right after dropping by Dave's house. Since Dave was the runner, he had to distribute the coke to the three spots. Shawn had five people working for him. But Tony, Dave, and Markus each had three workers. Before Shawn left, he handed me $1,000.

"Don't worry, there's more. You get the rest, later on," he said. "I'm running to the city tomorrow morning."

"For what?" I asked.

"I'm going to pick up walkie-talkies for us. And a police scanner.

"You're going mobster tech with this."

"Yeah, real gangster Scarface, Tony Montana style."

"Ah, you're crazy. I'll see you when you come back." I laughed.

"Also, I got check in with my uncle to make sure the problem was taken care of."

"Just be careful."

"Always."

His uncle had told him to lie low, that he would see to it no one fucked with a Carter. He blew me a kiss then drove off. Inside my house was boisterous; I could hear my mother's voice before I even locked the door. They were yelling at the TV show Dynasty, playing, and Crystal and Alexis were fighting with their designer dresses on and rolling around in the mud. Two socialites. I guess money couldn't buy you class. Here they were acting like Mucky and Booker from the projects and arguing and fighting over a man. I sat down next to Elisha, who was laughing at the whole thing. My mother and aunt were yelling for Crystal to knock Alexis out. Reruns.

Justina wasn't home, so I went upstairs to take a shower and get ready for bed, even though it was only nine thirty. I felt like I haven't had a moment's peace since I got with Shawn. My days were always full and fast, and now my nights were too. The old handball gang was now coupled up; everybody doing their own thing. I came out of the shower and I went into my bedroom to get dressed. Since Justina wasn't home, I could be by myself and take my time drying off, lotioning up my body. I looked at my nakedness in the mirror. I liked my shape—my small waist and round butt and my perky breasts. I had a flat stomach considering I ate like a pig. But all in all, I had nothing major to complain about. I put on a fresh pair of jammies, and was about to hit the bed when my mother knocked on the door. She peeked her head in.

"I'm just checking in on you. How's Penny?"

"I'm fine, just a little tired. Penny is OK, you know, always running off at the mouth. I have a slight headache from her," I replied.

"You need an aspirin?" Mom asked.

"No, I'm all right."

"Maybe some rest will do you good then, well, good night, honey. I'll check on you in the morning before I leave for work." Then she closed my door. How could I tell her that I'm not tired from Penny's big mouth, which sometimes does end up giving me a headache. Instead, I was with Shawn at the hotel having sex. Then hanging out with him in drug spots, helping him bag up—and he was a drug dealer.

No, I couldn't tell my mother that or anyone else for that matter.

I was a straight A student, I was already in college. I knew better, but something kept pulling me to him. No one would understand. Shawn's life and mine were on two different paths. I could hear my mother saying. So the less she knew, the better. Penny and the rest of my friends that knew Shawn knew he was a street pharmacist. But they didn't think I was one too. With the one thousand dollars he'd given me for pay, I was involved, and it was about to get thick.

My mother woke me up, telling me to call her at work if I still wasn't feeling well. I told her I was feeling better, didn't want to worry her since I was going out later on.

Shawn came by and gave me my walkie-talkie and a police scanner.

"What's this? I mean, how come you're giving me one?"

"You are still down with me, right?"

"Uh-huh."

"So, what's wrong?" he said. "In case I need you to bring me something, or if the cops, come you would be on the move, hopefully with the stuff and cash. That's why I want you to keep a low profile. I don't want you hanging out there. "You know sometimes, especially around election time, and these fucking cops get on their jobs. Shit starts taking pictures and shit, pulling up on us for no good reason. Just toss your ass up on the wall, have you do a lineup, just fucking with you. So that's why you have to lie low, like you just my girl."

"Yeah, I got it. All right, come show me how to use this damn walkie-talkie thing,"

I said. That should have scared me off; it drew me to him more.

"One more thing I have to tell you. Sandy called. She wants me to come to see my son."

"When are you planning on going?" I said, sitting up on the black leather sofa.

"Oh, maybe this weekend. We'll drive over there to Queens. I'll drop some money, then we'll split."

"I hope she doesn't start no shit cause I'm you."

"Naw, she knows all about you, ain't nothing between us. I'm just taking care of my son, and she cool with that, so everything is cool. You are my lady—everyone knows that."

"What? Did you put an ad in the papers?"

"Yeah, I did, right in ghetto weekly." Shawn finished showing me which frequency to keep my walkie-talkie on, and which channel we should use for privacy.

"You're going hi-tech."

"Yeah, I'm taking this to a whole new level. I want people on the roof."

I chilled in the spot all day with him, asking him about the double date. I wanted to hang out with Penny and take a break from this drug world. I was going with him to pick stuff up from his Uncle Pete. Then bag it up after making rounds collecting money, counting it, and counting drugs. I needed a change of scenery; I nudged him for his answer.

"Baby, you know money is rolling in. We have over four hundred thousand in three banks, not to mention what we got in stash we can't take a break not right now."

"What are we doing now? Now listen, I want to go out and have a good time and do it soon, like this week." It was almost the end of summer; I spent all of my time with him.

Shawn closed his eyes as Eboni was talking. "You call Penny and let me know when. You're making me a pushover."

"Yeah, but you're my pushover," she said then kissed him. In the weeks that passed, she knew everything about his business. How much Tony, Dave, and Markus made; how much Shawn paid them. Even down to how much Shawn was spending on the spots, the cost it took to rent it. And what he paid the lookouts, what he paid the cops to inform him about a bust so he could clean house.

Here we were, sitting on four hundred thousand dollars, almost five, that they built from his business. We had clothes, money, and a car. He brought his mother her house, but the deed was in my name. Shit, I was in too deep. How could a seventeen-year-old own a three-hundred-thousand-dollar home? I was paying rent for my mother, and told her I got a job. I got up every morning at seven and headed over to the spot with my keys and waited for Shawn. He usually came around nine, which was fine with me since I got there at eight. That gave me time to go over the books. Shawn wanted to buy a clothing store that was going out of business in the neighborhood.

He came in very upset, yelling about Markus getting shot by his home last night. He said he was taking a trip back to Harlem to visit his Uncle Pete, who always handled these types of mess for him. He was keeping Shawn's hands clean. He needed to prove a point before he became the next target. Or me, he said.

"When are you going?" I asked.

"Right now."

"OK, but who was the guy who shot Markus? Is he all right?"

"Yeah, stayed overnight at the hospital. Cops came asking questions and shit."

"What did he say?"

"Told them some shit about going to see a girl and ended up getting robbed. How he gave up the money and they still shot him."

"And the cops bought that?"

"Wouldn't you? The guys who did that told him it was payback, for Flip and them."

"You're talking about the guys from the party?"

"Yeah."

"Didn't your uncle take care of that?"

"Yeah, I guess they were looking for me, so that's why I need to go uptown. We need more people, and guns."

"I want one too."

"I got you, got one already, didn't know how to give it to you."

"Well, give it to me."

He handed me a sliver-plated .25 automatic with an extra clip. "Baby I'm going to show you how to use it. Put it away till I get back. Don't want you blowing your head off. Don't know what I'll do if I lose you. So put it away please. I'll be right back." He kissed me then he went out the door.

She sat looking at her gun; she knew she needed it—for her protection ever since those three gunmen came busting in on Dawn's party. She wanted one but didn't want to ask Shawn. She didn't like being scared, could never forget that feeling when those guns were pointing at her and Shawn. She didn't want to be at that side of the bullet. I better be pointing the gun and shouldn't be afraid to use it when it came down to my life, I choose every time.

She put her gun and bullets under the sofa and flipped the TV on, trying to take her mind off of it. What if it was Shawn or me just that quick? Let me call Penny and see how things are going. She was about to dial Penny's number when Shawn came running back in.

"Baby, cops are all over, stopping everyone, knocking on doors."

"Because of Markus?" I asked.

"No, a little girl raped and murdered from across the street."

"How old was she?" I interrupted him.

"I don't know, maybe around ten to twelve."

"The same age as Elisha, oh my god," she said.

"Baby, baby, listen. If the cops come knocking, just tell them you live here with your mother, and she's at work. I doubt they'd even brother this far. I hate to leave you like this, but I gotta catch him."

"Just go. I'll be OK. I can handle things."

"You sure? 'Cause I gotta go."

"Go, I'm fine. I got this."

He left out again.

Elisha… How could someone do this to a little girl? What kind of animal could harm a baby? Instead of phoning Penny, I called my sister. To hear her voice and to find out where she was going. And to warn her not to leave the block by herself. That there was a sicko out there. That could have been any one of us. You get so worried about trying to put food on the table, making a living, now, we have to worry about predators and pedophiles. Boy this shit really hits hard. I phoned Penny to shake my mind from this.

"What's going on, how's Shawn?"

"Good, he's out getting food, so I figured I'd give you a call. What's up?"

"I was thinking about the four of us going out."

"Oh yeah. Let's do it," I said.

"When?"

"Tomorrow."

"Cool," she said, then added, "You heard about Markus, right?"

"Yeah, that's fucked up."

"Yeah, well, he's all right. Got shot in the leg. Only a flesh wound."

"Oh, he was lucky."

"True."

"How's Tony?"

"He's fine. He was with me when it went down. Then Markus's mother called his cell. We met her at the hospital. Doctors called it a flesh wound. His mother said he was OK, he'll live. Anyway, about us going out at what time? First, we'll stop by and see Markus then go on to the city, around seven."

"Sounds good to me."

"All right, I'll call you later." Then I hung up. I felt a little better.

I closed my eyes and let the TV watch me as I doze off. Shawn came back four hours later. I was in a deep sleep when I felt his kiss on my face. I opened my eyes to see him standing there, smiling.

"Sleeping beauty, you must get up," his voice softly said. I reached up and pulled him down on me; I didn't feel like getting up. I wanted him close to me, especially after what happened.

"I want you right here next to me."

"Ahh, I'm not going anywhere."

"Well, I'm just making sure. So how did it go with Uncle Pete?"

"He's going to take care of this, sending my cousin Curtis down here."

"For what?" I asked.

"There might be a war brewing, so we need more guns, and Curtis is the man for that."

A war, guns—shit was getting real thick. It's like the more money you made, the more problems you face just to keep it, I thought.

He asked if the cops came by, asking questions about the little girl no. I told him they probably had all the information they needed. "You know this neighborhood had a lot of Peter Jennings and Barbara Walters. I'm sure somebody's seen or heard something and did the right thing, hopefully, and told the cops," I said.

"You know this neighborhood has an oath when it comes to police, but when someone hurts children, that's a whole other story, yeah. No love," said Shawn. Then he added two things a woman should know how to do. Drive and handle a gun.

"When are you going to show me how to use the gun?"

"Look, I don't want you caught in the middle of gunfire."

It's not like he didn't try and reassure me, but I wasn't having it. "You're going to show me how to use it," I told him. "I would hate to fire it and have the blast knock the gun right out my hand."

"Yeah, well, if that happens, that means you didn't have a secure grip on it," he answered. "We'll do it later, and we have work to do right now."

"Yeah, I bagged up some. It's in the kitchen cabinet."

He got up and brought in the rest then pulled out some more coke that needed to be cooked and bagged. "Since I was at Uncle Pete's, I figured I'd kill two birds with one stone. I was going to re-up anyway."

"Yeah, like next week."

"Anyway, it's cool, money's coming fast. Now let's stay ahead," he said.

"Oh, I phoned Penny, and we're hanging out tomorrow."

"What do you have planned?"

"Nothing fancy—movies, dinner," I lightly mentioned.

"Let's do something different, like a comedy club."

"Bet, let's do it."

"There's one in the village we could check out."

"Yeah, whatever."

We spent the rest of the day bagging up the stuff, talking about his empire he was building in his mind and wanted it to come true. How he was taking a trip to Miami. Next week, he was flying down, taking fifty thousand dollars with him, buying a return ticket, booking the flight for two weeks' stay, thinking of renting a car to drive the coke back up, and he wanted me to fly down to help with the drive back up. "Who, are you buying this coke from, can you trust them."

"Yeah, they're down with my uncle."

"So why don't you just buy from him like you've been doing."

"Because I don't want to keep depending on him, and suppose something happens to him? And once you start making money—he knows how much I got—people act funny when you blow up. Then there goes my business. I got to make my own connections."

"Babe, remember the next level."

"If you're not sure you could make it, I'll take Tony with me."

"That would be better since this is your first deal, and I'll keep an eye on the spots." He wanted to do a Miami vice drug deal, and I was scared shitless. I love him. So far, I've been smart about my actions. I felt that was a dumb move on my part out of state. But I wanted to learn the business, so I had to go.

CHAPTER

4

Now the problem was convincing her mother; she knew it was time to tell Penny everything in hopes she would join her. Penny had a lot of heart and wasn't afraid to take a risk.

She told Shawn she was going later on that night as he drove her home. Eboni walked into her mother's room as Gail was reading Ebony Magazine and look up at her daughter. Eboni looked around the room for courage, knowing this was a difficult situation she was going to ask of her mother into letting her go with Penny and Shawn to Florida. "Mom," she began slowly. "You know I've been working hard."

Gail put the magazine aside to give Eboni her full attention.

"Working hard, saving my money."

"Yes, and I'm very proud of you for that," replied Gail.

"Yeah, well, I've been thinking before school starts, I'd like to go on a trip to Disney World."

"Yeah, well, I'd like to go to London myself."

"No, Mom, I'm serious, I've been saving, look!" And she pulled out nine hundred dollars to show Gail.

"Don't you think you're a little too young to travel across the state by yourself?"

"Penny's going with me," she blurred out. "Besides, I was thinking of transferring to college out there." She tried manipulation.

"Oh really, when was all of this?" Gail said, not wanting to lose her daughter too. She calmed down a little to hear her out. Penny's been saving the money Little Tony has given her, she thought. Her mother looked at her. "Disney World, just how long you think that money would keep?"

"Mom, I'm not staying long, just a week, Penny has money too," she pleaded. "So could I please go?" She was expecting her mother to argue but was shocked when she said she could go.

"All right, Eboni, you could go to Disney with Penny only because I trust you. And you haven't given me any reason not to." She hugged and kissed her mother, told her she would bring back something for her. "Just as long as you come back, that's enough for me," and kissed her again. She hated to lie to her mother, but it was for her own good. She then phoned Penny to see if she could go. Since she and her mother didn't have a close relationship, there was no one to ask.

"When are we leaving?" asked Penny. Penny's mom drank a lot and spent her time watching soap operas while sipping on a can of beer, smoking weed, ever since her husband walked out seven years ago. Her house stayed messy, and there were clothes piled up in the middle of the living room floor, mixed in with garbage, while her mother sat there drinking. Penny's room was the cleanest room in the house—the kitchen sink was filled with dirty dishes. Penny always busted her ass trying to keep the place clean; she cooked for her little brother, Steven and her mother because usually, her mother was too drunk to be bothered. She said she would have to leave some money for him so he could buy fast food while she was gone. She's in.

I packed my suitcase, kissed Elisha and Mom good-bye. Penny was outside and packed. We took a cab over to the main spot and met up with Shawn and Tony.

They were sitting around the living room with their feet up when we walked in. Tony was talking about needing a gun. "You know those Cubans can be tricky, and we're going into their woods unarmed with cash."

"Don't worry about that. I got a friend at the airport, who smuggles in anything we need. I'm telling you," Shawn said, "we're all set."

"You know you 're not allowed to travel with more than ten thousand cash on us," I said.

"Oh shit, that's right," agreed Tony.

"How many people are traveling with us," Shawn asked and answered his own question. "It's four of us, right, and we'll split it up. The rest could go to my airport contact," Shawn added then walked over to the window to look for the cab he called. We landed at Miami International Airport and was greeted by a beautiful line of palm trees with tiny lizards scurrying about. The four of us got into a rental car with fifty thousand dollars cash and with one 9mm Glock and a .45 revolver, headed to the hotel so we could check in. Palm trees were everywhere, Florida was like something you'd see on a postcard. With its postcard-picture view came humidity. New York was hot, but as soon as we stepped outside of the airport, you're rushed by a heatwave. Hoping it was just passing by, as it circled over our heads, forcing sweat to leave our bodies, I missed the shade of the forty-story buildings that shielded us from the sun. As we drove along I-95, the main route, leading to our hotel with the AC blasting, Tony pulled into the Hilton Inn, parking lot where we had reserved two rooms. We planned on meeting up for dinner; around six. This left us with three hours to relax and freshen up from the flight. I went straight for the shower, and Shawn joined me.

We made love under the waterfalls. The shower was large enough to cool down our steaming Florida sweaty bodies. Feeling less stressed, Shawn turned up the AC. We got under the covers and took a nap. We were meeting Penny and Tony later on. Shawn slept with an inviting smile on his face, and I wrapped my arms around him and tried to join him, but was too excited and worried to relax or sleep. The room was lovely with basic furniture they provided. But the view was breathtaking. Florida looks like a deep-green blanket of grass. I fell in love with the landscape, manicured lawn, flowers in bloom divided along the highway. Not in New York, there would be garbage all up in there, and if not that, then you would have homeless people living right there. You could see vast, endless lines of restaurants, and one could get full while exploring the vast array of eatery that Florida offered. And on the other side was a strip of clubs—South Beach. If I were into dancing and partying the night away, this would be the spot. I crept back in the bed only to find Shawn staring at me.

"What's wrong?" he asked.

"Just worried about the deal, if we could pull it off."

"Baby, we're not robbing a bank."

"I wish we were. That would be easier. Bank tellers don't carry guns."

"I'd understand if you want to stay here while I and little Tony go."

"No, he's your lookout, and Penny's our getaway driver. And I'm your extra gun in the room while we're making this deal."

"Damn, baby, I'm glad you're so on point," he said.

"Now aren't you glad you showed me how to use the guns? And I'm not afraid to use it. My life vs. theirs. I win."

"Slow down, Foxy Brown," he joked. "We just got to remain on point and calm," he said.

"Well, I don't know these cats, and they don't know me."

"Yeah, no love, and no loss of blood." He pumped, trying to see if I was ready.

Was the amount of money we were about to make getting me crazed, or was it the love I had for him making me wild? I felt like a mother tiger protecting her cub; he was my baby. Bonnie would go all out to protect Clyde. But I'm not foolish, I thought. I went over to the bed to kiss him, and I wanted him to know that I was calm and serious. "This is all new to me, this whole drug game, but you stand firm. You ain't no duck niggah, and it pushes me to be strong. I'm with you on this, do you understand what I'm saying?" He started to answer, but I put my hand over his mouth to shush him. "Look, I'm for real with you. Just listen. I see your visions in my dreams. Now, I want to live it, but only with you." I had a tear I was fighting to contain; I had to be brave.

Shawn saw that tear welling up and wiped it with his hand. "Come here, girl. I'm so lucky to have you." Lucky was his nickname for her. "I was blessed not because you're here in Miami with me, but because of how you are. Let me tell you the difference. Some women pretend to understand the pain or the trouble you're in, but you do know. And you're right here with me. When Dawn had her party, you know what I did? I told the fellows to come strapping not just for me, but I was thinking of you. That's why I went to that hood party to make sure you were safe. You were on my mind, baby. I love you. Do you even know? Can't you feel it? Let me put you on to something. I don't know smack about women's intuition, but I do know feelings. When you care for someone and they don't care for you, and they pretend that they have feelings for you. Trust me, you know, you feel it. Just listen to your soul. It's always talking to you, but when it's real, your soul sings to you. Do you understand? I'm singing right now."

I looked at him. I felt it too. "Baby, we are doing a duet." I smiled and got under the covers. It was five o'clock, almost time to meet Penny and Tony, I thought. But I wanted to love him, not for the last time. "You're my drug, and I am addicted," I whispered to him.

"And I will always supply you," Shawn whispered back.

I was lost in my feelings for him. I was breaking laws, risking my life. He was worth it, I thought as I spread my legs further apart so he could go deeper in me. We exploded at the same time with his passionate kissing. We took a shower with only ten minutes to spare. We went down to the lobby, only to find them waiting for us.

"What's up man," said Tony as we walked up.

"Ain't nothing." Then turn to face the three of us.

"So where are we going to eat?" Penny asked.

Because we were surrounded by the beach, water, and smell of the sea, I was in the mood for seafood. "Seafood," I mentioned.

"Naw, we could always go to Red lobster," Tony replied.

"I ain't talking about no Red Lobster. Did you see that view of restaurants out there?"

"Nope, we never made it out of bed," Penny hinted and rubbed Tony's chest.

"Yeah, well, there's a whole bunch of them. All right, well, let us just get in the car." I was starving as we drove along Miami Ave. Judging by the different restaurants, I was expecting to see a rush of UN officials, heading towards their prospective cuisines. We finally decided on a little seafood eatery. Seafood by the Sea it was called. It offered an oceanfront view; after dinner, we topped the night off with drinks. I was glad the waiter didn't ask for ID, not that I needed to drink, but didn't want to be embarrassed. Shawn ordered strawberry daiquiri for me; two daiquiris later, I was ready for sleep. Shawn asked the waiter for the phone; he needed to call Santos with the meeting set for tomorrow afternoon. Shawn and Tony went over the plans once again. More with us. Everyone played a life-keeping part, he added. We all decided tomorrow was so dangerous. Everyone needed to be at their best. We called it a night. I phoned my mother to let her know we were having a good time, to not to worry. Shawn paid the bill. On the drive back to the hotel, Shawn drove on South Beach. Which was a paradise of night clubs. There was something for everyone from straight clubs to gay too chubby chaser. Florida had a nightlife outside of Disney World that I knew nothing about. Penny wanted to stay and people-watch but knew this was not a vacation. We had business to get though.

Back in the room. Shawn went over the plan. He handed me my gun. "Since they would probably search me, I can't carry a gun. They're not going to check you, I won't let them," he said.

"So you're going to be unarmed. How many of them will be there?" I asked.

"Well, Santos said him and some cat named Carols."

"And you trust him enough not to carry a piece?"

"No, that's why Tony and you are packing. With the two of you armed, I'll say my chances are pretty good."

"Where's the meeting? I mean, how far is it from the hotel?"

He got up out the bed and went over to the window. "Come here."

I went over to look.

"Look right over there, you see a row of small houses."

"Uh-huh."

"Yeah, well, right past that, you'll see a green-and-yellow motel. Well, it's in room 6. Santos is already there, that's why I drove down to the South Beach. So I could get a feel for the area. Don't look so worried. I told you my uncle always buys from them."

I was concerned but trying to hide it. All I could see was the Scarface movie, the scene where they were sitting at the table with one of the top Colombian drug czar sipping on coffee talking with Tony Montana. When the helicopter comes above them and Tony looks up, only to see his friend Angel's body is hung and thrown from the plane as they look on. Even though we weren't in Columbia we were in Florida and didn't have the luxury of the mansion or the distinguished drug czar who made his fortune by being ruthless. This was a lower-level motel meeting that was just as dangerous. I knew one thing: I could not freeze up. If it came down to using my gun, this was no movie, no director to yell, "Action, cut!" No stuntmen, basically no do-overs. The only film we would be on would be the eleven o'clock news. I was worrying too much. I rolled over on Shawn's chest, and let the sound of his heartbeat ease me to sleep finally.

I know I didn't sleep well. I got up first and ordered room service while he slept. I woke him up so he'd be ready when they came. The meeting was this afternoon; Penny phoned to invite her and Tony over. Shawn reluctantly went into the bathroom, rubbing his eyes like a five-year-old like when it's time for school. I chuckled.

By the time he came out, two waiters were exiting the room. Rotating in was Penny Tony. Shawn flopped back down on the bed. "Not quite up yet," said Penny. "Well, me and Tony been up walking on the beach," she added.

"How romantic," I joked. We ate. Shawn gave Tony his gun; I put mines in my waist. My jeans were tight enough to keep them in place. I threw on my jean jacket over my red tube top; hopefully, they wouldn't think I had a gun on me. "Now, do I look strapped?" I asked.

Penny looked at Tony, who then turned and looked at Shawn. Well damn, not everyone answered at the same time. "Please, it's not a jeopardy question, yes or no will do," I told them.

"Baby, you look beautiful, and no, I don't see a gun, to answer your question."

"Thank you, baby." Then kissed him on his lips, tasting eggs he'd just finished eating.

"Yo, we need to get over there early so we could be in place," Tony mentioned.

"Yeah, we better roll," Shawn said as he pickups the car keys.

We drove over to the motel; it was early, but Shawn knocked on the door anyway.

"Que pasa?" a voice said from the inside.

"It's Shawn. What's up, amigo?" Shawn answered while Tony stood by the ice machine. Soon as we pulled in the open parking lot, you could smell that the air changed. Even though the motel wasn't far from the beach, I guess the look of this motel told you they didn't verify ID. You could tell what kind of people stayed here. The place smelled of urine, stained hallways, and cheap cigars. Not that I knew what an expensive one smelled like. But I don't think anyone who could afford the expensive kind would be renting a room from this place. Two little Spanish boys ran past us, chasing a cat. One of the boys was yelling, "Bien gato!" while the other one was following with a string. We passed several rooms and could see through one that had moth-eaten curtains that this place did not offer room service or a decent maid for that matter. The garbage cans in the hallway were overflowing. Cigarette butts and stains decorated the worn carpet.

Roaches were playing lookout and guiding you through the halls. I didn't want to touch anything, afraid I might bring company back with me.

The door slowly opened, and there stood a Spanish man in his late twenties. No shirt on, pants crumples like he slept in them, scratching his head. "You Shawn?" he asked in a thick accent. Shawn nodded yes.

"I'm Carols, come in, come in," he said, stepping aside to let us in.

Soon as the door closed, Carols went over to Shawn to search him.

But then Santos came out of the bathroom. Said he was fine, no need to search him, he deals with Peter all time. I leaned up against the wall next to the door—one way in, one way out. I had them in perfect view in case I needed to get my gun. The room was no bigger than a closet. But the 9 mm would make room, if necessary. How could two grown men move about in such a tight space? But I guess when you're dealing below the law, the less attention the better.

Santos reached under the bed and pulled out a duffle bag, opened it, showed Shawn the stuff. Told him to taste it, which he did. Shawn then tossed him the money. He caught it and stuffed it down his front pants without counting it. All the time, my heart was racing to get out of there.

A knock came at the door. I turned to look at Shawn, who then came by my side. Santos went over to the door, opened it; he said something in Spanish. All while my hand was on the gun, which was first at my side and now pointing at Carol's back. Shawn tucked the duffle bag under his arm tightly. Santos then handed who was at the door a twenty-dollar bill. He said he pays a junkie to bring him food and forgot that he was coming. A slip of his mind almost turned this into a bloodbath, I thought. Santos patted Shawn on his back, said, "Nice to do business with you, amigo. See you again," then opened the door for us to leave.

Once, outside I welcomed the smell of the not-so-fresh air. Tony was at the ice machine, and he waited for us to pass, then he followed. As we drove to the hotel, no one said a word. Penny, who was driving, said she needed a drink, her nerves were shot. She then pulled into a liquor store, came back with Hennessy, then drove on to the hotel. Inside, Shawn told Tony everything. Tony said he had seen the man, but he didn't look like no junkie. And maybe we should change hotels now that our business is done.

"Yeah, you're right," Shawn agreed. Penny then poured all of our drinks into the glasses the hotel supplied. I went to the ice machine. A good thing there was one on every floor. I returned only to find Shawn pulling out kilos of cocaine, with a street value of just over four hundred thousand, in front of them. He was sharing too much information with them, I felt.

Penny was my girl, but this was my living. "Why don't we go and get something to eat then change rooms instead of hotels," I said. "I'll register in my name. Come on, Penny, let's go down to the lobby." We came back up to pack our suitcases. The bellhop, showed us our new rooms, which was only a floor lower, right above our old rooms. At the beach, I spent my time lying down on the white-grayish sand while Shawn and Tony swam out past the bowing, testing the lifeguard, daring them to blow their whistles or earn their keep. Penny went in the water just enough to get her feet wet. Black women's hair and saltwater didn't mix. Rain on a good hair day was our enemy. I kept my distance. Penny came and sat next to me.

"I want to make money too. What do I have to do to be down?"

"There's no audition, girl. I'll talk to Shawn. Shit, even Tony could put you on. Why don't you ask him?"

"'Cause you're my home girl."

"Yeah, well, let me talk to Shawn first," who was out too far. I heard the whistle blow and the lifeguard waved them in. After some time had passed, Shawn swam back to shore. They brought their dripping bodies over to us and dog-dried off on us. Patting his stomach, Tony expressed he was hungry.

We drove to the Olive Garden for a late lunch. Penny and Tony wanted to go sightseeing. Shawn and I wanted to go shopping. Miami is known for the best summer fashions. They had one of the world's largest malls. So we decided to rent another car; with that settled, we headed our separate ways. Since the deal was finished, he needed to get in contact with his flight attendant who was flying back to Miami today. He said we should leave early and not draw attention to ourselves. I needed to pick up gifts for my family. I told him, "Can you trust him?"

"He got the guns and money though, why not? I've known him for a while, and he's worked for my uncle. So I figured we can trust him. I like the way he refers to us as we. After all, it wasn't just his ass if we got busted."

We must have hit every store in Miami. By the time we got back to the hotel, Penny and Tony were at our door. The look on their faces told me something was wrong. But before I could ask, Tony burst out, said, "One of the guys from the motel, the Cuban who knocked on the door, asked for the money to buy food. We saw him walking away from the hotel. Told you let's switch hotels."

"When?" said Shawn.

"When we pulled in the parking lot." Shawn knew what I was thinking; we both jumped up, went to the window. Shawn asked what he was driving.

"A Buick Regal, dark blue, with one missing taillight on the passenger side," Tony replied. Shawn ran into the bathroom and came back out with all the coke. He packed it in his suitcase and made a phone call and told Tony and Penny to go pack. We checked out and left a fat tip. At Miami International Airport, I watched as Shawn handed over our future to this stranger. Then we four boarded the plane.

I dozed off. The only thing I felt was the plane bouncing off New York turf, making another safe landing at JFK. All the passengers exited the plane before us. Shawn said he was waiting for another contact. A man came pushing the cart, picking up trash that was left behind. He bent down and reached in the cart and pulled out the suitcase. It was the same suitcase Shawn had given to the other man back in Miami hours earlier. With everything intact, Shawn checked then handed him an envelope filled with cash. In the cab back to the spot, I finally took my first breath, still trying to shake the feeling of almost being killed, probably execution-style, or busted by Miami vice. I felt like kissing the filthy New York street.

"Here's to more money," Shawn said as he handed me my drink, with everyone with their hands held high.

"Cheers!" Clink, clink. "More money," We all yelled. Penny asked if I had talked to Shawn. So I made a toast instead of answering her. "Here's to having four corners to make a square. May the money pile in. And we are all about to live large."

And before I could finish, Shawn came over and kissed me. Then whispered, "Shut up," with a smile.

"It's going to take more of your kisses and body to keep me quiet," I said. "But we're partners."

Shawn went to call his uncle to let him know that he was back and went into the other room. We all looked at the door where the yell came from then Shawn came rushing back out, yelling something about his cousin Curtis was dead and his uncle shot up and in the hospital, and he needed to be there quickly as his uncle was not doing well.

CHAPTER

5

On our way to NYU Hospital to visit Uncle Pete, who was in the ICU, trauma unit. Blue uniforms and suits covered the white walls. Shawn whispered to me how fucked up this was as we walked past the cops. We walked right up to the nurse's station. Shawn asked the nurse which room Peter Carter was in. That freckle-faced white bitch look right past him and asked who we were and that visitation was just for family members only. She had that look of one of those DMV workers like she'd rather be fishing or watching soaps. Like we were keeping her from them. Shawn politely told her who we were. Then she directed us past the officers to the room where Pete was. A cop started to stop us then, though again, Shawn then entered the room, alone. Ten minutes later, he was back out, saying how bad he looked, but he would live but might never walk again. How there were tubes everywhere and how fucked up this was. His whole stomach was bandaged up. And he's then told for us to wait here. He disappeared through the doors again. It was like he was just rambling on and wasn't really seeing us as he spoke. I knew he was in shock. Pete was like a father to him, the only man who cared enough to raise him. I was so worried about Shawn. But I needed to be stronger.

Tony and Penny were sitting in the waiting area, next to where the cops were standing. Four policemen and two detectives stood joking around; I'm glad they could find humor when it's not one of their own who's going through a crisis. I stood at the door, waiting for him to come back out. I was too scared to go in. I didn't want to disturb them. An hour passed before he came back out, and when he did, he looked different. His eyes were bloodshot filled with tears.

"Oh baby." I pulled him to me, hugging so tight. He was crying and punching at the wall when one of those New York finest (I guess) comedian one said, "Take it easy. You wouldn't want to get locked up for destroying public property." I could have spat at those callous words the fucker just said. But instead, I grabbed my baby's hand as I asked him if he was ready to leave? He said yes. I told him to let Tony drive so he could lie next to me in the back seat.

"Baby, I'm so glad you're here. I'm in no condition to drive, you're right."

"I know. Is Pete all right?" I asked.

"Yeah, I just can't take seeing him like that, and Curtis is dead. My empire was falling before it even stood," he said then closed his eyes. I could hear his heavy breathing and knew he was sleeping. I didn't want to wake him, so I whispered to Tony to take the scenic way home from Manhattan back to Brooklyn. There wasn't much of a shortcut; only cabbies knew it. It was called the sucker route or the sucker view straight fare hike. We reached the spot. I told Tony to use the car so he and Penny could get home safe. We were only gone a few days only to find our world upside down.

Shawn woke up as soon as Tony parked the car. I told him Tony was using his car and would bring it back in the morning. I was going to stay the night with you. "Yo, man, catch up later on," Shawn said. Tony nodded then drove off with Penny.

Upstairs in the bed, he kept talking about Uncle Pete. The man who shot him, how Leroy was coming up from South Carolina, and now shit was about to get thick. Leroy was one badass. He sliced one of his homey's fingers just for pointing at him at a card game, when he said something about cheating. And he's shot, even killed, people. Basically, he's a killer. And the only son left of Uncle Pete. Raymond was dead. Curtis, dead. Almost the whole family wasted. "The Carters is not a family to be fuck with," he yelled out.

"Calm down, Shawn, let's get some rest. Tomorrow is another day, and we need to find out what beef and from who is out there," I said, lying next to him, rubbing his head soothing him to sleep. Slowly, he drifted off. I followed only to be woken up by him talking in his sleep. I tried to listen, tried to make sense of what he was saying, but all that was mumbling. I closed my eyes back and let his mumble be my radio, like a foreign station, and went to sleep.

I awoke to Shawn's kissing, and his erection told the story. We made love, took a shower together, then got dressed. And we headed over to the hospital to visit Uncle Pete. This time, there were no cops around decoration for the walls; only Pete's right-hand, an ex-cop himself stood guard; he looked at Shawn, shook his head as if saying, "This is war." I went inside with Shawn to find a powerful man lying helpless in bed with tubes, monitoring his vital signs. There was a good-looking dark-skinned man in the room holding his hand. Shawn walked over to the bed, put his arm on the man's shoulder, then spoke.

"Leroy when did you get here, how's he doing?"

"Drove here all night, just got in. Damn, Curtis is dead, he's gone," he said with tears dropping down on the bed sheets that were rolling down from his check. "This is so fucked up, Shawn," Leroy said.

I walked over to Shawn, stood there, looking at Uncle Pete, who was resting. While these two men grieved over Curtis.

The same freckle-faced nurse from yesterday came in the room to check on Uncle Pete. She took his pulse then blood pressure and charted it down, then checked his bandages to see how much blood was visible then said she would be in shortly to change his dressing, and we would have to wait out in the hall till she was done. Then we could come back in. Leroy asked how he was doing, addressing the nurse, who just answered that he was in stable condition.

"What the fuck does that mean?" he shot angrily. By the shocked look on her face, you could see she was frightened, and she could not give out any more information.

She replied calmly that the doctor would be in soon to speak and answer any questions that he has. And she quickly left. Ten minutes later, an Asian man came in. Said his name was Dr. Lee and he was Mr. Carter's doctor. Then he was told that his father had been shot five times, and he removed all but one of the bullet fragments that were lodged too close to his spine. And he would do more damage if he tried to remove it. There was a possibility that he might not walk again and how there was so much blood loss. Still, there's no sign of brain trauma. Then he went over the results from the CT scan, MRI, and the sonogram. "He's out of the woods, and very lucky to be alive—considering his age and the extent of the injuries he sustained." Leroy turned from the doctor and said thank you as he was looking at his father, who was now waking up. Dr. Lee went over to Pete, asked him how he felt. Pete spoke very low and slowly said he was in pain. Dr. Lee pushed the call button and the same nurse, who Leroy spoke harshly to, came in.

"Yes, Doctor?"

"Bring me 25 cc's milligrams of fentanyl For Mr. Carter, thank you," as she handed it to him. After injecting the I.V line. Dr. Lee went to the door, opened it, said, "The nurse would be in to apply a fresh dressing, on you, Mr. Carter." Then he turned and closed the door after him. "This is not a family reunion," Shawn said to Leroy, while standing there next to Jimmy. Pete's right-hand man. We were waiting in the hallway for the nurse to finish. Shawn told Leroy that his mother was coming by to sit with Pete. The nurse came out, told us we could go back in now. Pete was feeling and looking a little better.

He told Leroy not to do anything. Leroy said to him that the rest of the family was flying and driving up for Curtis's funeral. Pete started to cry. The pain reliever was taking control, and the tears were rolling down. Uncle Pete was a handsome man in his sixties. With strong, handsome features, he stood six foot four, weighed about 250 pounds, and was in good shape. Leroy was a younger version of him. The Carter men grew like trees; I remember Shawn telling me that when we first met. Now they were being chopped down, like bushes, and stepped on like grass, I thought sadly. I felt Shawn's pain, and there was nothing I could do. But I'll help him get through this. I've been back for a whole day, and I haven't seen my family. I would stop by to see them. I really didn't want to leave his side and leave him like this but knew he would understand. Leroy said to his father that he was going to check on something and would be back later to see him. He kissed his father on the forehead, told Shawn and me bye, and left. We left shortly after him so Uncle Pete could rest.

We headed back to Brooklyn. On the drive back, Shawn was so quiet, that I fell asleep.

"Eboni, Eboni, honey, wake up. I'm dropping you home. I need to get up with Tony, Markus, and Dave and the crew. Find out what's up and how things are moving."

"All right, I need to spend some time with my family."

"Yeah, do that. I'll see you later."

"Shawn, don't do anything stupid. You know we have too much to lose."

"I know, I won't. Just need to find out what happened and who's behind this mess."

"Curtis is dead," I yelled. "And you don't want to end up like that. Be smart out there. Shit is thick your words."

"Damn, babe, I know what I'm doing. Call you later." Then he quickly drove off. I went into the house with my suitcase and him on my mind. I heard my mother's voice laughing with my Aunt Nancy. Everyone was home. Elisha came running up to me.

"Eboni, what you brought me?"

"Nothing, you didn't give me any money." Opening my suitcase, I gave her, her gifts, a couple of Florida tee shirts and a doll, playing cards. Then I handed everyone their gifts, which consisted of tee shirt, ashtrays, key rings. After all, I spent time in the gift shop waiting for Shawn, picking up reminders for them, they all had the same thing. I hugged and kiss Elisha then kissed my mother and aunt. Justina said she was going out, and she loved my gift, 'cause I really didn't have to.

"You're right, it's the thought that counts," and hugged her anyway. Since I've been dating Shawn, I haven't spent much time with my family. I realize how much I've missed them. My mother asked if I had a lovely time. Elisha asked if I saw Mickey. Justina asked about the nightlife. I answered all the vacation questions I could then went upstairs to lie down.

Elisha came upstairs with me; she jumped right in my bed. I told her on the weekend, we were hanging out together. "For real?"

"Yep, just us girls. No Penny, Justina."

And with a smile, "No Shawn," she said.

"Yep, only the two us." I haven't spent any time with my sister; she was growing up right before my eyes.

"Where are we going?"

"We will go to the city, go to the movies, dinner, shopping."

"I could use some new clothes. I want those new seven jeans everyone is wearing.

"Everyone like who?"

"Ruby and Maria."

"All right, but let me get some sleep, oh, and if the phone rings and it's Shawn, bring it for me."

"OK, Eboni, I miss you and glad you're back." Then she left. I felt better about my plans with her. I thought about how much money we were making and banking and buying real estate. I decided I would tell Shawn I wanted a car now. After Uncle Pete, I didn't feel too safe if I had to wait for a bus like a target. Toyota or Honda were cool enough; nothing fancy like his BMW or like the Benz Tony was getting. Tomorrow, we could go to a dealer. Funny how things change. I remember I didn't want no car, didn't want that type of attention. But with this war shit, what choice did I have? Shawn phoned late to say he was with Leroy and his boys and would come over tomorrow. I told him that was fine and mentioned I wanted to go car shopping.

"Yeah, well, tomorrow then." He hung up in a rush. He said more information was coming in about some cats in the Bronx who wanted Pete's action then decided it was better to take the whole thing. As fine as Jeff was, I never spoke to him; he died right on the corner the same spot where they all still stood. Day in and day out. I heard his death was over drugs. Shot up by a crackhead fiend who felt shortchanged on a pack. And in a high state of mind unloaded a .25 automatic right in his chest. Shawn said he wasn't even there when that took place. He was uptown. But the rest of his crew was there and how the chase that crackhead beat the shit out of him. By the time the cops pulled up, he broke down and confessed while Jeff lay there bleeding to death. That was the buzz for the rest of the summer.

A Latino artist created a portrait of Jeff that's painted right there on the same corner store, daring someone to disrespect it. Shawn and the crew paid him for his talent. Like so many street corners, there's always somebody painted on the walls living on for the friends and family. No matter the life you lived, it is still a loss, I thought as I passed Jeff's picture.

CHAPTER

6

Later on, Shawn took Eboni car shopping. They went to several dealers from Honda to Nissan. He wanted her to get the smaller version to his new 750 BMW. Gutted out, suede seats trimmed with leather, out of respect. A player hater sound system, TVs in the headrest. They were sitting on the '22s. spinner's stop at the light, and he was still spinning. He'd convince her to get the 650i coupe convertible in white just like his 7 series. He would later take it to get gutted out. With the car in her name, after signing the necessary papers, he followed behind; they parked his car on her mother's block—Shawn jumped in. Eboni floated down Fulton Street. She was in control, she told him. He lay back in the cut. "Do your thing, girl. Flip the station to Hot 97." While 50 Cent played. Up "In da Club." "It's your birthday. Go! Go! Drop the top!" It was on. She felt like everyone was staring at them. "It's called envy get used to it."

She had wanted to keep a low profile, but here she was, blazing in Brooklyn, a brand-new 650i. BMW. The New (Black Man's Women). Loving it. They drove to the city, Forty-second Street. Shot up to Harlem. Making no stops, she continued to Soundview. Then bounced back to Canarsie Pier. Shawn was telling her about his plans for Markus and Dave. "I had them handle things when we were in Florida. Leroy and his boys from the south flew up and took care of the Bronx situation, he wiped them out. Plan on expanding Pete's business there. And offer it to me to run."

"And what did you say?"

"I told him I would think about it."

"Yeah, maybe Markus or Dave could run things there, for you," said Eboni.

"True, but right now, it's still hot. The dust didn't even settle yet. Leroy had murdered Doggie's whole family, including the kids. Didn't want any paybacks popping up. No loose ends," he thought. "I also need to get in contact with Santos, and them for Leroy."

"We need them too," said Eboni, being his silent partner.

She drove over to Burger King, got their food, then parked in front of the spot. They sat in the living room eating, with TV on, talked some more. He wanted to take it to the next level. Shawn fixed them drinks, brought the bottle and ice in the bedroom, where he waited for Eboni to come out of the shower. She came out wrapped in a towel, dripping wet, smiling at Shawn. He started removing his clothes. He sat up in bed.

"Is that your spot?" she said, teasing him.

"It seems like it," he quickly said. He reached out to grab her as she started doing her dance. She jumped back, slapped his hand away. He smiled, took another sip of his drink. He had moved up to Hennessy, on the rocks, but knew to mix hers. She dropped the towel, stuck out her round behind to him. "Shake your tail feather." He sipped on. "Ahh, you're killing me, girl, bring your fine ass over here I need you."

She strutted slowly. He pulled her on him, and they knocked each other out with their passion.

Eboni had learned how to control her body; she moved her hips while clutching Shawn a little tighter. Each time she bounced on him, he moaned and palmed her beautiful round ass and felt her booty jiggle under his grip. He traced his hands up and down the slope of her back and along her spine, exploring the dip in her back. She drummed harder on him. Eboni had a beautiful body. She had full breast, 36Ds, a small waist, and a plump round butt.

When she wore her jeans, she fitted them well; they didn't sag by the pocket side. She was apple bottom. Shawn was in love with her, and her body was just the blessing. She was his beautiful black queen. "You have been taking control all day let me drive." He wanted to please her; he got on top. "Start it up," she seductively said. He whispered in her ear, "Open," and started nibbling on her she ran her fingers over his head guiding him. Then he started sucking on her breast, she was moaning so loud, he had to take his time diving himself deeper in her. She cried out from the pleasure. Eboni loved the way Shawn felt inside of her. As she wrapped her arms around his muscled back, she slid down to his waist, controlling his movements. She was telling him that she loved him. The sound of her voice almost made him explode. He remained in control and continued to please. He saw she was cumming, with both hands planted firmly on the mattress. He arched his back and pumped harder so he could join her.

"AHH!" They clasped.

When he went to kiss her, she fell asleep in his arms. He stayed up looking at her while she slept. She was a real beauty, he thought as he traced the outline of her full lips. With his fingertips, he rubbed his hands across the side of her cheeks, and she was smiling in her sleep. He started kissing her, and she kissed back, still asleep. He wanted to love her again; he could never get enough of her. He was whispering in her ear, trying to wake her. She mumbled, "Let's rest in a minute." He lay down beside her, inhaling her scent. With a hard-on, he knew it would be a while before he fell asleep. Turned the TV on hoping to wake her, got out of bed to fix his pillow; still, her eyes were close. Plopped back down on the bed, tried to shake her; he decided to let her be, cut the TV off, closed his eyes and thought about the first time he made love to her. How much she's changed and how much better she is. She was leaving him wanting more. He was a player; when he was dating Sandy, was never faithful to her. Always had women, but when he met Eboni, all that changed. And when he started having sex with her, he was changed. The thought of another woman was the farthest thing on his mind. Eboni had matched him sexually, mentally, and physically. They had things in common; he wanted to spend more time with her. Made her his partner to have her on lock. When before with other women, he would just leave when the sex was over. Give them some money or buy them some designer clothes, dropped an expensive bag or jewelry and step out. He left them happy, but he felt nothing for them; it was like burning money. She was different. Unique, he thought. Not because she was a virgin; he had them before and didn't really care for them—too much work. But with her, he was willing to wait. I don't want to push her away. As he lay there, thinking about how he changed. She moved closer to him; she opened her eyes to see him looking at her. "Did you sleep?"

"No, been thinking about something."

"Anything wrong?"

He nodded no.

"Like what then?"

"How I still want more of you."

"Well, you're going to have to do all the work."

"That ain't nothing but a word," he said then climbed on top of her. She loved him some more; this time, they both fell asleep. He heard his beeper go off. He gently rolled, Eboni off him with ease not to wake her. Got up to check it, knocking his cell phone under the bed. Damn. He sat up. He only answered his beeper because of all the trouble that was taking place around him, and he became a light sleeper. "Fuck!" Tony wanted him, who was already downstairs. He got up to open the door. He wondered what he could want at 3:00 a.m. as he looks at his Rolex. Tony rushed past him. "Yo, son, seven of our spots got knocked by blue. They got at least one hundred Gs, of paper and powder combined." Shawn looked at Tony before he spoke, he could see that he's covered in sweat and was nervous. He spoke calmly. "Yo listen, find out who's busted, how much their bail is. 'Cause we take care of our own. And get word to them to keep the traps snapped."

"A'ight, but I ain't going anywhere near a po-po station," he said, shaking his head. "Not you, man. Let Penny or another chick do it."

"Yeah, 'cause I don't even know if these fucking cops are walking around with my picture in their back pocket," said Tony.

"Naw it's deeper than that ever since that Bronx shit went down, killing that whole family like that," said Shawn.

"Yeah, we fucked that family up," said, Tony.

"Shhhhh!" said Shawn. "Eboni's sleeping back there. And I'll like for her not to know that I was even down with that shit. And that's real. That shit might bug her the fuck out, get all scared."

"You think she might tell the cops?"

"Naw, I ain't saying all of that. She ain't no snitch, kill that right there. Yo, but jump on that and make sure them dolgers keep their mouths shut. Otherwise, the body count in Brooklyn will be going up too," said, Shawn.

"A'ight." Tony asked if he could crash till dawn. Shawn knew the cops didn't know about this spot, or they would have stomped through first. The apartment was in an elderly Spanish woman's name who he sublet from. And the landlord was making a cool thousand-a-month profit to not care. The neighbors were elderly living on a fixed income, so they minded their own business.

Damn, seven spots chalked out, and I didn't even get a chance to finish unloading my Florida keys. He had to relocate and keep a low profile like he was on the lam. And Eboni had that brand-new BMW. I should have waited. I'm moving too quick. I need to slow down. Let me get up with Leroy to find out what's happening in Harlem and the Bronx connection. We moved the Doggie family out, and the Carter family was going to move in when things cooled off. With Dave and Markus running it—Eboni's plan. Yeah, she's down. With all the spots combined, they had about two million dollars a week. He needed to get in contact with the cops he had on the payroll to find out what the fuck was up, why no one told him. I guess you can't trust a crooked cop, he thought as he was lying next to Eboni, his mind was racing while she slept. He knew the kid from the party was history, laid up in a wheelchair. He was trying to sort out who else needed to be dealt with before he went on another trip. Time was dragging by so slow. Eboni turned to wake up then fell right back to sleep. Her eyes opened for a minute when she heard Shawn tell Tony to deal with it. She was too drained to get up and see what was going on out there. Shawn thought about his money situation, told Tony to give him a few minutes, he was rolling with him in the morning.

"Eboni, listen, I'm going with Tony to check on things. He's dropping me to my car."

"What's wrong, baby, you look worried?"

"I am, but I can't talk right now. I gotta make moves. You are going to be here or at your mom's crib?"

"I don't even know. I'm not up yet, but most likely at home."

"Aight I'll call you later then." He kissed her bye and left with Tony.

Shawn was carrying a gun; he and Tony stayed strapped now. They drove over to Eboni's mom's block. Shawn hopped in his whip. Tony followed him, and they were heading uptown. Get with Leroy, find out how Uncle Pete was doing. He phoned Leroy from a payphone, spoke with him briefly. Leroy was going to the hospital, so Shawn would meet him over there. They parked four blocks from the hospital and walked. Leroy was in a private room with his father since Uncle Pete had moved from ICU.

———————————

Jimmy stood guard outside. Jimmy was dressed in a blue suit; he looked more like a boss than an ex-cop-now-bodyguard. They've been friends since boyhood, well into manhood. He has been working with Pete for years. They both committed crimes when he was a cop; he was the muscle when it came down to robbing number spots, gambling houses, whorehouses—did a bid together. He knew everything about Pete; they were more like brothers. He advised him on traveling certainties and handling business. He'd brought the product. Yeah, he was more than an employee, he's like a brother. But Leroy was his son. He had built his business in the South and connected it to his father's for a united front. The north and the south were at a civil peace with each other on a get-money business that was family owned and operated.

"Leroy, Pete was saying he heard about the heat you brought down on us 'cause you couldn't wait. Now what are you going to do?" Leroy was telling his father of his plans to shut down those dirty cops and put his people on, setting their ass up, talking about taking it to war.

"Hold on, hold on. This war shit is over," Pete said. "You, done, took out the Doggie family and his boys. That's cool because it's over, but know you want a bloodbath with cops," said Pete. "Shit, they drop just like everybody else." Leroy was the spitting image of his father, six foot four, silk black, and smooth with a devilish smile but could get buck-wild at the drop. Just like his pops.

"But they keep coming like roaches. You know, when you kill the momma roach, and the bitch already stashed her eggs, then you got a million motherfuckers running around—twice the problem you had in the first place. You know we don't need this shit, so cool off on that bloodbath shit. Bury that shit or put on the self, but please put it to rest."

Uncle Pete was an old-timer; he's a classic gangsta and a reasonable man with sense. He worked hard to support his family, legally, until his background caught up with him, and he got fired from his job at the phone company back in his twenties. Since then, he told Ma Bell to go fuck herself and never looked back. Harlem was his for the taking. Now in his sixties, going into his seventies, he had three sons from his wife, Lucinda, who died giving birth to Raymond, his last son, who passed from a drug overdose. He raised them with Shawn's mother's help. He thought Leroy was always the strongest, the smartest of the three. Gully, just like his pops. So he knew he had to make him see the bigger picture before he lost him too. Pete was staring at Leroy when Shawn walked up to them.

"What's up, Leroy?" Tony nodded their way then left the room. Shawn hugged his uncle then kissed him on the forehead. He went and pulled an extra chair up to the bed. Sitting next to Leroy, he could see how tense he was. Leroy was a killer and enjoyed doing so. But Uncle Pete was a man with common sense and knew the outcome. He stood to lose more than just his freedom and money; he stood to lose his last and only son. Curtis's funeral was tomorrow; the family was here. Uncle Pete was attending the service. He had a private nurse to accompany him. "Your momma just left. She went out to the house where everyone was. Had about twenty people in here." He pulled his cigar and lit it. He puffed and talk about who came to see him.

All the while, Leroy's mind was elsewhere. He finally snapped out of his trance. "You're right, Pop, we don't need any more heat. There are already closing down spots busting our people."

"Same shit in Brooklyn," said Shawn.

"Look it's slow out there. Money is barely coming in, and war might destroy us. Point-blank," said Pete.

"And besides, you need to get better, Pop. I took care of the Doggie fam, so once this punk cop crackdown blows, shit should pick up soon," said Leroy.

"Because it's election time, they want to get on their jobs and fuck with us. Let's not give them any more reasons. The people they had busted, bail them hook them up with legal so we don't have any rats. Take care of their families so they won't starve. And let's ride this bitch out."

"Yeah, I'm with that, Shawn," said and Leroy, gave him a pound. Uncle Pete shook his head in agreement.

Shawn called Tony in the room so they could finish working out the small details, discuss the money situation. Shawn told he had two kilos left, but not about the Florida stash. How much his operation was losing. Tony talked about how many spots marked off, said Markus and Dave reported the same thing.

Uncle Pete spoke first. "Look, the first thing we do is look after our own, in other words, cover our ass. Bail them out, call Jimmy in here too," he told Leroy, who then got up and motioned for him to come in. "OK, partner, we need your legal, but no connection on our part, of course. We'll pay for it, you handle that end. The rest of you, move your spots around. Don't clean them out, just leave enough bullshit then get the fuck out of dodge. Take a trip, go on vacation, get some out-of-state pussy, and no business."

With that clear alignment insight, Shawn and Tony left. They headed back to Brooklyn, to take care of business.

Eboni's car was gone. He drove over to the next spot to get up with his boys. Made some calls, got the boys involved, they reported back to him, told exactly who was busted. Information was coming in if they had seen the judge; they had an eye in the courtroom—waiting for them to appear. Shawn phoned Eboni. She wasn't home. She was with Elisha in the city, her mother told him. He had forgotten she had mentioned that to him, shopping with her sister so she could spend some time with her. He decided to go over to Tony's and chill with him. He drove over to Tony's Condo apartment. He had just moved out of his mom's and moved to Queens, Cambria Heights. A quiet neighborhood. Penny answered the door. Shawn went inside, sat in the living room. "He'll be right out," she said, swinging a head full of weave and went back in the room. Then Tony emerged dressed in a wife beater, And blue jeans, picking his small 'fro. "What's good?" he said.

"You know I'm still gonna pump my keys," Shawn said.

"I hear that," Tony replied.

"Yeah, we'll make a killing. Especially since there's a demand more than ever."

"So what about your Uncle, and Leroy?" he then asked.

"Go around them, that's all."

"True, I'm down" was Tony's response.

Shawn was looking around Tony's apartment. He commented on how phat his leather sectional set was with an open bar. Tony's apartment was laid—marble and glass end tables, Italian-style lamps trimmed in gold with a marble setting, showcasing black art deco. From Martin to Malcolm, Meager to Douglas. Every black home had a black Jesus hanging, so did Tony's. His kitchen was tiled dark green and beige. Everything matched. He looked around.

"You know, I've never been here." Shawn knew his next step was going to be big getting Eboni to move in with him. And their own home somewhere in Long Island. Can't have your people living larger than you, he thought. The next level. He still lived at home or a hotel. He stayed more at the spot with Eboni, the one he subleased from the Spanish woman while she was in Puerto Rico. He had the cash but wanted a large home with a pool. The real estate agent was already looking; he told them how much he was willing to spend, planned on putting it in Eboni's name. Or his son's because there was already so much property, his lawyer advised him, and would be moving around the rest so the IRS got paid, wouldn't look too much at her income, and red flag it, realizing she had no job. He thought about calling his lawyer, Mr. Alan Myers, since he was always in his office. Decided to stop by the next time he was in the city since his office was right by the Brooklyn Bridge, on Gold Street. Shawn and Tony went over to the main spot to bag up some of the Florida keys. There they talked about the women in their lives. Freely. Tony told him that Penny might be pregnant and how he wasn't ready to be a father, how they were waiting for the results from the Doctor.

"Penny's cool and everything, but I don't want no kids right now," Tony said. "I rather wait. I hope she didn't plan this."

"Just calm down, wait till the results come back."

"Yeah, but a father and with her, I mean she's a good fuck, big-ass tits, and sucks the shit out of me, but she ain't up to par as a mother. And you know the girls I've been with were all flyy phat asses. She a'ight, she ain't a winemaker. I don't drink from that."

"But you're with her, and she's been loyal," knowing that he was talking about Eboni's best friend. Tony looked at him then answered, "Yeah, true dat, I'm superficial just keeping it 100 and I love dimes with phat assess. Ever since I got my own place, she's been hanging out here, cleaning and shit, trying to make herself useful. 'Leave it up to me, I'll have dishes up to the fucking ceiling and then cope a dishwasher.'"

"So you got yourself a fucking Suzy homemaker," Shawn joked. Tony laughed at his comment then replied seriously, "Man, I just hope she ain't pregnant, but if she is, I'll do the right thing by her."

"What's that?"

"You know hit her off with dough, take care of mines. And make sure three-pack always, never slip—that's my word."

"Well, you have the money to do right by her and the child."

"Yeah, but she ain't no Benz or BMW material, that's a fly-ass car Eboni has."

"Yeah, I should have waited to buy it for her, 'cause I'm making her a target now—cops, Stickup kids they're all the same. I guess if Penny is pregnant, you'll be doing the station wagon or minivan thing," he joked. Tony threw a balled-up napkin at him but missed his aim, which was Shawn's mouth.

"Damn, it should have landed," Tony said. "Naw, but I'll get her a ride. Let's get off that subject," he then said.

"All right, just take it easy. Hope things work out for you, man. Shit, Sandy has my son. I've been there, I know what you're going through," Shawn mentioned, trying to let him know it's not the end of the world it's just an unplanned beginning. Man-up, Bro you got this. Then he got up and walked over to the bar to pour himself and Tony a drink.

"Make mines a rum and coke, strong on the rum," Tony said. "There's this place in Flatbush I checked out that we could use as another spot," said Tony.

"How deep?" Shawn asked, handing Tony his drink. "Did you check on who's running things if anybody pumping?" Shawn added. Flatbush was heavy with West Indians, which meant weed sellers and small-snails coke runners. Tony figured, "We could bring the coke trade on a large and cut out the small-timers. Did all of that, and it's clean. If there one thing I know is potential, and the Bush was full of it."

"A'ight then, we'll move a couple of spots out there and see how it rocks."

"Cool consider it done."

"And if we step on toes out there—" Before Shawn could finish his sentence, Tony cut him off.

"They just get stepped on, mashed up 'cause I ain't sweating no rude-boy West Indians."

"Who were known knife fighters. They always carried a blade," Shawn joked.

"Yeah, true dat that, but this is America where we run. Gats barracks is the sound we make, and besides, I haven't shot the fair one in a long time," Tony joked with his fist in the air, throwing jabs. "Yeah, you can't bring a knife to a gun battle," said Tony.

"True, but don't sleep on them either. Shit, they love their MAC-11 and TEC-9s."

Tony nodded his head in agreement.

After talking with his boy Tony, Shawn felt better about unloading his keys. Miami would be flowing through the streets of NYC in no time. Uncle Pete and Leroy wouldn't know. No one was going to stop his future plans.

◆◆◆◆◆◆

Eboni was hanging outside with May she had been home. Now going on two months from jail. Was telling her how hard it was to find work, and she was open for whatever. When Shawn pulled up.

He always looks fine, Eboni thought. He carries himself well. He had on his True Religion jeans suit, grace by white Jordans, just the right amount of jewels. He smiled as he walked up to them, kissed her on the lips. They spent too much time together for her to be shy around him. She was entirely past that stage.

"What's up, May, how are things?"

"Same o', same o', still broke."

"Tell me about it. Shit is tight all around, but I got something for you and my boys. It's in the Bush. It's new, but you can handle it. I'll let you know when."

"Sounds good. I just want to get my feet wet in some dough, you know what I'm saying."

He looked at her, knowing she was hungry, and it was all good. "Yeah, I got you. Here, my number. You got some way I could holler at you?"

"Naw, just my mom's phone."

"Don't sweat it." He reached in his pocket, peeled off ten crisp hundred dollar bills, and handed it to her. "Here, get yourself a beeper and a cell and give Eboni the number, OK? That should hold you till I'm ready for you. You'll work that off, so I ain't worried about it."

"Thanks, man, this dough is right on time, and I'm getting on that for sure," she said, leaving.

Shawn watched her walk off.

"Smart move, honey. May's going to prove herself big time, I feel it," Eboni said.

"Yeah, I know." They discussed Curtis's funeral and how much he spent on bail for his lieutenants and workers.

CHAPTER

7

Uncle Pete was now in rehab. He was learning how to walk again. The nurse was going through her range of motion routine. Then she started rubbing and excising his limbs. While he was stretching out his legs, she then asked was we ready to walk today. He tried to pull himself up using the wheelchair so he could bear his weight. When Leroy walked in, he didn't see him standing there. He managed to stand entirely on his feet and take a small step. Then the nurse pulled the wheelchair under him, in case he stumbled due to the fact he was still weak, unsteady gait. "You can sit back down now," she said then began massaging his legs. "You did well. I'll tell your doctors that you're making progress with your ambulation." Pete smiled then reached inside of his silk pajama's shirt pocket for a cigar. She frowned but knew not to say anything 'cause she knew who he was. "You ready to go back to your room?" she asked him.

She turned to exit then noticed Leroy standing at the door, staring at them. She smiled and said, "Hello, Mr. Carter, your father is improving. Soon, he'll be running around this here place."

"Yeah, I've seen some young pretty nurses I'd like to catch," he joked, looking at his nurse.

She blushed at his comment then spoke. "I'll be taking your father back to his room now." Leroy held the door open and followed behind them. Again, in the room, Leroy was asking about his father's health and how his therapy was coming along.

"Pop I'm so proud of you. I saw you take that step. You are doing much better."

"I feel it too," said his father. He spent most of the morning with him then left right before lunch.

"Next time you visit, bring me a decent meal," said Pete.

"Sure, Pop, next time. I got to go." He then kissed him on the forehead to leave. "Hey, what's the rush?"

"I got to take care of something. I have an appointment, that's all. Then left."

CHAPTER

8

Shawn was moving some of the spots to Flatbush. Whatever moved, he made sure Eboni knew about it, except for the killing of Doggie. He recalled that night when he, Leroy, and Tony drove out there with two of Leroy's boys, Hush and Whisper. "Ambush the family while they ate dinner." He remembered Doggie sitting at the head of the table, cutting up his steak, every finger on his hand filled with rings, his neck full like Mr. T. Doggie was a big man, wrestler status. So a fair fight would be like signing your own death warrant. Leroy picked the front door lock and signaled. His boys crept around back and took out Doggie bodyguards, Doke and Tune. Then ran around the side; they entered through a side window. While Shawn and Tony, Dave with Leroy walked in the front, all of them strapping. They came in like SWAT. Leroy, that's one cold motherfucker. He walked right up to Doggie with his gun aimed, put it right in his mouth. "The last thing you eat will be this here bullet," he said. When Doggie was looking around for his boys, only to see Leroy's boys, entering the dining room from the kitchen, that's when he knew he was a dead man.

Leroy was the only one to speak while Tony and Shawn held their guns on his family. His wife was crying the whole time, shaking with tears. "We have money," she yelled out. "Yo, somebody shut that bitch up," said Leroy. They then turned their guns directly on the kids, who were all crying by now. And Doggie was pleading with Leroy to spare him and his family. That's when Leroy spoke, "Like you spared my father and killed my brother?" he said bitterly. "I'll spare them the way you spared mines."

"Come on, man, I'll give you anything money, turf, drugs—just name it. Have mercy on my family," he pleaded.

"Shut the fuck up 'cause when you're dead, this shit, it's mines anyway. A dead man can't promise me shit. Now lay your fat ass fingers on the fucking table."

"Yo, halo this motherfucker," he told his boys. Who was just as gangsters, as he was. They had Doggie's brains held hostage with their guns, getting ready to send him to heaven, waiting for his word.

As he laid his finger on the table, he said, "What you want, man? I didn't mean for Curtis to die. My boys fucked up, and I dealt with them, I swear."

"Shut the fuck up, otherwise, this shit is going to go down real quick, and that's my word." With Doggie tight-lipped, Leroy sliced off his trigger finger. Before Doggie could scream out, his wife fainted. Leroy, in killer mode, walked over to her and put a bullet in her head. Then told Shawn and his boys to do the kids. Shawn ain't never shot no kids before, but Curtis was blood, and he's gone. He emptied two shots; Tony then pumped the rest in the kids.

While Doggie was now screaming and bawling his head off, he was covered in his own blood. Leroy sliced his neck. His boys freed Doggie's brain, sent him to heaven. "Now die with that memory and, I'll live with mines," Leroy said as he wiped his bloody knife on Doggie's shirt. His body was slumped over the table, his eyes wide open. Tears stuck in the corner of the whites that he never felt leave his body finally hit his cheeks.

"As we were going?"

Leroy picked up his trigger finger, took the ring, cleaned it off, tossed the finger to his dead kids, and they left.

Shawn was still sweating and nervous but knew it had to be done; it was payback Carter style. He must have drunk a case of Hennessy that night. Too hungover to function. He called Eboni to let her know he wasn't coming that day.

"What time is the funeral?" Eboni asked, snapping Shawn back into the present.

"Aw, it's one o'clock."

"Did you get your suit?" she asked.

"Yeah."

"I got my dress while I was with Elisha shopping. Shawn, what's wrong? You look worried."

"Nothing, I just can't believe Curtis is dead," he replied then squeezed her close to him.

"I love you, Shawn," she said then rubbed his head.

Shawn knew he could count on her to be his rock. That's why he was glad she was attending the funeral with him. She only met Curtis a couple of times on her trips uptown, but he was family. And now, so was she, he thought as he held on to her. Then told her how he wanted to move out of Brooklyn, or even better New York, and go down south somewhere, how this drug war was over. Tony, Markus, and Dave could run things. Leroy would take care of Uncle Pete with his mother's help. How she would be taken care of and her family. "Just say yes," he pleaded.

"Give me time. Shawn, that's a huge move, I need to finish college."

"You could do that anywhere."

"Yeah, but I also have a life here."

"Whom Eboni, who's your life?"

"Baby, it's not that easy. Please, just slow down a minute, let's plan this right."

He looked at her as she spoke on.

"Like where we would live, and what we would be doing."

That's when Shawn jumped up. "Baby, I'm upset, stressed right now, you know... you know, Curtis and all. I need time. I was just telling you what I've been thinking about. That's all. A man can dream, can't he?"

"Yeah, but you're not dreaming. You mentioned moving before. We don't have to leave. The beef is over. Leroy took care of it, right?"

Shawn turned his back to her; he didn't want her to see his face as he focused on the kids he had killed. "Yeah, Leroy took care of it." Then sat up in the bed next to her. Eboni talked about the killing of Doggie had brought chills. If it were just Doggie and his wife, he would have slept easier. But when you kill babies, you are going to have nightmares. Except that he wasn't sleeping.

"Boo, let's go get something to eat," he said, trying to shut her up about the whole thing.

She got up and headed for her car. Shawn was in no mood to drive. He felt like relaxing and letting her take control. He heard about the problems she was having with her mother and how Justina was getting on her nerves stealing her clothes and returning them dirty or ripped up, promising to pay for them. Eboni talked so much that she ended up running a red light and almost collided 4×4 truck. Shawn asked if he should drive.

"No, I got this."

"A'ight, let's just make it to dinner. We're in no hurry." He smiled. "I know my baby got skills the way you whip that shit. Whoa," he added.

"Yeah, I'm just lucky no cops were out here." Composing herself, she talked about Donny and Johnny. And how Penny said she was pregnant. She went to the doctor, and her mom kicked her out. And now she's living with Tony, and how Tony has been cheating on her, having girls call the house. Shawn closed his eyes because what she was saying he already knew. "You know, Tony asked her to get an abortion?"

"And?"

"What do you mean, and? That's fucked up, 'cause if I were pregnant, you would ask me to do the same."

"Naw, baby, that's them. That's what and means. Shit, if my baby were having a baby, I would be picking out names."

"I know, babe, I'm just tripping over them with their problems, we're fine."

"Yeah, we're more than just fine, we're solid. No other women can make me as happy as you do, or as brave as you. Shit, in Florida, you were more on point at the party, you jumped up."

"Yeah, my heart was beating so fast that if I thought about it, I would have been too scared to react."

"Yeah, but here we are back, in fucking NY, millions richer, and with our own Miami hookup." Shawn leaned over and kissed her plump on full lips.

"Shawn, I'm driving."

"Go ahead, babe, do you." He smiled then lay back in the cut. She turned off the Belt Parkway exit for Sheepshead Bay, which was known for their Italian restaurants with an ocean view.

"I feel like some privacy," she said as she parked her chrome-white BMW next to a red Porsche.

"Privacy? We could've ordered in," said Shawn.

"You know how white people are. They go out their way to ignore you, which only means they see you," she laughed.

"Yeah, well, let us just hope they don't run us out like Yusef Hawkins." (RIP)

"As long as we're out before sundown."

"Shit don't sleep. Most of those so-called racist white people are creeping over to our side of town for parties women and drugs."

"Well, let's hope those undercover driftwood crackers are in there and recognize us," she joked.

They entered the restaurant only to see four more black couples dining and enjoying themselves. They respectfully nodded towards them and were led by the maître d' as he seated them at their table and handed them their menus, asked if they wanted something from the bar, how the waiter would be over, then politely left.

"We must look like money to him," Eboni said.

"Well, we did pull up in a brand-new—black most wanted—BMW," he joked.

After dinner, Shawn left a nice tip. They cruised back over to the spot, which was now his apartment. He rented another one to cook up the product. "Don't want to shit where you rest if you can help it." Eboni took a shower, first calling Shawn to join her, which he did.

He threw his clothes on the floor, next to hers in the bedroom, stepped in the shower with Eboni, and began caressing her breast. "The soap," he whispered with that hazed look in his eyes; his horny haze was taking over. They made love in the shower then finished up in the bed. Eboni told him she had to leave early in the morning so she could get her dress for the funeral. "So you could sleep in while I run home and pick it up, and I'll just get dressed over there."

"No, babe, boo, let us go get it now and be done with that." He drove her over to her house. While inside, Justina had on her white Gucci sweatsuit. "No, the fuck you don't, take my shit off."

"Calm down, just calm down," she said with her hands in the air for her defense. "I'll take it off and have it cleaned."

"That's all right, just stay out of my fucking things." Eboni stormed into her mother's room and told her how she was kicking Justina out of her room they shared.

"Why?" her mother asked.

"'Cause every time I come in, she has on my clothes, and I'm tired off it. She could sleep in the living room."

"Go ahead and remove her things."

"Yeah, Mom, but I can't do it tonight, I got plans."

"With Shawn," her mother finished.

"Yeah, that's right, but don't say anything to her. Give me time, don't want her stealing or hiding my things."

"You just make sure you pack up her stuff and not her."

"All right, Mom, I gotta go. Shawn's out there waiting on me in the car."

Her mother shook her head; she'd known her child was involved in something dangerous, but every time she tried to discuss it with her, they would just argue, and she was pushing her away and right to him. I got to pray for her, Gail thought as she heard the front door slam close.

Eboni got in the car. They bounced back over to the apartment, ex-spot. "Yo, May came over while you were in the house." And how he was putting her to work.

"Good, about time," said Eboni.

They made love again then slept the rest of the night.

CHAPTER

9

It was raining during the burial of Curtis Chris Carter.

After the service, they went over to Uncle Pete's house, where everyone was gathering to pay their last respect. After the service, Shawn and Eboni left. They had to meet Tony and Penny. Shawn spoke to Pete and Leroy while Eboni waited in the car. On the drive back to the apartment, he told her about the private conversation he had with them. How Leroy was moving more people up from the South to run the Bronx, the same area Dave and Markus were supposed to manage. How they would be moving back down to Brooklyn and Queens.

"What's wrong with that?" she asked.

"I'm cool with that, just don't know how Markus and Dave might take it."

"They will be all right. They're moving back to the same place they left. They should be cool," she said.

"Leroy is running everything, I mean everything from what spot, gets what to who travels. He even manages to combine my shit with Pete's own."

"You need a meeting."

"Yeah, I know, let me call him and set it up," Shawn said.

"Do it once you calm down, 'cause right now, you're too upset," she added.

"True, 'cause right now, I could blow his head off. He's trying to control everything—shit, basically cutting my throat. And punking me at the same time. I started this Brooklyn shit. I was out there standing on the corner, selling crack and powder to the fiends, running from cops, battling it out with stickup kids. And now that it's making money, when we got workers and underdogs and lookers, spotters, he thinks he's just going to take my fucking business, my baby. Leroy is fucking with me, nigga trying to disrespect me and stressing my shit. I ain't having it."

"Honey, just calm down, talk things out with him, let him know you make your own moves. And Uncle Pete business and yours don't mix, and it's still all Carter."

Shawn walked over to Eboni and sat on the black leather sofa. He clasped his fingers together in a praying fashion and spoke methodically calmly to her. "I'm going to call Leroy now and set up a meeting."

"When is Uncle Pete getting out of the hospital?" she asked.

"I don't know, not sure. Heard something about physical therapy. As soon as he heals up would be using a wheelchair for a while. Why you ask?" Shawn barked at her.

"Because maybe you should go to the hospital and speak to Uncle Pete first, that's why." Eboni leaned in on Shawn's shoulder and bumped her forehead up to his lips, to keep them close, so he would think about what she just said then mention. "You can't think when you're talking," she teased.

He laid her down on the sofa and began kissing her; she started tickling him. He then grabbed both of her hands and tickled her back; she was laughing so hard.

"Shawn, wait, I have to use the bathroom."

"OK, but don't try anything, or you're gonna find yourself pinned down like the Rock did triple xxx."

"A'right, Mister Tough Guy, now get up."

Shawn got up off her; she ran down the hall to the bathroom. When she returned, she tried to sneak up on him, but the wood floors told on her. Shawn pretended not to notice and stayed sitting on the sofa, unmoving. The same spot he was in while she was in the bathroom. He was thinking about Leroy and the meeting if he should talk to his uncle first. Eboni sprang on him.

"You want me to tickle you again?" he said, pinning her back down on the sofa. "This time, I won't let you go to the bathroom. You will go on yourself," he joked.

"All right, all right, I was just trying to lighten the mood."

"Yeah, I know. Thanks. I decided to talk straight with Leroy."

"Just remember that if he pisses you off, you remain calm. After all, this is not little boys arguing over matchbox, cars, or Tonka trucks or a dick pissing contest. Keep that in your head. Stay calm, Shawn don't be a hot head. Have you ever noticed when two people get into it, that the person who always listens always come out on top?"

"I know, boo, thanks for your advice. You always come through on a positive tip. That's another reason why I love you." Shawn rubbed Eboni on her leg and kissed her hand.

"Babe, I love you too," she replied while hugging him. "You're my Clyde."

Shawn stood up over her. "What you Empire Stating me. Stand up, girl, I'm ready to make the call."

Eboni stood up and wrapped her arms around his neck. "All right, baby, I'm right here by your side. Do your thing."

"Wait, are you sure?"

"Yes, I'm sure. Don't second-guess yourself on this," while still having her arms around his neck.

"Let me make that, call." He walked over to the glass end table and picked up the receiver and dialed Leroy's number. Leroy picked up in mid of the third ring. "What's up, man?" said Shawn.

"What's up, cuz."

"Yo, we need a meeting on this biz shit. I don't feel too cool about it."

"A'ight, let's talk cuz. You coming to Harlem or what?" Leroy asked.

"Yeah, I'll be there tonight."

"See you then, peace."

"Peace."

Then they hung up. Shawn turned to Eboni, who was just staring at him while he spoke on the phone. He turned to her. "It's all set."

"All right, you want me to come along?" she asked.

"Naw, I'm cool."

"Well, I want to go with you, we could do something later."

"Yeah, OK, all right, come on then, let's head up there."

CHAPTER

10

Leroy was sitting in his father's chair; he stayed at his father's home since he was in the hospital and was arranging the family business, grooming it so he could take over. He was second in command, even though he had to share it with Shawn, and still had Jimmy to deal with. If anything happens to his father, he would be the boss since Curtis was killed and Raymond was gone . He was the only living flesh and blood Pete had left, even though Shawn was raised just like if he was their brother, instead of a cousin. He would have to share the business with him. And he wasn't too happy about that. Too many chiefs. Somebody had to be the fucking Indian, and it wasn't going to be him, he thought.

Leroy thought about all the problems that face him and all the situations he gotten out of. He was never one to back down. Growing up in Harlem, you had to be about it or you were labeled as a sucker, and he wasn't having that. Nobody respects those types. Since he was young, he'd been running the streets, been making his own money, running up in spots, kicking doors, taking what he wanted, plain old housing shit.

Wicked, with the fist game, he remembered the time his girl Tammy, back in the days, told him about some dude who had disrespected her when she told him she was Leroy's girl. He responded by saying he could fuck her better then grabbed his dick and winked. She walked off mad. The niggah then called out to her, "You fucking freak bitch" in front of his boys. They all started laughing while slapping each other five. When Leroy heard, he stormed around there and beat that niggah to a pulp, right in front of his boys. Asked if anybody wanted some while circling around the guy who was on the floor. They all went momentarily deaf and dumb with the quickness.

The cops came; they didn't have to look far. He was still shouting as they took him to the precinct. From there, his pops picked him up. That was when you could shoot the fair one, and the cops didn't try and bury your ass under the jail cell. They knew what it meant to protect yourself and defend your honor 'cause living in the ghetto, pride was all you have. He learned that lesson early in life when he was just a teenager. Now a grown-ass man, in his thirties, he remembers serving time in prison. He done a seven-year bid; it was there he met his homeboys Greg, a.k.a. Whisper, and Trayvon, a.k.a. Hush. And when he was released, Hush and Whisper came to work for him, which was over 15years. They were his right hands; they killed for him, didn't hesitate to pull a trigger. He depended on them; that kind of loyalty was hard to come by.

Leroy phoned his wife Keisha, who was over at his Aunt Dorothy's house, Shawn's mother, with the kids. He spoke to his daughter Kizzy and son Leroy Jr., who was a handful at the age of nine, like he'd spit him out was already gunning for the streets. Kizzy was his pride and joy; he spoiled her. She was only six and had him wrapped around her finger. He smiled. Keisha told him she would be at his aunt's house for the rest of the day. He explained he had some business to take care of and would see her later on at his father's house. So then he phoned his girlfriend, DeeDee, and told her he would be spending some time with her, after he met with Shawn, he figured. He would head over there to dip his dick, he thought. He loved his wife, who was by his side while he was in prison, the mother of his only kids. But DeeDee was his freak, and he hasn't seen her in a while. His dick swelled. Every time he came up to New York, he would check in on her for a swim. That was his second home, but since his wife flew in for the burial of Curtis, his place was with his family. But DeeDee was one bad bitch; he couldn't resist the creep. She did things he would never ask his wife to do. DeeDee made moves on the high-price scale, stash his tools, did little pickups, even played on other teams when asked. She wrapped in Prada, but she was framed in Gucci. One that he could afford. He bought her furs, jewelry, and paid her bills. She drove the latest expensive sports cars, also paid by him. He knew he wasn't the only man in her life that did things for her, but as long as he didn't see them, and she made sure they didn't call when he was there, he still took care of her. Even though he has other women, like Lisa Tina, DeeDee was his favorite.

She was sexually free and knew how to greet him. He anticipated his arrival. He looked at his Rolex. Shawn should have been here. He phoned Shawn's house and got no answer, then called his father told him about the meeting that was going to take place. His father advised him how Shawn was like a son to him and how he lost Curtis and Ray, and that almost destroyed him. After he hung up, he began to reason with the idea of partners.

Shawn was parking the car when Leroy walked over to the window and saw him. Then he went to open the door. "What's up, cuz?" he greeted in a friendly manner then kissed Eboni on her cheek and escorted them into the living room. Shawn began, "I am not too happy about this monopoly you're doing on my business making your own Carter cartel."

"What do you mean by that? I was protecting you, that's, all bringing you into the fold."

"Well, I feel like I'm being choked out, and it's my baby—mines," Shawn replied.

Eboni sat on the plush off-white leather butter cream sofa of Uncle Pete. She always loved the way it was decorated and the portraits that hung on the wall displaying the Carter men and family. Most of the pictures Shawn was in. She sat staring at Ray-ray's pictures and wondered what kind of person he must have been like. Curtis was a reasonably calm man, Leroy was ruthless, and Shawn was sensible. You could reason with him, and he always had a good judgment on people as well as business sense.

"Damn, Shawn, you know I wouldn't do that to you. You're fam, it's just that right now, everything is hot. And it would be in the best interest if I handle the heat while you lie low," Leroy said.

"Bullshit, man, this is fucked up, and you know it."

"Calm down, cuz, what you wanna tell me?"

"You know what I want, cuz." Shawn met Leroy with the same demeanor. No one spoke for a while. Eboni wanted to say something but decided to hold her tongue. "Leroy, look, you have most of the south on lock where you supply and run the streets. When Uncle Pete gets out of the hospital, he would be running Harlem again to an even larger scale. He's got Doggie's turf as well. Now you want mines. No way, it ain't even going down like that."

"All right, man, I could see your point. Knowing it's better to have people sleep than to be awake and full got make 'em starve a little. It's all Carter baby. Man, I was just tripping, I guess," Leroy said then walked over to the window and looked out, his mind drifted for a second to DeeDee. And he then turned back to Shawn and Eboni who was staring at him. Leroy shook his head in disbelief at what he was saying. A'ight, man, you got it, what was done is now undone," he said. Shawn walked over to Leroy and extended his hand. Leroy shook it then wrapped Shawn in a bear hug in an embrace. "Yo, man, we're fam, everything is cool. You're right, it's all Carter." Shawn then agreed. Eboni stood up, walked over to them.

"All right, boys glad, everyone came to their senses. So you're running Uncle Pete's and yours. While Shawn and I are running ours. Good, that's simple. So we live to bake more bread," she ended.

Leroy looked at Eboni, smiled she's official how gangster, with the nod of his head; she was young and beautiful, with a head for business. He had people watching them, and that's what they reported to him.

But now he was seeing her in action, for the first time. Because every time he'd seen her, she was always quiet and watching studying everyone, he figured. He got wind of their Miami trip and the deal they made with Santos.

When they got back in the car, Eboni asked Shawn if he trusted Leroy to keep his word 'cause she didn't. Shawn stood to make a hot one-million dollars from the Miami keys heading back to Brooklyn. Why would he just turn that back over to them, walk away without a fight? She knew Leroy was a powerful, ruthless, and greedy—a deadly cocktail. She asked Shawn the question again. "Do you trust him to keep his word?"

"I don't know, baby, I just don't know."

"Well, I don't," she said flat out. "We need to protect our own backs."

"Yeah, boo, and we will."

11

Leroy headed over to DeeDee's house. She lived in a beautiful three-story brownstone in Harlem he owned and paid for. It was on Riverside Avenue drive, off of Ninetieth Street. A quiet, clean neighborhood where no one hung out on the corners. He knocked on the door even though he had a key, which she didn't know about, since he didn't live in New York anymore. He didn't see the point in letting her know, in case he wanted to surprise her. This might end up in leaving her homeless, so as long as he didn't see, she still had a rent-free home.

She opened the door; she had on four-inch red heels, a yellow bow tie tied around her waist, and nothing else. "Well, hello, Captain, welcome home," she said with a big smile on her face, showing off her dimples in her cheeks. Her face was beautiful; she has gorgeous, dark, brown-eyes shaped like a deer's and sparkled. A beautiful, strong African nose and full luscious lips that she always painted red. Just juicy, Leroy thought while taking in her look. She wore a short hairstyle cut right above her ears, like Tony Braxton. He loved her skin tone—dark with an even tone complexion, with no scars, considering women hated on her. He stood looking at her body while she started undressing him. "Baby, come in and shut the door," she said in that sexy tone. She was high maintenance in the wardrobe department—from Versace to Chanel. He loved the fact she was nude. She wore no makeup, only lipstick, and that was one thing he liked about her—natural, the Carter men called it.

"Hold on, Bambi." That was his nickname for her. "Let me get a good look at you, girl, shake something for daddy."

"Oh, big daddy, I've missed you," she teased. Then walking over to her French King Louis XIV-style cut sofa he paid eighteen grand for it and sat down and motioned for him to join her, he sat down next to her.

"I didn't come all this way to just sit."

"Shhhh…hush." She rose to her feet, kissed him on her way up; she pushed the glass coffee table out of her way and began to dance for him. He eyed her body from head to toe.

"Babe, wait, let me fix you a drink, first. Get you comfortable…the usual?" she asked.

"No, fix me something mellow, make it a brandy."

"You got it, big daddy." She had a bar setup in the living room, which was set on a cart, she rolled the cart next to him. "I don't want you to move," she joked.

"Paralyze me," he said.

She made his drink then fixed herself one. "Brandy all around."

"Bambi, do your dance, for me."

DeeDee had a lovely body; she had full breasts and a picture-perfect round ass and a flat stomach. She didn't have any kids. Her waist was small. He loved to fuck her, and while enclosing his hands around her waist to control her, DeeDee began to dance once again. She had the music on, Maxwell's "This Woman's Work," stroke the mood. She was slow-dancing, moving her hips from side to side. He was mesmerized. Then she bent down to the floor while squeezing her own breast; her nipples were hard and poking up at him. He stopped her and this time led her to the bedroom. "Girl, I'm going to give it to you real good."

"Bring it on, big daddy, oh, I miss you. You'd stayed away too long," she pleaded.

"Show me how much you've missed me, baby."

She then took his shirt off, unzipped his pants, and gently pushed him back on the bed while licking her lips. He pushed her head toward his manhood. She popped her head up, smiled, looked him in the eyes, they sparkled, then delved right for it. "Oh, baby…oh, baby, I've missed this. This is what I've wanted," he moaned as she sucked and gagged like she was choking; tears rolled down her cheeks. After two minutes of strokes and one long hard suck, he closed his eyes and burst right in her mouth, which she swallowed.

She was nursing on his dick, sucking for more; she begged. The freak in her was coming out, and he was enjoying every bit of it. She looked at him, licked her lips, and wiped him off her chin with the back of her hand. She got up to take a sip of her drink. "You taste so sweet, I could do this all night. I want some more.

"No one does it better, girl. I need a drink after that. Fix me one too."

She got up to get him a drink; he lay on the bed, watching her ass shake. Looking at that ass shake in those red pumps, he was ready. It was turning him on to see all that jelly move. His dick began to grow. He knew he was not staying long, just came to dip his dick; has his wife and kids to go home to. She came back with drinks in hand, just shaking everything, and he started up again with her. Damn the drinks after taking a quick sip.

"Bring your fine ass over here, come get this big daddy. You want to ride this?" he asked while grabbing his manhood.

"No, I want to eat it she said, lowering her head to it."

"Ride it first, and if you ride it good, I might let you eat it again. Show me you could ride, baby."

"Oh, I can ride," she said while mounting him. The headboard was banging, beating into the wall.

"Ride it, baby, ride it, bring daddy home. I know you've been bad. I'm going to spank that ass." He was about to flip her over, but the feeling had him stuck.

"So bad I've been dirty," she called out. He came again, and she did too, then she sucked him off still. Before he left, he handed her an easy peel-away two grand.

"Baby, when will I see you again?"

"I'll call you. Just stay ready. I'm going to be in town for a while, you got that?"

"Yes," she answered sacredly, which meant no dates. He kissed her bye then left. On his way home, he stopped to pick up a bottle of wine for him and his wife. After that fuck, he was in the mood to make love.

DeeDee always knew how to relieve him of his tension; he'd been so upset lately. Now with things easing up, he missed his wife that way; and since she would be leaving with the kids in a few days, he wanted to spend a little special time with her. He knew just how to please her. A massage and some wine would relax her and do the trick, he thought. Jewelry, furs—she had all of that and didn't wear them. She wasn't that kind of woman. She was a family woman from the South, who enjoyed taking care of her man and the kids, not the type who needed flashy fancy diamonds and furs to feel loved. The real things in life matter to her: health, family and friends, cookouts, birthdays—not the Joneses. That's why she had everything, 'cause she wasn't looking for it. She was his angel, his good girl.

⸻ ✦✦✦✦✦ ⸻

Shawn and Eboni went out to dinner in the city, called the Cafeteria, a swanky little place in the village, for their famous chicken and waffles. Then they shot over to the movies, booked a hotel room at the Hilton. Deciding to call it a night, they made love and talked about Leroy some more.

"We are going to keep an eye on him," Shawn said.

"Yeah, well, maybe we should have him watched."

"What do you mean, private investor a tag?"

"Naw, I'm not going that far, babe, that's TV shit."

"All right, you're right. How about, just to make sure he stays in Harlem, some low-profile shit."

"Look, boo, I don't want to talk about this anymore, feeling a little agitated." Shawn then said, "Let's just get some sleep."

"I hear you." She rolled over and cut the light out. She knew she was going to hire someone to watch him from afar, taking matters in her own hands so she could sleep at night. You don't change from being ruthless to reasonable; it didn't make sense. To her, she couldn't feel any truth in Leroy's words. Shawn was too forgiving; he was weak in that department when it came to family. When he slept, she would be awake, she thought. Now she had to figure out who could handle that particular job. She didn't like going behind his back, especially since it was his own cousin. But that was one person you couldn't sleep on. You slept on him, you might not wake up. He'd put you to rest. I'm too young to rest, she thought.

"Babe, you're right, Leroy gave you his word."

"I know him, he's my cuz, so don't sweat it."

"You're right, babe, let's get some sleep. I want to get back to Brooklyn and get with Penny and May. Ever since she got pregnant, she's been staying in Tony's house. I hardly see her."

"A'ight, boo, get some rest."

They didn't bother to order room service this time. Shawn jumped in the shower while Eboni was brushing her teeth.

"I'm going to get up with the boys. I might have a surprise for you." He knew the real estate agent finally came through. Then he went to Long Island and found the perfect home for them, the agent told him on the drive out there. It was a large corner home with a pool and a two-car garage. With its long driveway, he knew she would love it. Five bedrooms, five and a half baths, master bedroom with private bath, walk-in, his and, hers closets, panoramic windows overlooking the pool, a large kitchen with a pantry, a vast living room with a fireplace and bay windows, private dining room, and family room. Enough room for a large family and more room for just the two of them. He loved it, and she will too.

He signed all the necessary paperwork and bought the home outright. No note, no mortgage. Shawn couldn't wait to show it to her.

"Boo, come join me in the shower."

"Naw, hurry up so we could get back to Brooklyn."

"Come on in here and let me wash your back."

She looked at him; she could see he wanted more than just to clean her back.

"Come, boo, the water is getting cold."

"Just my back." She jumped in.

"Yeah, and your front," he teased.

"You are too much."

"Boo, you know how sexy you are in the morning. I can't get enough of you. I love being like this. I could do this every day," he said.

"Me too, I love being like this with you."

"Well, let's be together, right now."

"Shut up and give me some. Who's the boss of this?" she played.

"No one. We're partners, boo. Let's meet up around six. Don't forget. I have something I want you to see." He pulled up on her block.

"All right, six see you then." She kissed him and went inside to see her family. Justina had moved out and was now living with Donny in a one-bedroom apartment in Park Slope, Brooklyn. Donny was working at some big-time radio station as an assistant or something for a disc jockey or program director. She couldn't remember. And Justina was a receptionist at a fashion agency while going to fashion school. She wanted to be the next top black fashion designer, what Jay-Z did for Rocawear or P. Diddy for Sean John, Russell Simmons for Phat Farm and so on, especially like Karl Kani, the pioneer of it all. She was going to burst on the scene like FUBU but remain. She was going to give Kimora Simmons of Baby Phat a run for her money. She was putting a spin on her clothing line, made for the big-butt sisters. Justina had big dreams for her future, and Donny had too. They were working toward it one step at a time. She didn't miss her.

Elisha and Ruby were playing with their Barbie heads. Elisha was putting on makeup on hers when Eboni walked in.

"Hey, Elisha, what are you all doing playing with that doll? Aren't you all too old for that?"

"No," they said in unison. "It's the Barbie head so we can practice hairstyles. It's not a doll, it's a hair model, and I'm giving her a day of beauty in my spa salon," said Elisha.

"Your spa salon. Well, OK," said Eboni.

"Yes, it's called Elisha and Ruby's spa salon."

"Do you have an appointment?" asked Ruby. She was the spitting image of her big sister May. Being black and Asian, with a Chinese father and a Black mother they both were fluent in Mandarin. And had beautiful Asian eyes that we're green and light skin with long wavy hair. The only difference was Ruby's hair was longer down her back. May wore hers corn-braided,and dyed blonde and it rested on her shoulders.

"Yes, I do," joked Eboni. "Where's Mom?" she then asked.

"In her room."

"That Eboni down there?" her mother called out.

"Yes, Mom, it's me. I'm coming up. Let me just get something to drink first." She poured herself a tall glass of juice then asked Ruby if May was home.

"Yes, she's home. You want me to go get her for you?"

"Yeah, I do."

"OK, I'll be right back." And left while Elisha stayed, doing her doll's hair. She was using the Ebony Magazines for the hairdos. Eboni smiled and went upstairs to her mother's room.

"Hey, Mom." She walked over to kiss her on the cheek.

"So you finally know how to come home."

"Yep, I'm here."

"You really think you're grown?"

"Aw, Maw, don't start that. How's Paul doing, got any letters from him?" she asked, trying to change the subject and bring some light to this mood that was trying to set in.

"I have a shoebox full over there. He's been traveling. He wrote about all the different countries, places he's been to, and how he's dating some nice women he'd met in Germany, where he's stationed at right now. Her name is Kim, a real nice girl. I spoke to her on the phone."

"That's good for Paul, well, where's Eric?"

"He's over at Johnny's house, with Keith. They still going on with that rap mess. They been up all night outside, on the stoop, rapping and carrying on. You know, I had to pour water down on them one night."

Eboni burst out laughing at what her mother just said. "No, you didn't, Maw."

"Yes, the heck I did, keeping me up all night when I got to go to work in the morning. I can't wait till school starts and they can get their butts in the house at a decent time."

"Well, did you get them?" she asked, still laughing.

"You know me."

"Yeah, you're something."

"Keeping me up all night making noise, after they move up the block to Johnny's house, let them keep his folks up. A damn cat in heat, done, come and took their place. Aw, no such luck, all I need is an old shoe."

"Mom, you're too much," she said, still laughing.

Gail looked at her daughter and started to laugh too. "Girl, it's a mess," she said, wiping the tears from her eyes. "So how's Shawn doing?"

"He's fine, he's coming to pick me up around six or so."

"Oh, I've seen Penny. Her belly is round and big. She must be carrying a boy."

"Guess, so. I haven't seen her, so she is showing."

"Yep, you can't hide that. You still taking your pills?" Gail asked seriously.

"Yes, Mom, I am."

"Good, I'm too young to be a grandmother, from you or even Paul for that matter. What about college, are you getting ready to go back? You are almost done, about to be a graduate. It's right around the corner."

"Yeah, Mom, I'm prepared for it."

"Good. Shawn's your first boyfriend, but he's not your whole life. You still need an education."

"I know, Mom, and Shawn knows I'm going to finish college. He is not trying to stand in my way."

"I hope so. You know, some men get jealous and act funny when a woman wants to better herself, start calling her names, trying to tear her down. Trust me, I know what I'm talking about. Been there with your father. I guess that's why he drank so much. His self-esteem was already low and…and to make themselves seem and feel better, they try to put you down. Break your spirits. Your father almost crushed me, but a little voice inside told me differently, and my children—all of you showed me different and made me strong. Now I had my days when I didn't feel like getting out of bed. But one of you would come knocking on my bedroom door. And I knew a man was not my whole life, just part of it. Now your kids, they're your whole life. They come from you, you gave them life. Men come and go. Your kids could disappoint you, but as a mother, you can forgive them. But a man knocking you down deserves no forgiveness. You leave his sorry ass alone before he makes you feel worthless."

You didn't, Eboni thought but did not dare say it out loud, afraid she would hurt her mother's feelings.

"And education, being self-sufficient are your keys to this big mystery of life. That's what unlocks doors. The more you learn, the more keys you get, and the more doors you unlock. You'd be walking around like a janitor," she joked. "And, baby, that's a good thing. So you finish up with school. Now, Penny, it's not too late for her. It is just a little harder but she can do it also."

"I know, Mom and I'm going to finish. I have plans for my future, I'm not thinking about no babies right now, and Shawn knows that. We've already discussed that. Mom, how are you doing?" she asked, concerned.

"I'm fine, working hard. Thanks for the money you gave me. I really appreciate it."

"Anyone special in your life?"

"Kind of been seeing this fellow at work, he's divorcé."

"How about that, does he have any kids?"

"Yeah, two boys, older, grown and living in LA somewhere. One's a teacher and the other is a dentist."

"Oh, that's good, I mean he could spend more time with you," she said, feeling a little awkward about her dead husband, Eboni's father, Henry. "All right, enough about me. And Charles."

"Charles," Eboni teased. "When can I meet him?"

"In due time. Right now, we're just getting to know each other, and I have to see if it's worth introducing him to you because you're worth it to me."

"All right, I'll back off, Mom." She heard Ruby and May come in downstairs and got up to leave.

"Hey, what's up, May?"

"Nothing much, just chilling."

"I need to talk to you, let's go up to my room." Eboni sat down on the bed with May sitting next to her.

"What's up, Eboni?"

"I need you to do me a favor."

"What's this, The Godfather?"

"Yeah, exactly. Now I need you to do something for me."

May looked at her and could see she wasn't joking. This shit was real, so she changed her whole attitude. "What's up, boss?"

Yeah, I like that, thought Eboni. "Here's what's up. I need a babysitter for this fucking asshole, Shawn's cousin, Leroy, for me. But they have to fall behind, be discreet. I mean, I don't want this information out there like that. Tell me and only me what he's up to. Shawn, you bypass, come straight to me on this one. I want you to be my right hand. Now, I know you're smart and shit, you got brains. I've seen the work you put in and how you handle yourself under pressure, and I like that."

"Yo, Eboni, thanks, and don't worry, I got this. I owe you. Look at me. I'm chilling 'cause of you, so no problem." May looked at Eboni, and her eyes sealed the deal. She knew she could trust May from day one, that's why she wanted her to handle this. She felt it would be done right. She has been wanting her to come work for her.

"Naw, you don't owe me shit. You've proved yourself off back." Eboni knew enough to know not to ever let a person feel they owe you; there's no loyalty in debt and even less in credit. No one likes to pay up when asked. May shook her head.

"Aight, I got you. When do you need this?"

"ASAP."

"Cool, consider it handled. Let me put a fire on this." And she got up to leave.

"Hit me on my cell or pager."

"A'ight, one.

Any for me?" she asked Elisha, who was making her homemade heroes.

"You could have this one."

"Thanks, I'm starving." They sat around talking. Her mother came down to join them; this was what she missed. She was moving her family out of Brooklyn; her mother was telling her about the moving date. She wasn't going to sell the house, planned on renting it out. It was the first home she owned since Henry died. And it was paid for, so why sell it? Eventually, Brooklyn will make a comeback, Gail thought. They discussed the rising price of rent. Eboni told her she would cover the cost of movers.

"Just make sure you are ready on that date, Mom." Her cell went off; it was May phoning to say she took care of it, all the players were in place. Good, she thought. "Mom, I am going to Tony's house to see Penny. If you need anything, let me know."

While driving her BMW, heading to Queens where Penny lived, she felt a little concerned about going behind Shawn's back having Leroy tagged, but what could she do? Just close her eyes to the stunt he pulled, trying to push them out and believe him when he said it was undone? What the fuck is that? That it's over just like that? Momma didn't raise any fools, I know better. Shawn was to relax when it came to his family, and his boys. She'll catch the knife before he ever sees it. Her motto: trust no one unless proven otherwise. Still, you keep one eye open. That's just what I was doing, an eye placed on Leroy, so if I blink, I still see but no regrets.

CHAPTER

12

Penny opened the door. She had a big smile on her.

"What's up, Mommy, look at you! All showing belly, sticking straight up."

"Yeah, and sick as a dog, girl, I've been throwing up and shitting every way, just lose," Penny complained.

"Well, you look good, and when you drop that load, we are going to do it upright," Eboni said then rubbed Penny's belly.

"Uh-huh, and leave Tony with the baby and have a girls' night out," Penny said.

"We're going to put the wild in girls gone wild and boogie all night."

"Boogie, I haven't heard that word in a good minute, now I know we need to hang, they both laugh."

"Ain't it the truth," said Eboni. She looked at Penny, who was walking across the living room heading for the kitchen. She couldn't help but laugh. "Girl, you got that cute pregnant walk."

"Yeah, every minute, I'm running to the bathroom. I swear this baby is sitting on my bladder. And as you could see, I'm eating like a pig. Eat, throw up, eat again. I'm caught in some Twilight Zone special," Penny joked. The truth was she loved the fact that she was carrying Tony's first child out in the world, so when he'd had suggested an abortion, she'd nearly flipped her wig and bust him upside his dome. As her belly grew, he came around. The fact that she got kicked out of her mom's crib, he couldn't have the streets talking, or Penny for that matter a big get money niggah. His seed is homeless a Brooklyn niggah. Oh hells no! So he told her to trash all her old shit 'cause he was doing it upright for her and his seed. After all, it flowed like that.

"Your skin is glowing. You're not all that big and shit."

"Thanks, but I feel terrible. I'm counting down the months till I get my body back. I'm ready to evict this baby girl."

"So it's a little Penny that's going to be ripping and running. Have mercy on all the ballers when she gets big."

"Big! I ain't waiting that long. Soon as she hits the playground, Imma teach her how to scope out the little ballers with the fresh Nikes on, trimmed in Burberry and Gucci, stomping through on their motorized Bentley Benz ,and BMW, owning the playground, not the kids in their played-out Jeeps and Barbie trucks."

"Girl, you really need to stop before you're a grandmother at thirty-two."

"And I would be the hottest granny out this, bitch."

"Just quit, you're a mess." They both laughed.

"Oh, it's been so long since I'd kid around like that." They were catching up on old times; she hasn't seen Penny in a while. She looked at her Gucci watch then realized it was getting late.

"Well, I gotta get outta here. Shawn's coming to pick me up."

"Since when'd you rush for him? Don't tell me dick got you jumping and shit. I know you ain't going for that shit."

"And you're right. He's got some surprise for me, so what the hell."

"At least he still does the little things like that. Me, I'll be lucky if Tony even comes home." She didn't feel like hearing her complaints about Tony. She knew what she was getting into, and she still tried to trap him. Like, my momma always says, a baby makes a man break into a marathon, or take on several different personalities, like Kyra, Ashley and Beverly, and so on and so on. "I'll check you later."

Back in her ride, she decided to call Shawn; she was about to dial his number on her cell phone when it rang. She pulled over to speak to him.

"Boo, I'm at your mom's crib. Where are you? Be there in a few."

"So how's Penny?"

She looked at him like, How he knew?

"Your moms."

"Oh. She's pregnant and miserable."

He kissed her as she closed his car door.

"So what's the surprise?"

"Just wait and see."

She could see he was in a good mood and decided to go along. "Lead the way," she said as she lay back in the seat. Forty-five minutes later, he was parking his car in somebody's driveway. "I'll wait in the car," she said.

"Your surprise is in the house, so come on." Shawn walked up the driveway as if he lived there with Eboni following close. This looks like a nice neighborhood, and this house is beautiful who lives here. Shawn reached the French double doors; he unlocked it and gave her the key to hold for him. "Just keep that for me."

"Shawn, who lives here? Look, the last thing we need is a burglary charge."

"I got the hookup, it's cool, boo." He flung open the French double doors then stepped inside into the parlor. "We do. Surprise!" he yelled.

"For real?" She then ran past him into the empty living room. "Whoa, this place is enormous," with him on her heels.

"Yeah, boo, we made it. This is us, our first home," he said, smiling in his Versace suit with fresh Jordans.

"When did you do this? Let me see the bedrooms. How many rooms?" she yelled out from down the hall.

"Slow down, boo."

She was so excited, asking so many questions. She ran through the first floor in a minute then pushed and rushed past him for the staircase.

"Slow down," he yelled after her.

"Damn, this is fly, so many rooms."

"Yea, one day we'll fill them up, one day soon," he mumbled.

She was too excited to notice. "Ooo, it got a pool too, this is the bomb! I can't wait to have my friends over, can't you just see me chilling out by the pool, getting my tan on?" she joked.

"That and making love in the water at night, or some 'sex on the beach' type shit, yeah, I see it."

She came up to him and kissed him. "Baby, I like it. When we can move in?"

"How fast can you pack? This is ours. We live here, we're calling the shots, so whenever."

"I'm ready now." She had calmed down, and now she was walking through the house, deciding on what type of furniture she would purchase. She taught about that chic place she'd seen in the city and decided that each room needed its theme or it should flow from room to room. From Pier 1 for knickknacks Fabio Exchange for big-ticket items.

Shawn sat on the window seal, watching her. "You just pick out everything. I trust you on this."

So many rooms they had that needed to be furnished. Shawn went to his car for a blanket and a bottle of crystal and two champagne flutes and laid down some cover in the master bedroom.

"Crystal—you think of everything, don't you?"

"I try. Now, let us break in our new home."

"You're reading my mind." And they made love.

CHAPTER

13

One Year Passed.

"Finally," Shawn said after he finished throwing away the last TV box, his seventy-five-inch, RCA plasma surround sound, the only thing Eboni let him have. The whole house was furnished. And it only took forever.

"Now, it's home sweet home," she added.

The phone rang. It was May calling to report to her; she checked in on a weekly. "No news, is good news," she said then hung up.

CHAPTER

14

Leroy received a phone call from his wife, Keisha, Telling him his old friend White-Boy Joe just came home. And he's hungry, he thought. His timing couldn't have been better; he had the perfect job for him too.

Joe served eight years in jail for robbing and beating a man to near death, who had shorted him on his money after a robbery they had pulled off. Joe was an old New Yorker head, now living in the rough part of Chicago. "If it ain't ruff, it ain't right." He always told him when he moved out there. Keisha gave him the number to where Joe was staying. He remembered Joe was dating this fine ass, black chick Nayla—sexy dark chocolate—before he got locked, then she bounced on him. He did the eight years by himself writing and calling him and Keisha, so when he got released, the first thing would be to call them naturally. And he was a down-ass white boy as hard as they came. "Yeah, my team was back together, all players accounted." White-Boy Joe, a.k.a. Black Shadow—a little joke, nickname he'd given him, saying, "Deep down your ass black." "Yeah, only at night," Joe always responded. Plus Hush and Whisper, now we could change the game, set our own rules, he thought.

He quickly phoned Joe, told him he was needed in NYC. "Yo, I got something for you, time to bite the apple."

"Yeah, cool. My pockets are lint, I could use the money. I'm on the next red-eye, player."

"A'ight, that's what I'm talking about. Yo take this info down," Leroy said then hung up. "One!"

Leroy went over to DeeDee's house since his wife and kids were back home in South Carolina. He needed to stay in New York; he spent most of his nights with her. She was always shopping, in need of something like the latest fashions. He didn't mind spoiling her. He had it like that, and he enjoyed the way she got it out of him; she had her tricks when it came to taking care of him. He gave Shadow her phone number; after all, he paid the bills.

Shadow would be arriving at JFK Airport within the next hour. He sent Hush and Whisper to pick him up. He was going to take over the Brooklyn and Queens operation and move Shawn and Miss Eboni out. His hands would be in the cookie jar, but he wouldn't drop any crumbs. He'd be in the cut while Shadow did all the dirty work. He would still respect his father wishes when it came to Shawn: was not to be touched, no harm would come to him. But Eboni was a whole another story. Shadow would move in and rush them out, by any means. This was business; and it was necessary. He had his dreams, and besides, he couldn't let these two young heads run the BQE. He had too much respect for the boroughs.

Deedee was out shopping; as usual, he had given her ten thousand dollars. With that, she broke ass trying to spend it. He got up from the sofa, where he had fallen asleep. Someone was ringing the doorbell; she probably forgot her keys or her hands were too full to look for them, he thought with a smile.

"Hold on, who is it?" he asked.

"Police! Open up, Leroy Carter," the voice on the other side said.

"Shit, I'm clean," he said as he approached the door. "Yo, don't even talk that crap," as he opened it to see Joe, Hush, and Whisper standing there.

<hr />

The phone rang again.

"I'll get it." Eboni ran for the cordless, which was on the marble dining room table. "Hello."

"Yo, it's May, can you talk?"

She looked to see if Shawn was where she left him, in front of his new love: fat-ass seventy-five-inch. Saw him reaching for the remote to change it from Oprah to the BET the Basement. "Yeah, what's up."

"Yo, Leroy's been stuck over there in the nineties, while his boys roam."

"OK?"

"Well, they just got this delivery from JFK."

"Speak to me."

"Some muscle-head white boy."

"Leroy is more trouble than he's worth."

"What do you want to do about that?"

"Nothing for now, just keep me posted." Click! With Shawn in the dark, she would handle things when needed. She knew he would be upset if he knew about the tag.

"What's up, man," he said, bear-hugging Joe.

"Shit, eight fucking years, man, eight years of COs telling me when to eat shit when I could go piss. I want to thank you and Keisha for being there for me on the strength for real."

"It's all fam, don't sweat that. I could see you weren't wasting your time, been working out pumping those irons."

"Yep got to keep it tight." He flexed. "Niggahs been testing me up in there."

"Damn, what you were pressing?"

"Niggahs" Joe said. "Shit you all pump up and shit" Leroy respond. Yeah, I got to keep busy. A niggah like me go crazy in there. That was my focus…that and reading. I practically breezed through the library while busting heads."

"Yeah, I heard that." As he poured Joe and them their drinks; they then sat around, talking about old times. He brought Joe up to speed on things. About the job he had lined up for him. "Yo, Hush and Whisper are going to take you over to the hotel I set up for you."

"Hope there's a big-booty dark chocolate chick laying butt-naked waiting for me, I ain't have New York pussy in a long time. Bump that, I haven't been with women in so long I damn near forgot what the hell they smell and feel like," said Joe.

"What you been having?" Leroy said with curiosity.

Joe stood up and walked over to where Leroy was standing, within inches from his face, looked him in the eyes, and responded, "Myself."

"That's, what's up. Well, get on over to the telly and get your nose open." Joe smiled and gulped down his drink, turned, and placed the empty glass on the coffee table. He hugged Leroy and left with the boys. Leroy phoned Lisa. He called in a favor. "Just make sure you take care of him, he goes way back." Then hung up.

Later on, DeeDee came in loaded down with bags. "Hey, babe," she called out to him as she closed and locked the door. "Wait till you see what I just brought. It's the sexiest little nightgown." She dropped the bags and packages on the floor, rummaging through the pink bags. Leroy was stretched out on the sofa. She went into the bathroom to try it on. It was a red lace teddy. "You like?" she asked.

"Turn around, and let me see it better."

She was strutting her stuff.

"Damn, girl, you sure know how to tease a man."

"This is all for you, big daddy."

"Well, bring your fine ass over here." They had sex.

CHAPTER

15

Chilling with Shawn

"Come here, boo, with your bad-ass self," Shawn joked while tickling Eboni onto the bed. "How, you get so tuff on the outside?" he teased. "Bet you used to kick ass back in the days."

"Shawn, let me tell you about my back in the days."

"Go ahead, I'm listening."

"There was this time I was in the fourth—wait, maybe fifth grade," she started while rolling herself on her elbows to look in his face, who was still on top of her. "I remember there were these two girls, sisters. New to the school. You're right, I was bad back in the days, and I guess they saw it and tried to try me. So the older sister stepped to me when I was on the lunch line, talking about her younger sister wanted to fight me."

"For what?" Shawn asked.

"Just out the blue, and it was going to happen at three o'clock. These girls look mean and shit, bald head and all."

"The Damager," he said.

"Yeah, terminator-like. Well anyway, three o'clock came and went, no girls. So I went home, thought I'll catch the after-school movie or something when my doorbell rang. My brother Paul got up to answer it, called me to the door like I had company. All I heard was, 'Come on out here, come on. So we could kick your ass.' I thought they were going to jump me, so I ran to the kitchen for a knife, brought back the biggest blade, I could find—you know, a cleaver."

"Damn."

"Yeah, but my brother took it away from me."

Shawn rolled off Eboni, sat up, looking intensely at her. "Then what."

"I was so scared of how the girls looked, bald head and all."

"Like some Grace Jones, the warrior," he said.

"Yeah, that's it, the warrior. I scratched the shit out of that girl. I clawed her damn near to death while screaming the whole time. I scared the shit out of her."

"You mean to tell me I got myself a cat woman?" he joked then made the sound, "Ahhh."

Eboni looked at him with his hands clenched like claws and burst out laughing. "Eboni doesn't it look like one of those Chinese movies, hah yah!"

"Shawn, stop it, my stomach hurts," with tears rolling down her cheeks.

"Come here, cat woman," he joked.

———— ·+·+♦·+·+· ————

She loved to watch him sleep, the way his face was at peace and the way his lips stuck out.

She rested her head on his chest, hearing his breath, letting hers mimic his. She thought about having a family. One day like, Penny and Tony, but the time wasn't right. With all the problems, how could she plan? With the light beaming in on their naked bodies, Shawn was the first to wake.

"Boo, I have to run out."

"So early."

"Yeah, I have something I got to take care of with Tony, I'll see you later on." Markus and Dave had traveled down to Florida to get up with Santos and Carols on Shawn's orders and were due back today. He had made a nice chunk of money and decided to flip it over. His airport contact had grown; he was moving keys on the regular.

Their spots were being targeted, even setup. She heard about this dude who was working with the cops, breaking in, locking people up. Some of the workers had even been murdered, plucked down right on the street drive-bys. Shawn's reaction was he put rooftop snipers out there for coverage. They were at war. Rumors were circulating; it was Leroy's boy who was behind the whole thing. She heard that from a reliable source. She quickly phoned Shawn's cell. He said he wanted a meeting with him.

"No," she protested. A meeting with Leroy? For what, to warn him? No! "Shawn, use your head. If you call a meeting, you're giving him heads-up, a time to plan his next move on us," she screamed into the phone. "And also, who's to say we'll leave that meeting alive? It's way too risky."

"Leroy is family, just leave it up to me. I'll call my boys and pay him a little visit."

"Shawn, Shawn, please come home. I want to talk to you first, please!" Eboni begged into the phone.

"All right, let me just go over some things with the fellows, then I'm on my way."

"You promise?"

"Yeah," he said while putting the bullets in his gun. He would pay Leroy a quick visit. He and Tony drove out to Uncle Pete's house, where Leroy was staying. The nurse opened the door for them. With their guns tucked behind their backs, Shawn began combing the house for Leroy. The nurse was telling him that he wasn't home and that his uncle was sleeping.

Shawn pushed past her, with Tony doing the same. They searched the whole house, peeked in on his uncle, then left.

Two weeks had past and no Leroy.

CHAPTER

16

Shawn and Tony were sitting on bleachers outside across the street from the main spot. They were dressed in sweatsuits, trying to catch their breaths. They had just finished playing some high school kids and got their assess kicked and served in basketball. They were watching the new champions of the court play, giving LeBron and Carmelo a run for their status. When a blue Escalade pulled up and blew his horn at them.

"Yo, who's that?" asked Tony.

"Fuck if I know," Shawn replied. The driver rolled his window down to reveal himself.

"What the fuck does that white boy want?" said Tony.

"Might be po-po," Shawn said.

"Fuck him, I'm clean, you're clean," Tony said while drying his face from the sweat with the end of his white tee shirt.

"Yeah, you're right, fuck him," Shawn said in between sips of water, then wetting himself down to cool off.

"What the fuck? Am I invisible?" said white boy, Joe, then got out of his truck wearing a black and white Akademiks velour suit, sporting unreleased retro IVs, stepping up on the court and coolly walking over to where Shawn and Tony were sitting. He stood over them. "You're Shawn, right?" he asked, looking at Shawn.

"Yo, who, you?" Tony jumped up in his face.

"Shadow from Chi-Town." He lit his cigarette and blew the smoke in Tony's face. Shawn, knowing how Tony's temper was, stepped in and pulled his boy back.

"Yeah, the fuck you want, Shadow from Chi-Town?" Tony spat those words out. "This here is fucking New York, so fuck that shit."

Shadow smiled at Tony then looked straight at Shawn. "I'm looking for some action, thinking of setting up shop in this Big fucking Apple." He shot a look to Tony.

"Whatever." Tony smirked.

"You, Shawn," he asked again.

"Yeah, what's it to you?"

"What's it to me? I want some of your action. There's enough in this apple for the both of us to bite," Shadow said to them, like playing chess. Shawn took a step back and looked at Shadow up and down.

"Who the hell do you think you are?" he blew at him. "You think you're just going to take over my shit and I'm just going to step the fuck aside? Do you know who you're trying to fuck with?"

"Yes, yes, I do," Joe said then started to walk back towards his truck, taking one last look at them. Then he got in and drove off.

"What the fuck was that?" Shawn said as he threw his hands in the air.

"Yo, you want me to smoke that white boy?" asked Tony.

"Man, I ain't sweating it. He's out of his league. Look, the first thing I want you to do is find out whose he working with, 'cause a white boy is not going to step up to two brothers in the hood."

"You crazy!"

"Naw, he's working with somebody. Believe that shit, somebody is backing his ass up, son," said Shawn.

"I know that's right. That boy got heart tho'. Imma check him out all right and see who's the vein pumping that heart. Then Imma check him out for good," Tony said. "Then his ass will be a Shadow or a ghost for real," Tony laughed.

"Yo, What's popping Joe?" asked Leroy. Answering his phone.

"Man, perfect timing. I just left your little cuz, and his little man Tony out there in Brooklyn," replied Joe while heading into his hotel parking lot waiting for the valet.

"What's good"

"Smooth like butter, baby, those cats don't want it."

"A'ight one!"

"It's almost time to place my pawns and take the little prince that wants to be king." Leroy smiled as he slowly drove past their Long Island home in his black Benz with NY plates that read BLK Knight. A year later!

CHAPTER

17

Eboni thought about how they were now settled in. Her mother didn't live too far from her; she was now living in Queens. And how it felt good to see her smile; she had Charles to thank. Gail was married for the second time, but she was happy this time in her life. May had also moved her family out there, and May's parents. We're on the next block. May had moved in with her new woman, Linda, a cute blonde and had dyed her hair even lighter so they matched. Elisha and Ruby were going to the same high school. Shawn was spending more time with his crew. Santos had hooked him up with a Florida furniture store that made expensive marble Greek statues and was shipping drug statues on a larger scale. The drugs left Miami South Beach, Tampa, and Orlando and arrived at a warehouse Shawn had set up. He paid his informants at the police department who would contact their people at Customs; they all got a piece of the pie. Money was flowing in. He had to invest in dummy companies so that he could funnel it. He brought out vacant lots, hired out welfare moms and untrained fathers, trained them to do construction, all the while they collected a legit paycheck, thanks to Allen Myers, his lawyer. He made sure the IRS got paid. He had surpassed his uncle with the Doggie operation combined. May had informed her on Leroy, and this white boy they called Joe and Hush and Whisper.

She knew of his whereabouts. Shawn was still blind to the tag. Years had passed. If she wanted to make a move on Leroy and his boys, it could be done. Since everyone was still making money, and no toes were being stepped on, Leroy was free to walk and, breathe. Spending time with Penny and the baby took her mind away. Watching Tonita run and tear up things, she looked just like Tony, she thought. And she enjoyed spoiling her; she had everything she needed and then some. Penny was going to night school at York College, working on her AS degree in early child care, she mentioned how she wanted to open up a daycare center with Tony and my money.

CHAPTER

18

Shawn woke up early. Eboni was still asleep. He looked over; he wanted to wake her, couldn't wait to surprise her with the engagement ring he had just brought. It was a beautiful pear-shaped, six-carat diamond set in platinum. He'd had it especially made by some ex-jeweler that used to work for Harry Winston—referred by his attorney Allan Myers. Then he went downstairs to fix breakfast for them. This should wake her up, he thought. With his grand slam, he made some eggs and English muffins, turkey bacon, and a fruit salad. Eboni no longer ate pork, so there was no pork in the house. He had given up eating it as well and found he didn't miss it. She was into eating healthy. She'd read all sorts of books on health and nutrition and always joked about how you are not going to die of a stroke due to pork when she would be cooking and he complained about not having pork chops. So with the breakfast made, he went back upstairs. He rested the tray down on the dresser. He then placed the ring on the tray, walked over to her side of the bed.

"Hey, baby girl," he said as he kissed her on her face.

"Let me sleep, I'm so tired," she said.

"Baby girl, I made something special for you."

"Oh yeah, what makes it so special?" she said, still with her eyes closed and with the cover now pulled overhead.

"'Cause I made it just for you."

She could hear it in his voice that he wanted to talk to her. So she stumbled out of bed and went to the bathroom to wash her face and brush her teeth. "OK, I'm up," she said as she walked back over to the bed and lay back down.

Shawn brought over the tray with the ring staring right at her. "Baby, honey, boo, you are all those things to me my love." He got down on one knee. "All that is good is what you have shown me. Now we've had some times, but we always made it back. You are truly the love of my life."

Eboni had tears in her eyes. "Oh, Shawn."

While he spoke on, the tears were just running down her cheek. "You make me complete. I'm not trying to rhyme, but you are right on time, so with you always by my side..." While holding her hand, he placed the ring on her finger. "I need you to be my wife." He kissed her lovingly, like he always did.

"Yes, I would love to be your wife. What took you so long to ask me?" she teased and wiped her eyes.

He got up, smiled, and walked over to the minibar they had built in their bedroom. He opened the mini fridge, pulled out a bottle of golden crystal champagne and two Lenox crystal flutes glasses he had chilling. Filled one and passed it to her then filled his. "This is to us for we are one, you bring out the corniness in me, and I love that."

"Yeah, leaves the thug in the street." She smiled. "And here's to... you are my life, and I truly love you...for I...no, no other, and I am complete," she said. They spent the next few days in bed.

"I'm going to Brooklyn, to get up with fellows," Shawn said as he threw on his Quarterback of the Century jersey; he paid three thousand for it and rocked it sandblasts jeans, with tan Timberlands. "Be back later." He kissed her and the ring bye. She smiled then sat at the kitchen counter to finish her OJ, looking at her ring. She was still sitting in the same spot. Leroy, Leroy, she thought as she watched Shawn leave, you have to be stopped.

She went upstairs to her bedroom, clicked the TV on the Oprah show, something about men cheating on their wives and girlfriends, and buying expensive gifts to cover up. She was lying across the bed, not really watching it; her mind was racing for answers. She needed to end this war.

Leroy and this white boy were starting. She was scared; she had to admit it to herself. With a lot of "what if" dancing on her brain, she needed to relax; she turned the water on to fill the tub, added her favorite bubbles by Donna Karan, and decided to take a long bath while Shawn was out. She undressed and wrapped her hair in a doobie. Then she slipped into the tub. "Ahh, this is more like it, time for dolo." How could Leroy do this? Greed was the ruler in the Carter family; it didn't matter he gave his word. Well, greed would be the end of him. She was trying to relax, in the tub when the phone rang. Shit, I forgot to bring the damn, cordless, in here with me. She went slipping and sliding on the marble-tiled bathroom floors. With her skin dripping wet, she almost fell. She grabbed on to the Roman-style sink to steady herself. Fuck, all I need is to break my fucking leg. "Hello," she said on the fourth ring, trying to catch her breath.

"Eboni, I have some bad news for you, it's Shawn.

"What, about Shawn?" she yelled.

"He's...Shawn's in jail."

"What the fuck are you saying?" Eboni kept yelling at May on the phone.

"Take it easy, boss. The cops picked him up a few minutes ago."

"The police!" she screamed as if she wasn't hearing right. Tears were rolling down her cheeks, her body was trembling. What's happening to me? she thought.

"Listen, I'm on my way," said May then hung up. Eboni was holding the cordless in her hand. She forgot to click it off. She heard the buzzing sound on the other end and realized May had hung up.

Penny, let me phone her. She dialed her number and got a busy signal. Damn! She paged Shawn then called his cell phone; it just rang. I know this shit ain't happening. Someone is fucking with me. Any minute, Shawn's going to come walking through the door, clowning, and I'm going to whip his black ass for real. 'Cause I know life can't be playing a cruel joke on us, she thought as she looked at her ring.

Penny phoned her. "Girl, I just heard what happened to Shawn. Are you OK?" she asked?

"How did this happen? What went down?" Eboni asked while getting dressed. She threw on her DKNY sweats and a white Nike tee and matching sneakers.

"I don't know. Tony phoned to say he was following Shawn down to the precinct, the DEA, and ATF—damn, girl."

Eboni was crying; she could hardly talk.

"Calm down, Ebb, it's going to be alright."

"All-right, you said? How the fuck it's going to be alright with Shawn's ass in jail? Look, I got to go." Then she hung up in Penny's ear while she was talking, trying to reassure her, mad at the situation. Penny knew she was venting and figured she'd give her time to deal with things in her own way.

Her mind flashed to Leroy. Somehow, I know he's behind this. I know it. I could feel it.

May was ringing the bell and banging on the door. "Eboni, it's me, May. Open up," she yelled out. "Let me in."

In a trance, she opened the front door to let her inside.

"You OK, boss?" May asked sadly, looking at Eboni. She could see that she was falling apart.

"What went down?" Eboni asked.

"Shawn was in the main spot, counting money with Markus and Dave," May was saying when Eboni asked if they got them too. She interrupted. "No, just Markus. Dave went out to do a run. He had all the product with him, so the only thing the cops got was Shawn and Markus sitting around with a pile of cash, and some fresh vials and all the shit we used to cook it up on," said May.

"Girl, they got my boo! And I bet Leroy had something to do with this." She already knew about the white boy. May told her. "I know he's to blame, and I'm going to fix his ass for good," Eboni said angrily.

"Yo, whatever you want to do, I'm down for it, boss. You know you can count on me."

"Oh, I got something for him." They drove over to the jail to see Shawn. The cops informed her that he would be arraigned at central booking in the morning and that there's nothing she could do so she might as well go home.

She must have tossed and turned all night; she awoke to find May standing over her. "What, you want?" she asked May.

"No, I heard you just screaming. I came to check on you."

"Oh, I'm fine thanks. I mean, I'm alive, 'cause my better half is not with me, so I guess I'm just existing."

"He's going to be alright, so don't you worry."

"So how did you sleep?" Eboni asked her.

She was staying in one of the spare bedrooms that was a guest room since they didn't have any kids together; one of the rooms was for Shawn's son. He only came over every other weekend.

"Not so good. I'm too worried to sleep."

"Yeah, me too, I must have been up most of the night, crying."

"Yeah, I know. I heard you." She put her head down, avoiding eye contact with her. "I got to make some calls," said May.

"Go ahead, I'm going to get dressed." It was 6:00 a.m. The courts opened up at 9:00 a.m. I better call Estevan. Shawn always told her if anything happened to him, whatever she does, her first move would be to get in touch with him.

Estevan was a tall, beautiful Dominican man in spirit and character. He grew up with Shawn. He was Shawn's left hand, and the boys were his right. Estevan took risks, like a daredevil or something. Everything he did was extra. He was shaving when he heard his phone ring. He stayed in a small studio apartment in Brooklyn. He quickly rinsed his face off and grabbed the towel to pat dry his face. He stepped out of his bathroom into his bedroom slash living room, took three steps to his sofa bed, picked up his receiver. "Hello," he said.

"Estevan, it's Eboni."

"Yes, I heard what happened, what can I do?" he asked, fully aware of the bond he had with Shawn.

"I'm going to the courthouse this morning."

"Say no more, Mommee. Shawn is my homey. I'll be there if you need me."

"Good. I'm leaving at eight," she answered.

"OK, see you then. And, Eboni, take it easy," he said.

"Thank you," she said then hung up. She finished getting ready. May was already downstairs in the kitchen when she walked in. "Estevan is meeting us over there," She told May, who was eating toast and jelly.

"I'm ready to go. You should eat something."

"Naw, I'm too upset to keep anything down. I need to find out what's happening to him."

After court, Eboni, May, and Estevan went over to dinner to discuss charges they had pending against Shawn and Markus. Shawn had twenty thousand dollars on him when the cops busted in, but no product was found. Traces of cocaine were detected, but not enough to convict him on, so they wanted to hit him with parole violation. The police would be going back out to the scene to conduct a full investigation. The cops didn't have a leg to stand on. Still, Shawn did violate his parole for even being in a drug spot; he was remanded. Markus's bail was set at, ironically, twenty thousand.

"Yo, this is how the cops operate. They have been watching Shawn for some time now, trying to gather their shit on him."

"Yeah, I figured that much," Eboni said.

"That means your phone or even your house might be tapped. That's how the task force gets down."

Eboni thought about all the telephone conversations she had with May; she had talked openly about dealing with Leroy. She started looking around the diner to see if she could recognize anyone. But this diner was filled with lawyers and cops and courts officers. Now hating her surroundings, "Let's go," she told them. "I can't eat with swine and devils." Then paid the check since the diner was right across the street from the courthouse and the Bail bondsmen.

It wouldn't be a problem to bail Markus out. All she needed to do was get to the bank. She withdrew a cashier's check in the required amount; she gave Estevan the money for Markus's bail. How could they deny Shawn a bond? she thought. The next court date was three months from now. She had to call Allen Myers so he could hire a brilliant defense attorney.

Back at the house with May, they went over a plan to deal with Leroy, a lure and kill. Tony was back from Miami and would be leaving in the next couple of days on a turnabout reload, she said while the music was blasting from her Alpine stereo. The doorbell rang. Eboni answered the door and let Estevan in, led him to the living room.

"Markus's out but lying low," he said.

"Good, good looking."

"One more thing. There's this white boy named Joe who's been asking a lot of questions about you and Shawn. One of my homies named Jose said he was from Chi-Town and was trying to move in on your turf, talking to the workers and shit-talking some 401k benefit pay hike to them."

"What does this white boy look like?" Eboni asked.

"My homie Jose said he seemed like a cop," said Estevan.

"Yeah, yeah, I saw some white motherfucker out there one day down at the number 26 spot. He ain't no cop unless they're paying them better these days, 'cause this bitch was sitting in a brand-new blue Escalade truck, rim out on some Speedwells while smoking some weed. His shit was all fogged up. He had some fine black bitch in there with him," May said.

Eboni already knew that, so May played along, wanting to see if they both were bringing the same news or did he edit for her ears only.

"Keep an eye on him, find out how long he's been coming around my business, and find out who he is working for, 'cause it seems like he got some heavy backing. To go in the hood asking questions and he ain't police, some things don't add up. And I want everybody on point with his Casper ass. It's strange how Joe somebody comes to town, and Shawn ends up getting locked up on some bullshit… Don't make any sense."

Estevan agreed. He was making himself at home' he walked over to her fully stocked bar and poured him some Hennessy. Then he sat back down on her leather sofa. "Yo, Eboni, Shawn could have been set up since the cops and DEA are watching him or this white boy," said Estevan.

Eboni already knew that this white boy was with Leroy, and his name was Shadow or Joe from Chi-Town. Her people were watching Leroy and his boys. She knew when he arrived. Her peeps followed Hush and Whisper to JFK. What she couldn't figure out was why would Leroy be so sneaky about the whole thing. So if he couldn't have

Shawn's business outright, he'll fuck it up for good and get Shawn out of the way. So he's on that destroy-and-build kick. But what did the white boy have to do with things? He had Hush and Whisper for backing.

Eboni was home alone, trying to cope with Shawn's incarceration. She was going over the books when she noticed that some money was missing. It was a small amount that could have been easily dismissed, but with the cops watching her every move, she had to be careful of her finances. She would talk to Tony about it now that she was sitting in Shawn's seat. Markus was still holding down the Flatbush area from a distance on her orders. Tony was by her side; she switched the travel. Dave was now busy flying back and forth to Miami and checking on the warehouse with Tony overlooking things. So she would correct him on the shorts.

Penny was stuck in the world of motherhood. And May was her eyes on the street; she was not going to make the same mistake Shawn made by going back out to the hood like that. Making money makes you a target. Sometimes there was love, and sometimes there was hate. He should have remembered the old green eye or crabs in a barrel, her mother always called them. It would be every blue she'd pop up on the Ave. It's time to pull myself together, she thought. No more crying. While Shawn was doing time, he was not alone; she was doing time too. His sentence was mine, and the fucking cops got a two for one and they knew it. The phone was ringing.

"Hello, Eboni," the voice said, sending a bolt of chills and anger down her spine.

Stay calm, girl, don't blow up. Only untrained women got emotional and blew their cool. "Hello Leroy," she smoothly said back, unfazed by his audacity to call her. Like he's innocent in this whole mess. Did he think he was dealing with a moron? Shit, why do dumb niggahs always thinking they invented the game? Two can play that. Like the Vivica Fox movie, "Collect yourself."

"How are you doing? I mean holding up. Stay calm."

"Good."

"Well, I'm calling to tell you, I'm going to be taking over the business. It will be in the Carter family waiting for Shawn."

"Leroy, we need to talk."

"Your place or mines?" he coldly said.

"Mines," she replied. She set the time then hung up. Then she quickly dialed Estevan's number. Damn, he's not even home. Then she tried his cell; it went straight to voicemail.

She then paged him and May. Since Leroy was coming to her house, she needed someone there, knowing he wouldn't come alone. May called her back. She explained her situation and the meeting with him.

"I got you, boss, I'm your lookout, for sure. I'm on my way." Then May hung up. She then went upstairs to get her gun; she still carried the same .25 automatic that Shawn had given her years ago when Markus got shot, then tucked the gun down her back, in her dress slacks she was now wearing, threw on her gray camisole top, and her jacket. The meeting was within the next hour. She stood in front of the mirror, looking at herself, trying to see if she noticed the gun, when the phone rang. It was Estevan, returning her call. She told him of her plans with Leroy; he agreed to be there at the time.

"Eboni, make sure you unlock the back door". It leads straight into the kitchen.

CHAPTER

19

May was sitting in Eboni's well-furnished living room in front of the big screen, watching the basketball game when the doorbell rang.

Eboni was in the kitchen on the phone with her mother, who's been calling her every day since Shawn's incarceration, being supportive, when she heard the bell. "Mom, someone at my door. I have to go. I'll call you later. Love you." Then she hung up. Click.

May was at the door; she opened it to see Leroy grinning at her.

"What's up?" he told her. "Where's Eboni?" he then asked.

She looked him up and down steadily. "Yo, check this out. I got to pat you down," she said to him. His boys were outside, watching the whole thing.

"It's cool," he told his boys. "Yeah, go ahead. I see how you all treat family members," he retorted.

"Yeah, well, it's always business, so don't take it personally," she said and patted him down.

"You enjoy that?" he smirked.

"Naw, you just reminded me why I'm gay," she shot back with a smirk.

He tried to brush past her, but she caught his elbow.

"Hold on, man, let's have some respect up in here," she said, staring straight at him.

"You should come work for me," he tried to joke. "Then again, you are working for me, so back the fuck off and go get Eboni," he said, he was provocative, and explosive towards her.

Eboni came out of the kitchen, just in time to extinguish the situation. She nodded to May to let Leroy past.

"Damn, Eboni, girl, you sure got yourself one badass bitch, I was just telling her how I could always use another thoroughbred worker," he spoke to Eboni.

"Well, let us get down to business. That's why you're here, not to insult my people." She then told May to leave them.

"Damn, it sure is cold in here. All this pussy, and you bitches want to get hard as a dick," he said as he grabbed his cock. "Whatever happened to that warm moist feeling when you first entered?" he shot at Eboni as May was leaving.

"Look, Leroy, let's talk, or you could get the fuck out." While she was pouring her a drink, "Now, the only thing you're going to tell me is if I need another glass, or am I drinking alone?"

"Yeah, I'm good. Fix me what you're having." He walked over to get his Hennessy that she was pouring for him. He was behind her and whispered in her ear, "I'm going to give you a good fucking. Take care of Shawn's shit while he's in jail, keep it sizzling for him because we're family." He grinned.

She calmly walked away from him like he hadn't said a thing, left his drink on the bar, and went and sat down on her leather chair. She knew she was strapped. She had protection for this occasion, so she wasn't worried. Leroy sat down on the leather sofa across from her as he was looking around. "Yep, the business has sure been kind to you," he said while sipping on his drink. "Well, Eboni—Eboni, that sure is a pretty name. I remember when I first saw you right there at the hospital, right by Shawn's side while my father was fighting for his life from gunshot wounds Doggie and his crew pumped in him. And I handled that situation and then at my Brother's funeral," he said and shook his head.

Eboni thought she had seen a sign of humanity in him, but he opened his mouth again.

"Damn, but there you were, looking all fine and tender." He took a long sip of his drink then licked his lips at her in a vulgar manner. "You sure are beautiful, Miss Eboni, that's the Southern, in me." He smiled.

"Look, let's get down to the business at hand."

"Yeah, of course, in a minute. I drove all this way over here, and you are trying to rush me off without giving a brother a little something, like a conversation."

"Yeah, Leroy, I'm going to unleash everything I have, if I find out you had anything to do with Shawn getting locked up," she said unsympathetically to him. She was now seeing Leroy, how he really was a misogynistic asshole that had muscle, and with Hush and Whisper outside, she sure was tempted to put a bullet right between his eyes. But knew it would be a suicide mission.

"Yo, yo, what's with all the ugly words for? From such a beautiful woman. I'm going to ignore that because he's my favorite little cousin. Miss Eboni, I was just teasing you, no harm done."

Yeah, well, he's going to say "Miss Eboni" and mean it right before I pull that trigger, she thought with pleasures. "Now, Leroy, you mentioned you wanted to take over Shawn's part for him. Well, let me just come straight to the point. It's not necessary so it's not going to happen. What's next? I mean, what, else you got?" she said with confidence.

"Look, I didn't come all this way to have some bitch tell me to fuck off. Now, I'll still give you part of the action, and whatnots you can't have. Shawn's bitch starving and shit and going on welfare, you're his queen" he said as he got up to fix himself another drink. He turned and walked over to the sofa and sat back down. "Now, Eboni, it pains me to say this, but it is about the money, so I must. Now you could step down or bend down or even fucking lay down, and if you lay down, you're staying the fuck down, you got me? Am I making myself clear?"

"No, Leroy, I'm afraid it's me that's not making myself evident to you. The game has changed its a new fucking day. You want to play this game with me? You got time to study, so you want to play?" she asked. "Because I'm staying right where I'm at. That's on top. You and your boys keep your shit in Harlem. That's yours. After all, Uncle Pete started that, that's his baby. But Brooklyn and Queens—that's my baby, so you step the fuck back 'cause I ain't going no fucking where, and take all your motherfuckers with you. And stay the hell out of my womb. I gave birth to Brooklyn. I'm the queen. Shawn planted the seed, and I made the shit grow, so you're right. I am a bitch. And like a bitch with a litter of spots, a bitch running my own shit and a bitch about it, now get the fuck out of my house. This meeting is over, bitch," she said to him.

And he got up to leave. "You sure you want this? You just started some shit, baby girl." As he walks, toward her front door and opened it, he shook his head. "I'm giving you three months." He smiled. Then he walked out.

Eboni poured herself another drink. I need a double shot of Hennessy coated with Jack, she thought. May and Estevan came into the living room. Estevan made himself and May a drink.

"We are with you, boss," May said as she sipped on her drink.

"Well, we're all in the fire with you," said Estevan as he downed his drink in one gulp.

Eboni went over her plan with them. She explained why she couldn't and wouldn't back down from Leroy, how she wanted this matter handled. "I'm going to be the one to pull the trigger on this motherfucker. He's mine, out of respect for Shawn. He wouldn't be able to accept it any other way," she said.

"OK, what about his boys?" asked May.

"You could have them. Well, however it goes down is fine with me, but Leroy is all mine," she said again, looking at May then Estevan. "Am I making myself clear?"

"Yeah, boss."

"Yeah, boss," they both said in unison.

"Good. He wants to play games, well, I got one for him, a real good one for his ass," she said to herself but just loud enough for them to hear.

"Hey, boss," May said. "You handle his ass right."

"He's one rude motherfucker who could learn some respect for women," Estevan added. "I'm in the business of the giving lesson, and he looks like he's got a hard head.

"All right, you guys, he's going to learn," Eboni ended.

Leroy was heated on the drive back to Harlem. The meeting with her didn't go how he planned. The words they exchange… Damn! She looked soft as shit innocent, but was as cold-blooded like him. She didn't even look scared, like my treats fell on deaf ears. Damn, I want a piece of her, lick or licks, he thought as Hush was driving and Whisper rode up front. He rode in the back of his black big body 600SL Mercedes-Benz tinted. "Damn that bitch! Who did she think she was? This is a man's world. Now women had their parts. Their place is in the kitchen, like my mother, or with the kids like my wife, shit, or like the bedroom like Deedee. But Shawn's bitch Eboni wants to sit at the head of the fucking table like she's some boss or don bitch. Queen on the throne," he told his boys.

Hush was driving, then started to laugh. "Yeah, she sure is fine. Wouldn't mind having her on top of the table," Hush said then finished laughing.

"Yeah, sure your right,'" said Whisper. "What do you want to do?" he asked Leroy.

"Teach that bitch what time it is, that's what I want to do, like kidnapping her ass and see if she still got a big fucking mouth while she's sucking on my dick," spat Leroy.

"Shit, whenever you give the word, I'll change that bitch's address for you," Hush added.

"I'll let you know when it's time to forward her ass," Leroy said, rubbing his chin.

CHAPTER

20

The next day, Eboni was on her way with May to Rikers Island to see Shawn. She would have gone to all of his visits, but she shared them with his mother and Sandy, his child's mother. Sandy had gotten married and had another child from her husband, Bryan. So she allowed her to visit. She'd been with Shawn too long to worry; she was not one of those sorry-ass emotional chicks. Weak women, she called them. Guess that's why she and May got along so well. May was hard as nails; that's why she respects her intelligence and her actions. She went over to drop another thousand in his commissary, which stayed full. He lives just like he was free, a king on his new throne. The inmates all knew who he was. And the correction officers and those who didn't were informed, plus his bust was an embarrassment to the police department. The spent x amount of taxpayers' dollars and had nothing to really hold him on. He was labeled the New York kingpin by the press. So everyone had their hands out for him. He got special privileges from the COs, for a fee. She was sitting at the table, waiting for Shawn to come down.

"Hey, boo" were the first words that came out of his mouth, and a smile on face. They were hugging when one of the COs in a blue shirt, Shawn knew, came and tapped him on the shoulder.

"Sorry, partner, but you have to take a seat. My captain is watching." And nodded toward him in his crisp white shirt.

"All right, man."

"Damn, baby, I want you home. The house is so empty," she said.

"I miss the shit out of you," he said as he was rubbing her cheek.

"Any trouble in here?" she asked.

"Baby, I'm not worried about any motherfucker. Nah, everything is cool. I'm just worried about you and how you're holding up and keeping things. I heard about you and Leroy. Baby, word gets around."

She looked surprised at him.

"Boo, prison has its own pipeline to the outside world. Baby, just be careful. Leroy is one sneaky bastard."

"Yeah, I know that now. Don't you see how you ended up in here?" Eboni told Shawn about the white boy that Leroy brought in from Chi-Town and his plans. Shawn then told her how he and Tony were at the park when he first stepped to them.

"Damn, boo, I was slipping when I was out there. I was too caught up in the money and shipments. I wasn't on point at all. Damn, baby. I'm sorry I failed you," he said with a sorry look on his face.

"No, you didn't. I'm your Bonnie, and you're still my Clyde, and this is our foolishness. I understand that sometimes, it's hard to see through family members. We always give them the benefit before the doubt, and that's what you did. Now, your cousin, he's just one greedy—" She bit her lip and kissed Shawn lovingly on his luscious lips. "Hmm, I've missed that," she said with her light-brown eyes looking at him.

"Baby, how'd you get so strong?" he asked.

"My strength comes from loving you. You sure look fine in that khaki green prison uniform," she tried to joke.

"Damn, boo, I'm sorry. Now you're dealing with Leroy and his shit by yourself. I fucked up." He slammed his hands down on the table. The COs looked then went back talking to each other. "Baby, listen, you got to create your own game then change the rules when too many motherfuckers learn it, or the game will play you and you'd be trying to catch up. Baby girl," he said, pleading, "I love you. Don't let the game play you the money's not worth it."

Eboni told Shawn everything—her plans, how she kept tabs on Leroy and his crew, the moves he was trying to make on their business, how she sent Dave back down to Florida instead of Tony. How Markus was running the Flatbush area, how the warehouse was stocked and ready for transfer. Tony was helping her, May and Estevan had proven themselves and were by her side. She asked him about the lawyer Allen Myers had hired for him; he talked about the conversation he had with him and was trying to get his sentence reduced. He'd only end up serving six months to a year for a parole violation 'cause no drugs were found, and how half of the cash was Markus's, how he sold a business. He needed them to make it look like that.

"Consider it done," she said.

"Yeah, I'll be out in six months, then I'll deal with Leroy," he said.

Eboni thought about what she was hearing from him and trying to make sense of it, trying reading behind the lines. Was she supposed to hide out or lie low for six months while Leroy took control of things and moved his people to Brooklyn and Queens and pushed them out? She knew she had to be strong for Shawn.

"Look, baby, six months is a long time out in the world, and I'm not waiting. Now I'm not saying I'm ready to make a move on him, but if he steps my way again, that's a whole different story. Remember, the game does change, and six months—you know how behind we will be if I waited on you."

"Eboni, you're talking about striking on Leroy, but it's not just him. There's Uncle Pete and his crew."

"Yeah, Shawn, do your six, and when you do get out, let's hope your babies are still intact. While we're hoping, let's hope Leroy and whoever this white boy is just go away."

"Look, baby, all I'm saying is that I'm in here, you're out there with them. I'm worried about you. Shit, I'm scared for you." Shawn thought about that night. He and Leroy murdered the whole Doggie family; he knew his cousin was ruthless and cunning and didn't want her to deal with him. "Alright, baby, you need to know what type of person Leroy is and just how quiet Hush and Whisper are." He knew he had to tell her about the whole Doggie murder and his part in it. He felt she would be strong enough to handle his part. It was for her own protection to know the whole truth and get the full understanding of things. He looked around the room at the other inmates and their families to make sure no one was watching them. The exits posted the guards on the other side of the room, and since they sat by the cage window on the far side, he focused his attention on the inmates since this was jail and everyone was a potential snitch, for a favor. With no one close enough to hear, he unloaded the story to her, right down to his role in the mix. The blood that was on his hands.

Eboni was shocked to hear what was being said; she knew she had to step to Leroy first. Otherwise, she could end up like Doggie. She remembered how couldn't get in contact with him and Penny couldn't get in touch with Tony. How drunk he was when she finally saw him, he was mumbling in sleep, tossing and turning the whole night. She thought he was still upset about his cousin Curtis's death. She knew Leroy had handled Doggie and his crew, but she didn't know about Shawn's involvement in it.

"Now, do you understand why I don't want you to do anything?" he said to her. "Hush and Whisper are professional killers," he said. "Kidnapping, rape torture that's their shit, their motive of operation (M.O.) And I don't want you dealing with them."

"So what am I supposed to do, take a fucking vacation, out the country go see the world while my world is crumbling?" she asked. "I heard what you said, and thank you. I know a little more about what I'm up against, but I can't back down now. I could use your support on this. Here's my plan."

Eboni left with Shawn's words ringing in her ears; he's murdered children! He was being punished for it everyday. Shawn felt better unloading that deep dark secret to her, that's been eating at him. He trusted her with his life and now his freedom, which he just placed in her hands. That was nothing new to him. She knew everything about me, he thought while lying in his cell.

"Light's outs!"

CHAPTER

21

Shawn was sentenced to five years for parole violation and other trumped-up charges.

––––––––– ·⬩⬩⬩⬩⬩· –––––––––

Eboni called a meeting with Tony, Dave, Markus, May, and Estevan. With everyone thinking out the same box, she knew her plan would work. It was time to end an enemy.

––––––––– ·⬩⬩⬩⬩⬩· –––––––––

Leroy heard about Shawn's sentence. It's time for Miss Eboni to get a change of address. He smiled to himself. Yeah, smart pussy, time to forward that ass right, certified that bitch.

––––––––– ·⬩⬩⬩⬩⬩· –––––––––

Eboni phoned Penny. She planned on spending some time with them—Tonita, her goddaughter, she missed them. She then phoned Elisha, told her she was taking her shopping. She hadn't seen her in weeks, and this was an excellent way to catch up. She thought about

Donny and Justina. She'd missed her little brother Eric as well. And Johnny. Eric and Keith was away at college in Georgia at Morehouse; she was paying their tuitions and had hooked them up with a four-bedroom house ten blocks from the college campus, and they had matching white Navigators. You'd think they would know how to call, she felt as she opened up the bills.

CHAPTER

22

"Damn, that son of a bitch," she said to herself while packing her suitcase. She knew after meeting with Leroy and talking with Shawn Leroy was still talking about taking over. She needed a stronger hold in Miami, so she booked a flight for South Beach, where she herself would meet with Hector Ramirez, the Cuban drug lord. Santos and Carols had set up the meeting with Estevan. He would be meeting her at the airport within the hour; she was a little concerned with the orders that were given to her. She was to stay at the Hilton Plaza in the penthouse suite and only use the car and driver that Hector Ramirez would send for her. And she was only allowed one other person to accompany her to the meeting. So May flew out a couple of days early to set things up. She would still be staying at the same hotel, just on a different floor.

She would be using a utility truck from their warehouse to follow them. Ramirez was the big boss. She was stepping into the big league. He didn't meet with just anybody; you had to purchase your appointment, and she had made the purchase mark. So he agreed to meet with her when Estevan had phoned Santos and set everything up. She traveled with two million cash; they still had contacts at the airport after all. Tony, now Dave, has been flying down to bring back powder. And because of that, she was making a cool ten million a month.

She finished packing, and she'd brought a twenty-thousand-dollar Rolex watch, which she planned to give to Ramirez—as a gift of good sportsmanship, she told herself.

The phone rang in the hotel suite. Estevan got up to answer it; he looked at Eboni, who was refreshing her drink at the full-stocked bar courtesy of Ramirez.

"All set," he said then hung up. "They're sending a car now to pick us up," he then said.

"Good. The sooner, the better," she replied and handed him his drink. "Once we have his word that he will continue to do business with us even if I go to war with Leroy, the stronger I will be. So Uncle Pete or Leroy can't change that," she told Estevan.

"You know, Eboni, I don't see why he would care. Just as long as he still gets his money, what difference does it matter who pays him?'

"Yeah, I would like to think it was that easy, but it's a respect thing. Uncle Pete paved the way for us in the beginning, and one might see it as if we're ungrateful like shitting on family, and that's disrespectful, and for that, you get no love or business. Not seeing it was Leroy's greed who started this whole shit. Because of that, he might just cut both of us off until things settled down. Then what? We both will be hungry. Shit, not me. I like being full I gotta eat," she said and raised her glass.

"Yeah, I got you. I liked seconds myself." Then raised his glass with a smirk. They finished their drinks and left the hotel. The car was out front. Santos was standing outside. He waved them over to him. They got inside the silver Maybach Benz.

May was in a utility truck and in uniform, following three cars behind them.

They drove for an hour and forty-five minutes and she kept time on her fifty-thousand-dollar Rolex before the car came to a stop in front of wrought irons gates. The gate had an emblem of an eagle engraved in black marble, that swung open for the car to drive in, leading to a multi-million dollar mansion.

May parked outside the gate, on the bend, then quickly ran and climbed over the stone walls and waited. As Eboni entered the home. The living room was four times her living room, she thought, looking around. Estevan went over to the window to look out for May, saw him and made her way up to the bushes at the window.

Carols reentered the room. "He will see you now, so please follow me," he told her. "Mr. Estevan, you can wait out in the hall, or in here if you like."

"That's fine," Eboni said then followed Carols down the hall, with Estevan behind them. They walked down a large hallway with portraits by Vincent Van Gogh and Claude Monet and a Jean- Michel Basquiat and Pierre-Auguste Renoir. At the end of the entrance were two gold and white marble Roman-style chairs placed side by side double massive wood doors with leather trim. Carols gently knocked then opened it to let just Eboni in.

She walked in, took two steps then felt the air behind her from the heavy doors closing. Hector Ramirez was a handsome Spanish man in his late sixties, with a gentle face. Why are most drug lords so fucking good-looking? she thought.

"Aw, Mrs. Eboni Reid, come in, please come in and have a seat if you like," he said in a thick Spanish accent.

"Thank you!" she said, sitting down on the leather-and-wood-trimmed chair in his office.

"Would you like a drink?" he offered.

"Yes, a Rémy Martin please."

He got up from his massive wood and ivory carved desk. And fix her one. "Well, Mrs. Reid—"

"Call me Eboni," fixing her Alexander McQueen jacket to her matching pantsuit, she interrupted.

"As you wish, Eboni," he said, smiling and handing her her drink. "I am surprised to be doing business with you, on this scale."

"Surprised?" she asked, taken off guard by his tone and choice of words.

"Yes, I don't mean to seem insulting. I'm just surprised that not many women can hold their own in this trade, especially in this world of finance."

"Oh, I see what you're saying. Well, I'm from New York, where it's just a little faster and audacious." Then taking a sip, she smiled.

He looked at her, then he smiled too. "Yes, New York, but faster doesn't always mean ideal," he added.

"I agree, but ideal could mean change, like idea, progression then you have your faster."

He smiled then spoke sternly. "I must say, Mrs. Reid—sorry, Eboni, you have been doing a lot of business with me and it's been well for the both of us, do you agree?" he said, still looking at her while holding his crystal goblet in his hand.

"Yes, it's been well, I would agree. That's what brings me here, and I'm glad you allowed me to visit with you. And I would like to continue doing well with you. As you know, I'm having some problems with some people."

"Yes." He shook his head.

"Well, I flew all this way to say it doesn't have any effect on this end. My problems are within a misunderstanding, sort of like a surprise that a woman—a black woman—could be in this world trade and make money. Some would think I should be having babies or some domestic work. But I want to assure you I can handle doing business with you in the future. And please accept this gift as a token of the future. Plans to continue in times to come," she said, handing the twenty-thousand-dollar Rolex watch and the two million dollars cash retainer.

Ramirez took the watch and money then told her to call him Hector. "I must say I like your style. Your husband is a lucky man, and I'm sorry for your troubles and problems. I am a wise man. You don't live as I do if you are not, agree?"

She shook her head, looking around the beautiful room they were in.

"My gut is telling me you are a wise woman too. I accept your gift of the future and what the watch represents in time. I like your style, Eboni, you must join me for dinner."

"I would like that."

"Good, we dine, we talk. How's dinner on the patio?" he said.

"That's fine, but I must get back to my hotel room first to rest up from the trip. I'm afraid I have a little jet lag.

"Oh, I understand." They shook hands. "Allow me to walk you out." He escorted her to the car he had arranged for her. "Please use this car as long as you need it, my friend, it is going to be good to be doing business with you."

"Thank you, Hector, I feel the same way."

Estevan shook hands with Carols. Then got in the car. Hector was still talking with Eboni when she noticed May climbing back over the stonewall. Then she got in the car seeing that May was safe, then they drove off.

"Boy, that went well?" asked Estevan.

"I sure hope so."

The driver asked what time to pick her up for dinner. Eboni told him at six. She then told Estevan that she was going to get some rest.

Hector and Carlos went back inside. "She sure is beautiful and smart," said Hector. "Wouldn't mind adding her to my team."

"Yeah, she's very beautiful," Carols agreed.

Later that evening, Eboni dressed in an elegant red classic Vera Wang cocktail dress with cream satin Prada shoes with a matching satin bag. She had dinner with Hector alone, while Estevan ate with Carols and Santos. Hector told her of his plans to expand his operations to New York on a larger scale. He needed someone to guarantee supervision, and he also needed police and political backing. And she could be a part of it. Then he presented her with a platinum two-carat diamond ring, a similar version he wore on his left pinky that had the same emblem that was on his wrought iron gates of an eagle engraved but in a black diamond. "You see, Eboni, I too have a custom. This ring represents me and my power. All my associates bear this crest. It's protection. I do intend on continuing doing business with you."

She thanked him for the ring. They ate and drank and talked some more. He told her how he lived when he first came to this country and how he'd lost his family in a revolutionary war in his country back in Cuba. How his wife and only son was murdered at the age of ten. And to add to his pain he was expelled from his country. Eboni listened while he talked. "You see when you don't have money, I don't mean like this"

—waving his hands around his beautiful gardens—"I mean money to eat to buy clothes and feed yourself, people treat you like an animal. No, change that—worse than an animal. Even a dog gets a bone or scarps by begging at a restaurant or on the streets. But a man, he will starve before anybody tries to feed him. Trust me, I've been there. I like and respect you, that's why I'm telling you this."

"I understand," she said.

"When you first come to this country, you are called every name out there, from spick to wetbacks. Then used and exploited as cheap day labor. Believe me, I know this to be true," he added sadly. "I've heard them all."

"Umm, and when you are born in this country, they still call you names," she said "I've been call nigger to black bitch."

"Yes, that is my point," slamming his hands on the glass patio table. "But who Eboni is the one calling us names?"

She said, "Crackers!"

While he said, "Gringos." They both laughed. "And when you make money your way, on your terms, they have their hands out trying to take it, from you. Then comes the initials like the FBI, DEA, ICE—let's not forget the IRS. So fuck them," he spat. "No disrespect to you for my language."

"None taken." She smiled. "I want to see—you know what my dream is, Eboni? I want to see Billy Bob on his fucking tractor cutting his fucking grass high on coke. The little missus coked up, trying to feed their little fucking gringos and losing their fucking farm in Kentucky, Montana, somewhere what they call the Heartland, the blue belt, but they have no souls. A man with no soul I call a vulture. We are eagles." Then held up his hand, wearing the ring. "We take only what we need. But they destroy everything. My point to you is to stay focused. Don't ever—I mean ever—use this stuff. You see me twenty years doing this, and not once had I ever used this shit."

"Oh, I have no intentions. I too want to see Billy Bob cutting grass high. That's a vision."

"Good, good girl."

Eboni thought about her meeting with Hector as she looked at her ring she now wore on her right middle finger. Mrs. Don, then smiled, I'm on my way. She slept on the plane the next morning back to New York City.

Estevan stayed behind to tie up any loose ends. May flew back with her; she was more confident her ties were getting stronger. She had taken Shawn's dream way beyond and made it reality. There was no turning back, and why would she? Money was right. She was now part of a drug syndicate. The next time she would fly back out there would be for the calling of rings a,sit down. La cosa nostra style, she smiled.

Eboni was feeling pretty good about herself, and the meeting with Ramirez had gone better than she expected. Still wearing the ring, which was his gift to her, during her visit with Shawn and told him all about it. Shawn wasn't too happy to hear she was planning to go to Florida to meet with the top drug lord, the kingpin. He felt that was his place, not hers. He remembered how nervous she first was when they were dealing with Santos and Carols. Now, she was going right back in there. Even though May and Estevan would accompany her, he still worried.

She showed him her ring. He looks at it. "Guessing that makes you a don, huh?"

"No, Shawn, it makes me a smart businesswoman. Look, Shawn, I didn't come all this way to fight with you on this. I'm just holding down things. I went to Florida and met with the damn man. Things went well, you should be happy for us."

"For us, Eboni?" he said angrily. "I'm not the one with a fucking ring on my finger like a boss. Are you connected now?" he shouted.

"Shawn! Please lower your voice, people are watching us."

"I don't give a fuck."

"Well, lower your voice, or I'm leaving."

Knowing that she would and he couldn't stop her without the turtles, the jealous and overzealous correction officers, jumping on him and giving him a beatdown, this was not the time to be in the hole for that matter. "I'm sorry, boo, I just miss the shit out of you—us, and was bugging from the whole ordeal. You know, being locked up."

Eboni looked into Shawn's eyes. She felt his pain. "Baby, I'm sorry too, forgive me." She kissed him quickly so the Officer's wouldn't scream them out. "Baby, do you need anything?"

"Naw, I'm good. I just want you to be careful out there, you understand?" he said while stroking her hair. He traced his finger over her lips, and she closed her eyes remembering his touch.

"It's been so long since you did that, it's not fair," she cried.

"Shh, babe, just relax and think of me and only me."

"I want no other,'" she said, grabbing his hand; she placed it on her breast.

"I want to, but I can't disrespect you like that. You're my queen." He slowly removed his hand from her. "I sleep with you in my mind. I can even smell and feel you here with me. No bars can hold my love, and that's from the heart."

"I feel the same way, baby. I wish I could make this all go away and have you back home with me. I need you." Tears were rolling down her face. "Why is this happening to us? We were just starting to live."

"Babe, and we'll live again. No bars could stop our love," he whispered.

"No bars," she said back.

After she visited with Shawn, she decided to ease her mind with a little shopping. The house was so empty, it was like living in a museum. There was no hurry to get home. Drove over to Manhattan's Fifth Avenue, parked at a public garage and walked into Coco Chanel dressed in Prada from head to toe. The saleswomen smelled money and rushed to assist her. "No pretty women here," she chuckled.

She dropped a cool ten thousand plus a tip and didn't miss it. Then she went to Gucci to drop more money, feeling her mood picking up a little, but couldn't shake the feeling that someone was watching her. She turned around once outside, but this was New fucking York City busy. She stopped at Starbucks for her favorite double mocha with half-and-half and sprinkled it with a cinnamon swirl with a hint of whipped cream for ten bucks, with a chippy cookie. She decided to sit down and pay close attention to her surroundings, see if anybody stood out to her. Girl, you're tripping, making yourself crazy, she told herself. She people-watched for another hour or so since she was having all her packages delivered; she decided to walk around the city and take in the sights, which most New Yorkers take for granted.

The next day, she was having dinner with Elisha and Penny and little Tonita. She called May to check on the last shipment that Estevan set up. It was supposed to be thirty keys in the form of ten Greek statues. The only time she felt safe was in the comfort of her home. She would have preferred to cook or even have the occasion catered when Penny heard about this restaurant. She insisted she go out.

"If I wanted to be in the house, I would have stayed home. Girl, you know I need a break with Tonita screaming in the background."

"All right," she laughed. "I'll meet you guys there. First, me and li'l sis are going to hit the stores and offend them with black purchase power, fuck their thoughts up, drop serious cash on them prissy asses," She told her over the phone. She'd already double-booked herself. She was trying to stay busy in order to keep from falling apart, missing Shawn. Later she'd phone Dorothy, Shawn's mom, to see if she needed anything.

"Sorry, Mom, I haven't had time to visit, but I promise as soon as I wrap things up on this end, I'm coming to spend a week with you."

"Good, I was beginning to wonder if I'd lost you too, but I figure you were dealing with the situation in your own way. So, baby, how are you?"

"I'm OK, Mom, just, you know, day by day."

"I'm hanging in there myself."

"That's why you really shouldn't be alone right now. Went to see him the other day, he looks good as can be expected."

"Yeah, I just miss him so much," she bawled. "Eboni, my son loves you a whole lot, and I love you too. He knew the lifestyle he lives would eventually catch up also, so don't you feel sorry for yourself. 'Because of you, he's able to hold on, so, honey, stay strong and pray like I do that he makes it back to us in one piece."

"I've been praying every night since this ordeal. I even prayed for that heartless judge, the prosecutor, and those crooked cops, but I'm not losing faith. I know my baby will come back to me."

"That's right, honey. Now that's what I want to hear from you 'cause I'm all cried out, but full of prayers. Hey listen, when you come for that week, we are going to march right into my church and speak to the Lord directly, and with both of us asking for the same thing at the same time, I know he will hear us 'cause I'm going to shout for my baby boy," said Dorothy.

"I will too. Next week, it's a date. I'm going to save my tears and use my voice."

"Amen, honey, that's what I'm talking about. It's too big for us, so we'll put it in The Lord's hands," said Dorothy.

She prayed before she went to bed.

Hush followed her around the city; he would stop short, dash into a store or hide behind those oversized potted plants that lined Fifth Ave. Anything so she wouldn't see him. He and Whisper had been trailing her since her encounter with Leroy didn't go as he planned. Now Leroy wanted to know her whereabouts. They slept at the airport and got cut down for that one.

"No more sorry-ass excuse." Leroy warned them to get on their jobs. Whisper was living in a truck right outside her home, and Hush would then follow her in another truck. Eboni would always have company with her; she didn't know it. So early in the morning, Whisper would be babysitting her if she went to visit Shawn. Hush was close by, tracking her movements. They were waiting for Leroy to give the order.

CHAPTER

23

Penny and Tonita were already seated at a booth off to the side, overlooking the bar and not too far from the ladies' room that she insisted was for Tonita's sake when Eboni and Elisha walked in.

"Hey, girl," Penny called out over the crowded restaurant, causing people to turn and roll their eyes at her. She flicked her manicured fingernails at them and continued to wave them over. Eboni and Elisha calmly walked past all the hate stares as if she'd disrupted their loud conversations.

"She hasn't changed," said Elisha, chuckling.

"You know Penny is going to be herself no matter where she is," Eboni replied as they approached the booth. Penny was dressed in a red halter top, exposing her still-flat stomach with True Religion jeans that were clearly too tight, and Tonita had on a pink and blue Gucci sundress with pink Gucci sandals.

"You just came from the office?" Penny teased.

"Girl, I know you're not trying to ride me on my outfit. What's up, how long have you been here?"

"Not too long, just enough too down my second drink" as she sipped on Long Island iced tea.

"You ain't never change," Eboni said as she sat down and hugged her. Elisha went over to Tonita and played with her when the waiter came up with two more menus, giving them a few minutes to settle in.

"I'll be back to take your order. He took their drinks orders then left again.

"How fancy," Elisha said. Elisha had on a funky brown DKNY skirt with a beige D&G top and riding boots. Eboni had on one of her favorite red Chanel suits (she had so many of them) with a white Chanel blouse.

"Girl, I'm starving. I haven't eaten anything all day."

"Eboni, you know that's not smart," said Penny.

"Yeah, but sometimes, I get so busy, and well, you know."

"I know that's right, but I have Tony's little rugrat to remind me. Girl, if I even try to sleep in, she's in the fridge, pulling out shelves of food. I tell you, sometimes I feel like just tossing some bits on the floor, but I know Tony would have my ass, and I don't want any mess or to hear Tonita's tantrums." Tonita looked at her mother when she heard her name mentioned. "I'm talking about you." Penny smiled at her daughter. "See, she's into everything," Penny jokes. The waiter brought their drink order over again.

Eboni was heading home after she dropped her sister home. She could barely keep her eyes open. A beep from another car made her jump, woke herself up by turning on the radio, and forced her to sing along. Forty-five minutes later, she was pulling into her Long Island home. Clicked the garage open, kicked off her shoes at the foot of the staircase, stumbled and plopped down on her bed.

CHAPTER

24

"Bingo!" Hush told Whisper after flipping off his cell phone. "Just got the call."

Eboni was home; she had just come back from shopping and had dinner with Elisha, Penny, and a very energetic three year old. Hush was with her the whole time.

"Let's move," Whisper told him as he got out of his truck that was parked on the next block. Hush waited by the shrubs for him. Three minutes later, Whisper was at his side.

"Let's go around back," said Hush. Whisper nodded then followed behind him. One of the motion-detector lights came on. Hush and Whisper quickly dashed around back to the side of the house, making their way to the back kitchen door. Hush was about to break the window when Whisper stopped him.

"Wait! Check for the alarm system—a place like this has one."

Hush was looking around. "Man, it's too dark in there, can't see a thing." Whisper motioned that he'd be right back then slipped around the side of the house and found the main panel, but it wasn't armed. He went back to tell Hush. Hush was trying to pick the lock.

"Break the damn thing, it's not even on, he told him. He thrust his elbow into French glass doors, causing the glass to shatter to the floor. He unlocked the door from the inside. Crack! Crack! Their shoes were mashing the glass from the pressure of their weight. They tracked the broken shards of glass upstairs to the master bedroom.

Where they found her sleeping, then the phone rang.

Leroy should be outside, said Hush as they were heading back downstairs with Eboni knocked out. Leroy's black Benz parked on her driveway. Leroy got in the back seat.

"What about our rides?" Hush asked.

"Man, just come on, we'll come for them later once we unload."

--- ✦✦✦✦✦ ---

She was trying to reach for the phone, the last thing she heard. It rang four times before the machine picked up. "It's the Carters. Leave you biz but don't eat up my tape," Shawn's voice commanded.

"Eboni, call me if you need me, Estavan, all right one."

He and May were counting the money and cooking up the product on Eboni's orders in the main spot. It was back to business as usual.

"I'm getting a bad feeling," said May in between counts of piles of ten thousand; she was fixing the money pile.

"Naw, she's fine. I spoke to her early. She was going shopping with her little sister, and Penny too, I guess, besides, she would have phoned me if something was wrong or out of the way."

"Yeah, you're probably right," agreed May.

"I'll call her when we finish here. That way, we'll have some information for her," said Estevan.

"All right, that's cool, let me phone my wifey. I need a break. All this counting money is giving me a headache."

"Yeah, go ahead, give wifey a call," said Estevan. May was on the phone with Linda, her life partner, while Estevan started to bag up the coke.

"You want a hit?" he asked May.

"Hold on, babe. Man, I don't fuck with that shit," as she waved her hands at him, saying no.

"Well, excuse me, don't mind if I do a little sniff. Ain't going to hurt no one," he said then made six lines to snort.

May rolled her eyes at him then got up and took some of the coke. She started to measure it, but Linda was playing in her ear. "Yeah, babe, I'm hearing you."

It's been months since Eboni slept well. She quickly fell into a deep, relaxing sleep; she didn't even hear the kitchen door, back window break, and when the glass came crashing to the marble tile floor. She was so tired she didn't hear the footsteps on her stairs ascending towards her or when Hush and Whisper were standing over her. She had an alarm system and close circuit TV monitors that Shawn had installed. But forgot to turn them on, even though he would always lecture. It was for their protection. You're the reminder. She used to tease. When she fell asleep, only to be awakened for a quick second by the phone, Whisper placed the chloroform cloth over her mouth, and she was knocked out before she knew what was happening, Hush quickly carried her downstairs then placed her in the back of the black Mercedes-Benz, where Leroy was waiting. He tied her arms and blindfolded her. Then duct-taped her mouth with Whisper behind the steering wheel. Hush went to the trunk for a blanket to cover her up. Leroy sat holding her while stroking her hair. He smiled to himself. "Let's get out of here," he said to Whisper, who then started the Benz and shifted into drive, and slowly drove off her driveway.

25

Leroy was planning this for weeks, ever since his last encounter with her and especially when he got wind of Shawn's sentence. So with him out of the way, he didn't see the point to leave her to run things, and with only her to deal with, the time was his to strike. It was the perfect storm. They drove over to New Jersey where he had a warehouse on the waterfront he recently just purchased for this. It contained a small room with a bed and a working bathroom. All the windows had bars on them, and the door to the room where she would be staying was steel. The room was soundproof; he planned well. He wasn't worried about her yelling and any morning jogger hearing her.

They drove up to the garage door. Hush got out of the passenger side to open the doors so the car could drive right in. And any passing cars wouldn't see their precious cargo.

Eboni was moaning. She was starting to wake up. Leroy motioned for Whisper to carry her to the room. I'll be joining her soon, he thought.

Eboni woke up but could not see a thing; she knew she wasn't dreaming. She could feel the pressure pinning her eyes shut and tasted the sticky tape glue over her mouth. Her hands were tied in front of her, so she peeled the blindfold off from around her eyes. She sat there, blinking her eyes and adjusting them to the light then took the tape from around her mouth, chewing on the tape that bound her hands and heard a key turn in the cylinder. That's when she stood up from the bed wanting to face her handler, who had her caged up like an animal, head-on and outmaneuver him, hopefully escape. Wishful thinking, she told herself, but doable if given a chance. The steel door opened, making a sound like a prison cell; it was familiar to her—that was the sound she always heard when visiting Shawn at Rikers Island. It echoed in her head. Leroy stepped calmly in; and in his hand he had two empty glasses and a bottle of Hennessy. He kicked the discarded tape pieces aside and smiled.

"Oh, let me rest this down so I could lock back this door. Would you mind holding this for me?" he asked politely, trying to hand her the glasses.

"Fuck you," she shouted back at him. He nonchalantly said.

"Suit yourself." He bent down to rest the glasses and bottle on the floor then turned and locked the door again. "There'll be no disturbance. You could yell, scream, kick all you want, no one will hear you. This room here is soundproof. I had it built just for you, Miss Eboni." Then he winked. "You see, our last meeting had me thinking you needed a change of address, so I moved you since you wouldn't move away by stepping down. Think of me as your personal U-Haul." Leroy then sat down on the bed. Eboni stayed standing, looking down at him in disgust. He poured himself a half glass, drank that down, then poured another one for himself and made hers. "Oh, I got manners. Here's yours. This place has some of the comforts of home. Hennessy, I didn't forget."

"No, thanks."

"Suit yourself. Now let me tell you what's going to happen here, but first, let me say it didn't have to come to this. It didn't have to be like this. I tried to be kind to you and told your ass I'd take care of you while Shawn's in jail. No, not Miss Eboni, you wanted to be Miss Boss Bitch sitting at the fucking head of the table with me."

She changed her mind and took a sip then spoke. "Look, I'm not going to beg, I'm not even going to cry, so whatever your sick fucking ass has planned for me, just do it and make it quick. 'Cause you are a dead man, a fucking dead man!" she yelled at him.

"Oh, I am going to enjoy you sucking my dick, you got a big fucking mouth, and I'm going to stuff it up." Leroy was on his third drink while Eboni was on her second; she was scared shitless and was drinking to gather courage. "I run this. When I finish my drink, we're going to have a little fun. I'm going to fuck your fine ass."

She was more mad than scared. "That's the only way you could get a woman is by force."

"Save that TV, soap opera drama shit, it's not going to work, not going to work," he said while sitting more on the bed, sipping on his drink. Leroy sipped his last sip then rested their empty glasses down on the floor away from her reach. Then he moved the bottle next to it. He stood up again and walked over to her. He reached out and touched her breast. She stood still with a cold stare on her face. "Take your blouse off—fuck that, take all your clothes off right now," Leroy said then pulled out two sets of handcuffs and handed one set to her. "Then I want you to cuff your right hand. You see, I thought this out, it's all for you. I planned after our last encounter, the meeting motivated me." He then kissed her hard on the lips. "I want you, Miss Eboni Boss," he teased. Eboni froze with fear of the handcuffs. I'll be more of a sitting duck, she told herself. "Look I'll take my clothes off and fuck the shit out of you, I won't even fight you."

"I don't mind angry pussy," he said menacingly. "I can tame a snake. I'm quite a charmer," he joked.

"Look, I won't fight you," she pleaded.

"I tell you this: if you go back on your word, I got some heroin, you know, smack out there, and I will shoot you up. Turn your ass into a junkie and let my lower-level workers then crackheads have their way with you. Shit, you'll be so high 'cause I'll keep you doped up. You wouldn't even know your name anymore, Miss Eboni," he teased. "So if you fight me now, forget the handcuff, 'cause you just been told your fate, you can make your future now. Take your clothes off."

Eboni began taking her clothes off, wondering how the hell this was happening to her. Shawn just told me Leroy was nefarious, capable of murder, rape, kidnapping. How the fuck could I have slept? I should have killed him. Damn, now I'm fucked! She then removed her Chanel skirt.

"Nice, very nice. Turn around and let me see that hundred-million-dollar ass."

Eboni turned for him; she knew she needed to relax so she could get him to trust her. She took off her bra and matching Christian Dior lace white panties set. Leroy stood up; he'd place his gun on the side of the bed where the bottle of Hennessy and glasses were.

"Don't even think about it, 'cause if you make it past me, Hush and Whisper are out there. Do you really think you could make it past them too? Shit, when Shawn comes out, he's going to thank me for making you a pro. He's going to get all this good loving you're about to learn. Shit, you'll be doing tricks with your shit. So after me, my boys got next. I'm going to turn you out make you a professional pleaser."

She couldn't see any way through this. Leroy had her at a disadvantage. "Make me another drink, since we're going to party, and since I'm the guest of honor."

"See, that's what I'm talking about, getting with my program. I'll fix you a drink." He handed her the drink then took off his shoes then pants; he stood next to her in his silk navy boxers. "Eboni, lay down. I want to taste you."

She was slowly sipping her drink when he took it from her.

"You can have it back when I'm done. Wouldn't want that glass slipping and bashing me upside my head while I'm down there, getting to know you better. Shit, I might just keep you for myself if you're good for real. I don't have to share you with them. Now come on and lay next to me."

I don't believe this shit, she thought as she lay down next to him.

"Now spread your legs. I've been waiting to dip into this cookie jar the very first time I've seen you. We could have been good together, Eboni. Now open your legs." Shawn was the only man she had ever been with. Now, she was being raped by his cousin.

If I live through this, I am going to cut his dick off and make him eat it! she cried inside

"Damn, you taste good, young and sweet, just the way I like it."

Eboni's body was reacting to him, and the alcohol was wearing her down.

"Grab the back of my head," he said as he came up for air. She did like she was told.

He was biting on her lips and licking around the man in the boat; she guiltily enjoyed it. I'm going to kill him myself, she sang over and over in her head. She was cummin'. Leroy looked up at her then smiled devilishly. She forced a phony smile of satisfaction on her face.

"Told you I could tame a snake. Now tame me I'm wild."

She wanted to bite his dick off but knew it wasn't the right time.

Leroy sensed her hesitation. He jumped up and reached over the side of his bed for his gun. "You do anything else but suck and you will catch a mouth of lead. You'll be picking up your teeth like tic tacs 'cause I will take this gun and knock all your teeth out and have better access, I will fuck a bloody mouth."

"I told you I'm not going to fight you, so just relax and enjoy," she said in a sexy voice.

He looked at her ample ass and sexy full lips, took one of her breasts in his hands and gently squeezed it. She moaned. He popped the nipple in his mouth and began to suck it till his hard-on returned. "Bow your head," he ordered while cupping her breast. Eboni closed her eyes with her head down, she swallowed hard, trying to fight back the tears. She placed Leroy inside her mouth. The tears came rolling down. Leroy grabbed the back of her head, his fingers now locked around her hair. He forced himself deep, his tip banged against her tonsils. She gagged; he held tight while she was choking then grabbing her breast so hard, she started to flare her arms. But she gave her word. He thrust deeper and deeper. Then he exploded in her mouth. She spat it out on the floor, gagging and gasping for air and wiping the tears.

"You will come to crave it when I start to starve your ass, wasting my shit, but damn, that was satisfying fuck around. I might just keep you and make you mines." Leroy was touching her between her legs, trying to get her wet.

She moved away from him and sat up, wiping her mouth off with the back of her hand. "My drink, I'm really thirsty and need to rinse out my mouth, I got a bad taste in it," she said.

He looked at her, shook his head. "You got spunk. I like that," and handed her the drink he just refreshed. It was less than a shot left in the bottle. "Tomorrow, I'll bring two."

Did he say tomorrow? Oh hells, no, I gotta get out of here. "Leroy, I'm hungry. All this drinking and good loving you're putting down got me starving. A girl needs to eat," she played.

"Yeah, when we're done. Now lay back and open your legs wide for big daddy." He entered her cat. She moaned not because she was enjoying him, but she was a woman in a fucked-up situation and needed him to relax. She hadn't been touched in such a long time. Damn, I miss Shawn. She closed her eyes and tried to pretend it was Shawn stroking her, making her cat purr. But the smell of him and his cologne made her know it was a nightmare.

Leroy was looking at Eboni. Though her eyes were closed, he could see she was enjoying him and he pumped harder, beating at her pussy walls by going deeper.

Eboni started moaning louder, begging for more. "Give me more! Give me more!"

And he arched his back pulled up on his arms to hold his weight, digging his knees deeper into the mattress for support then banged away at her, going deeper and deeper. Sweat was dripping down off of him and landing on her face.

"Rain on me," she cried out, excited he grabbed her hair with his free hand. His finger was twisted up in a knot around her hair, and she screamed from the pain in her head that excited him more. She placed her hands on her breast and started to squeeze them. Leroy was getting more excited. Eboni peeked up at him; he was lost in lust.

The gun, where the fuck is the gun? she reached out with one hand, searching over the sheets, twisting and turning, trying to feel for her freedom the gun would offer her. Time to change the game, if only she could find it. Leroy was still pumping away. Eboni grabbed Leroy's head and pulled him down to her breast. "Suck them," she told him. She needed to pick up her head so she could look around for the gun. He was sucking away at her breast, while she was breaking her neck looking for the gun.

Where the fuck. Is the gun! There it was, next to Leroy, lying beside his left foot, and she needed to get on top of him. Eboni grabbed the back of his head, and with her free arm, she was trying to reach for the gun, but it wasn't possible. She smacked his ass.

He pumped harder then came, rolled him off, and got on top of him. "Wait, wait, give me a minute to catch my breath," and lay back down.

She started kissing his neck, not giving up. "You're a tiger in bed." She gently climbed on top of him with him limp inside. She began rolling her hips like she always did for Shawn. Forgive me. She felt him growing as she reached back to his foot then, with her fingertips, was able to touch the gun.

Leroy's eyes were close; his hands were spread-eagle, gripping the sheets, while Eboni rode him. He moaned, "Damn, girl, you're mines."

"Say my name," Eboni told him. "Say my name and open your eyes. Say it to me," she whispered. Eboni brought the gun up to his head, a few inches lined it up right between his eyes. He was now in her crosshairs.

She laid the automatic, fully capable of blowing his head off. Leroy said her name then opened his eyes when he felt the cold steel press up against him. "Oh shit, what the fuck you doing? All right, all right, baby, calm down." He tried to inch back some.

"You stay calm, motherfucker! You make any move, I'll blow your ass away and take my chances with your boys once they see your brains all over me. They are going to want to cut a deal for their lives, all right. I'm going to get up off of you, and don't you fucking move," she warned. "One move, and that's your ass, you got me, motherfucker?"

"Yeah! Yeah! I'm cool."

"Good." Eboni eased herself off Leroy, still holding the gun on him. She bent down slowly and picked up her blouse. She pulled it over herself then buttoned it, all the while keeping the gun aimed at Leroy's dick. "Now, get the fuck up and open this door." He did like he was ordered butt naked.

Hush and Whisper were playing cards when Leroy marched out naked. Hush drew his gun; then Whisper drew his and stood looking at Leroy then Eboni. "Good. Everyone's strapped. Now tell your boys to slide their weapons over to me."

"Do as this bitch says," he ordered them. They slid their guns halfway to her. There were now three vehicles parked in the warehouse. A black Benz and two SUV trucks.

"Now we're going to have a little fun." She fired a shot in the air. "I'm not afraid to use this gun, especially when it comes down to my life. You all will lose," she said, pointing the gun at Leroy's boys while using his body as a shield.

"And no one make a move," Leroy said to his boys.

"Good, you finally understand me." Then she slapped him on the ass. He cringed. "Don't even try to flex," she said. Turning her attention back to them, she ordered them to strip. "Join your boss in the nude."

"Do as she orders."

Then she pointed the gun at Leroy's head. "Does this gun have a hair-trigger?"

"Do it," Leroy yelled.

Hush then Whisper took off their clothes. Eboni walked Leroy over to the table. She stood next to it then picked up the knife that rested on it. Just a few minutes ago, they all sat playing cards, awaiting their turn; they were going to run a train on her before she'd rock their world. With the knife in her hand, she sliced Leroy across the face then wiped the blood off on the other cheek. "Theirs and your blood are on your hands. You brought them here."

"Bitch—" Leroy started to say while holding his face.

"Save it," she interrupted him. "Now, where's the keys to the car?"

Whisper slid his keys over to her. "You will never make it out here alive," he said. Eboni looked at Whisper and knew he could be trouble. "You're right. She shot him square in the head. Then whispered to Hush mockingly, "He's right, he will never make out alive. Is that what he said?" She smiled. Only Leroy heard her. She grabbed the knife a little tighter and glance at Leroy. "You raped me and put your rotten nasty fucking dick in my mouth and bust."

Hush, seeing that Eboni was distracted with Leroy, he quickly made a dash for his gun still lying on the floor. Before he could pick it up, she shot him in the arm. It's like shooting cans, thanks, Shawn, for the lesson. I'm quite a marksman. She told him, "Now get your ass back over there by your dead friend." Whisper's body was still; his head was covered in blood. You could see the whites of his eyes turning red.

"Damn, you killed him!" Hush yelled at her.

"No, Leroy killed him and you from the minute you dealt me this hand. I'm just playing this motherfucker out. You know the rules, my game, my rules." She told Leroy to lie down on the floor and keep still. "You want to rape me? You like angry pussy?" You don't deserve to keep your dick! She picked up the knife then brought the blade down on his manhood.

His dick dropped down on his legs. Leroy started screaming and kicking while holding himself. It all happened so quick; he didn't think she had the guts to do that. "You're dead, you're dead!" He was yelling but no longer looking at her; he was in a trance.

She walked over to Hush. "How do you want it?" she asked with coldness. He knew he was dead. He then lowered his head, closed his eyes. "Lights out!" she said. Pop! And bust one single shot execution-style in the back of his head. His body dropped.

Leroy was still yelling. Eboni picked up the drink that was on the table. It was Hush's. "Well, he won't need it," she said. She sat down looking at Leroy. She took a sip. "You want a drink?" She took one of the other glasses. "See, I got manners too," she joked.

"Fuck you, bitch. You cut my shit off, Shawn's a dead man soon as I—"

Cutting off his sentence, Eboni calmly walked over to him. She reached down, still holding the gun. She picked up Leroy's dick with the tip of the knife. "Do you remember what I told you?"

"Fuck you!" he spat, rocking himself back and forth. The pain was so intense, but his anger kept him motivated all the while thinking how he was going to murder her and her whole family while she's watching. She had just killed his manhood, not to mention his boys, and she was still talking shit, he thought. Oh, hells no way was this bitch going to live another day.

"Do you remember?" she repeated. "I told you I would make you eat your shit, and here it is, so it's, fuck you."

"Oh hell no, I ain't going out like that. Fuck that shit, kill me right now."

"No, fuck yourself, motherfucker, so it's fucking you," she laughed.

"You are a crazy bitch."

"Open your mouth," she ordered him.

"Kill me, just kill me."

"Now, Leroy, what fun would that be? You enjoyed yourself with me, I played along. Now you want to flip the script on a sister? It spoils the sport. Whatever happened to sportsmanship?"

"Fuck you!" he spat.

"Look, I'm getting sick and tired of the whole 'Fuck you shit, fuck me, fuck me, yes' 'cause right now, I'm fucking you with your shit. So take this dick and eat it!"

"Fuck no!"

"You think this is a game?" She slapped him upside the head with the gun then shot him in the leg. "I'm not fucking around. I ain't playing." He crawled up into a ball. Tears came rolling down once again. He was breathing so hard she thought he would go into cardiac arrest and die from a heart attack before she could kill him. "The next one is your ass, understand? Now eat it!" she yelled.

His hands were trembling as he reached out to take it from the tip of the knife. "I can't do this. I'm a man. You can have everything... I'll bounce, and Harlem—it's yours, just don't make me do this, I'm a man. I can't go out like that. You have my word. Just think about it, or kill me with dignity, not like this, all messed up and shit," he pleaded. He looked in her cold eyes then heard words that no man should ever hear.

"No, negotiations. I don't compromise. Fuck all that. Now eat it," she said.

Leroy put it in his mouth. She took a sip of her drink, and offered him once again, this time, he took it after he spat.

"Should have made your ass swallow. Guess you got a nasty taste in your mouth too."

He drank the half glass of Hennessy.

"Now when I go home and remember this night, somehow seeing you eat your shit, I know I'll sleep better. No other women would have to endure what I went through." She stood up, aimed the gun toward his chest. "Tame this motherfucker!" Pop! Pop! Two shots to his chest. Leroy was silent.

Eboni went back into the room he had raped and imprisoned her in. She picks up the rest of her clothes, smashes the glasses and bottle on the ground. "I need to burn this bitch down. Lighter and lighter fluid, that's what I need." She grabbed the lighter from the table. She couldn't find any lighter fluid and was pressed to get the hell out but didn't want to leave any traces of her in there for the cops to see as she left them three nude bodies. She then took Leroy's shirt and found the keys to the Benz and five thousand cash. She popped the gas lid to the truck, stuffed a shirt down in it, leaving enough sticking out. Drove the Benz outside and started the ignition and lit the shirt. Poof! The truck caught fire then exploded.

Eboni drove away; she didn't even know where she was. With no directional destination in sight, she drove all morning till she spotted the New Jersey path train. She wanted to drop the car in the river, but it was too much traffic. She then parked, then cleaned herself up a bit, trying to look decent for the morning commuters, boarded the train bound for Manhattan.

White-Boy Joe was on his way over to the garage for some of the action. Hush and Whisper had phoned him in on Leroy orders. He was just turning the corner when he heard the explosion. "What the fuck is going on?" He jumped. And seeing Leroy's black Mercedes driving away, he could barely make out the driver when he noticed it wasn't Leroy or one of the guys driving. He saw a head full of wild hair, that's when he decided to follow the Benz. He was shadowing the car and got close enough to make out it was a woman behind the wheel. "Is that... that Eboni?" he said. He continued to tail, giving up the right amount of distance to the morning rush. He watched her park and dipped out and boarded the path train.

When he drove back over to the warehouse garage, he heard the sirens echoing in the far distance finally arrived just in time to see the coroner loading up dead bodies in the wagon. Leroy was dead. Hush and Whisper gone too. He swelled with anger. She is going to answer for this with her life, he promised Leroy as he dove away just as more police cars were arriving. Not wanting any attention on himself, back in the city, he lay there, planning his attack while remembering how Leroy was like his brother. The only family he ever had, years of friendship gone. He cried.

Before she reached home, she stopped at a payphone then phoned Estevan, told him about the Benz, how she wanted it to swim forever.

"I'll take care of it. I'll make it a fish. Are you all right, boss?" he asked.

"Yeah, fine, take care of that." Then she hung up. She rode in a cab and had the driver drop her off four blocks away from her house.

Once inside, she studied the place and went into the kitchen. She saw the broken glass and realized that was how they entered. Checked her alarm system then set it, went upstairs double-checked all the rooms, then went into the master bedroom. The bed was unmade, how she left it. Nothing was out of order. Shawn's picture was still on her nightstand. She stared at it then broke down crying, unraveling, began shaking as she lay curled up in a ball on the bed, holding the gun that was under her pillow.

"Girl, pull yourself together, get a grip, you killed those bastards. So just get a hold on things," she told herself in between sobs. "The worst is over. You're in one piece" as she dragged herself in the bathroom and took a long hot shower, still crying. She then threw on a sweatsuit, pulled her wet hair into a ponytail, fixed herself some Jack hard-core, and sat down to call her mother. She needed to hear her voice. "Come on, Mom, pick up the phone. Three rings later, "Hey, Mom."

"Hey, baby."

When Eboni woke up, she didn't realize she'd slept the whole morning and was too late to visit Shawn. She decided to phone Penny. What took place was her secret. Leroy was dead, and so were his boys Hush and Whisper. The only one left was Uncle Pete and Jimmy. "I'll take care of them later."

She watched the news later that day when she heard about the warehouse fire and a burnt Mercedes-Benz they discovered and pulled out from the river. How the Coast Guards were now setting up a diving team looking for bodies. The police stated that since this appears to be drug-related, no information would be released until they contacted the family members. They would release the names to the public. She switched off the television and phoned Estevan. He picked up. "Thanks, the fire was a nice touch."

"Glad you're pleased," he said.

She hung up with him, then her house phone rang; it was May. "Hello, boss, are you OK?"

"Yeah, I'm alive," Eboni said. She didn't feel like going into details with May or Estevan. The less they knew, the better, she figured.

She then phoned Uncle Pete later on that evening. His nurse answered. "This is Eboni, she said."

"Hold on."

Eboni heard the nurse call out to him. He picked up the other end. She waited for the click of the nurse's phone then she spoke.

"Hello, hello?" Uncle Pete was saying.

"Hello, Uncle Pete, how are you feeling these days?"

"Ahh, Eboni, it's so good to hear from you. How's my favorite nephew doing? You are taking care of him I hope?"

"Of course, I am."

"Good. Shawn got himself a good woman. I always told him that as soon as I get better, I'm going up there to see him. He'll like that. Have you seen the news?" he then asked. "When I find the bastard who did this, I will kill them!"

"I'm so sorry for you. Good luck and take care of yourself." Monster's, make monsters, Eboni, thought. Then she hung up.

CHAPTER

26

"Clear the way! Clear the way!" shouted an EMT five thirty in the morning when the ambulance arrived at memorial hospital in New Jersey.

Leroy was hurried in on a stretcher where he was then wheeled to a triage trauma unit, where three doctors worked steadily under pressure to stop the bleeding. They reattached applied stitches to his groin area where his reproductive organ had been removed and the surgery was a success. He now needed a bowel bag to alleviate bypass stress to the body. His body began convulsing. He had a minor stroke, then he lapsed into a coma. The doctors finished removing the three bullets from his body. He was sedated and placed in a medically induced coma.

Leroy was in the hospital; he was lucky to be alive. He had lost a great deal of blood due to the botched amputation of his penis Eboni had performed on him. When he woke up after passing out, he managed to drag himself into the same steel cell he had created for her; it saved him with three gunshot wounds. He was a few feet away from the explosion; he could not hear the sirens or the firefighter yelling, asking was anyone in there. He was passed out again, unconscious, when he arrived at the hospital wrapped in a blanket—the same one he used for Eboni just a few hours before.

Two detectives were outside waiting in the hall to talk to him and the doctors. He was burnt so bad and didn't have any ID on him, you could hardly make out his face. They needed the doctors to sign off so they could attain Leroy's fingerprints when he was more stable since he was brought in nude five hours had passed. They were still waiting for the doctors to come and talk to them.

Detective Hunter asked the young doctor who stepped out to talk to them. The doctor had a young face; he appeared to be in his early thirties. He was a young black man with a soft-spoken voice. "Did he say anything?"

Dr. Jamison answered, "He kept mumbling something, I'm not quite sure of what I heard, but it sounded like, miss. He mumbled again then finished with 'Bitch, she did this to me,' then he went into a seizure. Sorry. I hope that helps you because whoever did this to him needs to be punished." Doctor Jamison then explained Leroy injuries and condition before he was called back in.

Detective Hunter wrote down the information he had just received; another hour had passed before they were allowed to take fingerprints and photos needed to ID him. "After we send the prints off and receive a positive ID, we can address the family members," said Detective Hunter.

"Yeah, providing he's in the system."

Hunter was three and a half years from his retirement. He was looking forward to it until this case was dropped on his desk, being a twenty-two years veteran cop on the force with a great turnover when it came to solving cases. He didn't want to just walk away. This was a big case, he could feel it. His gut told him so. The big one, this case was becoming a high profile. The news was already speculating that it was a serial arsonist, or was it a drug deal gone bad? Every news channel was reporting different theories. Where do they get this stuff? Detective Hunter thought.

Detective Winfrey was an excellent cop, one of the few who had been trained by Hunter. They had been partners for ten years and trusted each other's judgment. He was a little amidst, as he recalled when he joined the force that Hunter took him under his wings and had been flying since.

Winfrey glanced over at his partner, who was going over his notes while Winfrey was driving. Ten years together now, I'm about to lose my mentor! he was thinking then commented on Leroy's condition.

"What kind of person could do such a thing to cut off a man's... ouch, it hurts to even say it."

"A sick bastard," replied Hunter.

"Yeah," Winfrey sighed.

They arrived back at the station. Five minutes later, they were headed over to the Carter resident in Harlem, New York. Leroy was a career criminal. The computer printed out a rap sheet, a book full, dating back to his first incident when he was a teenager charged with assault and battery from Jersey to Harlem. Knock, knock.

"Good luck," Uncle Pete repeated, then placed the phone back on its cradle. He was watching the five o'clock news when he heard about the Jersey fire on the waterfront warehouse. A black Mercedes Benz with NY plates that read BLK KNIGHT was also burnt up. They had recovered three bodies. Two hours later, two plainclothes New Jersey detectives were knocking at his Harlem front door. His private nurse, Josie, answered. She advised them of Mr. Carter's heart condition then led them into the living room where he was watching the news earlier. They had pictures of the bodies. He was asked to verify their identity. Leroy was burnt up so bad and was in a coma. Then he needed to come down to the hospital—that was standard procedure.

"That's my son," he told the police detectives. "Who did this to him?"

"Sir, we're investigating it still. Does your son have any enemies you think we should know about?" said Hunter.

"No, no, I mean I don't know," he answered in shock and disbelief that Leroy and his boys could all end up like this. His mind went first to Douglas Mason but knew that wasn't possible. They were wiped out for good.

"Please, gentlemen, Mr. Carter needs to rest. The strain, I'm afraid, is too much for him, so I hope you don't have any more questions for him 'cause I have to ask you to leave."

"No, madam, we're done. Thank you, and once again, we are sorry to deliver such unpleasant news," Hunter said to the young pretty black nurse who was walking them out.

Later on that night, Pete was rushed to the hospital. He suffered a massive heart attack. Jimmy was by his side, along with Nurse Josie.

Eboni was in bed all morning with the TV on when the news broke with a picture of the Jersey waterfront fire. She was glued ever since. Then the reporter said how the firefighters were recovering bodies from it. Two dead bodies and one unconscious, the lady reporter said.

"Who, who?" shouted Eboni. "No, he couldn't be alive," she said then jumped up and started packing her suitcase. The news continued that the third person was in severe condition and not expected to live, he's burned beyond recognition. He lost a great deal of blood and hemorrhaging with gunshot wounds due to the trauma in his groin organ area.

Eboni clicked off the TV. Good, she thought. I need to see Shawn and tell him the whole thing. The news was still unfolding—who the people were, why the fire started and the gunshot wounds, who was the culprit behind such a heinous crime, and why.

White-Boy Joe was also watching. He knew all the answers to the questions. And if I were there, the outcome would have been different, he thought. I should have killed that bitch when I saw her driving Leroy's Benz. No, I should have been by my boy's side instead of with some hoe, he blamed himself. One thing is for sure: she will suffer a hundred times more, I promise you Leroy, Hush, and Whisper. I owe you all that much.

CHAPTER

27

The next day, Eboni was up and dressed, and she threw on her blue Coco Chanel suit with a matching bag and shoes and a white silk tank top underneath it. She ate a light breakfast then got into her brand-new white G-Wagon she just brought. Then she drove over to Rikers Island.

"Mr. Carter," she heard the COs say, then Shawn came in. Eboni got up, and rushed over to greet him, she hugged him tight, kissed him on his lips, and then sat down.

"Hey, baby, you look good," she said as she touched his face.

"Eboni, I want to talk to you. I've been watching the news."

She knew where Shawn was going with this. "Yes, baby, it's all true, I did it. They came to me while I was sleeping, and when I woke up, I was in a cell blindfolded and gagged."

Shawn shook his head and started to cry. "You, all right, baby? That bastard got what he deserves. I'm just glad that your OK. Don't you worry bout a thing. Tony and Dave will take care of the rest."

"I called Uncle Pete, Shawn, and his nurse told me he was in the hospital for another stroke when he heard the news."

"My mom came to see me. She was so upset about her brother I'm worried for her."

"Don't worry, I'll look after her. Baby, I had no choice. You do understand?" Eboni told Shawn the whole story, including the rape.

216

She cried. He held her. A CO started to interrupt and break them up, but Shawn's eyes pleaded with him, so he let it slide.

"Damn, baby, I wish I was with you."

In between sobs, Eboni cried harder. "But it is all over now." She told Shawn how she was putting Markus and Dave to take over Uncle Pete and Leroy's operations. "And Tony would still run the Brooklyn and Queens till you get home, baby."

Shawn looked at her. He didn't recognize this person who sat in front of him. She had evolved onto a hardened woman that was strictly about business and dressed the part, and her mind made the moves just in that fashion, knowing what she'd been dealt with. Here she was, going on like nothing had ever happened. Gangsters respected her for that. He wasn't surprised at how well she functioned under pressure. He remembered how back then she'd put his money first in the bank and made it pile, how she toted the gat in Florida, sealed the deal with Ramirez. He smiled. "Baby, I love you. I'm so proud of everything you'd done for us."

Eboni felt a weight being lifted off her shoulders as he spoke to her. "I needed to hear that," she said. They spent the rest of the visit planning their wedding and honeymoon.

"Yeah, but first, I need a vacation until things cool off. Give me your right hand, Don Eboni," he said then kissed it. Giving her props, she'd championed over everything. He thought it was her due, the accolades, and his duty to respect her even more.

CHAPTER

28

"Oh, Ebb, girl, you know I'm here for you. Tonita, go and sit your ass down, you see I'm on the phone."

"Penny, Penny."

"Yeah, I'm here."

"You handle that, I'll talk to you later."

"Naw, girl, I'm here, shit. You still ain't tell me why your ass is running to Aruba. What's the rush? Did something happen?"

Eboni wanted to scream out, "Yes, I've been raped!" But not by a stranger. Raped by Leroy, and she'd just killed his boys Hush and Whisper and left him for dead. But how could she bring herself to say it?" Yeah, she and Penny went way back, but some things were better just left unknown. "I need to get away, you know with Shawn and in jail, this house is becoming a damn prison cell for me."

"Uh-huh, so you're telling me running off to some fly-ass spot in the sun is the answer?" Penny questioned. She knew her girl loved Shawn and vice versa. But women have needs, and Shawn was gone. What's a woman to do? "You sure you're not running to someone?"

"Look, Penny, don't ever come at me with some hoe-hopping shit. Respect me because you know I don't get down like that," she snapped. "It's what I said it is, just trapped and wanting a change."

She could hear in her friend's voice that shit was not straight, she was stressed and very upset. And here I was, thinking like askant. "You go on your trip. I just wish I could go with you. Shit, I need a break from my life too. Tonita, sit down now."

"Mommy, mommy, I want to talk on the phone."

"No, go sit down, and as soon as I get off the phone, I'll fix you something to eat. Eboni, let me go. She's driving me to knock her out, and if I don't get a chance to speak to you later, just have a safe trip and relax 'cause Shawn is still waiting and counting on you."

"Thanks," Eboni said with tears. She quickly hung up before she had to sniff. Stay strong. You went through too much crap and made it through to punk up and break down, so pump those tears and handle it.

Bring!

"Hello?"

"Hey, sis, what's up?" asked Elisha.

"Nothing much, how was school." School has been out, thought Elisha. "Eboni, you don't sound too good. Is everything OK?"

"Yeah, I just have a little cold." She sniffed. "I washed my hair and went outside while it was still wet, so I got a head cold with the sniffles—sniff, sniff."

"I've done that a million times too. What you are doing today 'cause I was thinking of coming over to spend some time with you."

"You should bring your passport 'cause we're going to Aruba."

"Aruba! Why? I mean how? When?"

"You just bring your stuff. Don't pack. I'll buy you new gear. Just bring your passport, OK?"

"Yeah, for real?"

"For real, so hurry up." Eboni lay back in her bed, thinking about spending time with her baby sister. She was just the chatterbox she needed to distract her. Get her mind off things.

"Elisha, where are you running off to, in such a hurry, leaving your Louis Vuitton bag with all your money, and what you are doing with your passport, you plan on going somewhere too?" asked Gail. She was dressed in her Sunday outfit even though it wasn't Sunday, and she wasn't going to any church meetings. She had a date with her husband.

"Thanks, I'll lose my head if it wasn't screwed on. With Eboni," she squealed. "We're going to Aruba."

"And when were you planning on telling me?"

"Maw, I just found out today when I called her, and she invited me."

"Oh, that's nice. You two sure need to spend some time with one another. Lord knows she needs it with Shawn still in jail. She has been so depressed lately, I don't know how she stays in that big ole house all by herself. It just ain't right. Well, you look after your big sister 'cause she needs you right now. And when you all get back, the Reid women will do something."

"OK, Maw, I will." Elisha left wearing just a pair of Frankie B jeans and a red Prada tee, red-silver America cup Prada sneakers, and passport in tote, heading for Eboni's house.

Later that evening…

"Tony, I'm worried about my girl Ebb."

"What are you talking about? Did she say something?"

"Naw, it's the tone. You know, a woman knows this shit," she said, crawling into the bed with him. Tony sat up, waiting for Penny's tongue twister. She could wrap his dick into a pretzel. But instead, she lay her head on his chest.

"What's this? What the fuck?" with his hands glazing over his privates.

"Calm down, I'm taking care of you but, first I want to talk about Eboni. You work with her, has she been acting strangely in any way?"

"Naw, why?"

"Oh, 'cause she's going to Aruba on the drop, that's why."

"And so, what's so bugged about that?"

"I don't mean it like that. I'm just saying I know Shawn is locked up, and shit is tight all around."

"Yo, chop that shit. My boy's girl is a real trooper, down for him. Look what the fuck she did when shit got thick? She ain't run and start tricking with the next baller nigga like some hoe. Shit, she took the cake and started baking and open up shop! So fucking what if she bounces to the island? It's all good, and don't you go saying no stupid shit like that for my man Shawn too, hear you got me?"

"Yeah, Tony, I'm just worried for her, that's all. Ain't nothing sway about her downness and love for Shawn. I mean, she just seems a little stressed."

"Shit, if your ass were out there with your hands dirty instead of laying up relaxing, you'd be stressed, bet that too."

"So, you're saying it's all business?"

"Yeah, what else could it be? She ain't fucking no one 'cause you'd be the first to know," he joked, lowering her head. "Come on, baby. Poppa missed this."

"Yeah, well, Tonita, needs—"

"Don't even talk to me about my daughter 'because she gets everything and your ass too."

Penny got up early and headed over to Eboni's crib to check on things. It's been over two weeks now. She promised to do the usual and water the plants, let in the Happy Maid company to dust and vacuum, pick up her mail so her box wouldn't get too full. She still didn't trust her neighbors. It was the Brooklyn mindset. And Long Island was still New York. So Penny did the walk through and landed in the master's bedroom while the maids were downstairs, cleaning.

"So this is Shawn's place," she said, staring at his picture that Eboni had hung over the bed since he was gone. Damn, he's fine. She smiled. "But my girl got you, you passed on this prize," she said. She checked out Eboni's walk-in closet, from Gucci to Channel to Louis to Prada bags, shoes, clothes. "All a nigga wants," she sang from Biggie, trying on one of her minks then sable too, fox coats. Damn, she's large, she thought, from the stoop to the stars. This shit should be mine's. Why, Tony never stepped up on this scale? Or was he holding out?

CHAPTER

29

"Mail call, mail call."

"To my love, I hope this letter finds you at your best because we both know we are still blessed as I lay here in the sun with Elisha, wishing you were here. Things are a sail all around from one spot in the island to the next. This beach has the most beautiful sand and, divi trees. I could hardly see the shore, so I figure I'd stay a while longer and enjoy the sun some more. AK.A. All spots are flowing," he read from the letter, "from Flatbush to Queens Bridge and looking beyond." He kissed then burned the letter even though the COs already had their copy in his file.

CHAPTER

30

Eboni returned from her trip to Aruba. She needed some time to find herself after Leroy was found alive, she had to get away. When she returned, she thought about going into a legit business for herself she created. She phoned Penny for some brainstorming. They talked over a few ideas, and news was still unfolding about Leroy months later. They reported how he was a known drug dealer and how his father was a top New York gangster. Whoever did this, it had to be drug-related.

"Give it a rest!" she yelled at the TV. He was a fucked-up person. I did you all a favor if only the bastard had died, she thought. But the cops were no closer to catching this person. Now they believed it was a mob hit, perhaps somehow related to the Doggie massacre, or was it a serial arsonist. My luck is changing. She smiled.

CHAPTER

31

The fourth year Shawn was in jail, Set Life Realtors was born. She married Shawn while he was in prison. They said their "I dos" with inmates and COs watching them. I'm going to make this up to her. After all, five years is a long time to wait for me, he thought. Shawn wanted her to have a five-carat diamond ring on her finger at the wedding, so he'd asked his boy Tony to pick it up for him so that he could surprise her like old times. A carat for each year. Eboni bought a solid gold band for herself and Shawn to wear. She figured when he came home, they would have time to ring shop. He surprised her with the five-carat ring.

"How did you do this? I mean how did you manage this?" she asked happily, blushing.

"I have my ways." He smiled back.

"Now, man and wife, you may kiss your bride," said the preacher.

"Yeah!"

"Yahoo!"

"Yahoos!" yelled out the inmates.

"Tony picked it up for me."

"Oh, I love it." She glanced at her hand. "But I love you more," she replied.

"Baby."

"Yes, Mr. Carter?" she answered.

"When I get out of here, I'm going to throw you the biggest and baddest wedding 'cause, you deserve it," Shawn promised.

She had on a Vera Wang off-white summer dress and white sandals while he was dressed in a fresh, crisp blue state-issued uniform.

Four years had passed, and with Shawn still in jail, unscarred Eboni had spent her time traveling out the country. After hearing Leroy was in some private hospital recovering. He didn't die, she thought. While Shawn's behind bars, she'd enrolled in a trade school and took some courses in construction. Then at a local real estate agency where she obtained her license; she was now a bona fide real estate agent. She already had her Master's Degree in finance from the University. So she went shopping for office space. Then she found a prime property space in the MetroTech Brooklyn section, not too far from the city just, five minutes over the bridge. It was a spacious five-suite luxury office building for rent in a ten-story building. She rented the top two floors. Now all I need is a name. She had the money to buy the place outright, but never really earned an income, didn't inherit, and she wasn't a Rockefeller. The IRS would be on her back in a NY minute. So she decided to rent with the first option to buy. With Century 21 and ReMax out there, she wanted a catchy name. She'd figured Set Life Realtors. Yeah, that would work. It had a chic NY flare to it that people with style would notice and wonder about.

She phoned the painters, and when the architect finished, she then called in a top Manhattan designer to help out with the furnishing. She wanted a contemporary European look. With everybody doing New York, I'm in a box cubicle. This is my space, and she was not impressed with it. She didn't want to feel like a mouse going through a maze every day. You couldn't tell if you enter a corporate office or a real estate office; she wanted it to stand out.

So she has a living room slash waiting room. The sofa and chairs were soft cream white suede with white and gray marble glass-top tables being caressed in stone with a white marble-tile floor finish. She wanted a splash of color. It was almost looking like an upscale Beverly Hills doctor's office, so she added red paintings and red lampshades and red drapes and one solid red stone coffee table with a white-and-red marble top. She had it specially made, which gave it a luxurious look as well as comfortable. She'd spent weeks searching for the best artwork to grace her office walls when she came across a painting of New York City without any people. It showed the subway empty. Offices bare, once-crowded streets were exposed as well, no street vendors, no cars and cabs, and best of all, no people. A blank canvass, she thought. The concept of the name of her business was perfect to showcase this portrait of Set Life. How opposite still attracts. She smiled. She decided to do her whole office in oak wood. She had a huge oak table with leather trim and leather wallpaper, adjoining matching conference room large enough to hold twenty employees. She didn't want her office to look too feminine. Ramirez had taught her that much, so she copied his style. She wanted a very manly, masculine look to it that would give her the look of strength, not frills and doilies. She wanted to play with the boys. Now she needed employees. She phoned Penny and hired her as a personal assistant—only temporarily. Penny had plans of her own, for her future, with her own office. She went through sixty applicants to fill her office and needed people who could run it without her present. With two floors to fill, she found her special twenty. Jordan Moore was a twenty-three-year-old college grad with a master's in finance and business. She would become Eboni's floor manager. She needed to make her street business more legit; she had already informed her street staff how she expected them to conduct themselves when they visited her. For Tony, May, Dave, Estevan, strictly suits, ties—just like the basketball players at a press conference. No street wear attire, and she wanted them to blend in when entering Set Life. Had a little reputation; she was creating an image. It dealt with out-of-towners looking for that exclusive little million-dollar apartment to working mothers receiving Section 8: everyone will be treated the same. They were offered food, drinks, then fine wine once you made it inside her office…if they made it that far. You had to purchase that mark.

Her receptionist was a Spanish girl named Janet Ruiz, and she was a mother of three, divorced, and only twenty-seven years old. She was bright. Eboni liked her off back when they first met. They talked for hours like old friends; she felt comfortable around her.

"Mrs. Carter, there's a gentleman out here waiting to see you," she buzzed in.

"Does he have an appointment?" Eboni asked.

"No, but he says he traveled a long way to meet with you, and he's looking for a luxury apartment in the city."

"OK, tell him to wait for a few minutes. I'm wrapping up a business meeting," she said to Janet.

Janet then informed the handsome man, "She'd be right with you, Mr. Vincent Benzio." She smiled at him, and he stared blankly back at her. She offered him some coffee, but he refused. She got up, walked into the kitchen, came back with two coffee mugs, and excused herself to him then went into Eboni's office. Eboni was still eating lunch when Janet came over to her desk and sat her coffee down. "You have a hot hunky white man out there who looks like a model or something," Janet said excitedly. "I know you have a husband, but that is one fine man out there," Janet said, acting like a schoolgirl.

Eboni turned on her closed-circuit monitor TV. "Yeah, he looks all right," she replied to her.

"Could you find out if he's single, like how big a place, how many rooms he needs?"

"You want me, your boss, to snoop into this man's private affairs? No, I don't think so. You will just have to do it when he comes out of my office." She smiled at her as she took a bite of her Swiss and turkey sandwich. "OK, I'm done. Send him in."

Janet left. A minute later, Mr. Benzio was knocking and opening her office door. "Ahh, Mrs. Carter, so lovely of you to meet with me. Please allow me to take a few minutes of your time." He gently sat down in one of her chairs. "I'm looking for a spacious apartment on the Upper East Side."

Eboni thought, that's where she now lived. He might end up being one of the neighbors; she needed to investigate his background. "Oh that's a lovely neighborhood. I'm going to have my agent assist you in finding something to your liking."

"With all due respect, I would prefer if I had your assistant, Mrs. Carter. I do like the best, and why not start at the top. This is a top-notch real estate firm, I've done some homework."

"You have," replied Eboni.

Shadow sat looking at her; she was beautiful, he thought. Such a shame to kill someone this lovely.

Eboni smiled. "Very well, Mr. Benzio. I'll look into it for you. I'll be in touch."

"Good, I'm pleased to hear that."

"I'm sorry, but I'm swamped. You kind of caught me in the middle of something. Please leave all the information with my secretary Janet, along with your contact information to be reached."

He got up to leave; he opened her office door, paused, and looked at her. "We'll be in touch. Mrs. Carter, thank you for your time." He smirked then closed the door behind him, still holding that expression on his face.

Janet smiled again as he smiled back at her. He handed her his card that has all the contact information Mrs. Carter requested. "There's also paperwork that we need you to fill out, Mr. Benzio," and gave him a couple of sheets, and offered him a drink. He refused. She led him to a small conference room where he could sit at a desk. It was the exact design of the other conference rooms, only smaller. It was used by the heads of each department when they called their smaller staff meeting or had their lunches. Shadow sat there. He began filling out the necessary paperwork to get closer to Eboni. While Janet went back to her desk. Shadow had been watching Eboni for some time.

Eboni was in her office. Knock, knock. It was Janet. She opened the door and peeked in. Looking up from her paperwork, she just stated, "Yes, Janet?"

"Oh, I just wanted to tell you that before I leave for the day, Mr. Benzio's background checks out on him. And I have his file right here for you." Janet walked over to Eboni's massive oak desk and placed the file down.

"Thank you," Eboni said.

"Is there anything else you need before I leave?" Janet asked.

"No, oh, I won't be in tomorrow, so if you need to get a hold of me, call me at home, but Jordan would be here, so check with her first,'" Eboni added.

Janet left. She could see that Eboni was really busy and in no mood for office chatter. She'd wanted to ask her about Mr. Benzio but decided she was getting carried away with herself. The man hardly spoke to her, and he did have a coldness about himself that said, "Back off."

She was home going over the books Tony had just dropped off, making sure the amounts added up. Eboni received a call on her cell phone from Estevan. Leroy was still in a medically induced coma and had around-the-clock bodyguards to watch him, plus two detectives were buzzing around as well. Damn, she thought as she flipped her cell phone shut.

Set Life Realtors was making great money, and reputation was building; it was all positive. Tony was running the drug business for her; she came to depend on him in that aspect. Dave and Markus reported to Tony, who then came to her. And made sure no one was robbing and ripping her off. Estevan was her ears and muscles, so her hands were cleared and clean. And now, Leroy had personal police protection that her tax dollars were paying for how ironic. Estevan was there waiting to take him out. With all my ducks in a row, how could I mess this one up? Leroy, you are a lucky bastard. When the publicity fades and the police leave he'll sneak into your hospital room and slit your throat.

CHAPTER

32

May was following him; she was his trial,when he went to DeeDee's house. She went to DeeDee's house. She watched his movements and would report to Eboni. When he rolled with his boys; she was there watching. When they went into a strip bar one night and a white boy walked up to them. She noticed how relaxed Leroy was with him, which caused her to take more notice toward the white boy. They all were sitting around the stage. Leroy was tipping a big-bosomed beautiful coco-brown woman. Hush and Whisper were watching the ladies shake their breasts in Leroy's face, but the white boy called a dark-skin big-butt honey over to him. She came over. He whispered something in her ear; she giggled then sat down on his lap. She was rolling her hips on him. Leroy looked over to the white boy and patted him on his back, laughing. They didn't even notice her. May sat behind them drinking while Leroy and his boys got their kicks, feeling up the dancers. They were spending some serious cash 'cause four more girls came rushing over to them. How much longer is this show? she thought. As that little crowd grew louder, he tossed money up on the stage, commanding the girls to do something extra for it.

The girl started to dance, tease, and play with each other. Leroy ordered his eighth round of drinks, tipped the topless waitress another fifty. She smiled then shook her big behind for him Leroy squeezed it;

she laughed with him then walked off. May knew she needed to get a picture of this white boy to Eboni. But the flash would cause attention, revealing herself and location to them, so she waited two more hours before they left. Once outside, she was able to get the pictures needed. Anybody that came in contact with Leroy had their grill taken by her. They hung around the strip club, and the dancers came running out giggling. She followed them to a hotel where they checked in, decided it was going to be an all-nighter and didn't feel like waiting around, so instead, she headed to a twenty-four-hour drugstore for aspirin.

Once inside her apartment, she clicked the light on. Waking Linda up, she jumped and sat up in bed.

"Sorry, baby, I'm beat," she told Linda. May had been living with her for three years now. Linda was a schoolteacher at a junior high. She was a look-alike of Kim Basinger with her blonde hair scattered on top of her head. She was a real beauty.

Linda sitting up, rubbing her blue eyes. "Babe, what time is it?" Linda then asked. She was trying to adjust her to the sudden light.

"It's late, and I need to get some sleep." She came out of the shower smelling all fresh of soap, yawning. Linda had rolled back over to her side of the bed. May climbed under the sheets where she spooned up close to her, smelling her hair.

May woke up still feeling like she didn't sleep well, threw on her clothes, some blue jeans and a white wife beater with some tan Tims. She brushed her blonde cornrows back and picked up the photos she'd toss on the dressing table earlier that morning.

"I got to take care of something important. She kissed Linda lovingly they made love. I'll be right back, babe."

"You want me to fix you something quick to eat?" Linda asked.

"Naw, I'm pressed for time it's cool I'll just grab some Mickey Ds"her first stop was to visit her friend at the City morgue. She met him around back as planned he wheeled out her package, she needed help loading it into her car she handed him a envelope and was out. She had a scheduled to keep. Speeding trying to catch the light cause it was a slow yellow when a moving truck as scheduled came barreling down at the intersection, slamming right into the back passenger fender of her black Audi coupe.

———————— ✦✦✦✦✦✦ ————————

After the burial arrangements, Eboni went to see Shawn in jail. He agreed with her to take care of May's family and Linda too.

———————— ✦✦✦✦✦✦ ————————

In a daydream, Linda thought back on her first encounter with May and how she changed her life again.

"Excuse me, miss, can I talk to you a second? I need help picking out something special for a friend," said May, blushing and, smoothing down her blonde cornrows. Linda, the salesgirl, helped her pick out a present for Eboni. It was an old antique shop in the village. After she'd seen Linda in the display window, she had to step to her. Linda looked at May and was hooked. It was May's style that she was attracted to. Her rough and beautiful urban ways that seemed to impress an old-fashioned country girl from Lancaster, PA. She'd only been in the Apple for three months now; she moved, hoping to be a model slash actress but, needing to pay the rent, took the first job that came to her. Linda was a tall blonde. May looked over her frame and decided it was workable. She was on the prowl for someone she could chill with, so they exchanged numbers. May left with an eighteenth century picture frame and Linda's heart. That was three years ago. It was May who convinced her to go back to school and get her master and become a junior high school teacher. And May paid her tuition.

Six, months later, the phone rang. The digital voice beamed in. "Please leave a message..." Beep!

"Hello, Eboni. It's Linda. I know I haven't spoken to you in such a long time so I just wanted to say thank you for all you've done for me since May's funeral. She'd left something for you, so please call me," leaving a number where she can be reached. "Good-bye."

232

Linda finished packing; she was moving back home to Lancaster, PA, her hometown. With the money Eboni had given her, she was planning on opening a ladies' boutique shop and buying herself a home. She packed all of May's belongings and couldn't see herself parting with them. She just had one little thing left to do—to give Eboni May's package. The police had taken so long in releasing her personal items from the car accident, and the movers were coming around two o'clock. Maybe I have time to run this over to her office and still beat the movers here.

Ping! The elevators chimed, and a very tall good-looking blonde stepped off.

Look at this place, it's beautiful, Linda thought as she strode over to the reception area. "Hello, I would like to speak to Mrs. Eboni Carter," she said, holding May's package in her hands.

Do you have an appointment?" asked Janet.

"No, I don't, sorry, but we're old friends, so please tell her Linda's out here to see her."

"OK, Linda, please have a seat." She knocked on her boss's door and popped her head in. "Eboni, there's a woman out here that said she knows you. Her name is Linda."

"Oh, Linda, send her right in," Eboni said.

"Yes, right away." Janet walk out.

"Linda, how are you?" Eboni, asked.

"I'm fine. I just wanted to thank you for everything and inform you that I'm moving."

"You're moving? Well, good for you, where are you moving to?"

"Back home?"

"And where's back home?"

"Oh, Lancaster, PA, I'm afraid I'm not cut out for city life, and all my families are still out there."

"Oh, I understand. Well, good luck to you."

"Thank you. Oh, I almost forgot why I came all this way. May had this on her the day she passed. Guess this is for you," she said, handing Eboni the package.

"From May," Eboni said sadly.

"Yes, I would have brought it over sooner, but it took so long for the police to release it, and you know, May's death almost destroyed me. So I couldn't even face or deal with anything."

"How are you now?" Eboni asked, looking into Linda's eyes that were puffy and red.

"I'm hanging in there. Sorry, I gotta go. I forgot the movers are coming today." She hugged Eboni.

"Good-bye, take care of yourself, and if you need anything, please call me," Eboni said, hugging her back.

Eboni was looking at the package Linda had just left. Let me see what my loyal friend has for me.

Buzz, buzz!

Janet was calling her. "Yes, Janet. I'm calling to remind you of the staff meeting. Everyone's present, just waiting for you, boss."

Eboni opens the package and flips through about seven photos of Leroy. She dropped the stack. It's like watching a ghost. A flood of memories came busting in her head, the kidnapping the rape and the fire. She stood up shaking to leave for the meeting. She quickly threw the photos in her Gucci briefcase and locked it.

After her meeting, she headed home.

"Hey, Sam," she said as she passed her doorman. Kicking off her four-hundred-dollar Jimmy Choo shoes, she tossed her briefcase and purse on the sofa, went into the kitchen, and poured herself a cup of tea. Walking back into the living room, she clicked the TV on to CNN, where she sat watching all-day news. Her mind drifted back to that night on the waterfront. Leroy should have died. He's worse than a fucking cat. She got up to get her briefcase when the phone rang.

"Hello, baby."

"Hi, honey."

"What are you doing home so early?"

"How did you know I was home?"

"Ha. I phoned your office, and Janet told me."

While talking on the cordless, she picked up her briefcase, took out the pictures, and flipped, threw the rest of them and placed them in her kitchen safe that was behind one of the cabinets. Then back in the living room.

"Baby, I'll be home soon."

"I miss you so much."

"I know, boo, let us not bring this mood down," Shawn said.

"Oh, Linda came to see me."

"Yeah? How's she doing?"

"Not so good. She's moving to Lancaster, PA."

"Why, what's out there?"

"'Cause that's where she's from."

"Oh well, that's good for her, but what's she going to do out there?"

"Something about opening a ladies' underwear shop."

"She won't be lonely for long," Shawn joked.

"Shawn!" Eboni said. "That's not nice."

"No, boo, I didn't mean it that way."

"Yes, you did. I know you."

"All right, I take that back, but what did she want anyway?"

"Oh, to say her good-byes, that's all." Eboni didn't want to tell Shawn about the photos May had taken before she left. She was going to keep that buried secret in her safe. "Wait! Hold on, honey, I got another call. Hello."

"Hey, girl, what you are doing at home?"

"Penny, what's up?"

"I have Shawn on the other line."

"I'll call you back. You're home?"

"Yeah."

"Ok, then."

I'm back. That was Penny."

"How's Tonita, my goddaughter?" he asked.

"Just as spoiled."

"Well, I ain't going to let my goddaughter grow up without me because as soon as I get out of here, I ain't never coming back. I feel like I'm missing so much. Like life is just passing me by. You know what I was watching the other day on TV in the dayroom?"

"No. What?"

"The Shawshank Redemption. I have never heard of it before, but here I was, watching it, and when that older man Gus got out of jail, they had cars. And shit, life just passes him by."

"Shawn, honey, that was just a movie, baby," she said, trying to ease off this self-pity mode he was set on tripping on.

"Yeah, boo, I know, but there's truth in that. It doesn't have to be cars."

"Yeah, baby, but you'll be home soon. Then we could do all the things that we couldn't do."

"Like starting a family," he said.

"Yeah, Shawn, I would like that." They spent the rest of the time playing catch-up.

"Baby."

"Yeah, hon?"

"My time is up. It's time for the COs to change shifts, so I got to go for the bed count. But when you come to see me... Damn, you hear how fucked up that sounds? Silent pause.

"When I come up, what are you saying?" she said cheerfully.

"Yeah, when you come, we'll talk about our future."

"Yeah, we'll do that."

"Hey."

"Hmm?"

"I love you."

"Love you too."

"All right, baby girl."

She closed her eyes then kissed and said good-bye to Shawn. She placed the phone back on the charger. "Oh, Penny."

"What's up, girl? How's Shawn?"

"Not so good, you know prison, it's hard on him."

"True, but stay strong for him."

CHAPTER

33

After he met with Eboni the next week, he received a call from Janet, her secretary, telling him about a luxury apartment in SoHo, a lovely duplex. She wanted to make an appointment for him to see it.

He asked, "Would Eboni—I mean Mrs. Carter—would she be showing it to me?" only to be told she doesn't handle that part. That Jordan Moore would be showing him instead. Shadow was not happy with that. He wanted to get Eboni alone. He agreed to meet with Ms. Moore. The appointment was three days from now, he thought. He phoned the next day to cancel, to inform them he wasn't taking that apartment needed and wanted something with a view and a little more privacy he added. Jordan then said she would be in touch. Then he added he was leaving town for a few days, and if they have what he's looking for to leave a message with his phone service 'cause he would be checking in, then hung up.

Being in prison for eight years can either change a person for the better or the worse, and Joe fit right in the middle—never quite walking away from an easy buck like burglary or robbery. This time, this stretch changed him, making him more careful. Patience became his virtue; he learned to test the water's and to stakeout the joint, just don't dive in. So with Eboni, he wanted to do just that.

And he needed a new identity. Who better to deliver such a package while he nested than Jimmy, Uncle Pete's right-hand man.

Joe then phoned Jimmy that he needed a new ID, new driver's license, birth certificate, and most of all, a bank account set in the same name. Six months later, Mr. Benzio was born; so when Janet ran a credit check, it was all good. Thanks, Jimmy, you're still the best, he thought, sitting in the lobby of Set Life Realtors, waiting to see Eboni Carter, while Janet sat flirting with him. He was not interested in her. He'd instead wanted to wring her neck and leave her dead body for Eboni to see as a game, but being she knew of Eboni's whereabouts, she was starting to look better to him alive.

"She will see you now," said Janet, smiling leading him into her office.

Eboni called Tony; she invited him over to her apartment in the city to discuss business. She was dressed in a pink and gray Adidas running suit, with her hair in a ponytail and china bangs, when the phone rang.

"Hello,"

"Ahh, hello, Mrs. Carter.?

"Yes, who's calling?"

"Oh, I'm sorry, this is Mr. Benzio," Shadow said. "I was phoning to invite you to dinner. It seems like I'm not being taken seriously."

"What do you mean by that?" she asked.

"Well, for starters, I asked if you would be handling my affairs."

"You know this is a bustling company as well as a new one, and I'm a very busy person, so I'm afraid I cannot accept your invitation," she said.

"Well, Mrs. Carter, it would be of your interest I say that to express not only am I looking for a place to live, but I'm also looking to invest my money in a community."

"Oh, you are. Well, like I stated, I'm swamped, but call my secretary and make an appointment with me at my office."

"OK, so you don't eat dinner, not even a business dinner?"

She was going to say she didn't do dinner with new clients when her doorbell rang. "Mr. Benzio, I appreciate your interest in my diet. Call my secretary. Good day, Mr. Benzio," and she hung up the phone.

Shadow place the receiver down with a smile. Oh, I am going to enjoy this game of cat and mouse, he thought.

The bell rang again just as she was about to open the door to see Tony standing there. "Hey, what's up?" closing the door behind him.

Eboni wondered how he got her home number; she would have to check Janet. Tony was echoing in her head. "How's Shawn?" he asked again.

"He's fine, yeah, he'll be home soon. Yes, and I'm planning his welcome-home party for Shawn."

"Five years," Tony said, looking at Eboni. Wow, and you handled everything and blew it up. Shit, Shawn's coming home to an empire."

"And it's legit," she added.

"True that. How's the biz on your end?"

"Well, Dave and Markus are going back down to Florida and were doing about three to five million a week on that end."

"Damn, that's all we need to branch out, covering more ground and grow in other areas," she said. "Like small companies from taxi cabs to bus shuttles and car services."

"Yeah, that could work. We could even travel the drugs that way," he said.

"Yeah, but only passengers, not drivers."

"Oh yeah, I got you. Beauty parlors, barbershops, sneaker stores, even furniture stores up to supermarket chains—we could grow in that way too." They spent the next few hours discussing areas to invest. She ordered Chinese takeout.

CHAPTER

34

Shadow was a tall Italian with dark features. He could pass for a Puerto Rican with olive skin; he was a cross between a young version of Robert De Niro in the face and Sly Stallone when he played Rocky in the body. Prison time had served him well. His body was perfect, and his mind was sharp. With Jimmy's help, he was able to obtain everything he needed. He was enjoying his newfound self-control prison had taught him. The old Joe would have already blown her head off that day when he saw her driving Leroy's Benz; instead, he calmly walked into her office, sat down with her, and discussed his plans all to find out about her; he wanted to see her in person. The same person was responsible for killing Hush and Whisper and leaving Leroy all burnt up in a coma. Leroy was suffering, so killing her fast would be easy, like doing her a favor. No, he knew all too well about time. He decided to send her some flowers, knowing Shawn was in jail. All women like gifts; he would send a thank-you note for allowing him to see her and explain why he didn't take that apartment Jordan wanted to show him and apologize for being so forward, inviting himself to dinner with her, and she's a married woman. She kept the flowers but tossed the card in the wastebasket.

Dear Mrs. Carter,

Thank you for your time, for it was well spent on my part. For I now know this is the company that I would like to do business with in the future. Thank Ms. Moore for her time. She was all so gracious in her search for occupancy for me. Set Life is also a caring company where one could feel safe and comfortable where their money is in the best interest of all parties concerned.

"Blah, blah—toss it."

CHAPTER

35

Joe was getting dressed. He threw on his Versace blue suit and crisp Versace silk tan shirt. He tucked his gun in his waistband; he headed over to a meeting with Eboni, which took weeks to get. He was going to discuss his business deal plans with her since she also provided portfolio planning and income tax preparations her business offered. A lot of outside interest. He saw Tony there several times, picking the lint off his Versace suit. The last details were done. He hopped in his blue BMW 760. The truck was parked up with his lady of the month. The Beamer was parked at the Marriott Hotel, where he stayed a blocks away from her Manhattan apartment building. He drove over to her office and valet parked his car at Kinney's overpriced garage. Then he took the elevator to the tenth floor. Ping! was the chime the doors made when they opened.

Janet looked up at him and smiled. Joe walked over to her; he smiled back. "Good morning. I have an appointment with Mrs. Carter," he told her. Janet looked at her appointment book; she knew he would arrive this morning. That's why she decided to wear her low-cut blouse and thigh-high skirt, hoping to entice him. She pretended to look for his name, allowing her head to drop lower, giving her blouse more room for him to view her chest, which no straight man can refuse, or so she thought, counting down when to look up. She figured it only takes a man no longer than three seconds to drool over her bust line. One second, two, three, on the four—bingo! Got him. She smiled to herself. Looking him square in his eye, he looked away for a minute, feeling caught. He recomposed. He smiled again a little warmer this time.

"I'll inform Mrs. Carter that you're here, Mr. Benzio, please have a seat," she said, asking if he wanted some coffee.

"No, thanks," he replied.

He didn't even give me a chance to shake my rump in his face, she thought. She then picked up her phone, buzzed Eboni, and informed her that her ten o'clock was here. She placed the receiver down, glanced at Joe, who was staring at her. "Oh, she's ready for you. You can go right in."

Joe stood up then walked right over. Eboni's double woodoak doors. He knocked—tap, tap—then opened the doors, stepped in.

"Good morning, Mrs. Carter, so nice of you to see me," extending his hand for her to shake.

"Thank you!" she said; she shook his hands, which was cold. Weird 'cause it was 90 degrees outside. Sitting back down, "What can I do for you?" she asked.

"I have a business proposition for you. I want to invest quite a bit of money in a project. I was hoping that you could help me with that, 'cause I to have been busy. I found a building that I would like to buy and renovate. It's located in the Brownsville section in Brooklyn. I want to turn that into a rec. center for the community or a business link offering jobs and day care, medical and low-cost housing."

"That sounds wonderful, but may I ask why? I mean, why would you want to spend money on helping the poor?"

"Well, I must confess something to you." He paused, as to why a man with money would and should care. "I grew up in a foster home, which I ran away from. They placed me with a couple of drunks so I ran off so I could eat. They drank up most of the money, if not all the money they got from the state to care for me. When I ran away, I ended up on the streets dirty, smelly clothes, not like the man you see before you, until I met this man who had a son around my age who took me in. Dressed me well and fed me good, so you see the results of kindness, and I promise that man I would return the kindness, if given that chance.

So I have the means and opportunity to help hundreds, maybe even thousands, so, Mrs. Carter, that is why I want to help the poor, as you called them, but I prefer to call them people less fortunate or human beings without offending anyone," said Shadow.

"Oh, I see," Eboni managed to say. "I'm sorry to hear that," she added.

"Mrs. Carter, don't feel sorry for me 'cause I feel sorry for human suffering in the richest country in the world," he ended.

"You're right 'cause I too came from humble beginnings. No silver spoon was under my crib, so I do understand and would like to work and perhaps invest in your project," she said. "Welcome aboard." He said. And they shook hands once more—this time, she held his hand a little longer. "Please call me Eboni," she said.

"And call me Vinny."

"OK." She smiled, and he smiled back to her. "Let us go over your paperwork so we could phone the bank and secure the deed to the building," she said. "Give me a minute." She punched in the information on her computer, then phoned John Godspeed at Chase Manhattan Bank, who handled all of her big-money transactions. He worked for her personality with the money transfer confirmed. Eboni turned and smiled at Joe/Vinny. "We're all set. There's just one more little detail when it comes to the renovation. The government would put up a third or secure a loan, whichever is the lesser. Still, you have to go by their guidelines as far as licensed staffing and programs."

"That's fine either way," he said. Shadow looked at his clock. It read 11:45 a.m. He asked if she would like to join him for lunch; she agreed but only if they could order in. "That's fine." They agreed on Italian; they ate, talked over ideas. Eboni had a passion in business. Shadow respected and admired her passion. She scheduled the next meeting for him, this time with the architect and building planner. Zoning board members will meet; he agreed then left. He passed Janet with an even warmer smile, walked past her, and headed for the elevators.

Damn, he didn't get to see my legs. Where's the fire? she wondered. She knocked on Eboni's door, peeked her head in. "Is everything all right?" she asked, trying to read Eboni's mood.

"Yes, Janet, I'm fine. I was hoping you could contact these people ASAP to get me a meeting."

"One month from today?" asked Janet.

"Yes, so please get to it now. It's important to me," Eboni ended.

"Yes, will, do." Then she walked out of the office and picked up her phone, speaking to the other secretaries until she got her task done. Forty-five minutes later, she was finished. She was good at what she did, that's why Eboni hired her. Janet buzzed Eboni and confirmed everyone on the list.

"Thank you, Janet, you're the best," she said then clicked. Janet could only read that Eboni was all business, which meant Mr. Benzio was free and up for grabs.

CHAPTER

36

Leroy first opened his eyes, trying to adjust them to the light. It felt intense, and the bright white walls didn't help. He then looked at his surroundings, saw his wife sleeping half in the chair and half on his bed. He realized he was in a hospital in their infamous twin bed. He tried to say her name but managed a sound instead, waking her up. She hasn't slept since this ordeal.

"Baby," she said, touching his arm.

"Huh?" Leroy moaned.

Keisha was at his side; she was crying. "Thank the Lord, he's alive! Leroy, honey, you've come back to me and the kids," she said, sitting on the chair next to his bed, where she'd slept every night for the past two years. He saw his wife through the bandages covering his face, revealing only his eyes, nose, and mouth. He resembled a mummy.

"Baby," he tried to say.

Keisha filled a glass of water from the pitcher on the nightstand. "Honey, don't talk. Here, drink some of this first." She placed a straw in it then held it for him to drink. Leroy took a sip of water then waved his hand as if saying no more. "All right, baby," Keisha said, then placed the glass back down next to the pitcher on the night table. "Baby, let me call the doctors in to see you." She pressed the call button. A few minutes later, a nurse came tapping at the door.

"Yes?" she asked as she walked over to Keisha, who was smiling with tears of joy running down her cheeks.

"I need the doctor to come. My husband has awakened."

"Oh, I see," said the nurse.

Leroy was staring at the nurse and his wife. Awaken? How long have I've been asleep? he wondered, but his throat was too sore to talk. He tried to swallow his saliva to ease it before he spoke. He managed to ask the question, "How long I been sleeping and what happened to me?"

The nurse looked at him. "I will get the doctor, Mr. Carter; he will answer all of your questions. I'll be right back, Mrs. Carter." And she gently closed the door behind her. Within minutes—tap, tap—three doctors and the same nurse and another nurse came in.

"Well, welcome back," said the first doctor. "Do you know your name?" the doctor asked him.

"Yes," Leroy said, speaking his full name.

"Good," said the second doctor then charted.

"How many fingers am I showing you?" asked the first doctor, revealing four fingers. Leroy answered. "Good." The second doctor charted.

"Doctor, how long have I been here?"

"Two years," the first doctor answered.

"Two years?" Leroy repeated; a tear rolled down his bandaged face. Keisha squeezed his hand. She was sitting on the edge of the bed looking at him, trying to hold back her tears.

"What happened to me? I mean, why am I here with my face all wrapped up like this" he said, taking his free hand and feeling his face then addressing the first doctor.

"Well, Mr. Carter, you were in a fire. You were burned over 70 percent, and you're lucky to be alive."

"Agreed." The third doctor stepped past the second doctor. "I'm Doctor Taylor, a burn specialist, and I need to check burns and see how they healed. If you don't mind," he asked, pulling a pair of scissors from his white jacket pocket.

"Nope, no, go ahead, but I must see what I look like," said Leroy.

All the doctors turned and looked at one another then agreed. "Very well, I understand," he said." Snip, snip, snip, and snip—all the bandages fell, revealing Leroy's face. His skin had taken on a reptile's skin texture like a lizard fused with a human look. Keisha gasped.

She held her breath and wiped the tears quickly before he saw them. The nurse who was in earlier handed the doctor a mirror, who then gave Leroy the mirror. Leroy started to cry.

"Baby, what's wrong?" said Keisha.

"Nothing, I'm saying good-bye to my old self, that's all." Still holding the mirror without moving it. He held on to it. "I'm going to need some privacy," he told them.

"We understand," said Doctor Taylor. They all turned and left the room. "We'll be right outside the door," he said before the door shut.

"Baby, baby, you want me to stay?" Keisha asked with tears running down her beautiful face.

Leroy looked at her. "No, baby, I need to do this alone."

"All right." Keisha walked over to the door, turned back at her husband, smiled, said, I love you then stepped out.

"Good-bye," Leroy whispered. He slowly guided the mirror toward his face, stopping at his neckline, which was fused to his chest. He closed his eyes and placed the mirror in front of him. With his eyes still shut, "I'm strong I can do this," he opened his eyes staring at someone he couldn't recognize. He touched his face, feeling it through his hands, letting it sink in. "Shit, this is my shit, this is me." He dropped the mirror on his lap, closed his eyes again. The memories of that night came rushing back like it was yesterday. "Damn, that bitch. Eboni will die. Eboni will die, die, die," he sang over and over.

He was once a ringer for Morris Chestnut, like his evil twin on the dark side. All that was gone.

The next day, the nurse informed the Carters that two Detectives were out in the hall, waiting to talk to them. Leroy agreed. The nurse let them in.

"I'm Detective Hunter, that's Detective Winfrey," said Hunter. Leroy and Keisha both shook their heads, as if saying OK. "Well, Mr. Carter, I've been waiting for this day, or should I say a chance to talk with you," flipping through his notepad. He had written down Leroy's last words two years ago. "You said something that leads me to believe that you know the person who did this to you," said Detective Hunter.

"No, I can't remember a thing, are we done? Detectives." Leroy, angrily said. Detective Winfrey was staring at Leroy's face; he had seen pictures of burn victims before but not to this extent. And lived. "Have, it your way but, when your memory comes back give us a call." Hunter, said. Leaving his business card on the bedside table as they left.

Keisha Calls Joe

"He's up, he's awake."

"What?" Joe said.

"He woke up. Leroy came back to us," Keisha yelled into the phone.

"That's good. I'll be right over," he said then hung up. He arrived at the hospital. Joe greeted Keisha, she had a big smile on her face. As she ran into His arms, crying. "He's back," she blubbered on to his shoulders.

Joe was holding her. "Can I go in to see him? Is everything okay with him."

"Yeah, sure, I told him you were on your way over. He's expecting you."

Joe walked into Leroy's room. He couldn't believe what he was looking at, what he was seeing. Leroy was awake and looking at him, and Leroy's face—the eyes were familiar, but the rest, Eboni had done a number on him. Something he would have to live with the rest of his life. Every time he looked in a mirror, he would see her.

Joe walked over to Leroy's bed. He reached out to hug him, his old friend, but was stopped short by his words.

"You see my face? Look at what that bitch has done to me. I'm a freak, a circus freak, a fucking carnival headline and I want her dead. But I want to be the one who does it."

"I understand," Joe managed to say. Joe spent the rest of the day visiting with him while Keisha went home to be with the kids, Shawn's mother Dorothy and the nanny watched them. Visitation was up, the nurse came in to inform them.

Joe wanted to ease Leroy's pain by telling him that he had gotten close. He was working with Eboni on a business deal, but he did stand to make a lot of money from it once the deal went through. He had met with the necessary people. The site was now being renovated. Leroy wouldn't see the big picture; he'd see it as a sign of betrayal or even weakness. Or worse greed.

I guess I should have taken care of her when I first saw her driving his Benz that morning in New Jersey after seeing the coroner bringing Hush's and Whisper's dead bodies out. No, Leroy wouldn't understand, he thought as he drove back over to his hotel. Once inside his room, he phoned room service and ordered a couple of cans of beer and steak well done, with eggs, realizing he hadn't eaten all day. Keisha had woken him up with the good news. But he needed more time. Things were working at a faster pace than he would have liked.

When Shawn's released from jail. Eboni was going to be dealt with. I will find a way to talk to Leroy, how could you tell a man who lost so much to be patient while I make this money?

CHAPTER

37

Eboni could hardly sleep. She forced herself by taking half of a sleeping pill her doctor had prescribed since her ordeal back then with Leroy. To settle her nerves, but who wanted to be in a coma-like state when your house was burning down around you? She thought and dropped them in the back of her nightstand top drawer. She awoke with no puffy eyes, looking fresh and excited. April 17th. Shawn's release and coming home, she thought as she quickly jumped out of bed, walked over to the mirror in the bathroom, brushed her teeth, filled the tub up with Yves Saint Laurent bath oil and body wash.

The aroma was intense and penetrating; she soaked her body for what seems like hours. She considered throwing Shawn a welcome home party but then decided that could wait. She needs some alone time with him first before she shares him with the friends and family, plus he needs time to adjust to his freedom and new home. She wrapped herself in a Versace towel. The whole theme of her bathroom was made for a queen. She smiled, looking around the marble tile floors and walls of black and gold.

"Now my king was coming home," she said as she trickled water across the tile floors. Music—that's what's needed. She hadn't played music since her kidnapping. She wanted to hear every sound, every bump that went in the night. She turned on her four-thousand-dollar acoustic bedroom system, found her old-school Kool & the Gang CD. "It's a party going on across the nation," she chimed in then dropped to the chorus, "Party over here, it's a party over there. Still, the real party is right here." Eboni sang in her own words as she got dressed. April 17th.Shawn's release date from prison. "Mix with you never going to get him never, never, never going to get him. I got to pick that one up next time I go shopping," she was floating on Shawn's embrace. Shit, cloud nine was too low for her. "Celebration" comes on, sings along while checking herself in the mirror, then chooses a red Christian Dior silk dress that splits down the front, giving her breast a peek-a-boo effect to anyone staring. The dress fitted her just right with her 36 Ds under a tent. It being the month of April in New York, still spring and winter mixed, she decided to wear her thirty-five-thousand-dollar white sable full-length fur coat. Eboni had been planning this day in her head from when he had first gone to jail. She tried on her white fur and slipped on her red Dior heels. "Perfect," she said as she spun around in her full-length mirror. She took off her coat, laid it across her bed, then touched upon her hair. No makeup, just a little lip gloss, the way Shawn remembered her and liked it. With her hair flawless and hanging pass her shoulders and her smack shining, she's set. Grabbed her fur and was in her Brand New Benz coupe on her way over to Rikers to pick up her king with Beyoncé's "Love on Top" blasting from the CD NewYork plates that read QUEEN.

She didn't anticipate the traffic 'cause when she arrived at Rikers Island, Shawn was standing out front in a caramel color Armani suit and white Gucci turtleneck with Gucci sunglasses, stepping on soil with his Gucci loafers. She'd switch his clothing prior to his release date and couldn't have her king coming home in faded, played-out clothes that sat in a laundry log room for years. "Oh hells no, not my king, my boo."

Shawn walked up to her as she pulled the Benz right in front of the jail, breaking their driving rules. She was supposed to park and catch the bus over the bridge. Shit, it's a celebration. She got out of the car, ran right over into his arms. He stood looking at her while hugging her close, smelling her woman's scent. "Damn, baby, I've missed you. I love you so much."

"I love you, I love you" Shawn said in her hair while holding her tight.

Eboni looked up at him; tears were rolling down his cheek. She grabbed the back of his head, pulled him down to her, and kissed him, and their tears bonded together like it was one. Not wanting to be separated again, Shawn whispered baby, "Let's put some distance between us." And they both looked at Rikers and agreed.

"How long have you been out here waiting?" she asked.

"Five years," he answered, then said, "Not long…a minute," as he got in the coupe.

The drive back to the city, Eboni talked about how much money the business was grossing and how much they had spread out in different banks in the States and islands throughout. "I was always on a working vacation."

Shawn looked at her in amazement. "Boo, I'm so proud of you, but right now, I need to feel you close to me." He laid his head on her shoulders for a minute then kissed her while she drove on. They made it to their luxury apartment in one piece as Eboni unlocked the front door.

"Damn, this place is tight, this shit is dope," he said, looking around the living room's panoramic windows.

"Yeah, wait till you see the place I'm having built for us upstate NY. It's a mansion, and it's almost finished."

"What about the house in Long Island?" he asked.

"It's still alive. We're free, Shawn, you're free, and now, I feel free. We don't have to be confined to one place to live. We got money coming out our ass. We could do that." She smiled. He smiled back and walked over to her and took her fur coat off, tossed it on the luxurious yellow Spanish leather sofa with pink dyed mink pillows. She kicked off her Dior heels. Shawn ran his hands down the front slit of her dress while his fingers played peek-a-boo on her breasts. Eboni closed her eyes and moaned. Shawn was kissing her over to the sofa, where her sable landed. He grabbed it and laid it down on the marble stone floor. Eboni lay down; he took his jacket, Gucci turtleneck sweater off. Ripped her dress right off, and a tear of passion formed in the corner of her eyes then rolled down her cheek while kissing him back hard and lovingly.

"I miss you," she cried. "I need you."

And he replied to her, "You're all mine." With their naked bodies snug up close to each other, they made love. With five years of their sexual passion locked up, Shawn popped Eboni's cherry again.

Penny's on the phone, telling Tony she needed some money. They were no longer together. Their daughter, Tonita, was seven years old, and Tony Junior was three. He'd told her he would be over later to drop some cash off. One thing's for sure, he was no deadbeat; he took care of his kids. The problem was, he also took care of the ladies. She then phoned Eboni, who she wasn't able to catch up with since Set Life Realtors were founded and Shawn's release.

Penny's daycare business was doing well; she'd opened the third one and now had one in Queens and two in Brooklyn and working on the fourth one to open in Manhattan in less than two months. With Sun Tots DayCare trying to pop up like White Castles, she was doing very well for herself. Tony, Eboni, and Shawn had all invested in her dream. Penny now lived in a beautiful five-bedroom house with a live-in Jamaican nanny in her late forties, named Margie. Penny drove a brand-new white 750i BMW and a new platinum Yukon Denali, which were both paid off. She worked from home, going over her payroll, while Tonita was in private school and Tony Junior was with Margie, who spoiled him. She had the company of her Pomeranian dog named Bones—cute, fluffy, brown, no bigger than a cat, sleeping in his bed in her state-of-the-art all-white marble-tiled kitchen.

On the fourth ring, the machine picked up; the digital voice said, "Please leave a message."

"Girl, it's me, Penny. I know, Shawn, but I just want a minute with her, so call me," she laughed. "Bye, you guys," then hung up. Click. She'd hung up before the tape ran her off.

Eboni and Shawn were in bed when the phone rang. Eboni looked at Shawn; he smiled as he pulled the sheets around her nude body. "You really should have let me get that," she said. "I feel guilty about not spending much time with her."

"Yeah, but we need time for ourselves too, and I know Penny can understand that," watching Eboni shake her backside, heading for the bathroom. "Hey, what's the cover-up for?" he yelled after her.

"The cover-up?"

"Yeah, the sheets."

"It's too much for you, baby, to take at once. Gotta let you have it in small doses," she joked. Shawn started laughing, he was looking around the bedroom where he was in a king-sized bed but still slept at the edge, only when Eboni wasn't in bed with him. Guess that's why he always called after her whenever he was left alone. He was still having nightmares of hearing the prison cell doors open and close and the inmates yelling multiple conversations going on at once. No quietness, tossing and turning, concerned that his newfound freedom could end. Learning to adjust and appreciate peace of mind and time to think. And relax.

CHAPTER

38

"I'm getting married in the morning, ding-dong, you hear the church bell rings," sang Shawn in a fake Jamaican accent while getting dressed.

Yellowman and Bob Marly would be proud," Eboni jokes.

"Four more days, then you're Mrs. Carter again. A promise is a promise, and you deserve the best," he replied excitedly while Eboni was combing her hair in the mirror.

She walked over to where he was and wrapped her arms around his neck. "I don't need a big fancy wedding. I already have my Clyde." She smiled.

"Yeah, but I want you to have the dress, the cake and guests, not a bunch of COs and inmates as a memory."

"Listen, the only thing I remember is the I, do's, not the surroundings and making you my husband—you know, bagging you." She smiled, assuring him then kissed him on the cheek. "OK?"

"Yeah, but I'm not in jail anymore, so let's do this upright."

The phone rang; it was Justina calling to say she was on her way over to drop off Eboni's wedding gown she'd made.

"That's excellent," Eboni said then hung up. "Oh, I almost forgot. Since the house is finally completed, the wedding planner along with the decorators and caterers are coming out tomorrow to set up things."

"I can't wait to move into that mansion," he said.

"That's my gift to you," she said.

"You mean a gift for us." He kissed her lovingly on her full luscious lips. Then the phone rang again.

"Hello, Mom," she said, dashing for the phone. "Yeah, uh-huh, yeah um-hah, OK. I know, I got that done" was all Shawn heard from the conversation.

"All right, wait, Mom, hold on, hello? Hey, girl, you home? I'll call you back, Mom's on the other line. Yeah, Mom, all right, I'll see you soon."

"Now, where was I?" he said, moving close to her again.

"Shawn, honey, don't hate me, but I have a ton of calls to make. Remember, ding-dong getting married in the morning and errands to run, so keep that fire lit for later, and I'll put it out."

Shawn grabbed Eboni around the waist, kissing her on her neck and ear.

"We can't," she moaned. "Not enough time," she moaned. "I must go, Mom's coming over, and I still got to call Penny back and Elisha and phone Janet, about the wedding planner and Paul and his family are flying in later today."

"Yeah, Um-hum..." Kiss, kiss. "What else you have to do?" he whispered in her ear.

"Noooo! Shawn, we can't."

"All right, calm down boy," he said to his privates. "You'll see her tonight," he told himself, looking down at his bulging pants.

Eboni smiled, enjoying his show. "Well, it's going to take Mom some time to get over here and Justina too. Let me just phone Elisha and Penny back quickly," she said, taking her clothes off and tossing her bra on the bed.

"Yeah! That's what I'm talking about." He jumped, tearing at his clothes.

Eboni phoned Penny while Shawn was in bed, all tented up looking at her naked body. "All right, see you soon." Click. "Now, where was I?"

"Right here," patting the space next to him on the bed.

Ding-dong, ding-dong.

"I'm coming, hold on." Damn, she said while running to the front door.

"Open up, it's me." She recognizes the voice on the other side, unlocking the door. "Look at that smile on your face, girl, hmm. Where's the lucky man who put it there?" Justina said, following Eboni into the living room.

"He's out, you just missed him. Went out to Brooklyn with Tony and them."

"And left you all alone, you probably need a break. Heard you been walking all cowgirl up," she joked and mimicked. "I just love this apartment no matter how many times I've seen it. It's like bam! Right at yah," moving on up to the deluxe, she chimed.

"Yeah, thanks. Now where's my gown, girl? Quit playing."

"Bam!" Justina said while taking the gown out of its garment bag. "Now go and try it on so I could see if I need to make any adjustments to it while I'm here."

Eboni went into the guest bathroom down the hall to change into it.

Ding-dong!

"Justina, get the door for me please."

"Where's Eboni?"

"Trying on her wedding gown."

"Ohh yeah, well, let me see if she needs any help," Penny said, walking toward. the bathroom. Tap, tap. "Ebb, open up."

"Hold on a minute," she said while pulling the dress over her head. Opening the door, "Well, how do I look?"

"You will be the bomb, that is a badass dress!" Penny said with tears forming in her eyes.

"Girl, don't even start that crap 'cause I'm about to cry too."

"Eboni, you just look so beautiful. Justina put her foot in that dress, girl. Where is that girl?" she then asked where Justina was.

"Justina!" Penny yelled out, who was in the kitchen.

"Yeah."

"Come here, girl, come see Eboni."

"Ohh, perfect. Look at you, you are wearing that dress I made for you."

The dress was a beautiful soft white creamy silk halter, showing off her toned arms with lace trim around the hemline that fell into a silk and Swarovski crystals spiral flare with an elegant chiffon fourteen-foot train that detached for the evening.

"Eboni, spin around so I can see how the back looks—ohh, child, Shawn is going to flip when he sees you coming down the aisle. It's perfect.

"Pop-pop, it's about to be on after the wedding. You'll be dropping out babies like me," Penny said, cutting Justina off.

"Justina, thank you for making this exquisite dress for me."

"Wait till you get my bill. Nah, just kidding. I'm glad you like it."

"I love it. Now, let me take it off so it doesn't get ruined."

Ding-dong!

"You mind getting that for me, it should be my mother?" she said to them.

"I'll get it," said Justina, who was leaving to answer the door. "Hello, Auntie. Eboni's trying her gown on for us."

"Hey, child traffic was hectic. First, I got on one train, then there was a small track fire, so we all had to get off and wait for the next one, which was so packed I could hardly get in. Whoa, let me just sit down a minute. Oh, and tell Eboni to come out here so I could see her."

"All right, I'll go get her for you."

Gail sat on the sofa with her eyes closed, kicking off her shoes.

Popping her head in, Eboni said, "Hey, Mom, I heard you complaining about the subway, why didn't you just drive in?"

"'Cause that's worse for me, and besides, the parking in the city is too expensive."

"I would have paid it for you."

"Oh, baby, I'm fine. I'll take a cab service back."

"Well, Mom, what do you think?" she said, stepping into the living room.

"Look at my baby, oh honey, you're beautiful—it's just…it's perfect, that dress. I'm sorry, but I'm about to cry."

"Mom, save your tears for the wedding." Clap! Clap! "Attention, everyone, nobody is allowed to cry in my house."

"Baby, you look, you look like an angel. Thank you for having a second wedding and doing it right so I could be a part of it, and, Justina, you have a real gift, just so talented."

"Thank you, Auntie."

"Now that everyone who should see me in this dress has seen me now, I'm going to take it off before I really do ruin it."

"Pick up that train," her mother yelled after her.

"I'll get it,'" Penny said, rushing behind her.

Eboni hung the dress up back in the garment bag. "I'm so happy for you," Penny told her. They spent the next couple of hours going over everything for the wedding to the reception. Eboni told them about their honeymoon. She'd wanted it to be a surprise, but Shawn already knew. The travel agent sent the tickets FedEx, plus Shawn needed permission from the courts due to his probation and a passport. "'Cause I'm planning an island hopping— Aruba, Arugula, Trinidad, Jamaica, Haiti, Bahamas and everything else in between. We'll be gone for two months."

"Two months? Who takes a two-month honeymoon?" asked her mother.

"Me, that's who. I mean the company is doing excellent. Jordan and Janet can handle things while I'm gone, and Shawn was talking about opening a nightclub, which will take some time zoning broad liquor and cabaret license and all that crap. The mansion is finished, so when we return, we'll be living there. I'm keeping this apartment and the house in Long Island, so with everything taken care of, why not? And besides, I need time away from things and more time with Shawn."

"What you need to do is make me a grandbaby. Don't you think it's time you had a child while I'm still able to run after one?"

"Yeah, Mom soon." And more sooner, she thought. She was late and wasn't feeling too well, so she took the day off and went to see her gynecologist, who told her that she was pregnant. She was keeping that little tidbit for Shawn after the wedding to surprise him with the news. It's been a month since she found out.

"Who's hungry cause I'm starving?" said Penny.

"Yeah, let's all go in the kitchen and pig out," said Justina, getting up leading the way.

"Speaking of food, what kind of food are you serving at this reception?" Gail, asked" 'Cause I can't eat no cucumber sandwiches. I need real food."

"Mom, I'm having it catered by two different caterers. One is that West Indian and soul food place you like so much, Sylvia's."

"Ohh, child, now you're talking. And the other place?" she asked.

"It's a local caterer from this neighborhood called Lala Chef."

"Oh, I heard of that," said Justina while rummaging through Eboni's fridge.

"Lala Chef? What kind of food they serve?" asked her mother.

"Everything, Maw, French, Asian, Italian, Spanish, and American, so I'm having a mixture of dishes for the mixture of people."

"Sounds good," Penny, said drinking down her cola.

"As long as Sylvia's there, I don't care what else you serve, and may I say more Sylvia's for me? Let me just get my Tupperware, and I'm fine," she joked. The rest laughed too 'cause they knew she meant it.

⁜

The night before Eboni and Shawn's wedding, Jimmy remembered that day when he was by his old friend's side in the hospital. Nurse Josie had to phone him with the news on Uncle Pete's condition.

"Jimmy, Jimmy," Pete said. "Well, old friend, we're at the end of the line. You have been a good friend to me, my brother."

Jimmy looked at Pete with tears rolling down his face; Pete was crying as he spoke on. "We've been through everything. I don't need to name it 'cause I wasn't by myself." He tried to lighten up the mood that was already setting. "And if I need anything, I can always count on you, my friend. I'm afraid I must ask you to do the unthinkable. I've lost a lot in my life, even though I have made more money than I could spend in three lifetimes. But I lost far more: my loving wife Lucinda, my youngest son Raymond and Curtis, my middle son. Now, I'm about to lose my oldest son Leroy, and I can't stand to bear that. Because of his pain, my life is soon ending," he said, sobbing. "Leroy is not the most reasonable man to get along with. He's my son, my last blood to flow. He doesn't deserve what has happened to him."

"I understand."

"No, I don't think you do. I started looking back on my children's lives and where they were headed, the path and choices they made, and my nephew Shawn, who is like a son to me."

"Shawn?" asked Jimmy.

"Yes, Shawn bears the family name." Uncle Pete passed away, leaving Jimmy with his last orders.

CHAPTER

39

"Ding-dong, due date," Shawn's singing, waking Eboni up. "Honey, its showtime."

"OK, OK, I'm up. Please don't sing. You've been singing that same song for the past four days. So give it a rest. I'm up anyway, I'm just going take a cold shower." She headed for the bathroom.

Shawn was packing his Louis Vuitton duffle bag. Tony was on his way over to pick him up have breakfast with the fellows and drive him over to the mansion, where they would be getting dressed.

"Honey, I'm leaving. Tony's here."

"Oh, OK." I didn't hear a bell, she thought.

"I'll see you there. Aren't you going to come out so I could see what I'm marrying again?"

"No," she yelled through the door. "You just have to wait. See yah at the house," while running the water over her body.

"All right, baby, I'll see yah," he said then waited, tiptoeing toward the bathroom. He gently turned the knob and popped his head in to get a peek of Eboni.

"Oh, shit, you scared me! I thought you had left already," she yelled at him while he was laughing at how she'd jump. Seeing that, she then threw cold water on him.

"A'ight, I'm leaving before you drown me."

———— ⋅⋅♦♦♦⋅⋅ ————

Jimmy getting dressed for the wedding.

He was still wrestling with the loss of his old pal. He was putting on his tuxedo, and was on his way to Shawn and Eboni's wedding.

The outcome wouldn't be the same. He didn't agree with what Uncle Pete had told him of what must be done, but that was his dying wishes. And he owed his respect and loyalty to him.

He fastened the last button on his white shirt clip-on his tie, checked the clip on his. 9mm, got out his silencer and tucked it in his inside pocket. He put the extra clip in his pants pocket. With that set, he left for the mansion.

———— ⋅⋅♦♦♦⋅⋅ ————

Leroy was on his way over to the wedding. He was wearing his sunglasses to protect his eyes from the glare of the light' because he'd suffered from severe migraines . After numerous surgery and skin grafts, his face was finally healing so that he was able to leave the hospital. The best doctors had worked on him, and for that, he was grateful but still filled with resentment. He couldn't wait for Eboni to see him in her new home in the pew with the other guest. He adjusted his gun that was poking him on the side. He didn't want to alarm any bystanders by adjusting his gun, so he bore the pokes—a very minor inconvenience, he thought as he slipped in with the other guests and took the last seat in the back.

Ahh, Shawn, smile now 'cause trust and believe me, you will most definitely cry later. No one crosses me and lives. No, they get crossed out, he thought as he sat there, watching Shawn and Tony clown around.

"Here Comes the Bride" played as Eboni walked past him. He cringed then clutched his gun in reaction to seeing her after all these years. The wedding was out in the garden, under a white tent with flowers lining the path. It was just a beautiful day.

———— ⋅⋅♦♦♦⋅⋅ ————

Elisha, Aunt Nancy and, Gail and her husband Charles, and Denise were waiting for May's li'l sister Ruby and mother Tammy and husband Lee.

When Eric and his cousin Keith and their girlfriends Kenya and Kente, they were identical twins, they met in college. Along with Paul and his wife Kim and his daughter Padina were in the kitchen, eating a light snack. They were all heading to the mansion.

"Where's Justina and Donny and Johnny?" asked Elisha.

"They are meeting us over there since Justina is going to help Eboni get into her dress," said Gail.

Elisha and Ruby got into their matching silver 540i BMW Eboni had just brought them. Steven, Penny's younger brother was following behind with his boyfriend Jason. In a red corvette.

Gail and Charles and Aunt Nancy rode with Denise. While May's parents, Tammy and Lee, drove in their Cadillac SUV. Gail had her own car a red Range Rover but didn't like to drive when she was nervous. The rest got in their respective vehicles and headed over to the wedding.

The house was finally completed. The cleaning crew company Eboni hired was pulling off the driveway when she and Penny arrived to inspect the home before the guests came. Eboni parked her Benz at the beginning of the driveway. She wanted to take in view of the gardens. As the wrought iron gates were closing, they had a crown emblem with a C crested for Carter.

"Wow, this is unreal," said Penny while walking through the Roman-style garden with Greek statues Shawn brought over from the warehouse that lined the driveway. "This place is enormous, Eboni. How can you and just Shawn live in such a place," she asked.

Eboni shrugged her shoulders as she looked around in amazement. Shawn is going to love this now that he's free, she thought as they walked up to the massive mahogany double doors encased in limestone exterior. This is what I envision for us. She had acquired the land through her real estate company. It was an old farmhouse attached with a rotting barn, sitting on three acres. She had the whole place torn down. She spent months with several different architects until she found one who could see and perform her vision. The house has cream Carrera marble floors and marble staircase, dating back to 1902s that was flown in from Italy in stages. That was overlooked by a hand-carved ceiling with floor-to-ceiling windows throughout the home that was installed with lighting motion detectors and shutters. It was an eight-bedroom twelve-half bathroom dream come true, with formal and central dining room fireplace in the master bedroom and living room and a state-of-the-art chef's-style kitchen, with his and her private offices, a large movie room that seats fifty, plus indoor and outdoor heated pools. She hired a decorator that gave her silk wallpaper in the bedrooms, suede in the living room, and leather in the halls and study, as she and Penny explored the whole house from top to bottom.

Eboni took notes of the secret passages that lead to a panic room without Penny noticing. They went on to the library; she kicked back on the Colonial-style burgundy leather sofa.

"Eboni, girl, you have arrived. Who's your neighbor, Oprah or Tyler Perry?"

"Both, girl," she joked.

"I remember when we used to sit on your mother's stoop back in the days in Brooklyn, thinking about those knucklehead guys on the corner. Who'd believe you and Shawn would end up living like this?"

"You are not doing so badly yourself, Miss Daycare Queen!"

"Yeah, that's 'cause of your help. We both know you climbed up the ladder of success and pulled me up with you."

"Huh, I don't know about that."

"You gave me the money to start my daycare centers when no bank would even look at my black ass."

"Yeah, but you made it grow, branching out in every borough—you did that. Sometimes we all need help, and a chance so don't look at it any other way, and besides, it was you who convinced my sorry scary-ass to talk to Shawn in the first place." Laughing, Penny said, "Yeah, I remember that day at Lucia's," holding her stomach.

"Uh-huh, when I ran out of there, knees all buckling."

"He must have thought you were worth it back then," said Penny. "Like I do too."

"Thanks, Penn."

Justina helped Eboni into her wedding gown. She was trying not to get any lipstick on it when Donny came knocking on the door.

"Shawn told me to tell Eboni its showtime. Everyone's in their places, we just waiting on you."

Eboni's mother spoke. "Go tell Mr. Shawn Carter patience is a virtue, soooo, wait," she yelled out with a smile. Penny was all tears; she was Eboni's maid of honor, falling apart. Dressed in a soft pink rose color with teal with thin spaghetti straps with teal pumps.

"Ebb, girl, you ready?"

"Yeah, been, ready."

"Well, let's go get them," said Penny.

With all the bridesmaids lining up— Ruby, Justina, Elisha. "Y'all ready?" Eboni asked nervously. They all shook their heads. "OK, showtime," she whispered breathlessly.

Ding-dong!

Shawn was at the podium with Tony, his best man, and Dave, Markus, and Estevan. They were all lined up in their black tux. Shawn was adjusting his tie.

"You scared?" asked Tony.

"Naw, man, I'm fine, ain't like this is the first time."

"Yeah, well, you sure you want to do this?"

Shawn elbowed Tony lightly in his ribs. "Quit playing, man, you think I'm a virgin at this?"

"Just trying to have a little play with you. Now, if you want to run, I'll stand guard. Think I could take the moms," he said, smiling at Shawn.

"Man, if you don't quit…," Shawn said, biting his lower lip 'cause they were on stage in front of the guests. "You're going to end up at the end of the line. Its showtime," Shawn said when he saw Ruby step out then Justina then Elisha then Penny. Then Eboni. All eyes with smiles were on her.

"Dearly beloved," the minister began, except two people she should have felt their hate.

CHAPTER

40

"Yahoo, it's a celebration," Kool and the Gang sang with Usher and a live band. They played a little Luther Vandross and Jaheim. The music played on, the waiters were serving; no one had an empty glass. The food was being served; she had the reception out in the garden as well under a lighted tent. Her guests dined. The decorator had built a platform dance floor that could hold two hundred of her guests—some people she didn't know but where her mother's friends. Everyone was dancing when Eboni noticed Janet and Mr. Benzio out on the dance floor. She held up her glass to Janet, who smiled back at her with her arms snug around his neck. She was happy to see Linda May's old lover there but a little surprised she was with a man, but glad she wasn't alone. As she and Shawn were sitting down overlooking her surroundings, they were on a built-up hydraulic stage.

"Excuse me," Shawn said to her. "I saw Jimmy over there." Then made his way towards him. "Hey, Jimmy," he said, giving him a bear hug.

"Congratulations, Shawn, she's a beautiful, and such a smart woman."

"Yeah, man, thanks, I know, but between us, I'm the lucky one. Jackpot." He smiled.

"Yeah, Shawn, let me talk to you in private for a minute."

"A'ight, sure we can go to my office upstairs."

Leroy looked at White-Boy Joe then nodded his head toward the house. Joe excused himself from Janet and followed behind Leroy.

Eboni looked at Shawn and Jimmy entering the house then froze, like she'd seen a ghost. Was that Leroy at my wedding? No it can't be.

Elisha came over to Eboni. "Sis, you OK? Is something wrong?" she asked.

"No, honey, I'm fine I, I need to talk to Shawn, that's all." Then she got up in a hurry to follow them.

Jimmy was talking to Shawn when Leroy and Shadow burst in.

"What's up, li'l cuz? Congratulations and shit on your big day. Sorry, I missed the other wedding, but I was indisposed and shit," he said, pulling out his gun. "I know you recognize me. Look at me! Look at what your bitch did after I fucked her!" he yelled with his weapon pointed at Shawn. Jimmy pulled his gun out too. He had the silencer on it and held it at his side. "Where's the bride? I want her to suffer when I blow your head off."

"Head off" was all Eboni heard as she raced past Shawn's office, heading to the master's bedroom for her gun that was in Hermès pocketbook. "Lord, please don't let Shawn die. We're about to be a family. I haven't even told him that I'm pregnant. Please, oh please, no more secrets," she begged as she crept back up to the door, trying to hear Shawn's voice with her head pressed up against the wooden door.

"You see my face? Look at it, man."

Shawn was frozen. Damn where the fuck is my GAT! I don't want to die like this, he was thinking. "Yo, Leroy, man, just calm down," he pleaded with his hands held up, at that point remembering the Doggie family.

"You, calm the fuck down when I blow your bitch apart."

Lord, please... Don't let Eboni come in here. Don't tell me you let me be free, marry her again just for me to see her die. Why? Shawn thought.

"Leroy!" Eboni shouted, busting in with her gun pointed at Leroy. "I should have blown your head off instead of taking your dick off that night at the warehouse, but I fucked up."

"This bitch still talking shit while I have a gun in my hand. Thought you were smarter than that, Eboni," Leroy spat! Shadow stood at Leroy's side behind Jimmy.

Jimmy then spoke to Shawn and Leroy. "I need you both to listen to me and understand what I have to say. It was your father's last words."

+ +♦♦♦+ +

"Where's Shawn and Eboni?" asked Tony to Justina and Penny, who were sitting at the table.

"I don't know. They're probably in the house," Justina answered.

"Yeah, newlyweds and all." Penny smiled.

Just then, Sandy and her husband Byron came over to them. "Where's the happy couple?" she asked while holding her son Tyrell by the hand.

"Don't know. Tony's looking for them too."

"Oh well, we've gotta get going. I told Eboni I would let Tyrell spend the night with them since they are leaving for that fabulous honeymoon tomorrow evening and all."

"Well, you can leave little man with me," said Penny.

"You, sure? 'Cause it's a long drive back to the city where we're staying."

"Yeah, I'll watch him."

"Well, all right then. Give momma a kiss. I'm coming to pick him up in the afternoon."

"OK, I'll tell her."

"Well, let's go look for them," said Tony, who started to walk off toward the house.

"Tony!" yelled Penny. "Why don't you give them some privacy? Just give them a few minutes. Come dance with me."

"I don't have any money," he said.

"It ain't about that. Just come on, boy," she said, pulling her reluctant ex, the father of her two children, to the platform dance floor, where Usher was singing his love song "Nice & Slow."

"Now, don't you go getting any ideas." Tony smiled.

"Fool, just dance." Justina stayed, sitting with Tyrell when Elisha came over.

"You saw Eboni? 'Cause she seemed a little upset a minute ago."

"Naw, she's in the house with Shawn."

"Oh, all right. I'll catch her when she comes out."

"Is something wrong?" Justina asked.

"No, just worried for her, but she's with Shawn, so everything is fine."

Eric and Keith were dancing with their dates while Paul was sitting with his wife Kim and was feeding his daughter Padina. Usher started to perform another song.

"How much is this wedding costing my baby?" wondered Gail While talking with her sister Nancy and her longtime friend Denise, waiting for her husband Charles and, Lee to bring them back their drinks. Dorothy, Shawn's mother, and May's mother, Tammy, were talking when the fireworks went off.

"Shit, where's Eboni and Shawn? They're missing everything they paid for as," she started to get up and look for them. She walked over to Elisha and Justina. "Have you seen Eboni?" she asked them.

"Yes, she's in the house with Shawn," answered Justina.

"For heaven's sake, there's guests out here!" as she marched off to get them.

"Come dance with me, Mom," Eric said, breaking away from his date Kenya then leading his mother to the dance floor, next to Penny and Tony.

"Usher can make enemies fall back in love," teased Penny. And Tony chuckled.

--- ·+++++· ---

"My father's last words," Leroy said, listening to Jimmy. "What! What's his last words, man, 'cause ain't nothing my father could say would stop me from killing this bitch, and I know Shawn. He's not going to roll over and take it, so Imma smoke his ass too." Shadow stood looking at Eboni; her eyes said, "Why the fuck are you here, Vinny?"

He avoided her stare and drew his gun out too but held it at his side. Then it clicked for her.

"Ahh, the infamous white boy, the Shadow. The same one she's been working with. I slept and slipped again, now fell, damn."

"Your father talked about both of you and told me how I should handle this war of blood, and I am here to end it. Joe, step out of the room and stand guard."

"Joe, who's Joe?" Eboni looked confused 'cause she knew everyone, but just the white boy left.

Shawn closed his eyes as Jimmy ordered Joe out the room. Lights out for us came across his mind. Jimmy talked about how there can no longer be spoiled blood, how his legacy, the Carter name, must live on. "Well, with that, forgive me." He pointed his gun.

Leroy lowered his and smiled. "My hands don't even have to get dirty. Good old pop from the grave sent Jimmy."

And Jimmy pulled the trigger. BANG! A single shot right between the eyes, causing the body to hit the floor. Then Jimmy looked at Eboni. "Sorry for your wedding day," then left out, leaving her in disbelief.

"It's over. It's over," she cried in Shawn's arms while Leroy's body lay still forever on the floor.

"Yes, baby, it's really over."

"Shawn, I have something to tell you, which this night has taught me one thing: never put off today because tomorrow is not promised to you. I'm pregnant and, May is alive. I know it's not the right time, but it's time you knew the whole truth I'll explain everything and my reason why I kept May a secret."

"Ok, you better. I can't believe this. And as life leaves, life comes again," said Shawn, hugging her. Focusing on his unborn child he almost lost.

Shadow looked at Jimmy when he came out. "It's over. You understand the family dealt with it their own way. It was Pete's wishes," Jimmy said to him then walked off.

Shadow looked in the room only to see Eboni in Shawn's arms and Leroy, his best friend's body lying on the floor full of blood. He tapped on the door. "Sorry," he said as he passed them with his head held down. "I'll take care of this, He was my friend, and now everything is done—The way the family wanted blood spilled blood. You will never see me again."

"Let's get out of here before people come looking for us, and you have a lot to explain." Shawn said, pulling Eboni out of the room. They went back down to their guests. Shawn sat, holding and looking Eboni and his son.

Eboni looked at him then took off her eagle ring. "Now, it's over."

"You're sure?"

"Yeah, Shawn, I'm sure." Then two white Rolls-Royce's Ghost pulled up in front of them, only stopping a few feet from the platform stage where they were seated. And the drivers approached them in unison, handing the newlyweds gold satin gift boxes. In timing, then a release of more fireworks and a black Range Rover drove up, and the two drivers made their exit.

"A gift from Ramirez," Shawn whispered and opened it, revealing sets of keys for Rolls-Royce's and a pair of Rolex presidential watches said, Eboni.

• • ✦ ✦ • •

Joe was giving a buyout on Jimmy's orders. Eboni and Shawn now controlled; everything the Carter cartel was theirs.

• • ✦ ✦ • •

"It's a girl!" exclaimed the doctor. Shawn looked at Eboni drenched in sweat. He held his daughter all covered up in a blanket. The nurse placed her in his arms. "My little Eboni queen."

"Yeah, but I'm naming her Shawnte' Princess Carter..."

"OH, my little Shawnee." Said Shawn.

The aftermath...

A brown UPS truck pulled up to the home of Hector Ramirez. Two armed guards detained him. "State your business."

"What's the problem?" said Santos as he was walking toward them after being called down from the house.

"Hey, I just came to deliver this here package, you know, just doing my job, working that nine-to-five, man," he stated, trying to relax the situation that could turn in a second, as he handed the package over to Santos while the two guards held the post.

"Ahh, Mrs. Eboni Carter," he said after reading the label, you may go, he waved him off and handed him a crisp one-hundred-dollar bill. "For your trouble."

"Thanks, man, appreciate it." Then drove away.

So Mrs. Eboni has sent a little token for Hector. He will enjoy it, he thought on his walk up back to the house.

"Who does she think she is?" said Hector then slammed the package down on his desk. Santos peeked at what had him so upset. The platinum eagle ring bearing the emblem of the family. "We were just in bed, making lovely fifty million, and now, she wants to get up before I'm done! Oh no, Mrs. New York Carter, for I am a Latin lover, and it's not over till I say it is, then it's over. Santos, you and Carols go to New York and find her. Just report back to me on what she's up to if she's cheating on me with another connection." He smiled. Hector was not going to take Eboni's rejection well. She'd been funneling his and her drug money through her real estate company, Set Life... the deal was too sweet to walk away from. He walked over to his bar and poured himself a glass of rum. He'd put the squeeze on Pete. "The choice is yours," he warned, threatening to wipe out everyone. His first meeting with her, he was impressed. And to protect his interests and investments by ensuring Eboni outcome he'd had given her the ring. She was under his protection as part of his syndicate. No harm shall come to her, she owed him her life and didn't even know it. "Get on that now," he ordered Santos, who was still standing there. He damn near jumped out of his skin.

"New York fucking City—this place is packed like a can of sardines, building on top of building," said Carlos.

"Yeah, I know. I hate this damn city too," replied Santos as they stepped off the plane dressed in their cream lining suits, heading for the hotel. "Taxi!"

"Let me phone Mrs. Eboni Carter and hear it from her own lips. It must be more than it appears."

Burr. Brrrng.

"Hello, Set Life Realtors, how may I help and direct your call? This is Janet speaking."

"Hello, Miss Janet, this is Hector Ramirez, may I talk to Mrs. Carter, please."

"One second, Mr. Ramirez, please hold," she replied knowing who he is.

Buzz!

"Eboni."

"Yes, Janet?"

"Ramirez is on the other line."

"Oh…" A lump rose in her throat. "Put him through."

"Hello, Eboni."

"Hello, Hector, how are you?" she asked.

"Fine, fine, but I could be better, like fifty million reasons better."

Another lump. She held her breath. Just breathe, she told herself as he spoke on, feeling a little guilty about breaking their deal. But how could she make him understand that after the wedding, when she almost lost what mattered to her most, and the birth of her daughter, her heart wasn't in it? She couldn't foresee doing any more business in this world trade. The risk was too high. She reflected on their first meeting. Some would say that women should be having babies.

"Life is funny," he quoted, reading and breaking her thoughts.

"Hector, I'm sorry, but my end is over. I have my reasons, please."

"Eboni, that's no way to treat an old friend. I'm not a happy man. You gave me your word. Now, now, relax chill, cool out, enjoy your new life and husband and bambino. Take some time for yourself to be happy, then we do business again soon. I'll talk to you later when I'm ready. Take care, Eboni for now."

Click!

THE-END?

CPSIA information can be obtained
at www.ICGtesting.com
Printed in the USA
LVHW020941030621
689238LV00004B/111

9 781637 284810